The Dragon, the Blade and the Thread

The Dragon, the Blade and the Thread

Book Three

of

The Star Trilogy

by

Donald Samson

Illustrated by
Adam Agee

For Raphael
Number One Son

Printed with support from the Waldorf Curriculum Fund

Published by:
The Association of Waldorf Schools
of North America
Publications Office
65-2 Fern Hill Road
Ghent, NY 12075

Title: *The Dragon, the Blade and the Thread*
Author: Donald Samson
Illustrator: Adam Agee
Proofreader: Ann Erwin
Layout: David Mitchell
Cover: Adam Agee
© 2011 Donald Samson
ISBN # 978-1-936367-16-0

YA Fiction

Acknowledgement

I am deeply indebted to my friend and mentor, David Mitchell. In his capacity as publisher for AWSNA Publications, he believes that these stories deserve to be read. I am grateful for his unique vision, unbounded support, and unflagging labor to bring these books to readers, both young and old.

PRONUNCIATION GUIDE

Several names of characters in these books are not immediately easy to pronounce using English phonetics. *Aina* is pronounced the same as the '*ai*' in a*i*sle. *Michael*, as explained at the end of Book One, is pronounced *My-kah-el*. The *o* in *Thos* is long, like the *o* in *go*. Both vowels in *Aga* are the open *ah*. The *g* in *Aga* is hard, like the *g* in *bag*. And always present in the background, waiting to appear again in a prequel, *Galifalia* has the main accent in her name on the very last syllable, as in the word *hurrah*, something we do not often hear in English.

CONTENTS

Prologue 9

Part I The Queen's Niece

One   Some Sleight of Hand 13
Two   The Magician's Dagger 29
Three   A Chance Meeting 37
Four   An Answer Only Straw Would Know 43
Five   Trouble to the South 52
Six   Flight into the Night 58
Seven   A Plot Uncovered 76
Eight   Escape 89

Part II An Unsettled Kingdom

Nine   An Unexpected Visit 99
Ten   What the King Discovers 118
Eleven   An Unexpected Challenge 137
Twelve   Aina's Secret Trysts 149
Thirteen   The Magician's Deception 154

Part III The Enclave

Fourteen	Precious Cargo.	171
Fifteen	The Writhing Dragon	189
Sixteen	*Naft Abyad*	205
Seventeen	A Blade in the Moonlight	223
Eighteen	A Sudden Departure	241
Nineteen	The Summons	251

Part IV Desperate Measures

Twenty	The King of Warrensfold	265
Twenty-One	In the King's Dungeon	279
Twenty-Two	The Black Lake	287
Twenty-Three	The Blade Strikes Home	295
Twenty-Four	The Deceit of Prince Corin	313
Twenty-Five	The Second Ride of Sound-the-Alarm	323
Twenty-Six	Elinor's Secret	333
Twenty-Seven	The Starry Sky	352

Prologue

The old man sat outside the city's towering walls, gazing into the quiet fields beyond the commotion of the city. The path that ran along the outer perimeter of the wall had no traffic, and the only noise was the morning chatter of birds in the apple orchards spreading into the fields. He did not mind that the stone he was sitting on was bumpy. He knew he did not have long to wait. To while away the time, he idly flipped a silver coin from finger to finger along the back of his hand. It was an impressive trick and he smiled at his nimbleness.

His head jerked up when he heard the sound he had been waiting for. He jumped to his feet and pressed himself into the deeper shadows of the wall's outcropping. He watched in silence as the great beast slowly lumbered into view. For weeks the old man had come regularly to observe the dragon and could by now see clear signs that it was losing the vigor it once had. Now it looked tired even early in the day. He followed the movement in the dragon's eye as it scanned the spot where he stood, but showed no sign of having seen him. *You are so sly,* he chuckled to himself.

The man looked up at the boy sitting on the dragon's neck. He was really too old to still be called a boy, although he had not yet grown to manhood. He was whistling to himself, lost in some reverie. He never noticed the stranger hiding in the shadows. *It's time to wake up from your daydreaming,* the old man reflected. His hand reached for the dagger at his belt, and his fingers followed the contours of the intricate design on its blade. He looked down at his other hand which still held the coin. With a quick flick of his wrist and a blur of fingers, the coin disappeared from sight, and the old man smiled.

Part I

The Queen's Niece

Chapter One

Some Sleight of Hand

*T*he boy looked up from the piece of cloth he was sewing. "This is *so-o-o* boring," he said, glaring at his mother. It looked like he had been holding it in for a long time.

In contrast to this young man's sour mood, the morning was particularly pleasant. The air was fresh, and the sun was already driving away the early morning chill. The two were sitting at a vegetable stand, surrounded by the noise and hurry of shoppers. The open market was awash with colors, smells and a confusion of sounds. Townsfolk milled around, stopping to greet one another and gossip. Many women had children in tow. Flies and wasps hovered in the air above the fruits and vegetables on display. Among vendors and shoppers there was a lively traffic of goods and conversation.

It was quiet at the stand where mother and son sat. Shoppers glanced briefly towards them and then hurried on. Occasionally someone stepped up to buy something. There was nothing wrong with the wares they offered. It had more to do with who was sitting there. Although the two did not look noticeably different than anyone else, it could not be overlooked that a woman and a man stood in attendance at a discreet distance behind them. And the man was armed in the fashion of the palace guard.

At her son's bitter complaint, his mother looked up and said, "If you don't like the sewing, then put it away."

"It's not the sewing," he said defensively.

His mother forced a smile, not wanting to react to the tone in his voice. "Would you like another bun? "

"No! I do *not* want another bun," he replied sourly. "What I want is not to be here. It's such a waste of time."

"I think you should eat something," the woman advised. "You won't be as cranky if you eat something."

"We have no business being here," he said bitingly, ignoring her suggestion.

"But it's market day," the woman said, surprised. "You have always loved coming."

"I've *never* liked coming to market," he muttered with a dark scowl.

"Now you're just being difficult," the woman said with a shake of her head. "Here, take a bun before they're all gone." She picked up the basket and offered it to him. "I put dried cherries into them this week. They're very tasty. I'm sure your father would love them."

"Mother, I don't want another bun. I've already eaten two. And I don't think it's right that you just give them away."

The woman tucked a loose wisp of hair back underneath her blue scarf. "I don't quite see it that way. But I suspect you are still too young to understand."

"Don't talk to me like I'm still a child," he snapped crossly, jabbing with the needle at the cloth in his hand.

"In some ways you still are," his mother said. "Fifteen is not quite altogether grown up. And could we have this conversation later?"

"And why do you have to dress like that?" he persisted, obviously not willing to wait for a later time.

"You are so harsh this morning," she sighed. "What's wrong with the way I dress?" She looked down at her clothes. She was wearing a light-blue blouse stitched with a design of flowers along the collar. A rose-colored apron covered her plain brown skirts. Over her hair she wore a dark blue scarf with golden stars embroidered into it.

"It's so *common*," he snarled. "And then you use that scarf. It's not right. They don't go together. And the vegetables you offer are so *ordinary*. The poorest of the poor. Why not grow something useful and harder to find like valerian or veronica, or even figwort, for goodness' sake. This is such lowly fare."

"How can you say that? We use these in every meal. Those other plants are not for cooking. Besides, these vegetables are a family tradition, my dear. You didn't use to mind."

He did not respond. He went back to his sewing, tugging at the thread, a frown on his face.

"Perhaps you should speak with your father. You used to beg to spend time together. You always got along so well."

"Not anymore," he mumbled. "That's all over."

At that moment, a young woman walked hesitantly up to the stand. She had two little children in tow, a boy and a girl. She made a small curtsey.

"Your Majesty," she said in a small voice, "forgive me for interrupting."

"You're not interrupting," Aina said kindly. "And I'm not *Your Majesty* here. I'm just selling vegetables from my garden, like everyone else."

"Yes, Your Majesty," the woman said with another small curtsey. She glanced to the young man and mumbled, "Your Highness," bobbing her head towards him. He only glared at his handwork in response.

Aina sighed. "What would you like, my dear? Would your children like a bun? I put dried cherries in this batch. I think they came out very tasty." She held the basket out for the woman, who quickly took two buns, keeping her eyes downcast.

"Yes, Your Majesty," the woman said with a third curtsey. "Thank you, Your Majesty. And a bunch of carrots and three potatoes, Your Majesty. And a ball of garlic and three onions." She bent down and handed the buns to her eager children.

"Any leeks today?"

"Yes, Your Majesty," the woman said straightening up. "It will go well in the soup. One, if it please Your Majesty."

"Yes, it pleases me. And I hope it pleases you more." She looked to the children. "Are you enjoying your sweet buns?"

The boy and the girl looked up and giggled. The young woman bent over and whispered something to them. The children looked at each other and giggled again. Then the girl made an off-balanced curtsey and the boy bowed so low he was comically doubled over. When they straightened up, they said together, "Thank you, Your Majesty." They collapsed into one another lost in laughter, and then hid behind their mother's long skirts.

"I'm sorry for their rudeness," the woman blushed.

"They've not been in the least bit rude," Aina smiled. "I find them very sweet. Here are your vegetables. That will be three coppers, please." The woman took the produce and tucked it away into the basket on her arm. She hastily passed some coins to Aina. Still blushing, with her eyes cast down, she turned and walked away, calling for her children to follow her.

"*That's* what I'm talking about," the young man hissed as soon as the woman was out of earshot. "*She* knows you don't belong here."

"She's young," Aina sighed. "She must have been but a child herself when Worrah was king. They don't all behave that awkwardly. You know that. You've seen many who come just to chat and visit."

"Looking for favors."

"Yes, some do come looking for favors. But they have good reason to. And if I can help, I do."

"I heard you swear to Father that you would never bring your court out here."

"And I will not," the queen said firmly.

"Yet you are the court, and if you support someone's petition for help, then you have brought it out here."

"Oh, Corin, you are too clever for your own good," she said with a dour smile. "I don't mean help in that way, and you know it. You are so quarrelsome this morning. Why don't you go and listen to the minstrel? I can hear his music from here. That will cheer you up."

"Fine," he exclaimed. He packed away his sewing into a leather wallet and jumped up to leave. "I can tell where I'm not wanted."

"Oh, Corin, you know that's not true," Aina sighed. She turned to one of the women who stood in attendance at a discreet distance behind her. "Would you please accompany Prince Corin—"

"Mother," her son cut her off sharply. "How many attendants did you have when you used to come to this quarter?"

Aina took a deep breath before answering. "I came with a donkey laden with food. Nothing more."

"So why must I be dogged by attendants?"

"You are the prince. You are in line to be king. It is only fitting that—"

"You were the princess," he cut her off. "You became the queen."

"Well, at least I knew how to handle a sword as well as a needle," she quipped.

"There you go again," Corin exploded. "Why do you bring that up? Do you expect me to get into a pitched battle here in the market? You know how much I hate sword fighting. And it was Master Ambroise who asked me!"

"Never mind," his mother sighed, waving him off. "Forget I said that. Go. Just go. Be back by the end of market."

As Corin slipped through the crowded street, she turned to the young guardsman who was standing behind her and gestured that he attend her. "Stay with him," she commanded.

"Yes, Your Majesty," he said, following after the prince.

"Don't let him slip away this time," she said to his receding back.

Corin was listening to the minstrel's ballad when the young man sidled up to him.

"You again!"

"Sire?"

"Don't *sire* me, Roddy. We're in the street, not in the court."

"Yes, sire," he said with a smile.

The prince sighed. "How do I get rid of you?"

"Sire?"

"I bet that when you were my age, they let you roam free."

"Yes, sire. That is how I met your father, the king. I am certain I've shared the story with you. However, we were living in the forest, not in the city."

"Where it was probably a lot more dangerous."

"Quite a bit more dangerous," Roddy said with a nod. "We were hunted by the trackers of King Worrah and had to guard constantly against discovery. It was a perilous time."

"So why can't I wander free in the city? The only person tracking me is you. I'd love to live in the forest. Imagine who I might be able to meet up with once you let me off your leash."

"It's not that simple. I am common born. I was a restless boy and I gave my parents grief with my wandering about. However, if I had gotten lost, it would have troubled only my parents, sad as that would have been."

"I'm as good as common born," Corin spit out. "My father grew up on the streets, and later he worked cleaning stalls, and my mother keeps a stand of vegetables in the open market. Mostly *foul*-smelling vegetables. And until a year ago, I was cleaning stalls as well. What could be more common than that?"

"The stalls you and your father before you cleaned hold a very special guest. I've been honored to spend time cleaning them myself."

"I'm doomed to forever follow in someone else's footsteps," the prince complained sullenly. "When will I be able to live my own life?"

"I beg your pardon, sire?"

"Just drop the *sire*, will you?"

"Of course, sire," Roddy smiled.

"Can we just listen to the music?"

"I love this ballad."

Gaily dressed, the minstrel was accompanying himself on a lute, slowly stepping back and forth before the small crowd that had gathered to hear him. He was singing with dramatic passion. "... *And the night was as black as his horse was white. Yet onward he rode, though great was his fright* ..."

"I'm so tired of this story," Corin commented.

"Sire?"

"... *Through thunder and lightning and punishing hail, yet Storm did not falter, his heart did not fail* ..."

"It's like they can't sing anything else around here," Corin complained.

"...*Sound-the-Alarm pulled his cloak even tighter, while lightning flashed, now closer now brighter* ..."

"I'm actually quite fond of it," Roddy sighed. "Even if it is exaggerated."

"How about *untrue*?" Corin challenged. Then he said, impatiently, "This is unbearable. I'm going to the plaza at the other end of the market."

"I'll accompany you."

"What a surprise. I thought you liked the ballad."

"Sire?"

"Never mind. Let's go watch the jugglers. This minstrel is boring."

"An excellent idea, sire," Roddy said.

"How did I know you'd be so agreeable?"

"Sire?"

"... *onward Storm rode and the boy's mind was set, despite hunger and thirst and his clothes soaking wet* ..."

"Such drivel," Corin sneered. "Never happened." His chaperon said nothing, but glanced regretfully over his shoulder as they left.

They made their way through the many stalls in the market. At some fruits were sold, at others vegetables, several held a selection of both. They passed by a bakery stand, crowded with shoppers. At one, hares and ducks hung upside down from a horizontal pole, and live chickens squawked and fluttered from crates behind the vendor's table. Another stand was devoted to dried herbs and spices. Behind it sat a shriveled old grandmother, all bundled up. Still another stand displayed large wheels of cheese from which shoppers had thick triangles cut off.

They passed by a woman wearing a colorful shawl and skirt, with shiny earrings dangling from her ears, a bright scarf holding back her hair. She had a naughty twinkle in her eye. She addressed the prince as he walked by, "Your fortune, young sire? Shall I read your fortune? One copper a hand. Your right is your future."

"I have none," he replied bitterly and kept walking.

There was a general buzz of people haggling, visiting, shouting and laughing. It was a colorful collection of humanity, and in spite of complaining to his mother, Corin enjoyed it. It was a mixture of men and women, with children dodging this way and that. Most were local townsfolk, with a smattering of travelers in their odd clothing and with their strange accents. Above the hum of activity the prince could hear snatches of music, both instruments and voices, from wandering minstrels. Layered on top of the music rose the sing-song offers of the vendors barking their wares.

He knew where he was headed. At the furthest end of the market was a space left open for street performers. The jugglers were well into their act when he and his chaperon arrived. The performers had a spot in the sun, and, as the day was already growing warm, they had stripped to the waist, exposing their muscular chests and arms. They were in the midst of tossing large, sharp-edged knives between them, and their bare skin was beaded with sweat.

"Have you ever tried that, Roderick?" the young prince asked.

"Oh, bless me, never, sire."

"Would you like to try it?" he persisted.

"Oh, no," he said, shaking his head. "It looks much too dangerous."

"I think it would be fun," Corin said flatly. "I think we should try it when we come home. Will you try it with me, Roddy? If we watch them carefully, I'm sure we could figure it out. We just have to follow every move."

The prince looked out of the corner of his eye and saw Roderick swallow hard, but he did not answer. His eyes were riveted on the blades flashing through the air. Corin had hoped for this. He tentatively took a step backwards. Then another, slipping behind the other spectators.

When the jugglers had finished that part of their act, the small crowd around them burst into appreciative applause. Still clapping, Roderick turned to comment to his young charge, and it was only then that he missed him.

"Drat the boy!" he cursed, turning in all directions to see if he could catch a glimpse of him. Corin, however, had long since slipped away. Then Roderick laughed at himself. "You'd think I'd know his tricks by now. Can't say I blame him. I would've done the same. But the queen will not be happy that I let him get away again."

When Corin reached the edge of the crowd, he glanced back quickly to make sure he was not being followed and then broke into a run. Markets in Gladur Nock did not happen every day in each of the quarters, but rotated around the city. He wanted to visit a market clear on the other side of the town. He knew the back streets well. Over the years, he had escaped often enough to explore them to his heart's content. Secretly, he envied his father for having grown up on the streets. He wished he could have been the one.

The streets, rarely straight, led him a circuitous route that snaked its way gradually to the market in the quarter called Rivergate. He entered a plaza filled with the temporary stands of the vendors. Panting freely, he stood a moment to look around, hoping that the one he was seeking had come to market that day. Then he saw him, with the usual knot of people watching his show.

Corin approached the back of the small crowd. Then he slipped into the gaps between the spectators. No one paid him any attention. Boys ducking under arms to get a better view was a regular occurrence. The front line of viewers stood tightly together, and Corin had to squeeze between two women, both of whom carried laden baskets. As he nudged one of the baskets aside as gently as he could, he heard its owner cluck her disapproval at his arrival.

Corin, however, did not care if he had annoyed her. Now he had a clear view of the old man. He was a magician. He was dressed in a rather untidy green tunic, tied at the waist. A cloak of a darker green hung loosely from his shoulders. His hair was white with streaks of black, unruly and wildly matted. He kept it underneath a worn velvet cap with long black feathers stuck into its band. The hat was sun-bleached and had lost its form, but looked as if at one time it had been quite stylish. The man's greying beard was equally wild and almost as badly matted at his hair. To everyone's delight, perched on the magician's shoulder was a large black bird, which Corin took for a crow. It balanced there, warily watching the crowd. At times, when the magician made a sudden move, it spread its wings and fluttered to keep its perch.

It was obvious that this old man did not live the well-ordered life that the young prince knew from the palace, with regular baths, clean, well-mended clothing and servants to prepare food and do the washing. This old man was well versed in the mysteries of the road. Oh, how Corin yearned for a chance to get to know that life. It rankled him that every minute of his day was prescribed with something that someone else had decided he should do. On the road, he would be master of himself. He sighed at that delicious thought.

The magician was in the midst of doing some sleight of hand with a matron. She stood beside him, her full basket of shopping protectively tucked beneath her skirts. He had already snatched a biscuit from her and, as everyone watched, made it vanish with a small flourish of his hands. Corin had arrived just in time to see this, and it thrilled him. He loved the magician's tricks more than anything else.

"Well, it looks like I found something to go with my lunch," the old man commented to the laughter of the crowd.

"I want my biscuit back," the matron squawked, causing even more laughter. "I paid for that."

The magician glanced over and, catching sight of Corin, winked at him. Corin's heart leapt with joy at being acknowledged. He tried never to miss the magician's act, and it was not always easy to throw off his chaperon to come look for him.

"You're quite right," the magician said. "I can't let you go away empty-handed. I must pay you a price for your biscuit."

"I should think so," the matron pouted.

"Now, where shall I find something you would like?" the magician mused. "Ah, I have an idea. Maybe we can get something worthwhile out of this boy's empty head." He took the two steps over to where Corin stood and reached out his hand. The bird fluttered on his shoulder. Corin ducked his head involuntarily as the old man reached out to grab something in his hair.

"Just as I thought," the magician said triumphantly. "The boy's been hatching eggs inside there. And I thought he was just a numskull." He held up his hand to the crowd and showed two eggs. There was appreciative applause. The magician stepped back to the matron and offered her the eggs.

"Would you call this a fair exchange for your biscuit?" he asked.

The matron stared at the eggs a moment in astonishment and dumbly nodded her head, but did not move. The old man chuckled and, picking up her hand, placed the eggs carefully into it. She glanced suspiciously from the eggs to his bird.

"Fear not," the magician announced, noticing the connection she was making. "They are not from my feathered friend here. However, seeing where they came from," and he nodded his head towards Corin, "make sure they're not already hard-boiled before you try cooking them." This comment delighted the crowd, and Corin laughed as heartily as the rest. The crow became agitated and fluttered its wings. It bent its head down and pecked at the magician's ear. It let out a long clicking croak. The old man bent his head to the side and appeared to be listening to what the bird had to say. The crowd tittered with delight. By now the matron had picked up her groceries and retreated back to the safety of the onlookers. The magician's eyes darted into the crowd, as if searching for something.

"I see," he muttered, and nodded his head. "Well, we'll do what we can. As always, we'll do what we can." The crowd waited with anticipation for his next trick. "And now I need a volunteer with a very sharp eye," the magician announced. "Someone who will not let me fool him with my little tricks." He scanned the faces before him. Many grew uneasy at his penetrating gaze and averted their eyes. "You, sire!" he announced suddenly, pointing into the knot of onlookers. "Please, do me the honor and play with me my little game." The crowd opened up where he was pointing and revealed a nobleman, recognizable by his fine dress and the pheasant feather stuck jauntily into his hat. He had a short sword at his side and a dagger stuck in his belt. That alone marked him as from the noble class. Other than the guard who was on duty, no one but the nobles carried a weapon openly in the street.

The prince studied this man. He was not from the nobility of Gladur Nock, of this he was certain. He knew all the noble families, had grown up seeing them come and go from the court, and their children had been his playmates. In fact, their children provided the bulk of the workers in the compound. He was certain he had never seen this man inside the palace. It was not uncommon for nobility from other kingdoms to visit Gladur. But sooner or later, they all made their way to the palace to pay their respects to the queen. Had he missed hearing about this nobleman's introduction to the court? His mother usually chatted about such things at meals. He was very curious to find him in the market watching a magician's show.

"Step forward, my well-dressed sir, you've nothing to fear," the magician encouraged him. "You are much too clever for me to trick you." The young nobleman stepped hesitantly forward. The bird on the magician's shoulder fluttered its wings, bent low and emitted low, throaty clicking sounds.

"Just tell your bird to mind its manners," the nobleman said, stopping in his tracks.

"You're not afraid of my feathered companion, are you?" the old man asked. He reached up and stroked the bird, smoothing its ruffled feathers.

"Just tell it to stay away from me," the nobleman said, going to stand on the other side of the magician. He looked uneasy, glancing around at the crowd.

"You aren't worried that I'll take something of yours, are you?" the magician asked.

"Not in the least," the nobleman answered. "I've seen through all of your tricks. Nothing but sleight of hand."

"Exactly!" the magician exclaimed. "I can trick only the foolish and unsuspecting. That is why I called a man of your deep perception to come forward and help me."

The nobleman eyed him suspiciously. "Don't try any of your tricks on me," he growled.

"Tricks? No," the old man said cheerfully. "But how about some *magic*?" He swirled his arms and with the last word held up a rose. Some voices in the crowd cried out in astonishment and several people applauded.

"I don't believe in magic," the nobleman objected, keeping his eye on the rose, which the magician was waving in the air in front of his nose.

"That's what makes it all the more magical!" the old man said brightly and tossed the flower into the crowd. There was laughter as several women scrambled to catch it. Next the magician held up a small, ornately decorated money pouch for all to see and was in the process of opening it up.

"Hey!" the nobleman said with a start. Both his hands shot to his belt. "Where did you get that? You've stolen my money!"

"Not so, good sire," the magician said handing him the purse. "Otherwise, I would have kept it hidden until you'd gone away. Your purse had gotten lost, and I am returning it to you. I recommend that you keep a better eye on it. I have heard that there are pickpockets in the market. Imagine that!" This was greeted with laughter from the crowd. "But for my trick, I require one of what you keep inside it. May I?" and without waiting for permission, he pulled out a coin with a glance at the nobleman, whose confident smile had now turned into a frown.

"Now," the magician continued, holding the coin up for all to see. "Keep your eye on the coin." He paused a moment to let everybody get a good look that the coin was made of gold. "Do you always walk around with such a richly lined purse?" the magician asked with a sidelong look at the nobleman.

"You won't buy me off with a pair of eggs if you make that vanish," the nobleman threatened.

"I would not dream of taking your money," the magician assured him. "It appears that you have come here to sell something of great value, and it looks as if you have been well paid." He watched the nobleman's reaction to his words. "Or perhaps you've come to *buy* something of great value." The nobleman glared at him darkly. "Or some service, perhaps?" The nobleman's expression turned into a frown and he opened his mouth to speak, but at this moment, the coin slipped out of the magician's hand and fell to their feet.

"How clumsy of me," the old man muttered, quickly bending over. The bird on his shoulder fluttered frantically to keep its balance.

"You can't even hold onto a little coin?" the nobleman scorned him.

"Ah, my hands grow old and stiff," the magician lamented, fumbling on the ground before straightening up again, accidentally bumping the nobleman, who looked like he was losing his patience. The magician's bird grew quiet again. "Forgive the delay. I promise to be more sure-handed from here on out." The magician displayed the gold coin again. "Here it is," he said, and passed his open hand in front of the hand holding the coin. In that moment, the coin disappeared. The crowd held its breath.

"I lied," the magician said with a shrug of his shoulders. "It seems as if it's vanished, after all. You never can tell with magic what's likely to happen next. But that it's gone is not totally the fault of magic. That's the nature of money, they say: Easy come, easy go. And then I recently heard another amusing saying: A fool and his money are soon parted."

The nobleman's frown returned and his face was getting darker by the moment. Corin was afraid he might reach out and strike the old man. But the magician's smile never wavered. "Perhaps you'd be content with this in exchange," he said, holding up a dagger.

The nobleman took one look at the dagger before his lips pulled back, showing his teeth, as if he were a dog about to bite. "It's my own dagger," he growled. "You're nothing but a common pickpocket. I should use it to cut off your nose." He snatched the knife back from the magician and brandished it threateningly before the old man's face before slipping it back into its sheath at his belt. The boy was amazed. He was convinced that he had watched the magician's every move, yet he had not seen him take the nobleman's money purse, and he had missed when he snatched the dagger as well.

"Where's my money?" the nobleman demanded, his hand held open.

"How about this?" the magician said, holding up a shoe buckle.

"I don't need a shoe buckle!" the nobleman spat out impatiently, raising his voice.

"But I believe you do," the magician said, looking down towards the ground. The nobleman followed his gaze and let out a cry of surprise. His left shoe was missing its buckle.

"How did you do that?" he exclaimed, snatching the buckle from the magician's hand.

"Magic," the old man said simply. "And now to return your money." He took the nobleman's hand and placed the coin into his palm. The nobleman stared at it to make sure he had not been cheated.

"Nothing but foolish sleight of hand," he grunted. He turned on his heel and stalked away, the crowd opening to let him by. He happened to pass right by the young prince as he left. Corin's eye was drawn to the dagger at the nobleman's belt. The handle was different! It had been switched. How had the magician done that? When he looked up, he noticed that the old man was beaming at him. The magician took the two steps over to him and leaned down to whisper in his ear.

"Here, hold onto this for me," and he pressed something cold into the boy's hands. Corin glanced down and saw a dagger with a design etched on the blade. He quickly shoved it into the folds of his tunic, glancing around, hoping no one had noticed. In a moment, the magician turned to an old matron standing in the front row and, to the crowd's delight and wonderment, looked to be pulling a long strand of colored silk scarves right out of her nose.

Chapter Two

The Magician's Dagger

"Corin, she's coming tomorrow afternoon. Messengers arrived today announcing her."

He looked up from the chicken leg he was gnawing on. "Already?"

"Yes, already. I've been telling you for a week, now."

"Why does she have to stay with us?"

"As I've explained, we are her next of kin. She's my niece. Her mother, bless her soul, was my sister Jewel, and that makes Elinor your cousin."

"I know that part. She's been here before, you know. It's not like I've forgotten."

"How well do you remember her?"

"Bits and pieces. Just that they came to stay with us once, and that I liked my aunt."

"She was very kind," Aina sighed. "I missed Jewel terribly when she married and moved away."

"And she had a son. His name was Farnwith, wasn't it? I liked talking with him. We played a lot of games together. What happened to him?"

"Farnwith perished with his parents," his mother said sadly. "There was a younger sister whom I had not yet met. I heard she was the first of the family to succumb to the disease."

"And then there's Elinor."

"She's about your age."

"Younger," Corin corrected. "I don't like thinking about her."

"Perhaps it would be better if you did. Unless I'm mistaken, the two of you did not get along very well together."

"She put slugs in my bed! And I jumped into the bed without knowing they were there. It made a gross mess."

"She was angry with you, if I remember. From what I understood, you had talked her into eating fumets."

"Only tasting! And how was I to know she'd be so stupid as to do it?"

"Obviously she trusted you. So perhaps you can understand why she took revenge."

"But then she smeared her breakfast egg into my hair, right here at the table."

"I believe that had something to do with getting her to climb up with you onto the dragon's back and playing hide and seek there. And if I remember the story correctly, you made her hide first, but it was just before Star went off for his scrubbing at the river. And you snuck off his back, leaving her behind. I'm told not even Star could figure out for the longest time where the crying was coming from. I think the egg in your hair was her way of letting you know that she didn't trust you any longer. And considering how you treated her, it was a well-founded decision on her part."

"I got the message," Corin shrugged. "I left her alone after that."

"I think she just wanted to play with you and be friends."

"I remember that she was whiny and annoying. And that she always had a runny nose."

"I'm sure she's changed," Aina said with a sigh. "Maybe you can start over. Act like it never happened. Your father and I often have to do that after we've had a disagreement."

"Hasn't seemed to work lately," Corin said under his breath.

Aina peered sternly at her son. He looked away and asked, "Doesn't she have anywhere else to go?"

"They've all perished. She's had a terrible shock, seeing all the people she loved die of the illness," Aina said, her voice heavy. "I want her to feel welcome here."

"How do we know she's not bringing the plague with her?"

"Corin! What a terrible thing to say."

"Well, it's possible," he insisted.

His mother sighed. "Just for your peace of mind, she's been living in the countryside for the past three months. Her parents sent her away when the illness first broke out. If she'd had it, she would have shown signs by now. Besides, Star would not let that happen, letting the plague break out here."

"Um, Mom, Star doesn't really work that way."

"Nonsense. Star is a Luck Dragon. He has brought us good fortune from the very beginning. All of our kingdom's prosperity stems from his presence."

"That's not what stopped the plague from breaking out here. We closed the frontiers so that no traveler or merchant could bring it here."

"And had Star not suggested that strategy in the first place, the plague would have broken out before it occurred to any of us to close the frontiers. So you see, Star *was* the one that stopped the plague from spreading here."

"Have it your way," Corin sighed.

They were silent for a while. Corin had finished eating and, after wiping his hands, took out the piece of cloth he had been stitching at the market and continued working on it. Aina picked at her food, watching him.

"Is that really what Ambroise wants you to do?"

"He wants to see how even and close I can get my stitches," Corin said without looking up.

"And you enjoy doing that?" she asked.

Corin did not break his concentration, merely nicking his head.

She watched him continue to work and then asked cautiously, "How is he? Has he gotten any worse?"

"Master Ambroise?" Corin asked, looking up.

"You know who I'm asking about."

"Who? Star? Why don't you just say so?" He went back to his work. "Mom, don't worry about him so much. He's a dragon. He'll be fine." After a few more stitches Corin put down his work. "About Elinor. If she's been living in the countryside, why can't she just, you know, stay where she is? I'm sure she's happy there."

"It's as if you don't want her to come," his mother said, arching her eyebrows.

"Well, if you want me to speak freely ... "

"I certainly do not," she replied sternly. "You will hold your tongue, be civil, polite and obedient."

"Yes, Mother," Corin said, lowering his eyes. He folded his hands in his lap.

They were silent only briefly before they both began to laugh. "I guess that's asking too much," Aina said lightly. "I never held *my* tongue. Why should my son be any different?"

"I'm glad I'm like you, Mom. We understand each other."

"Do I hear behind that remark that you and your father do not?"

"Can't I say anything without your reading something else into it?"

"Just tell me if it's true or not."

Corin grew silent and studied his hands. "It's different," he said. "He's changed. We used to have fun together. But now he just tells me all the time what I'm doing wrong." He had a pained expression on his face. "Sometimes I think all he wants is for me to become him."

"He cares for you very deeply."

Corin shrugged. "I just wish he wouldn't expect me to do everything his way."

"It's not a bad way. It brought him from living on the streets to sitting on the throne."

"But it's *his* way, not mine. And I'm not living on the streets." He bit back the desire to say that he wouldn't mind trying it out. Instead he said, "Nor does he spend much time sitting on the throne."

Aina's lips became a thin line before she responded. "There has been a lot of unrest. He's doing the best he can. And he only means well for you."

"But does that mean I always have to do everything his way? Why doesn't anyone else understand that? After all, living here how can I *not* get the best training? *He's* looking after me, not Father. Father's rarely here, anyway. You admit it yourself."

Aina grew pensive. She decided not to let herself get drawn into an argument. Instead, she changed the subject. "Does he talk to you about it?" she asked. "People are beginning to notice. I've heard that the barn workers are starting rumors. Have you gotten him to tell you anything?"

Corin had picked up his stitching again. He looked up. "Who? Star? Are you asking about Star again?"

"Yes, dear, of course, I mean Star."

Corin shrugged. "He won't talk much about it. All he says is that he's tired a lot lately."

"He's growing pale," the queen reflected. "His scales don't shine like they used to. You have noticed that, haven't you?"

"Of course I have," Corin said with an edge in his voice. "I'm the one scrubbing them, after all." What he did not tell his mother was that Star dragged his feet going to the river and coming back, occasionally stopping to rest along the way. And during their regular exercises, the dragon was not only moving slower, but not pushing the boy to learn with the same enthusiasm that had been there just months before.

"I worry about him," Aina fretted. "I didn't know that dragons could get ill."

"Maybe he caught something," Corin suggested. "Like the plague, only it just makes him tired a lot."

"I don't think so, Corin," his mother said firmly, sitting up straighter. She peered at him to see if he was being sarcastic.

"You never told me how long I have to stay at this," Corin said, not looking up from his sewing. "It's very tedious, you know."

"Are you asking about the sewing?"

Corin put his cloth down. "No, I'm not asking about the sewing. I already told you I enjoy this. I want to know how much longer I have to go every day and scrub the dragon."

"You don't go every day. Once a week you join me in the market."

"Just as bad," Corin grumbled.

"Corin, don't you enjoy spending time with Star?"

The prince hesitated before responding. It was not a simple answer. He did not know how much of what they did together he could talk about. "I'm just ready for something else," he said at last.

"You will go with the dragon until Star says that you are finished." Corin looked unhappy, but did not say anything. Aina continued, "Long before the plague struck, Elinor's parents had asked if she could come and help care for Star. They thought it would be a good experience for her. In the same way that Queen Alis of Nogardia sent her children here. Perhaps at one point Elinor could offer you some relief from looking after Star, once she is familiar with how we do things around here."

"That would be fine with me," Corin said. "Maybe it will get Father to give me a little more space."

"I don't know any boy in this kingdom who has more space than you do."

"Not *that* kind of space, Mom."

"As soon as you've figured out what kind of space you need, you let me know. Which brings me to ask, why did you ditch Roderick again at the market?"

"I didn't ditch him," Corin said innocently. "I just wandered away while he was caught up watching some jugglers. I was already somewhere else before I realized that he was no longer with me."

"It is not wise to lie to me, young man," his mother said severely. Corin pressed his lips together to keep from smiling. Then Aina shrugged her shoulders. "Well, it's a passable lie, at least. I'm grateful that I can still tell the difference. I want your promise that you will not include your cousin in this misbehavior. She will need a chaperon at all times in the city."

Corin nicked his head briefly but said nothing. Aina pursed her lips and commented dryly, "I guess that's as good as I'm going to get right now."

"Time for me to go to bed," he said, standing up, wrapping away his sewing.

"Not so fast," his mother said sharply. She was staring at his waist. "I want to know about that."

"What?" Corin asked. He looked down to see what his mother meant.

"That knife. The hilt is showing and I want to see it. When did you start carrying a knife?"

It was the dagger the magician had slipped to him at the market. He had stuck it into the waistband of his tunic and not thought about it again. He had forgotten that the hilt was showing.

"Hand it to me," she said. Corin drew the dagger forth and gave it to her. He saw his mother's eyes grow large as she took in the design on the blade. "Where did you get this?" she asked in a sharp voice, examining it carefully.

"In the market," Corin said, not sure how much to reveal. Then he saw a look of alarm and concern cross her face, and she turned pale. "Mother," he cried out. "What is it? What's wrong?"

"How do you have this?" she asked. Her voice was shaking. "Where did you buy it?"

"I didn't buy it," he stammered. "It was given to me."

The queen looked searchingly into her son's face. "Who gave it to you?" she demanded.

He hesitated, but decided to tell her. "A magician. He gives shows in the market."

"A magician?" There was alarm in her voice. "What did he say to you? Did he know who you are?"

"He … he said to keep it safe. No, he didn't know who I am. I don't think so. How could he?"

"That settles it," Aina said, her color returning and her voice growing firm again. "From this day forward, you will promise me to stay with your attendant. If you refuse or run off again, I swear I will set an armed guard around you. And you will keep your distance from this magician. Have I made myself clear?"

Corin's eyes were wide. She had never spoken so forcefully to him before. He nodded his head. "Yes, Mother," he mumbled. Then, after a moment, "Can I have the dagger back?"

"No!" she answered so sharply it made him jump.

"Is there something wrong with it?"

She stood up abruptly to her full height, clenching the hilt in her hand. He was no longer in the presence of his mother. A fierce light flared up in her eyes that made it impossible for him to meet her gaze. She stood before him fully the Queen of Gladur Nock, lioness and defender of her people, and she was frightening in her sudden grandeur.

"Hope you never have to know," she said severely. "Now, go to bed."

Corin realized any further questioning would be dangerous. Yet he was determined now more than ever to see that magician again.

Chapter Three

A Chance Meeting

*T*he next morning Corin kept a low profile. Instead of breakfasting with his mother, he grabbed his leather wallet and, tucking it into his belt, left early for the compound. He told his mother he would grab a bite at the commissary with the others. She barely acknowledged that he had spoken. It was obvious that she was preoccupied, and he was glad to get out without having to answer any more questions.

The commissary in the Dragon Compound was alive with subdued morning chatter. Groups of workers either stood together at the high tabletops or sat on benches at the wooden tables. Corin went to the counter to pick up a bowl and get some bread, grateful that none of the servers commented on his being there. He breathed in the aroma of the morning soup and felt his stomach growl in anticipation. The food here was simple, but always plentiful and tasty. He found two of his former sweeping mates sopping up their morning soup with a fistful of bread. "Sprout!" one of his friends called out as he approached their table. "You've returned to us."

"I'm here every day, in case you hadn't noticed. The same as you," Corin said, and he sat down with his food.

"But never for meals any longer," his friend pointed out. "It's like you've gotten too good to spend time with us. To what do we owe the honor today? All rise! Prince Corin of Gladur Nock has arrived. Oh, wait, I don't have to stand in your presence. I'm a prince of the house of Nogardia, next in line to the crown. And I'm older. But you, Balu," he said, turning to the other boy, "you are only next in line to wash dishes. You are going to have to stand up."

"Just shut up, Muck, or I'll punch you in the nose," Corin threatened.

"You and who else?" Muck asked. He raised his arm and flexed his muscles. He was in fact half a head taller and twice as broad as Corin.

"I will command you, as your liege lord as long as you are here in Gladur, to stand still," Corin said with a smile. "And then I will have Balu beat you with a stick." The other boy perked up and cracked his knuckles with a wicked smile. Although Muck was large next to the prince, Balu towered over them both.

"That would do it," Muck said with a shrug of his shoulders and went back to his soup.

"I needed to get away from my mom before she started in on me," Corin explained. "My cousin's coming to stay with us. I think I'm going to come eat here a lot from now on." He took his first sip from his bowl and commented, "The food here is really quite decent."

"Oh, quite," said Muck in a mocking tone.

"Your cousin?" Balu asked. "Is she the one you got to eat fumets?"

"Taste. I only got her to taste them. And yes, she's the one."

"I bet she'll be delighted to see *you* again," Muck said, and all three began to laugh.

"Is she going to come here to work as well?" Balu asked.

"I suppose so. I don't know what else she would do here."

At that moment a bell rang and the knots of workers began breaking up. "Time to go," Muck announced and quickly downed his last bite of bread.

"Will she go out with you to learn how to scrub?" Balu asked as they carried their bowls to the wash basins.

Corin quickly drained his bowl as they walked, keeping his bread for later. He hesitated at this question. "Why would she do that?"

"She's your cousin. Isn't that what all the royals do?"

"I never thought about it," he admitted.

The three boys walked together towards the barn. Corin hooked the lunch bucket that was set out for him every day, and he put the bread he was saving into it. The large doors of the great barn had been opened, and the bright morning light streamed into the immense space. The boys hurried past the dragon's tail, which was twitching and thumping on the ground.

"Let's get moving, Sprout!" a voice bellowed from near the dragon's front leg. It was Mali, waving him to hurry. "Star is getting restless. Barn workers! Grab your tools and line up."

The prince hastened his pace, stopping only long enough to snatch up a scrubber and two empty buckets from their places along the wall. He passed by Mali with only a quick nod in greeting.

"I will take his improved mood as a sign that his health has shifted for the better," Mali said to him. "Bring him back in good humor."

Corin did not respond. Why did they always think that he could influence the dragon's mood? He arrived at Star's head.

"At last," the dragon said in his chime-like voice.

"Are you feeling better, Star?" the prince asked as he began his climb up to the top of the dragon's head.

"It's a beautiful day," Star responded. "And it's all a matter of timing."

"What's that supposed to mean?" he asked as he heaved himself up onto the dragon's broad neck, hanging onto his scrubber and buckets.

"It means that we have to leave now to be on time. Did you bring your needles? We don't want to disappoint Master Ambroise."

"Yes, I brought the needles," Corin grumbled, feeling to make sure the wallet was still tucked under his belt. He scrambled up to the crown of Star's head and sat down comfortably in the narrow indentation between two massive horns. Normally they were relaxed and hung back against the dragon's neck. Today, however, they stood up straight, which surprised him. He saw them standing up only when Star was excited about something. Corin knew the dragon would tell him only when he was ready, so he gave up asking more questions.

He looked down into the barn and saw that the workers had formed an orderly line along the wall, each standing with his tool of the day: pitchfork, shovel, broom, mop. They were ready for their day's work.

"All right, my noble steed," Corin said. "Giddyap."

"You are far too familiar," the dragon groaned.

The boy smiled. "Let's go to this rendezvous of yours."

"Very perceptive," Star said as he heaved himself onto his feet.

"It was a guess," Corin admitted. "But now you have me curious. Lead on." He pulled out the bread he had stowed away and continued his breakfast.

Star cleared the barn and turned onto the path that led to the orchard gate. Once they had left the Dragon Compound, they were on the path that skirted the outer walls of the city, before it veered away to a place downriver where the water was diverted into a smaller estuary where there were shallows. Star liked this place because it was a good distance from the city and had shade trees that offered privacy from the prying eyes of the curious.

As they came to a stretch of city walls before taking the path to the river, the dragon slowed down. Corin noticed and quickly swallowed his mouthful of bread.

"I thought you were in a hurry to be somewhere," he commented. "Why are you slowing down? Are you tired again?"

"I am slowing down because we've arrived," Star said, coming to a halt. Corin then heard the unmistakable sound of Star's ringing purr.

"For what?" Corin looked around, but at first saw only the massive stone walls of the city rising high overhead to one side and the open fields and quiet apple groves to the other. Then a man stepped out from around the great head of the dragon. He had been standing so completely underneath the dragon's chin that Corin had not seen him. At first look, Corin's heart leapt up into his throat with surprise and recognition. "You!" he gasped. Before him stood the grey-bearded magician.

"Imagine that," the old man commented carelessly. "Here I was taking a leisurely morning stroll to stretch my old legs, and you just happened to come along." Corin did not mention that this had been Star's doing.

"I am glad to see you. I won't keep you long," the old man continued. "I realize you also have somewhere to go. But I have some business with you. You have something of mine. Tell me, what you did with that dagger I gave you yesterday to hold for me."

The prince panicked. "I ... I don't have it any longer," he stuttered.

"What did you do with it?" the old man asked with a frown, twirling his beard around his fingers.

"My mother took it. I didn't mean for it to happen. But I had it stuck in my belt and she saw the hilt. My mother is—"

"I know who your mother is," the magician said curtly. "What was her reaction when she saw it?"

"She was upset. But she would not tell me why."

"That'll do," the magician said, looking satisfied. "Now, you have a cousin coming, I've heard."

"How do you know that?" the boy asked, astonished.

"It's my business to know. Your business is to keep a close eye on her. Bring her to me when you have a chance. Go on your way now," he said with a sudden dismissive gesture of his hand and turned away from them.

"Will you take me with you?" Corin had blurted these words out so suddenly that he surprised himself. The question had popped into his mind, but he had not meant to say it out loud.

The magician turned back, amusement in his eyes. "Here you have a whole dragon to take care of, the envy of every kingdom from the mountains to the sea, and you want to go with an old wanderer like me who is never quite sure where the next day will bring him. Who would have thought?"

"Well, can I?" Corin heard himself ask.

"Not now," the magician said firmly. "I want you here. But you are welcome to come visit me some day. Now go before anyone notices you've stopped and wonders why." He turned and walked away from them. Without waiting for Corin to give him directions, Star continued along the path to the river. Corin let the dragon walk silently for a while before speaking. The dragon was walking slower now.

"Star, what was that all about?" he finally asked.

"It sounded straightforward to me," the dragon answered. "He wanted to know what you did with his knife."

"You know him, don't you?"

"I don't know what you're talking about," Star responded.

"That was our rendezvous."

"Not at all," the dragon said. "Just a chance encounter. I stopped so as not to run him over. The foolish fellow was standing right in my way. I was hurrying down to the river, where a robin has been sitting on her eggs. They are due to hatch, and I wanted to be on time to see them."

Corin did not believe a word of it, so he was all the more astonished and confused when, in the branches of a poplar at the water's edge, Star showed him a nest where a robin's hatchlings had just that morning emerged.

Chapter Four

An Answer Only Star Would Know

*L*ate that afternoon, after he had returned Star to the care of the barn keepers, Corin learned that his cousin had arrived. Uncertain of how she would receive him, he avoided eye contact when he was introduced and offered only a polite, brief word of welcome. They ate an early supper with his mother, who plied her niece with many questions, saving her son from having to make conversation. For once, Corin was grateful for the chattiness of women and that he was not expected to take an active part. He did, however, several times catch his cousin sizing him up when she thought he was not looking.

"I will introduce her to the court after the Spring Festival," Aina declared, turning to her son. "But for now, before it grows too late, take Elinor to see Star." Corin stiffened, because it meant he would have to be alone with her. However, once they got into Star's presence, he knew his cousin's attention would not be on him.

The lanterns in the barn had been lit and they cast a golden glow through the giant structure. Elinor stopped in her tracks and just stared. The dragon's scales shimmered dark green in the barn's muted light.

"There he is," Corin said as they walked closer.

Elinor gazed on him in silence. "He's every bit as big as I remember him," she finally said, speaking in a low voice. "I thought that maybe I had only imagined him so large."

An older, grey-haired man carrying a rake was walking by. When he saw them, he stopped.

"Who's your friend, Sprout?" he asked.

"Sprout?" the girl looked up surprised.

"It's just a nickname," Corin said, shrugging it off.

"I like it," she said. "It fits you."

And I hate it, the boy thought. Instead, he said, "Mali, this is my cousin, Elinor."

"Ah, the young Elinor," Mali said. "We'd heard that you were coming. I'm sorry for your loss."

"Thank you," Elinor said, averting her gaze.

"Mali is the Barn Master," Corin continued. "He's in charge of everything that goes on in here. He's known Star longer than anybody else here. Even longer than my father."

Mali greeted Elinor with a kindly smile. "I'd heard that you were coming. I remember you from your earlier visits, although you were quite a bit younger then. Weren't you the one who stole away on Star's back when he went down to the river for his scrub?"

"Don't remind me," Elinor said with an embarrassed smile, glancing at Corin.

"Welcome back to the Dragon Compound," Mali said. "Are you going to join us and help look after Star?"

"As soon as I've settled in. I think that's what my aunt wants," she responded.

"Then maybe you can help us figure out what's ailing him."

"Is the dragon not well?" Elinor asked surprised. "I didn't know a dragon could get sick."

"Neither did we," Mali said with a shake of his head. "He's not been himself lately is all we know for certain. I've spent enough time around him to tell the difference. It's like he's grown old and tired. I'm starting to worry, I must admit."

"Ah, Mali," Corin said, "Star's all right. He's just a little under the weather."

"You have your ins with him, I'll accept, but I've seen more. There is no such thing as *under the weather* for Star."

"Do you also speak to the dragon?" Elinor asked.

"We all speak to the dragon," Mali replied with a laugh. "But I don't ever get much of a response that I can understand. That privilege is reserved for the king. And young Sprout, here."

"Mali," Corin asked, "is it all right if I show her around?"

"Take your time," the Barn Master said. "We've finished our work for the day and most everyone else has gone off to supper. I'm just attending to loose ends and getting things ready for tomorrow. I'll give a call when it's time to put the lanterns out." Mali turned and continued on his way.

"I like him already," Elinor commented.

"Mali's great," her cousin said. "He worked with Star where my dad grew up, and when they set up the Dragon Compound here, my dad asked Mali to run the barn. He's very good at it. Nothing gets overlooked. You'd be working under him, if you work in here. Is it true, then? Are you going to work in the compound?"

"That's what your mom suggested I do. I'm just not so sure I want to spend that much time so close to the dragon."

"Don't worry," Corin said. "You do most of your work when Star is away. I take him every day down to the river for a scrub."

"How many of you go?" she asked.

"Just me. I take him alone. Supposedly, it's a family tradition. My dad used to do the same thing."

"How do you get him there all alone?"

"It's not at all difficult. I just ask him to take me, and we go. Star knows the way and does all the walking. I sit up on top," he added, gesturing towards the crown of the dragon's head. "It's a great view from up there."

"That's not my memory of it," Elinor said with a frown. "I thought it was very scary." She stared at Corin until he was uncomfortable. "So, is it true?" she challenged. "Can you really talk to the dragon?"

"Don't you remember? You must have seen me talk with him on one of your visits."

"I remember, but I thought you were just making it up. You know, just to show off. It just sounded like a bunch of bells to me."

"Chimes, not bells. Star's voice is like the sound of chimes."

"It's all the same to me," Elinor shrugged. "All I know is that it doesn't sound like words."

"To me it sounds like words. I can understand what he says."

She snorted. "Prove it."

Corin shrugged his shoulders and shook his head. "Why don't you believe me?"

"All I want you to do is prove that you can really talk to him."

Corin took a deep breath. He knew he had to get this said if he was going to clear the air between them. "Look, I'm sorry that I played those tricks on you. I was a stupid, young kid. I thought it was funny. I know now that it wasn't."

"You don't have to apologize. What you did was mean, and I'm not going to forgive you anyway."

Corin threw up his arms in frustration. "So what do you want?"

"I think you're just pretending. And because you're the prince, no one is going to doubt you. I don't believe a dragon can talk. Or that someone who can be as mean as you were to me can understand him if he can talk."

Corin's eyes bulged and he was about to storm away. But he remembered his promise to his mother that he would be friendly and make her feel welcome. He reminded himself that she was not likely to be going away any time soon. She had come to stay and this was now her home. He took a deep breath and let it out slowly. He glanced at Star. They were standing near the dragon's left shoulder. He was looking down at them over his leg, listening in at their conversation.

"Star," Corin called up. "I want you to meet my cousin. She's come to stay with us."

"Your mother told me she was coming," the great dragon replied. "I remember her. She's the one you tricked into taking a ride on my back."

Corin winced. "He remembers you," he said.

"How do I know you're not making that up?"

"Why would I do that?"

"I don't know. Maybe to feel like you're better than everyone else."

"Star just spoke to me. You heard him. Why don't you want to believe that?"

"I'm just not convinced, that's all."

"What would it take to convince you?"

She thought for a while. "He'd have to say something you wouldn't know. Something too clever or wise for you to make up."

"That is just so mistrustful," Corin scowled. "What's wrong with you?"

"Nothing's wrong with me. Look, if you had a horse that neighed whenever you spoke with it, and then you said that it was talking, I'd think that you were just trying to trick me."

"And you would have a good reason to think that. There is no such thing as a talking horse."

"So why should I believe in a talking dragon?"

"Why should you believe in a dragon at all, except that he's in front of you?"

"Exactly. So my eyes tell me that he exists. But my ears don't yet tell me that he can talk." She smiled. "But I will admit that he does make some sweet sounds."

Star had listened to all of this in silence, and chuckled.

"What did he say?" Elinor asked.

"Nothing. He was laughing. At our argument, most likely."

"See. That's what I'm talking about. You could have told me anything. I'm going to believe you only when I've heard something you couldn't know."

"That sounds like an idiotic game to me."

"It's not a game at all," she insisted. "And you're just afraid."

"Afraid of what?"

"Afraid that I'll prove that you're making this all up."

"I don't have to prove anything to you," Corin said crossly.

"You only say that because you're afraid I'll expose your little game."

"I'm not afraid. There's no game to expose." Again Corin had the impulse to walk away and have nothing more to do with her, but he stopped himself. "Oh, you are *so* annoying."

"Ask her what her question is."

Corin looked up at Star. "You're not really going to fall for this, are you? She's just being difficult. She's angry at me because I played tricks on her when we were younger."

"What did he say?" Elinor asked.

"He wants to know your question."

"At least *he* takes me seriously."

"I thought he can't talk," Corin challenged her. "Besides, I *am* taking you seriously."

"No, you're not," the dragon said. Startled by this comment, Corin looked up at him again.

"Are you taking her side?"

"This has nothing to do with taking sides," the dragon continued. "She wants to know if she can trust me. She wants to know if she can trust what you tell her I've said. I find that very reasonable. Now ask her what her question is."

"What did he say?"

"He said he'll play your game. What's your question?"

Both the dragon and the girl said at the same time, "It's *not* a game!"

Startled, Corin jumped and looked from one to the other. Elinor's eyes were blazing with defiance. It was a look similar to what he had seen in his mother's eyes the night before. There was no doubt that she was part of the family.

"All right," he said, resigned to doing what she asked. "I got it. This isn't a game." He took a deep breath. "I'm ready. What's your question?"

Elinor did not hesitate. "Why does everyone call Star a *he*?" she asked. "I don't think Star's a he at all."

Corin stared at her a moment, then blurted out, "That's a stupid question."

"Are you going to ask him, or not?"

"I don't have to ask him. He's got ears. But don't expect him to answer such a stupid—"

"She is very perceptive," Star said, interrupting him.

"She's *what*?" he exploded.

"What did he say?" she asked.

"Never mind!" Corin snapped. Elinor started laughing. Corin was annoyed that she was enjoying herself at his expense. "Now just everybody slow down and don't talk to me at once," he said, glaring first at the dragon, and then at his cousin.

"Well, what is he?" she asked. "A *he* or a *she*?"

Star's chimes rang merrily as he answered her question. Elinor waited patiently for her cousin to speak.

"Both," Corin finally said, shaking his head in disbelief. "And neither. Star is not of the earth."

"What does that mean?" She waited while Star explained it.

Then Corin spoke. "Star lives on the earth, but he is not a creature of the earth, so he does not obey earth patterns and rules. He does not reproduce like other creature, so he has no need of … Star, what did you call it?" The dragon's chimes rang gently in answer. "Oh, right. He has no need of a gender."

Elinor looked puzzled and considered this last comment. Finally, she looked up and addressed the dragon directly. "How do you have babies, Star?" She waited for the chimes to stop before she turned to Corin for an answer. He looked stunned, as if he had just fallen from a horse. He spoke in a quiet voice.

"He doesn't. He says he was made from stardust. And one day, when his time here is complete, it is to stardust that he shall return."

Elinor smiled. "I'm satisfied," she said. "There is no way that you could have made that up. You're not that clever."

Corin stared at her, but he was too astonished by what Star had just divulged to be irritated by her comment. Not yet, at least. He had to finish his conversation with the dragon.

"Star, why did you never tell me about this?" he demanded.

"Because you never asked," the dragon said simply.

"But you've told me a lot of things I never asked about," he protested.

"And they are all matters that are important for you to know."

"You don't call this important?"

"I do, but since reproduction on the earth is really in the hands of the female gender, it was not a subject that was essential we touch upon. It took a woman, or woman-to-be, to wonder. She has a right to have her questions answered, since she is also of the race of the Dragon Keepers."

"She is?"

"I'm what?" Elinor asked. "What are you two talking about now?"

"What did you think, boy?" Star continued. "Her mother was your mother's sister. You are descended from the Dragon Keepers on both sides of your family. She is as connected to me as the queen."

"Unbelievable," he muttered.

"Yet true, nonetheless," Star said.

"Are you going to tell me what he's saying?" Elinor demanded.

"I think we should go talk with my mother," Corin muttered, pulling her by the sleeve. When Elinor began to protest again, he added, "And I'll tell you along the way." But then he stopped himself and turned back to Star. "Does Father know about this? I mean, about not having babies and all."

"It never came up between us. I have been content to be referred to as a *he*, since there is no term in your language that clearly identifies what I am."

"We've got to go now, Star," Corin said, pulling Elinor along.

"Thank her for her questions," the dragon said. "Somehow they've helped me feel a little better."

"What did he say?" Elinor asked as Corin towed her by the arm.

"Nothing," Corin insisted.

"Why don't you want to tell me?" Elinor pressed.

"I've told you everything," Corin mumbled, pulling harder to keep her moving. Deep in thought, he did not speak again as they passed through the palace hallways.

Chapter Five

Trouble to the South

*W*hen they entered the queen's chambers, they heard someone speaking loudly. The king had returned, and he was in an ill temper. He was pacing back and forth in front of the queen, who sat in her chair looking alert, yet unmoved by the king's passion. The cousins kept to the shadows, waiting until they knew they would be welcome.

"Why does that man still plague us?" the king's anger flared up. "I spend all my time dealing with the mischief he's done. Why does King Bellek give him a free hand to stir up so much trouble? How does this serve him?"

"What has he done now?" Aina calmly asked.

"Three more farms were burned along the frontier! We could not even find a trace of what happened to the families of two of them. We tracked one of the raiding parties clearly into Bellek's territory, but they got away. It's like chasing a phantom. I thought that being king meant I didn't have to do this anymore."

"No, dear," Aina replied patiently. "It means that you don't have to do this *alone* anymore. You can take the army with you. Or you could just send General Korvas to chase the phantoms. I'm sure he could handle it."

"No," he said quickly. "I have to see to this myself."

"There are other affairs of state that could also use your attention," Aina said stiffly.

"I'm confident you and the council can see to them," the king said. "And Sprout can see to the dragon."

"Then you should know that he's been complaining about that," Aina said.

"Complaining? About looking after Star?"

"He said that he wants some variation from always scrubbing the dragon."

"What is wrong with that boy?" the king growled. "I'll have to have a talk with Star."

"Maybe a talk with your son would be more to the point," the queen said cuttingly.

"We rarely cross paths," the king said with a shrug. "I'm so often on campaign, and he has Star to look after."

"You should have plenty of opportunity during the coming week."

"Aina, I'd been meaning to tell you—"

"You're not leaving again, are you?" the queen interrupted him with a look of alarm.

"As we rode to Gladur, messengers reached me that there is unrest to the south. Impossible as it sounds, who else can it be but Worrah, under Bellek's orders, stirring things up there as well."

"But the Spring Festival is in two days. I thought you had come home for that."

"It was my full intention," the king said. "But I dare not let things fester elsewhere. A small uprising leads to a big one in very little time."

"But certainly you can spare just two days for the festival. You are the Dragon Master," the queen pointed out. "How can the Dragon Master miss the spring procession?"

"I don't have a choice," Michael said firmly. "I have to go. Besides, I have full confidence that you and Sprout will pull it off. You will have Star's full cooperation. Mali has done this so often, you can leave most of the details in his competent hands."

"But the people! They will see that you're missing from the procession. They want to see their king, know that you stand beside me."

"How can they doubt that if I am off fighting my queen's wars?"

"The nobles will grumble again," the queen warned. "It's happened before. They will spread the rumor that you do not want to be seen. That you do not like the very festivals that you initiated and brought to the people."

"If only they *had* taken them up," the king said abruptly, turning away from his wife.

"How can you say that?" Aina protested. "The people have embraced both the harvest and the spring festivals whole-heartedly."

"Yes, with excessive feasting and carousing late into the night," the king said bitterly.

"They honor the day in the way they know best," the queen replied defensively. "They mean no disrespect. You are the only one who knows how things looked in Nogardia when you were a boy."

"Mali knows," the king muttered.

"And he has the good sense to keep his opinions to himself. You can't expect the people of Gladur to recreate for you a childhood memory. They celebrate in their own fashion."

"I only wish it were with a bit more decency."

"Michael, you have no way of knowing how the people in Nogardia celebrated when you were a boy. You were protected by your life in the compound."

The king paused to consider this and finally shrugged his shoulders with a frown. "I don't understand why you defend them. It feels so much like a continuation of how things were when I first came here, when Worrah let the rich carouse and the poor starve."

"Well, we have certainly changed that," Aina said defensively. "The poor starve no longer. The homeless are gone from the streets. That is an accomplishment to be proud of. You couldn't claim that for Nogardia when you were a boy. We can allow the people to celebrate these two times a year in a way that satisfies them."

The king sighed. "I suppose you're right."

"So you'll stay?"

"I cannot, Aina," the king said, avoiding her gaze. "I must attend to our frontiers."

"And what about attending to us? To our relationship? These festivals were once a time when we renewed our marriage vows. You've changed so from the man I married."

Michael looked pained. "That is unfair," he said weakly. "The security of the kingdom depends upon me."

"Then at least speak with your son before you leave," Aina insisted.

"I can't linger," he deflected. "My talk with Sprout will just have to wait."

"It doesn't have to. You could start right now," the queen declared.

"What do you mean?" The queen gestured and the king looked towards the door. He saw Corin and Elinor standing in the shadows of the room.

"Sprout!" he called out, masking his surprise. "Come in, my boy. I've finally made it home, but it won't be for long, I'm afraid. I will have to return soon to the campaign road. King Bellek is allowing Worrah a free hand to harass the frontier settlements. I am leaving the Spring Festival in your competent hands."

The disharmony between the king and the queen lingered in the room. The cousins walked tentatively forward, acting as if they had heard nothing of what had just passed. "And you must be young Elinor," Michael continued. "When did you arrive? Aina, you did not tell me that she was here already."

"Had I not? We had other pressing matters to discuss, I'm afraid."

"My, you have grown since we last had you here," the king said, placing his hands gently on her shoulders. "I want you to know that you are very welcome here. Are you settling in well?"

"Thank you, Uncle," she said with a curtsey. "I arrived only today, and my reception and lodging are everything I could want."

"Excellent," the king said. "Have you been to see Star yet?"

"Yes, Father," Corin said. "We're just coming from there."

"He's magnificent, isn't he?" the king said, beaming.

"Mother, Star said something that puzzles me," Corin turned to Aina. "He said that Elinor is also from the Dragon Keepers. Is that true?"

"I'm what?" Elinor asked.

"Never mind," Corin said, trying to brush her aside.

"You can't talk about me when I'm standing right here," Elinor objected. "That is so rude."

"Elinor is right," Aina said. "You have to include her in the conversation."

"Just tell me, will you?"

"I'll tell you both," Aina said with a stern look to her son. "Elinor's mother was my sister. That means that Elinor, through our father and back to our grandmother, Galifalia, is also descended from the Dragon Keepers. So what Star told you is true."

"Who are the Dragon Keepers?" Elinor asked. "My mother never told me about them."

"It is the ancient race from which we are descended. It is why we are able to keep a dragon here. We have a special connection with him. Perhaps your cousin will be willing to share more with you later. Corin?"

"Yes, Mother," Corin grumbled, casting his eyes down. Then he made a face at Elinor.

"Which brings me to ask," the king said looking at Elinor. "How soon do you think you will be ready to start working in the Dragon Compound? It will be light work at first, I assure you. Nothing you couldn't handle."

"I'm not sure I want to do that," Elinor replied. It was not what she meant to say. She had wanted to say that she was not sure about spending more time around her cousin. However, at her words, the king's mouth fell open. The queen quickly took him by the arm.

"I think what she means is that this is much too early to speak of such things. She has only just arrived, my dear. We must give her a chance to get to know her new home. I have not even presented her to the court yet. Tomorrow I will have my own personal handmaids take her around the city, visit the markets, make some new friends. Caring for the dragon can wait until after the Spring Festival."

"Of course," said the king, recovering from his surprise. "What was I thinking? The city is filling up with visitors and the people are preparing their spring revels. Elinor, take your time, tour the city, enjoy the festivities. There will be a great deal to see and a marvelous procession. Unfortunately, I must attend to affairs in the south, so I will miss out on the fun."

"Elinor," the queen said turning to her, "I think it is quite late enough. You have had a very full day, and tomorrow will be filled with many new impressions. Off to bed." She caught the king's eye and nicked her head toward their son.

"Yes, Auntie," Elinor said, giving the queen a quick hug. She turned to the king and gave a small curtsey. As she passed by her cousin, she stuck her tongue out at him before leaving the room.

"Did you see what she just did?" he protested to his parents.

"Off to bed with you, too, Sprout," the king said with a laugh, slapping him on the back. "Nothing that can't wait until tomorrow to deal with."

When Corin had left the room, the queen turned to her husband. "Well, you side-stepped that one." The king shrugged his shoulders, pretending not to know what his wife was talking about.

Chapter Six

Flight into the Night

$\mathcal{T}$he next day passed quickly for Corin. He was up and out before his cousin had risen from bed. He was surprised to hear from a servant that his father had already ridden off to rejoin the army. He went to join his friends for breakfast in the compound. They plied him with questions about his cousin, but he was not in a mood to talk and gave them silly answers until they were annoyed and gave up. He took Star over from Mali and walked him down to the river.

Corin was happy to be alone with the dragon. While he scrubbed Star's massive back, he pondered the events of the past two days. He was glad for the quiet to sort things out. When it was time to practice sparring with Star, he was not at his best. His mind was distracted, which made moves that he already found difficult outright impossible. During their rest time, they were both unusually quiet, and Corin was irritated with himself when a second needle he was polishing went lost in the fine sand along the bank. Star commented dryly, "Master Ambroise will not be happy."

"I'll deal with it," Corin replied with a scowl. Master Ambroise always made a fuss when he lost needles. After that, neither of them spoke again, and for once, Corin was content with silence. Later, he returned to scrubbing and was immersed in his thoughts of Elinor and the discord he had witnessed between his parents. For once, he was comforted by the monotonous, rhythmical brushing. When Star commented that it was getting late, Corin was startled to see that the sun had already set behind a gathering mound of dark clouds.

The lanterns in the great barn shed a golden light, though deep shadows gathered where it could not reach. Outside, the thick clouds caused night to fall early inside the barn. On their way home, Corin had watched the weather and wondered if the approaching storm had made Star more than usually sluggish. However, Star never used to be affected by the weather.

Corin finished his last check to make sure that the dragon's bedding was well distributed. The barn workers had gone to their supper, and Mali was off looking for some tools to repair a broken rake. Corin picked up the cracked handle and, studying it, commented out loud, "I can do this myself." He sat down on a barrel and took out a long strand of leather he had found earlier lying discarded on the floor. He started wrapping it around the crack in the handle, creating an intricate weave to give it support.

Star watched him work. "Well, that at least is something that catches your interest," the dragon said flatly.

"Do I sense sarcasm?" Corin asked, not looking up.

Star sidestepped the question. "You could have tried a bit harder today, and left the repair of tools to Mali and his crew."

"I like working with my hands," Corin sighed. "I'm good at it. Besides, it feels a lot more useful than …" But he cut himself off before he said something he might regret. But he had already said too much, and the dragon finished his thought for him.

"More useful than scrubbing a dragon and being forced to practice drills to learn a skill you don't want?" Outside the deep resonance of thunder rumbled and its vibrations shook the barn.

"Maybe I should just work under Mali and you could train someone else," Corin suggested. He knew it was not an option, but it felt good to say it. "I'm sure that Roderick would love the chance. He idolizes you."

"I have given Roderick some training already. It is now time that I work with you, the heir to the throne."

"Of course," Corin huffed impatiently. "The heir."

"You don't like the sound of that, do you?"

"It's just that it's so—undisputed."

"Undisputed? What is that supposed to mean?"

"As in *no choice.* No one bothered to ask me about it, whether I was interested in being the heir to the throne."

"Well, no one asked *me* if I was interested in being a Luck Dragon."

"Come on, Star. That's what you *are.*"

"And heir to the throne is what *you* are. And I would advise you not to take *undisputed* for granted. I believe there are several members of the court who would fancy themselves on the throne and would not hesitate to replace you. Geron, for instance."

"Ah, Star, not with you around."

"That does not stop them from plotting. Which brings me back to asking you to try a bit harder during our practices."

"You're not terribly perky yourself these days," the young prince countered.

"Don't worry about me. I'm not the one in training. You are. At least, I thought you were. How about reviewing everything you seem to have forgotten how to do? We could go over it now, if you like."

"Can we talk about something else?" Outside, there was another deep roll of thunder.

"As you wish. How are things going with your cousin?" the dragon asked. "Are the two of you getting along any better?"

"Ah, she'll be all right, I guess," Corin said. "As long as I don't have too much to do with her. Of course, because of her, I did learn something about you that I might never had known. But I still find her annoying."

"I believe I overheard her saying something similar about you."

"Thanks for being on my side, Star."

"I'm on both your sides. In fact, I am on everyone's side. I'm a Luck Dragon."

"Well, if you're on everyone's side, then tell me this: Do you also bring good fortune to people who are up to no good? Like to Geron, who plots to usurp the throne?"

"I never said he was plotting, so don't go putting words in my mouth. Although, if he were, it would not surprise me. I bet he thinks his oldest son would be a far better heir than you are."

"Leprun?"

"Yes, Leprun. And as to your question, if you count that my influence could help them lead better lives, then yes, I do bring good fortune to those who are up to what you call *no good*. But if you asked them at the time, I suspect they would not recognize my influence as good fortune."

"Well, maybe you could do something to help Elinor be less annoying."

"I think I have my hands full with you right now."

"What? A big guy like you can't handle a kid like me?"

The dragon's chime-like laughter filled the barn. The boy could not resist joining in. The dragon's laughter, however, was suddenly cut off. His neck went stiff and his eyes stared blankly into the darker recesses of the barn, focused intensely inward. With a swooshing sound, he was on his feet in an instant.

Corin was knocked over by the dragon's sudden move. He scrambled to his feet. "Star!" he yelled up at him. "Star! What's going on?"

The dragon looked down at his small figure, blinking his eyes, as if coming out of a deep trance. "Open the barn doors," he commanded.

"Star, it's night time," Corin objected. "You can't go anywhere now. There's a storm about to break. And you haven't been well. Haven't you heard the thunder?"

"Open the doors," the dragon repeated. "Otherwise, I will break them down. I'm leaving."

"Star, I can't let you go," Corin stammered.

"You don't have to," the dragon said curtly. "You're going with me. Now open the doors and take some weapons. You're going to need them."

"Weapons? Whatever would I want—?"

"Now!" the dragon ordered sharply.

Star was too commanding for Corin to disobey. He unlatched and pushed open the large barn doors. He went to a closet that held a hodgepodge of items and where he remembered once seeing some weapons tucked in the back. He found most of what he was looking for. He buckled on the sword, although it was not full-size. He strapped on a helmet, but it was a poor fit, made for a man with a larger head. He slipped his arm through the straps of a battered shield that had seen better days. "Shouldn't we tell someone? Mali must be somewhere nearby."

"Climb on," the dragon ordered as he lowered himself to the ground. "We have no time to lose."

"Star, night has fallen," Corin pointed out as he clambered up the dragon's leg and onto his long neck. "It's going to rain. Wherever are we going?"

"To save your cousin."

"My cousin? Elinor is inside supping with Mother."

"Of that, you are mistaken."

"Explain."

"No time right now. I'll tell you more once we've arrived. Back down and sit between my wings. You will be best protected there from the wind." Star walked to the open door, spread his great wings and lifted off the ground into the night. Above their heads a muted flash of lightning flared, hidden by the looming clouds.

"Ah, just my kind of weather," the dragon murmured as he rose higher to skim the underbelly of the storm.

Corin heard this comment and thought darkly to himself, *Does anyone care what my kind of weather is?* The rain had not yet begun, but the air was moist. Bracing his legs, Corin tied his collar tight, as a roll of thunder surrounded them.

It was a wild ride through the darkness, the wind whipping at the loose ends of Corin's clothing and rattling the helmet against his ears. He learned the hard way that he had to keep the shield flat against the dragon's neck. He had let the edge of it come up, and the wind snatched it like a kite and nearly ripped it from his arm, wrenching his shoulder, the sudden pain taking his breath away. The only solace was Star's coat. In the darkness of the night it shone like the stars in the heavens. Corin imagined himself riding through the Milky Way. He had ridden on Star's back while in flight before, but never at night. In spite of his initial reluctance to be there, he was delighted with this new experience, and it took the edge off his agitation to be involved in this unexpected adventure.

The ride on Star was much smoother than riding on the back of a horse. However, without being able to see where they were going, Corin was aware that they had arrived only when Star landed. Taking stock of himself, he was surprised that his face, hands and clothing were wet. However, it was not raining where they were standing. They must have flown high enough to have passed through the clouds. He scrambled down to the ground from his perch.

"All right, Star," he demanded. "I'm listening. What's going on? I thought you weren't feeling well."

"The flight was more taxing than I would like to admit."

"Then what are we doing here?"

"Your cousin's been kidnapped," Star said tersely.

"She's just arrived! Who would do that?"

"It's hard for me to tell. We'll have to ask her when we have a chance. I know only that she's in trouble, and they're not far from here."

"Star, how do you know this? How did you know where to go?"

"She summoned me."

"She did *what?*"

"She told me what's happening and where to find her."

"How did she do that?"

"It's in the blood."

"But she can't talk with you. Yesterday, she couldn't understand a word you said."

"Yet she has brought me here."

"Can I do this? Summon you from far away?"

"We'll have to try it some time. Right now, you have to help her. This is about as far as I should go. As it is, I'm not at my best. Now it's your turn."

"I beg your pardon?"

"I've found them, and now I will stay out of the way while you deal with this."

"While I deal with this? Are you aware, we came out here alone, just the two of us?"

"That should be enough. You brought a sword."

"What do you expect me to do? Rush in there with my blade flashing and slay them all?"

"Something like that."

"I'm not my father, you know."

"So I've noticed."

"Look, Star, I just don't do things the way he does."

"Then do it your way. Isn't that what you're always insisting you want?"

"Oh, bother!" Corin flapped his arms in exasperation. But when he saw that Star was not going to help him any further, he took a deep breath and steadied himself. "All right, I'll do it. But you're not getting out of this so easily. You got me into this and you'll have to play your part. There'll be no hiding in the bushes."

"But you know the danger if it comes to blows. You're much better off doing this alone."

"I told you I'm not my father."

"Should I go get him?"

"Right, and bring the palace guard while you're at it."

"I'm on it," the dragon said, turning to go.

"Star! You're not going anywhere!" The dragon stopped and looked back over his shoulder. Corin glared at him. "You're enjoying this, aren't you? Go on, admit it."

Instead, the dragon said, "You know what could happen to me at the very first blow ..."

"I don't plan on there being any. Besides, it's a risk we're going to have to take. You're always harping at me to take risks. Well, this time it involves you. Just follow my lead, all right?"

"What fun!"

"I knew it. This feels like such a setup."

"Honestly, I had nothing to do with it."

"Indeed, on a stormy moonless night, you've taken us into a dense forest where my cousin is held captive and you managed to get me to come fully armed. You've had nothing at all to do with this."

The dragon ignored him. He was peering into the darkness. "I think I see their campfire."

"Then I'm relieved I won't have to stumble around in the dark too long. What direction is it in?"

"Turn around and walk through these trees. Then you'll see it, too."

"I can smell it already. All right, here's the plan. You will follow me and stay in the shadows out of sight until I call for you. When I tell them you'll eat them, you better look like you mean it," he warned.

"I promise," the dragon said, and gave the prince a gentle nudge from behind with his snout.

"Don't be so pushy," Corin complained, but he could not keep himself from smiling. He sobered quickly and whispered over his shoulder, "And be quiet."

The small band of rough-looking men that sat huddled around a meager campfire was startled at the noise of someone crashing through the bushes. In the darkness, it sounded like a whole army was headed toward them. Star had made no attempt at being quiet.

"What's that?" one of them cried out, and as a body, they jumped up and grabbed their swords, ready to defend themselves. The youngest among them pulled a slight figure of a girl to her feet and dragged her back into the shadows, despite her resistance. The men stood their ground as Corin emerged from the bushes. They peered around him, expecting more, but behind him it was now silent. Then they focused their attention on the youth. They noted the ill-fitting helmet, the tattered shield and the short sword, which he had not yet drawn.

"You the rescue party?" one of the men asked. Then he began to laugh. "They sent a boy alone as a rescue party?" And he doubled over with laughter. Relieved, the others joined in. Elinor took this unguarded moment to bite the hand of the man holding her. He cried out in pain and cursed, but he could not stop her from breaking free. She ran to Corin and held onto his arm for safety.

"I knew you'd come," she said breathlessly. Her hair was mussed up and her eyes were wide with both fear and relief.

"You're nothing but trouble, you know," Corin hissed at her.

"But it will all work out in the end," she said confidently, although her voice was shaking.

"What makes you so sure?" he leaned over to whisper in her ear. "We happen to be outnumbered."

"You came with Star, right?" Elinor said confidently. "And Star's a Luck Dragon."

"That's not the way he works," Corin hissed. "Why doesn't anyone around here understand that?"

"Well, boy, it's your move," the man who had first spoken now invited.

Corin stood up straighter and announced, "I've come to retrieve my cousin. She does not have leave to go with you. I am returning with her to Gladur Nock."

"Oh-ho," said another of the brigands. "We seem to have the honor of the young prince himself. Our prize is looking better and better. We've snagged two royals now."

"I'm taking my cousin back to the palace," Corin repeated, as if they had not heard it the first time.

"You and who else?" the leader asked, peering into the darkness behind the prince. "You're a bit scrawny to take on all five of us. And your sword is a bit on the short side."

"I didn't come alone."

"Really? And who came with you? Did you bring your pet dragon with you?" The men laughed at their leader's joke.

"As a matter of fact, I did." With these words, Corin raised his hand, and there was a loud rustling in the lower branches of the trees. The dragon's immense head emerged from between the leaves and into the circle of firelight. The men gasped and recoiled. Their leader recovered first.

"Steady, lads," he said. "He's just here for show."

"He makes a big showing, that one," one of the brigands said, his voice quivering.

"Steady," their leader warned. "I know all about that dragon. Tame, he is."

"Tame unless roused and angered," Corin quickly added. "And you've upset him by taking the queen's niece. He's not happy. I am the only thing that stands between you and sudden death. I am willing to spare your lives and let you go, if you swear never to set foot in Gladur Nock again." He glanced over his shoulder and gave a little nod to the dragon. Star yawned, and although it exposed his immense teeth and cavernous jaws, the gesture was too obviously benign. The brigands were not fooled.

"You're going to let us go?" the leader asked, glancing up at the dragon, and then he took a step towards the boy.

"If you go now." Corin's voice was quivering and he silently scolded himself for not being able to control it.

"That's so generous of you." The brigand took another step forward, and this time the other members of his band followed his lead and stepped forward as well.

"I'm warning you," Corin said. "This offer will not hold much longer."

"Then we should act fast," but instead of turning, the brigand continued to close the space between them.

"I don't think this plan is working very well," Elinor said quickly in Corin's ear, the panic rising in her voice. "It's time to try something else."

"I don't *have* any other plan," Corin hissed in a low voice. He took the sleeve of her tunic and began slowly pulling her back into the bushes.

"Grab 'em, boys!" the leader commanded, and the band lurched forward as one.

"Do something!" Elinor shrieked.

At that exact moment a flash of blinding-white light burst upon them, accompanied by a deafening crack as if a tree had been broken in half. The dragon emitted a roar that sounded like a storm rushing through the forest. Startled, the cousins jumped, their hearts pounding. At the dragon's roar, the brigands stared, their faces contorted with fear.

"Run!" one shouted.

"Run for your life!" yelled another. They turned as one and stumbled out of the clearing, falling over one another, getting up and scrambling as fast as the dark night and the dense forest would allow.

"Now!" Corin yelled and, dragging his cousin, disappeared into the dense undergrowth and beneath the waiting dragon. With another flash and peal of thunder, the skies opened up. A torrent of heavy rain suddenly poured down, drenching everything that was not protected. The cousins, their hearts still pounding, found the underbelly of the dragon the perfect place to stay safe and dry.

"That was close," Corin panted.

"Stars," Elinor said with wonder. "Where did all the stars come from?"

"Oh, when it's dark, that's what his coat does," Corin explained.

"That's the dragon?"

"That's where his name came from," Corin said. "That's why he's called Star."

"I always wondered," Elinor said. "It's beautiful. Why didn't you ever tell me?"

"It would have come up sooner or later. You only just got here, remember? Are you all right?"

"You planned that, didn't you?" Elinor said, still gripping his arm.

"You think I planned that? The lightning and the thunder?"

"Well, maybe not every detail, but the dragon took care of the rest. Didn't he?"

Corin moaned. "What can I say to make you understand?"

"How else can you explain it? You chased them away, and you never struck a blow. Just brilliant."

"Look, I'll prove it to you. Star! Can you hear me?" The sound of the pouring rain was loud.

Although they were no longer near the spluttering campfire, they could make one another out in the luminosity of the dragon's marvelous coat. Star's head now appeared upside down, as he bent over to talk to them taking refuge beneath him. "Yes, my young master?"

"Star, why did you roar?"

"I am almost embarrassed to admit it, but I was startled by the sudden flash of lightning and the crack of thunder. It was a very near hit. And I may be a dragon, but I have a very healthy respect for lightning. I prefer to stay out of its way."

Corin told his cousin what Star had said. Then he added, "Star had not agreed to do anything but stand there and hope the very sight of him would frighten them. You see, he can't be around fighting—"

"I don't know why, but you're making that up," Elinor interrupted him. "I don't believe you would have come out here without knowing that you could overwhelm them. You could not have left it to chance that they would be scared of Star just because he showed up."

"It was the best plan I had," Corin said with a shrug.

"It makes no sense that you want to pretend that you didn't know what you were doing. But have it your way. I'm ready to go home now," she said.

Corin shouted up to the dragon again to be heard over the storm. "Star, can you get us back to Gladur Nock?"

"With this rain," Star responded, "I recommend that we walk for the time being. You can remain dry underneath my wing."

"Accepted," the boy said. "Lead on."

The rain continued to fall hard as the two walked along under the protective shelter of Star's partially extended wing. It made the perfect awning to keep them dry. Corin quizzed his cousin to find out how she had landed in the hands of the brigands.

"You did what?" he asked astonished.

"I went with them," she answered meekly.

"Willingly?"

"I thought it would be fun. And they seemed so friendly. I didn't know they were going to kidnap me. And when I tried to make them let me go by saying the queen's my aunt, instead of releasing me, they hustled me right out of town."

"Where was your chaperon?" Corin asked.

"I gave her the slip," Elinor answered sheepishly.

"I sort of like that part," Corin chuckled. "But do you have any idea—" He stopped himself before continuing. "Look, promise me that you will never leave with strangers again. Or give your chaperon the slip." In the back of his mind, he had a glimmer of understanding about why his mother insisted that he never wander the city alone. However, he quickly pushed this enlightenment away. He was not ready to admit that she had been right. After all, no one had ever tried to kidnap *him*.

Elinor hesitated, but then nodded her head. "All right, I promise. At least for the time being."

"That'll have to do," Corin said. He knew he would get nowhere insisting on more.

"We're not alone," the dragon broke in. He had stopped walking.

"Can you tell who's coming?" Corin asked, his hand reaching for the hilt of his sword.

"Unless I'm mistaken, it is the queen's guard."

"How did they find us?"

"I thought you might want some backup," the dragon answered.

"Backup? You didn't trust that I could handle this?"

"I had full trust in you," Star said sincerely.

"Then why the backup?"

"What's he saying?" Elinor asked.

"I'll tell you later," Corin shushed her. Then he turned back to Star. "Why the backup?"

"To keep the queen happy," Star said.

"Go on."

"Well, there was no way she was going to overlook the two of you missing—"

"Oh, and it was easy to overlook that the barn was empty and *you* were gone."

"Let me rephrase that: She was not going to overlook that we all three were missing, so I gave her something to do. I couldn't just let her sit there and fret."

"And how did you do that?"

"What's he saying?" Elinor demanded.

"Not now," Corin insisted. Then he said to the dragon, "How did she find us?"

"I sent her a message."

"I didn't know you could write," the boy said acidly.

"I never said I sent her a written message."

"What's he saying?" Elinor shouted.

"I said, not now!" Corin shouted back.

Armed guards carrying sputtering torches suddenly swarmed out of the darkness ahead of them and took up position, protectively surrounding the dragon.

"Mother!" Corin called out. "We're here!"

The queen of Gladur Nock emerged from among her guards and strode up to the cousins underneath the dragon's wing. She wore a long, woolen cloak against the rain and a helmet on her head. "I know," she spoke. "I could hear you quarreling."

"We weren't quarreling," the boy objected.

"No, Auntie," his cousin added. "He came to save me."

"So it would seem," the queen replied. Corin could tell from the tone of her voice that she was far from happy. But how could he expect otherwise. She had not had the umbrella of a dragon's wing to keep her dry. "Well, I can see that you are both being well cared for," the queen conceded. She glanced up at the dragon that was peering down at her. "Thank you, Star." He chimed his bells in reply. She then turned and addressed a guard who was standing in attendance nearby. "Morik, take a patrol and go find these kidnappers."

"Yes, Your Majesty," he said and turned to go, but Corin held him back. "Morik, wait. Mother, they're long gone," he explained.

"And it really wasn't their fault," Elinor added. "I mean, it *was* their fault, but—"

"Morik," the queen broke in, "go look for them. I don't want word getting out that my niece will walk off with any handsome face that invites her." Morik strode off barking orders, and disappeared with a number of the guard.

"I didn't find any of them handsome," Elinor objected. "Well, with the exception of the one who had such a sweet smile. But he hardly ever said anything. I could not believe that he could be one of them. I think in the end he would have let me go."

"Is that the one you had to bite to get away?" Corin taunted.

"Well, he wouldn't let me go when you showed up," she said defensively.

"Enough!" the queen stopped them. "We'll talk more of this later. It's time to get you home and dry—and Star safely back in the barn." She turned her attention to Corin. "Considering his present condition, Mali is fit to be tied that you took the dragon out in such weather."

"I didn't take Star out," Corin protested. "He took me."

"That's just an excuse," the queen said with a dismissive gesture. "Is the dragon in your care or isn't he?"

"Yes, he's in my care—"

The queen would not let him continue. "Can you handle looking after the dragon?"

"Yes," Corin snorted. "I can handle it."

"Then don't take him out on stormy nights in his present condition. It's that simple."

"And just let Elinor be kidnapped?" he snapped back.

"We would have gotten her back one way or another. If you need to go ranging about the countryside, take a horse."

"You are so *unreasonable* sometimes," Corin complained.

"Better to be unreasonable than irresponsible," the queen countered.

"So, now I'm irresponsible? This wasn't my idea."

"And you just happened to be an innocent bystander, accidentally out in the forest, fully armed, for an evening's stroll?"

"Forget it, just forget it," Corin said flapping his arms in frustration. He turned to storm away, stopped himself, took several deep breaths, and then turned back to his mother. "All right, I promise. I'll never take the dragon out again without permission. Is that what you wanted to hear?"

"That'll do," said the queen. She turned to address the dragon. "Star, how can I thank you for looking so well after them?" The dragon's bells chimed merrily. The queen turned to her son. "What did he say?" she demanded.

"I don't think I ought to tell you." Corin was still pouting. The bells chimed briefly again, and it sounded like an order. "All right, I'll tell her. Star says he doesn't remember the last time he's had so much fun." There were some more bells. "And he hopes that we can do this again sometime."

"Wonderful!" the queen said bitterly. "I'm glad that we're at least keeping our dragon amused. Let's go home."

Once back at the palace, attendants helped the queen remove her soaked cloak. Elinor gasped and her eyes grew wide to see that her aunt was wearing full armor and a sword hung at her waist. As they walked to their rooms, she commented to her cousin, "Sprout, she looks so impressive in that armor. As if she could really wield a sword."

Corin laughed. "Just don't make her angry. When she hits me, it hurts even more than when my dad does. I think he holds back, but she wallops me with a full swing. Just don't get her worked up. It's not worth it."

"They *hit* you?" Elinor was aghast. "Your parents *hit* you?"

"Well, not anymore. But when I was younger, and only when I deserved it," Corin said with a shrug. "It's not like they smacked me out of the blue or anything."

"But they *hit* you?"

"Look, if I did something I shouldn't and I got caught, what do you expect them to do? Sometimes I made them really mad. I can't say I blame them." Then he added quickly, "But don't tell them I said that."

She had a worried look on her face. "Do you think... because I ran away... and got kidnapped ...?"

He understood where she was going. "Not a chance. She didn't even punish me for going with Star, and she was really upset. Besides, you're a girl. There's no way they would hit a girl. And you just got here. Just don't let it happen again."

"Believe me," Elinor said with a relieved laugh, "once is enough."

"The spring procession is just two days away," Corin said. "That will keep my mom so busy that she will forget all about this. Timing is everything, you know. At least, that's what Star says."

"Oh, I hope so," Elinor said earnestly.

Chapter Seven

A Plot Uncovered

*E*linor gazed at her reflection in the large looking glass and sighed with pleasure. She wore a full skirt that flared out due to the two starched petticoats beneath. It was covered by an apron intricately stitched with images of wild flowers in blue, gold, red, vermillion and yellow. White knee stockings covered her lower legs. Her blouse was white with a simple design of blue forget-me-nots stitched on the collar. Across her shoulders was spread a midnight-blue shawl that was embroidered with a random pattern of golden stars. Her hair had been braided, pinned up and decorated with sprays of white and lavender lilac.

"I look so beautiful," she sighed again. "Thank you, Aunt Aina."

The queen looked up from where she sat, holding still so her attendants could finish placing flowers into her hair. "Your beauty is all your own, Elinor. You needn't thank me for that. I simply provided some clothing."

Elinor laughed and blushed at her aunt's compliment. Still gazing at herself, her expression grew suddenly solemn. "Somehow, it's not right to look so beautiful so soon after they've … gone."

"I understand, my dear," Aina said quietly. "Although nothing can take the hurt away, you do not dishonor their memory by taking part in our ceremony today. Your mother would want you to be cheerful and beautiful. Our sadness cannot bring them back. If it helps, think that you have dressed up today for her sake."

Elinor looked long again at herself in the mirror. "Then, for today, for my mother's sake, I will be cheerful," she said forcing herself to smile. "And beautiful." Tears formed in the corner of her eyes.

"That's my brave girl," Aina said.

"Will I walk with you?" Elinor asked.

"Since I have not presented you at court yet, it would look odd and raise questions if you accompanied me. I will have you walk with the other maidens of the noble families. You will be with some of the girls who showed you around town the other day ... before you gave them the slip."

Elinor blushed under Aina's stern gaze. "I promise not to wander away again, Auntie," she said quickly.

"I certainly hope not," the queen said. "There are many foreigners in town for the festivities, in addition to our own populace from the countryside. I want you to stay with the other handmaidens throughout the festival. No mixing with the crowd this time. Promise?"

"Yes, Auntie."

"You will have plenty of mingling after the procession. Afterwards there is a grand reception where you can get a closer look at the nobility of Gladur Nock."

"Where will Sprout be?"

"During the procession, you will see him perched on Star's neck. Afterwards, it is anyone's guess what he will do. Most likely he'll find some mischief to get into. And for that reason, you might consider staying away from him until afterwards. Unless, of course, you like mischief."

Elinor bowed her head gently and curtsied towards the queen. "Yes, Your Majesty," she said with a broad smile. And then she blushed realizing what she had just said. "I mean, no, Your Majesty. I don't like mischief." The queen laughed at her confusion and directed one of the girls attending her to take Elinor to join the other maidens preparing for the festivities.

The queen's niece joined the handmaidens in their place along the procession. The girls chatted happily among themselves, admiring and comparing one another's costumes, commenting on the dress of the ladies of the court, many of whom were the mothers of the girls surrounding Elinor. Some of the talk was complimentary, some of it was snippish and hurtful, nothing that Elinor was unaccustomed to hearing among girls. For the most part, she remained silent, listening and observing. As it was, she was not prepared for the scope and grandeur of the procession, nor for the crowds cheering them on. She had never seen so many people in one place before. It felt like one enormous packed marketplace, yet they were walking out in the fields outside the walls of the city. Every free space was occupied by colorful pavilions, and banners waved in the breeze. Her head was swimming from the noise and the sheer immensity of it all.

Elinor found herself unintentionally lagging behind her group of handmaidens. She was distracted by all the colors and waving flags and cheering faces on both sides of the procession. However, she only noticed this when she looked up and saw that she was now walking among the adults. Both the men and the women were dressed in richly dyed velvets, while the women's headdresses and the men's hats were adorned with feathers and colorful silk bows. The men carried swords at their sides and wore self-satisfied smiles on their faces. Several of the women were more ornately dressed than the queen herself, and a few wore dresses with trains so long that youthful servants followed behind holding the expensive cloth off the ground.

One man in particular caught Elinor's attention and intrigued her. He was tall and, although he wore a short cape covering his upper body, he looked immensely strong. He had a hawk-like nose and eyebrows that ran together. His black beard was neatly trimmed and cut to a point, giving him a dashing look. She found him very attractive. He was walking beside another man, who had curly hair, a round face and a stout body. His smile was jovial and he seemed to be always ready to laugh at what his companion was speaking into his ear. Although he was not what she might call handsome, she was attracted to the mood he emanated, as if she would find something to laugh about as well.

Elinor sidled over to the two men, who were so involved in their conversation that they paid little heed to this young handmaiden who was suddenly walking beside them. She was curious what they could be speaking about that gave them both such obvious delight.

"... that her dress says it all, Geron," the curly-haired man was saying. "What further proof do we need that she is common born?"

Who could they be talking about? Elinor wondered.

"In truth," his hawk-nosed companion responded. "We need only observe where she spends her time when not in court. It is nearly shameful."

"She's out buying the support of the poor," the curly-haired man said quickly. "Low born, the both of them. At least he has the decency to acknowledge it."

"Curious that he avoids the very festivities that he introduced," hawk-nose said. "As if he's embarrassed to be seen here."

"Soon, Geron," his stout companion continued, "when the young buffoon of a prince disappears, the nobility will take its rightful place and have cause for celebration. Until then, we must smile and pretend..."

Elinor needed to hear no more. When it dawned on her who they were talking about, she felt a sense of urgency. She had to get to her aunt. She hastened her pace until she caught sight of the queen walking in the procession. Aina was graciously waving to the cheering crowds. Elinor saw that she would have no chance to get close to her.

She knew who she needed to find, even though it annoyed her to admit it. She looked behind, over the heads of those in the procession. Not far behind, towering over everybody, walked the dragon, acknowledging the crowds of people with graceful nods of his great head. He wore a huge garland of flowers around his horns and had an immense harness strapped to his body. Attached to the harness were long lines that pulled a wagon filled with cheering maidens and farmers. On Star's head, amidst all of the greenery of the garland, sat her cousin. She wondered if she should go to him now, but then changed her mind for a better plan. She watched until she saw a break in the crowd and headed into the gap.

Some time later, Corin was climbing down from the dragon's great neck. They were back in the barn and several workers were unfastening the harness from the dragon's body under the watchful eye of the Barn Master. The boy looked up and called out, "Thanks for the ride, Star." Then he turned to Mali. "He didn't have any trouble pulling that wagon."

"I think the festival and the crowds cheered him up," Mali responded.

"How can he not be happy on a day like this? I'm going to the festival. I don't want to miss the jousting. 'Bye, Mali, see you tomorrow morning."

"Don't get into too much trouble," Mali called back. Corin turned and walked quickly through the barn. He had arranged to meet up with Muck and Balu after the procession and tour the food stands on their way to the jousting grounds. As he was passing by a large storage cupboard, a hand reached out from beside it and, grabbing hold of his tunic, yanked him off-balance.

"Hey!" he called out in surprise. Corin found himself staring into his cousin's face. "You! What are you doing here? And what in the world are you doing grabbing me like that?"

"We have to talk," she said urgently.

"Where's your chaperon?"

"She couldn't keep up. Sprout, I've uncovered a plot."

"What kind of plot? Hopefully not one to kidnap you again."

"Look, Sprout, you have to take this seriously. It's against your parents. And you."

"Keep talking," Corin said. "I'm listening." Elinor described what she had heard while walking the procession.

"They're from the noble families? Are you sure?"

"They were walking with the others."

"Would you recognize them again?"

"I'm certain of it."

"Then let's go to the ball. They're bound to be there and you can point them out to me."

"There's a ball? Is that the reception Auntie was talking about?"

"It's where all the noble families get together and gossip," Corin explained. "There's music and some dancing. It's so boring, I don't know what they like about it so much, but most of the adults make a showing. We can grab a bite to eat there as well. I'm hungry. Come on, I'll take you there."

Corin led the way to the great hall in the palace. It was late afternoon, and daylight poured in through the large windows. Elinor stopped in her tracks as they entered the room. The space was gaily decorated with sprays and garlands, the musicians were playing a fast-paced piece, and dancers were skipping and twirling across the middle of the floor. There was an underlying buzz of conversation and people were standing everywhere outside the dancing. Servants snaked their way through the throng, carrying plates of food from which revelers helped themselves as they passed, while other servants carried large pitchers of wine, filling any goblet thrust in their direction. Elinor gaped in amazement. It was a lot for her to take in at once.

"You do everything big here," she sighed.

"What do you mean?" Corin mumbled, shoving a sweet bun he had just snatched from a passing tray into his mouth.

"Big hall, big dance, big noise, big crowds, big procession, big dragon. Everything is big."

Corin laughed. "That's Gladur Nock for you. Better get used to it. How do you want to go about finding these conspirators of yours?"

"I didn't expect so many people," Elinor admitted. "I'm not sure what to do." Her attention was drawn to a royally dressed couple who sat on a raised dais at the head of the hall. Something about them, however, was irregular. The man had a weathered look, his beard was wild and untrimmed, and he had piercing eyes. He surveyed the hall of noble ladies and gentlemen with what Elinor took to be a mixture of mistrust and hostility.

"Who are they?" Elinor asked, tugging at her cousin's sleeve.

Corin had also noticed them. He had the feeling that the man was staring straight at him, and it made his skin crawl. The woman was equally wild and uncombed, but had a flower garland in her hair. She had a broad smile and was thoroughly enjoying herself swinging the goblet in her hand in time with the music.

Corin forced a smile. "That's the Lord and Lady of Misrule."

"I beg your pardon?" Elinor was certain she must have heard wrong. "They're what?"

"They are the master and mistress of the revels," Corin explained. "A man and a woman are chosen by lot from the peasantry to be in charge of the festivities. They make a brief showing here in the palace, and then take a place of honor outside to preside over all the activities. Any questions or disputes are brought to them, and their word is final. For one day, they even have the power to place someone in the stocks or even in prison, so the people think twice before coming before them with any frivolous suits."

"What an odd custom," Elinor said.

"It works for the people. They all look forward to having one day in the year when one of their own rules over them. Anyway, they'll soon move on. They only come for a few dances—oh, look, the Morys Dancers are coming."

The music had changed and a large space in the middle of the room opened up. Into it streamed a double line of men, adorned with long ribbons, dressed in white and wearing colored waistcoats. Each of the men carried a stick and sported bells on his arms and legs so that they jangled merrily with every movement.

"Oh, I've seen them before," Elinor said. "I like how they smack their sticks."

Elinor and Corin watched as the dance unfolded to a lively tune that kept the dancers in constant movement, even hopping to the music when standing in place. They used the sticks they carried to either smack the wooden floor or strike against a neighbor's stick. When the dance came to an end, the revelers in the hall clapped in appreciation. Before Corin could ask how Elinor wanted to search for her conspirators, the musicians took up a new tune.

"It's a children's dance," Corin groaned. "Come on, let's get out of here."

"Wait!" Elinor exclaimed. "I love this dance. It's 'Jenny Pluck Pears.' Come on, Sprout, dance it with me."

"You can't be serious," Corin moaned. "It's for the little kids. We're too old for that."

Elinor grabbed him by the sleeve and drew him toward the circle that was forming around a girl dressed with colorful ribbons in her hair who carried a branch laden with pears.

"What about these traitors of yours?" Corin asked.

"After the dance," Elinor said. "It's just one dance. You do know how it goes, don't you?"

"Of course I know how it goes. What did you think?"

"Then, come on," she said, tugging harder on him. "Let's find a place." Corin let Elinor steer him into the circle. Included among the younger children were a number of Corin's friends who had also stepped out of the crowd to join in the dance. He nodded a greeting to Muck and Balu when he saw them come forward. Muck shot him a questioning look from across the circle, gazed at Elinor, looked back to Corin, and then back to Elinor. Then he smiled broadly. Corin wondered why he was acting so strangely when he realized that none of them had met Elinor yet.

It was a partners dance, but the boys rotated around the circle, changing partners in succession, so by the end, each of the boys had danced a turn with each of the girls. Out of the corner of his eye, Corin noticed across the circle that when Muck was dancing with Elinor, he had such a big grin on his face that he looked foolish. He could not figure out what Muck could be so happy about, and meant to ask him later.

When the dance finally ended, Corin grabbed Elinor by the sleeve of her blouse and drew her away from the dance floor. "Wait here a second," he said. "I'll be right back." And he slipped away through the crowd.

Elinor looked around while she waited, admiring the finely dressed women wearing intricately stitched sashes wrapped around the waists of their lovely gowns. She sighed and wondered if she would ever look so beautiful. As she stood there, she saw through the crowd that her aunt was nearby, seated on a slightly raised throne, overseeing the festivities and receiving guests and well-wishers. She wore a fresh garland in her hair and her cheeks were flushed from the warmth in the room. Behind her on the wall hung a large tapestry depicting a hunting party chasing a unicorn. Elinor was about to walk over and greet her when she froze in her steps.

It was at this moment Corin returned to her, again stuffing some bakery into his mouth. Elinor grabbed her cousin's arm and squeaked, "Sprout, that's him!"

"You found him?" he mumbled through his full mouth. "Your conspirator? Where?"

"That one," she gasped, pointing towards the queen. "Next to her."

Directly behind the queen stood two armed men, their arms crossed, surveying the crowd, watching every face, every movement. "Them?" Corin asked. "Aw, Elinor, that's Morik and Pommer. They're captains of the Queen's Guard. They've been with her since forever. They would lay down their lives for her. When you were kidnapped, Morik came with my mom—"

"Not them," Elinor hissed. "*Him.*"

"Who? I don't see anyone else."

"He's right there," Elinor said urgently. "Right next to her. You can't see him?"

"You don't mean the man talking to her, do you?"

"Yes," she said urgently. "The man with the hawk-nose. That's him. I'm sure of it. We have to warn your mother. Quick! Tell the guard."

Indeed, the hawk-nosed man from the procession was standing beside the queen, slightly behind her left shoulder. He had just bent over to speak something in her ear. Elinor was horrified to see him so close to her aunt, within easy striking distance. She was not prepared for her cousin's reaction to seeing the conspirator.

"Are you out of your mind?" Corin blurted out. "Do you have any idea who that is?"

"What? What are you talking about? That's him. I swear it. The man standing beside your mother."

"That man standing beside my mother is Count Geron."

"That's it!" Elinor exclaimed. "That's the name the other man called him. I told you it was him."

"Count Geron," Corin said slowly, as if explaining it to a child, "comes from a family whose roots run deep in Gladur. His father was Count Billum, who was already a commander of the army under Worrah. But after the Battle at the Straits in which Worrah was defeated and driven out, Billum swore fealty to the Queen."

"That wouldn't prevent Geron from conspiring—"

"Geron happens to be the commander of the city guard and oversees the protection of Gladur. When my father is on campaign, he is answerable to no one but the queen. He's a member of her cabinet. He is one of my mother's most trusted counselors."

"But what I heard him say—"

"Look, Elinor, everyone, sooner or later, complains about something. My mother says you can't expect to please everyone, and the more you try, the more people you will displease. He was probably just agreeing with someone else to let him blow off steam. I can't believe you got me here to spy on Geron. And then we had to be in that silly dance. Look, I'm off to skylark with my friends. Are you coming?

I can introduce you. They figured out who you were and want to get to know you."

Elinor was stunned that Corin was not taking this seriously. She was not convinced that Geron was harmless. She knew what she had heard, and he had not been agreeing just to let his companion blow off steam.

"The other one called you a buffoon," she said flatly.

"Ouch," he flinched. "I'll have to work on my image. But not tonight. Look, if you're not going to come with me, find your chaperon and stay with her. I'm leaving. The festivities are much more fun out on the green. There's lots of food and later there will be some jousting, although just for fun. If you change your mind, come look for me." He did not wait for a response. He wormed his way between the revelers and in a moment was gone. He had noticed that the King of Misrule was staring at him again, and he was glad to get away from those piercing eyes.

Left alone, it took Elinor only a moment to decide what she had to do next. Geron had moved away from the queen and was standing off to the side, speaking with the stout man he had walked with in the procession. She had to hear what they were talking about. Moving slowly, making it look as if the general mingling of the crowd was pushing her along, she made her way towards the two men.

Elinor felt very clever turning her back to them when she had come close enough to be able to overhear their conversation. She backed up a step more, just so she could hear better over the music and the many conversations around her.

"... through these spectacles to gain our favor," one of the men was saying.

"Have no concern. When the time to strike is near, we will have the support we need." That was the stout man's voice, she was certain of it. They *were* conspiring.

"But we must hold our counsel until the time is ripe," Geron said.

"Which will not be long, by my reckoning," the stout man added. "I look forward to the day this charade is over." Oddly, it seemed to her that their voices had become even louder, but before she could figure out this mystery, strong hands grabbed her under the arms and forcefully whisked her off her feet, dragging her backwards. She was too astonished to even cry out in protest. The next thing she knew, she was standing in a semi-darkened, confined space. She had been carried behind heavy curtains that covered the cold stone palace walls. She was separated from the revelers in the great hall by only the thickness of the heavy cloth, but she was too terrified to even cry out. Looming over her, staring down into her face with his penetrating eye, stood Geron. She felt two heavy hands pressing down on her shoulders from behind and realized that the other man held firmly onto her. There was no escape.

"This is the second time today that you have eavesdropped on me," Geron said in a slow, deliberate voice. There was enough light to see the malice in his eyes. "I don't know who you are, which makes me all the more curious, so I conclude that you are a guest here. For that reason, I will give you the benefit of the doubt." He paused to watch her reaction. She was too startled and frightened to say anything. Her body began to tremble, and she only hoped her captors had not noticed.

"The first time someone overhears my conversation," Geron continued, "I consider it an accident, and I forgive it." He paused, and Elinor's trembling became more severe. "The second time," he said, "I become curious. And you have made me very curious." He stared hard at her, and with the pressure on her shoulders, she feared her legs would give out underneath her. "The third time, I make sure that it will never happen again. Have I made myself absolutely clear?"

Elinor nodded her head, although it was more the movement of her trembling than her willing agreement.

"I'm glad we see eye to eye," Geron said with a wicked smile. "Because I would hate to see someone as pretty as you become ... less pretty." He reached out and gently patted her cheek. The action made Elinor suddenly sick to her stomach.

"What about this?" asked the man holding Elinor. She could feel him pulling on a corner of the star-embroidered shawl draped over her shoulders.

"Curious, most curious," Geron mused. "Make sure that you don't let the queen see you wearing this. Whatever misguided sentiment brought you to thinking this imitation would please her, you are sadly mistaken. She does not take kindly to impersonators. And if you think my displeasure is uncomfortable, you do not want to get to know the queen's." He had bent down towards her face as he offered this threat, and his breath smelled heavily of wine. Elinor could feel her heart racing.

"What do you want to do with her?" asked the stout man from behind. The very question made Elinor's blood run cold.

"I'd say it's time she went home to sit by the fire and do her stitching. Before she gets into any more trouble. Wouldn't you agree, young lady?" He did not wait for her response. The two men slipped away, leaving Elinor alone behind the curtain. Her knees buckled and she collapsed against the wall. She covered her face with her hands and succumbed to her tears.

Chapter Eight

Escape

*J*ust watch his face when I'm introduced to the court," she said. "That's all I'm asking you to do. You can do that much, can't you?" The cousins had been arguing about Elinor's suspicion ever since Corin had returned from the river with Star.

"He's the commander of the city's garrison, for goodness' sake," Corin protested. "My father trusts him with the safety of the whole of Gladur Nock. He controls the army stationed at home. If he wanted to raise a rebellion, he could have done so a long time ago. He could have had the whole royal family beheaded before breakfast!"

"I know what I heard him say," Elinor insisted. "And I know that he threatened me. Do you think I'm making this up?"

"I never said that," Corin said quickly. "I just think you're mistaken."

"So that's why I want you to watch his face. When he finds out that the queen is my aunt, he won't be able to hide his true feelings."

"Why don't you watch him?"

"Because then he'll know I'm on to him. Besides, he frightens me, and I won't be able to hide that if I look at him."

Corin sighed. "If you must. But I don't know what you think I'm going to see."

Satisfied, Elinor went off to get dressed for her introduction to the court. The queen had chosen for her a simple gown, something she hoped would prevent too much gossip among her fashionable ladies.

Once again, she placed across Elinor's shoulders the shawl that bore her royal crest, a field of blue studded with golden stars. She left Elinor's hair flowing freely, as a sign of her youth, and placed upon her brow a small, yet elegant silver diadem, embellished with cleverly crafted silver leaves.

"I wore this myself as a young princess," she explained to her niece.

"Auntie, why doesn't Sprout have any brothers or sisters?" Elinor asked, admiring herself in the mirror.

Aina self-consciously lifted her hands to her abdomen in a protective gesture. "I have had six pregnancies," she said in a low voice that was lined with sadness. "And I lost five of those babies before they could be born."

"Auntie," Elinor said quickly, taking her hand, "forgive me. I did not mean to pry. I spoke before I thought."

"I do not mind telling you this," Aina said with a kind smile. "I was injured once in a great battle and nearly died. My physicians told me I was lucky to have even one child. That is why I am so happy that you have come to live with us. Since I have no daughter of my own, I am giving the diadem to you."

Elinor blushed and held her aunt's hand to her cheek. "Thank you, Auntie. I am so grateful for everything you've done for me." Aina was touched by this gesture and lifted Elinor's chin. She saw distress in her niece's eyes. Elinor wanted to warn her aunt about the threat to the crown she was certain she had uncovered, but she did not know where to begin. The queen mistook her look for nervousness.

"Just hold your head high and don't let any of the gossipy women intimidate you with their wagging tongues," Aina encouraged. "Women can say brutal, unkind things. The trick is not to let it touch you, and if it does, not to show it. Once they see they've hit their mark, they will destroy you." Little did the queen realize that the least of Elinor's worries were the ladies of the court.

Once the queen sat on her judgment seat, she had the usual business to preside over. As part of the day's proceedings, she brought her young niece forward to be viewed and received. When she introduced Elinor, she explained what had happened to her family and added that Elinor had come to live under her protection and guidance. The ladies of the court were openly sympathetic to Elinor's loss and, for the time being, withheld any displeasure they may have found in her looks or attire. If the girl was coming to live as a member of the royal family, there would be ample opportunity to criticize her later.

Elinor hastened to find her cousin after her introduction. He was waiting for her where they had agreed to meet, in a small anteroom next to the hall where the court was held. He looked pale. Elinor carefully closed the door behind her.

She grew somber when she saw his expression. "Sprout, what happened?" she asked.

"It was as you said," he began. "At first when my mother brought you forward, Geron's face showed interest and curiosity. But as your story emerged, and your relationship to the queen was made clear, his whole expression changed."

"What did it look like?" she asked.

Corin pursed his lips and thought carefully before answering. "If I put it into words, I'd say it looked like a combination of fear and hatred."

They sat there in silence. Corin was stunned that Elinor had been correct about Geron. Star's warning came back to him, and he scolded himself silently for not taking it more seriously.

Finally, Elinor spoke in a quiet voice, "What am I going to do?"

Corin perked up. "I know who can help," he said with confidence.

"Who? Your mother?"

"No, we can't go to her. She won't believe you any more than I did. Knowing her, she might even want to get the two of you together to show that he holds nothing against you. That could be disastrous."

Elinor shivered involuntarily at the thought of being alone in a room with Geron. "But your father's gone on campaign," she said.

"And my father put Geron in the position of power he holds," Corin said. "He can't help us either."

"Then who can we go to?"

"You're forgetting Star."

"Of course!" Elinor exclaimed. "Can we go now?"

"I'm sure they have not yet put the lanterns out. I'll send Mother a message that we may be late for supper. Go change and I'll meet you at the door to the barn."

Once they were with Star, Corin had to wait until no one was around. This was not as easy as he had hoped, for Mali was in a talkative mood and wanted to get to know Elinor better.

"I hear you were presented to the court this afternoon," Mali said.

"Yes," Elinor said with a nod. She glanced at her cousin. "It's all very new for me, being here."

"Oh, I'm certain it won't take you long to make friends. I saw you walking in the pageant yesterday. You wear your nobility well."

Elinor blushed and curtsied. "Thank you."

"I look forward to seeing more of you," Mali said. "When will you be coming to work in the barn? You'll be surrounded by friends in no time."

Corin saw his cousin was at a loss for words, so he spoke for her. "I don't know what Mother has in mind. Elinor's still so new here."

"Well, I look forward to getting to know you better," Mali said. "For now, it's a good idea for Star to get to know her smell. I've got some work to finish up, so you two let me know when you're finished visiting and I'll put the lanterns out. Don't stay too long. Star needs his beauty sleep." Chuckling, he moved away towards the back of the barn.

Once Mali was out of earshot, Corin quickly explained Elinor's dilemma to the dragon. "I can't believe I missed this," he added. "You even tried to warn me."

Once Corin had stopped speaking, Star did not hesitate. "It's very clear what we must do," he said.

"What's that?" Corin asked, hopeful to hear Star so confident.

"Tell her to meet us just outside the gate tomorrow morning, the one where the path veers away from the city wall towards the river."

When Corin told Elinor the plan, she asked, "But what will I tell Auntie? And how will I get away from my chaperon?"

"You will tell your aunt nothing," the dragon said. "As to your chaperon, have you had any trouble evading her?" Before Elinor could respond, Star added, "Oh, and I want you to come dressed in leggings, like a man might wear. Have the boy give you something of his, if necessary. Go now, the both of you and get a good night's rest. Tomorrow will be a very full day."

As they left the barn, Corin called out to Mali that they were leaving. "See you in the morning, Sprout," he called back. "Bring your pretty cousin soon to visit again."

"Pretty?" Corin mumbled to himself. He had not thought of her in these terms, and he turned to see what Mali was seeing. What he noticed was that Elinor was downcast.

"Hey, cheer up," he said. "If Star has planned it out, it has to be something good."

"I guess so," Elinor shrugged. Corin described where to find them in the morning. Elinor listened, nodding her head, but made no comment. It was clear that she was uninterested in further conversation. She mumbled that she would be ready at the agreed upon time and went directly to her room.

The next morning, as usual, Star came out of the compound gates with Corin perched on top of his neck. It did not take long before they were outside the city walls and on the path that led down to the river. Suddenly Corin remembered Star's instructions, and he scolded himself that he had forgotten to offer Elinor some of his clothes. A moment later, he saw he had nothing to worry about. They turned a sharp corner of the road, and there in the shadow of the great city walls, with her knees drawn up under her chin, sat Elinor. The dragon stopped long enough for Corin to help her up Star's leg and onto the neck to sit beside him.

"We're ready," he called out once Elinor was settled. The dragon continued on his way with his long, rolling gait. "Where did you get the clothes?" Corin asked, admiring her leather pants and jerkin.

"My father had them made for me," she sighed, and grew silent, looking out at the orchards they were passing. "It's beautiful from up here," Elinor said with a catch in her throat. "Just like you said." There was wistfulness in her voice. Corin looked at her face and could see that she had been crying. He wanted to say something, but he felt awkward, so he remained silent.

Star brought them to the secluded grove along the river. He stopped briefly at the poplar tree with the nest of robins so the cousins could admire how they had grown. Elinor sighed. "They're so sweet and innocent," she said. Corin saw tears forming in the corner of her eyes and again felt at a loss to know what to say. For the life of him, he could not understand what was bothering her.

Star lay down at the water's edge so his passengers could dismount. Once on the ground, Elinor looked around at the river and the trees, and stared at the path that continued along the river beyond where they stood. She turned to Corin and it was obvious that she was struggling to hold back her tears.

"Well, Sprout, I guess this is it," she said, her voice hoarse. She pressed her lips together for a moment before continuing. "I haven't thanked you yet for coming to save me when I got kidnapped. I can't believe how stupid I was. You were grand to come and get me, and to do it without a fight."

Corin stared at her, wondering what had come over her. He shrugged his shoulders, still not at all sure what to say. It was Star who broke the silence.

"What's in the bag?" the dragon asked. He was referring to the small pack Elinor had slung over one shoulder. Corin had noticed it when they picked her up but had thought nothing more about it.

When Corin had translated, Elinor answered, "Some food."

"That was good thinking," Star said. "Boy, did you remember to bring extra?" Embarrassed, he shook his head, no. He had only the food he usually carried as his daily provisions when he came out to the river with the dragon. "What else is in the bag?" Star asked.

"Some extra clothing," Elinor said with a shrug.

"What for?" Star had Corin ask.

"For the road," she answered, but the words stuck in her throat.

"What do you think I've brought you here for?" Star had Corin ask next.

"So I can flee," she said. She took a ragged breath and raised an arm to wipe her eyes on her sleeve.

The dragon's chimes rang merrily.

"What's he saying?" Elinor asked, an unhappy expression on her face.

"Nothing," Corin explained. "He's laughing."

Elinor could not bear it any longer. She burst into tears. "Why is he mocking me?" she sobbed. "I like it here. I didn't mean to cause trouble. I'm *sorry*. I'm going already. You don't have to laugh at me. That's so *mean*." Elinor hugged her bag to her chest, but she did not move. The dragon spoke again. She drew in a ragged breath and held it, to make herself stop crying.

"Star didn't bring you here so you can run away," Corin related.

"So, why am I here?" she exploded, letting out her breath and surrendering again to sobs.

"To learn how to defend yourself!" Star exclaimed. Corin had to say it three times before Elinor could hear it.

"Does that mean I can stay?" she asked, wiping her running nose on her sleeve, her face streaked with tears.

"If you can learn how to handle a sword," her cousin related. "Star wants to teach you how to fight."

Part II

An Unsettled Kingdom

Chapter Nine

An Unexpected Visit

Corin sat in the shade of a large tree beside the water. He was overheated and glad to rest and cool off. He pulled out his leather wallet and began working in the fine sand, polishing his needles. He watched Star putting Elinor through exercises similar to the ones he had just finished. He admired how flexible she was and how quickly she could move. He gasped every time she barely escaped being clipped by Star's massive head, and once he was so distracted that he accidentally pricked himself. He wondered if it looked that frightening when he sparred with Star.

The dragon continued to work with Elinor until she cried out hoarsely, "Stop!" She collapsed on the ground breathing heavily, drenched in sweat. Star sniffed at her and then his bells chuckled.

"You're not going to like this," the dragon called out.

"Then don't tell me," Corin responded, looking down at his work, pretending to be uninterested.

"She's been doing this for only a fortnight and she is already as good as you."

"I asked you not to tell me," Corin pouted.

"Tell you what?" Elinor asked, propping herself up on one arm. Corin ignored her question. "What are you doing in the sand?" she asked.

"I was hoping it would motivate you to apply yourself," the dragon said. "You're slow."

Elinor stood up and walked slowly towards Corin. "What do you do all the time in the sand?" she asked. Corin quickly folded his work back into the leather wallet and placed it under his leg.

"I don't like swords," Corin responded. He was talking to Star, but Elinor could not know that.

"What does that have to do with what you're doing in the sand?" she asked. "I've seen what you have there. They're sewing needles. What are you doing with needles out here?"

"It's not like you have a choice," the dragon said, continuing their conversation. "It's the way of the world."

"What if I change it?" he said. "The way things work."

"Sprout, answer me," Elinor demanded. She reached to snatch the wallet from under his leg, but he grabbed it first to keep it out of reach.

"I'm polishing them," he said, annoyed and a little embarrassed as well.

"Polishing needles? Whatever for?" she asked.

"For Master Ambroise," Corin told her. "I apprentice to him, sometimes."

"Have I met him yet?" Elinor wondered.

"No. Hope you never do," Corin said curtly. Then he turned back to speak to Star. "And I will change things."

"Change takes time, and while you're working on it, I suggest you become handy with a sword. And that you learn to move faster."

"You never got close to me," Corin protested.

"What's he saying?" Elinor asked, still eyeing the wallet. "And why do you polish needles?"

"The day she realizes that she's better, you will never hear the end of it," the dragon warned. "And she will punish you. She still hasn't forgiven you."

"I'll deal with it," Corin said, and stubbornly crossed his arms, tucking the wallet underneath, hoping Elinor would forget about it. Then he looked at her. "Star says you are doing all right for a beginner, but that you still need a lot of practice." At this comment, there was a cascade of chiming bells from the dragon that sounded like a scolding, and Corin winced.

Elinor giggled. "I think you translated that a little too freely for him. But don't worry. I get the idea." She considered him a moment. "Why don't you want to show me what's in the wallet?"

Corin heaved a sigh. She was not going to forget about it. Resigned, he pulled the wallet out and unfolded it on his lap. Inside was a row of sewing needles of different sizes, stuck into the soft leather, and a twist of flax thread. There was also a piece of cloth with a variety of practice stitches. "Just needles, see?" he said.

"Odd," she commented. "Do you like sewing?"

"Yes, I like sewing," Corin said impatiently.

Elinor stood up. "You like sewing and you don't like swords." She laughed. "You should have been a girl." She walked to the water's edge and washed her face, then took a deep drink. Corin glared at her back the whole time.

"That felt good!" she exclaimed standing up. "I don't think I've ever enjoyed anything so much. I'm so happy that we started this. I feel like I could take Geron on single-handed."

There was a eruption of music from Star's chime-like voice.

"What did he say?" she asked.

"First he laughed, and then he suggested you learn some defensive moves before you take on the commander of the army who happens to be a seasoned warrior."

"Suggestion accepted," she said smiling with a bow towards the dragon. Star continued speaking. "What now?" she asked when he had stopped.

"Star wanted me to ask you how you're getting away from your chaperon every day," Corin said. "He's wondering why Mother is not getting suspicious that you disappear every morning and don't show up again until late in the afternoon."

"I was just honest with her," Elinor responded with a shrug.

Corin was astounded at her boldness. "You mean you told Mother what you're doing?"

"No, silly. I told my chaperon to stay out of sight in my room until I return in the afternoon, and that if she breathed a word to anyone that I was gone, I would send her back to her family an invalid."

"Elinor!" Corin shrieked. "You didn't!"

"I most certainly did," she said.

"Who's your chaperon?"

"Someone named Nellie."

"But I know Nellie. She's a very sweet woman who wouldn't hurt anyone. You must be scaring the daylights out of her."

"I certainly hope so," Elinor said with another shrug. "I can't afford that she say anything. I don't want to take the chance that Geron finds me. You heard from Star. I'm not ready yet."

"But how is what you're doing to Nellie any better than what Geron did to you? Don't you remember that this all started when he threatened to hurt you?"

Elinor stood in silence a moment and considered this. Finally, she asked, "Do you have a better idea?"

"I'll go speak with her."

"What are you going to say? You've told me more than once that Star doesn't want to breathe a word of what we're doing to anyone."

"I agree. I will tell Nellie that you are under my care and not to worry about you. And I will tell her it is important that she not tell anyone. And I will add that I will not let you hurt her."

"It will backfire on you," Elinor said. "People are more agreeable and willing to cooperate if they're afraid."

"You see, Star?" Corin said turning to the dragon. "That's why I don't like doing this *and* I hate swords. You taught her how to fight, and she goes and threatens a harmless, kindly woman. It always leads to someone wanting to dominate someone else. What good are swords, other than for hacking at each other? Give me one good reason why this is worth learning."

Star chuckled. "I enjoy your conviction. Just the same, I want you to practice. If for no other reason than that you are able to defend yourself on the day that someone attacks you and does not stop because you have politely asked him to."

Corin stood there with his hands on his hips and thought about what the dragon had just said. "You have a point." Then he shrugged his shoulders and laughed at himself. "A very convincing point."

"What did he say?" Elinor asked. "That sounded good and I want to know his response."

"Later," Corin brushed her off.

"And I agree," Star continued, "that you should have a chat with Nellie so that she is not living in fear of Elinor. Besides, I don't believe Elinor would hurt her."

"Why don't you want to tell me?" Elinor asked. "Was it about your sewing?"

"But a threat is still a form of violence," Corin insisted, ignoring his cousin.

"And now you have made a point which I accept," the dragon laughed. Then he added, "And you can't keep ignoring her and get away with it."

"Sprout, are you going to tell me what you're talking about?" Elinor demanded. "Sometimes you make me so angry, I want to ..." and she raised a balled fist.

"He said you should not threaten others," Corin said quickly with a glance at the dragon.

"And you expect me to believe that?" Elinor confronted him, her fist still balled.

"It's true," Corin said with a shrug, walking away from her. "Ask him yourself."

Elinor glared at her cousin and muttered, "Maybe I will."

Corin walked over to the brushes and buckets that lay at the foot of a tree. He glanced up at the sky to determine how late in the day it might be. "It's time for us to scrub Star down before it gets any hotter. Into the water," he said to the dragon, gesturing towards the river. "We'll take a break after his scrub and have a bite to eat. Then we can practice some more."

The cousins filled their pails and, with a scrubber in one hand and the pail in the other, walked up to the dragon. With their arms outstretched to balance themselves, they clambered up Star's leg. Corin climbed up to the middle of the dragon's back and stood beside one of his great spikes. "I think we stopped around here yesterday." He put down his bucket, spread some water and began brushing. Elinor joined him, and side by side they scrubbed Star's scales.

"Remember to always scrub *away* from his head and *towards* his tail," Corin instructed.

"I know, I know," Elinor grumbled.

"So that we don't scrub any dirt underneath the scales," he continued.

"I *know!*" she barked so sharply it made Corin jump. "You don't have to always remind me."

"You don't have to be so touchy," Corin said defensively.

"Just stop telling me every day something I already know. I'm not stupid, you know."

"Sorry," he said. "I just wanted to make sure."

"And stop keeping secrets with Star," she added. "That's really annoying. And rude."

Corin decided not to respond. Elinor's vigorous strokes with her brush were enough to let him know that she was angry. They worked silently for a while, the only sound the sloshing of water and the scratching of brushes against the scales. Then Corin commented, "I used to not like scrubbing the back half of the dragon."

"Why not?" Elinor asked.

"It was lonely work. Back here, I can't talk with Star anymore. Then I'm just scrubbing, and I feel like I'm wasting my time. At least with you here, I have some company."

"If you feel like you're wasting your time, do you ever think of running away?" Elinor asked. She was only teasing him, so she was surprised by his response.

"All the time," Corin said, keeping his voice low. "But don't tell anyone." He glanced over his shoulder toward the dragon's head. "Not even Star."

"What are you saying?" Elinor blurted out, surprised by what he had revealed. "You can't go anywhere. You're going to be king."

Corin looked uncomfortable and took a deep breath. "Of course," he stammered.

Elinor stopped brushing and peered hard at her cousin. "You don't want to be king, do you?"

Corin looked embarrassed. "It's not that simple," he said.

"You don't like fighting and you don't want to be king, and you don't even care that much for scrubbing the dragon. What are you doing out here?"

Corin's expression became stern. "I said, it's not that simple."

Elinor shrugged her shoulders. "Let me know when you've figured it out. As for me, I didn't come out here to scrub the dragon. I came out here to learn how to fight."

"The way I remember it," Corin said severely, "you came out here to run away, and Star offered to teach you how to defend yourself. And part of coming out here is to keep the dragon clean. So as long as you're here, that's what we're going to do. Scrub the dragon."

Corin had spoken so firmly that Elinor stood there staring at him. "Yes, Your Highness," she said with an obedient nod, and there was no mocking in her voice. They went back to scrubbing and worked silently for a while. Elinor realized that she had touched a sensitive nerve, so she chose a different approach. "Sprout, does anyone know what you do out here? I mean, besides scrubbing?"

"I think my parents know, although we've never talked about it. But Star was very clear that what we do out here is just between us. We don't always practice, though. When you joined us, we put aside our usual routine. After my midday break, we would sit a lot and talk. But since you can't understand him, he said we should put that on hold. Normally, Star teaches me about what it means to be descended from the Dragon Keepers. Has my mom told you any more about that?"

"A little bit. That it's an ancient race and that we have always taken care of dragons. And that's why you can talk to him."

"It's also why Star is willing to teach you. He says that, although you can't understand his speech, you can get ideas from him. Sort of like reading his mind."

"I can read his mind?" Elinor asked.

"That's what he says, anyway," Corin replied, continuing to scrub.

Elinor stood up straight, turned around, and stared at the back of the dragon's head. "So that's where it's coming from," she said.

"Where what's coming from?" Corin asked, concentrating on his scrubbing.

"This!" she said, and lifting her brush by its long handle, suddenly swung it at her cousin's ribs. He saw it coming out of the corner of his eye, but had time only to turn his body slightly before it struck him with dull thud.

"Elinor! he cried out. "What are you—?" But he never got his question finished before she raised the brush above her head and swung down, aiming at his head. He was able to get his own scrubber up to deflect this blow, though clumsily, and the force of it threw him off-balance. Next Elinor jabbed him hard in the chest, and, losing his footing, Corin tumbled down the dragon's side. He landed in the water with a splash. Corin surfaced in a moment. "Are you crazy?" he yelled up at her, shaking the water out of his eyes. He swam to the shore and heaved himself out of the river. He was furious. He ran up the dragon's leg, back to where Elinor stood. "Why did you do that?" he demanded, confronting her.

"Star told me to," she said with a smile. "I was trying to figure out why that idea had popped into my head, to swing the brush at you, and then you said—" but before she could finish her explanation, Corin picked up the scrubber he had dropped when he fell and swung it at her. She parried the blow, although the force of it stung her hands.

"That's the lamest excuse I've ever heard," he yelled at her, swinging at her a second time. He was angry that she had attacked him without any provocation. "Don't ..." he swung, she parried, "ever ..." swing and parry, "do that ..." swing and parry, "again!" With each swing, he forced Elinor to take a step backwards. He was quite a bit stronger than she was, and his anger fueled his strength with accuracy. After his last swing, he thrust his leg forward, catching hers from behind, and gave her a shove. Elinor lost her footing and cried out in alarm. She fell backwards, tumbling down the dragon's side into the water, the same journey her cousin had taken a few moments before.

Corin stood there holding onto the scrubber, his chest heaving and knowing that had she not fallen, he would have kept swinging at her. He was surprised at the feeling of exhilaration that filled him. He had never felt this way before, even when sparring with Star, and it gave him a sense of aliveness that was new to him.

He had no more time to ponder this further because a movement in the distance caught his eye. He looked up and saw horses in the distance approaching at an easy trot. They were riding on his own stream path and heading straight for him. He stared at the riders a moment and then looked down into the water where Elinor had just come spluttering to the surface.

"Elinor!" he shouted down to her. "Stay in the water. Stay hidden."

"Why?" she called back, shaking water out of her ears.

"Riders," he answered, careful not to look down again in her direction. "Riders never come out here. Something is out of place. Stay there and hide. Hang on to his leg. They'll come on the other side of the river from you. Star's body will conceal you."

Corin dipped his scrubber into the bucket of water and went back to work, acting as if he had not seen the approach of the riders. He only hoped that they had not rounded the faraway trees before Elinor had tumbled off of the dragon's back. He had taken a quick count. There were five riders, but he did not yet know who they were. He glanced up towards Star's head, but the dragon seemed unconcerned, and this helped him relax. If Star was not worried, he had no need to be, either. He continued scrubbing. He glanced over to the small grove of trees beside the stream. Raucous cawing in the higher branches attracted his attention. Then he looked down to the open space beneath the trees where they had been sparring earlier. Two wooden practice swords lay at the edge of the high grass. He hoped they were well enough out of the way, for there was no time to go hide them. The riders would see his every move.

He focused on his work until he could hear the hoofbeats of their horses. He looked up, ready to feign surprise. However, when he saw who was leading the party, he did not need to pretend.

"Commander Geron," he called out. He spoke louder than he had to. He wanted Elinor to know who had arrived. "Is there some emergency that you seek me out here?"

The riders pulled up their horses. Count Geron glanced around, as if looking for something—or someone. He then addressed the prince. "You have no need for concern, young master. All is well with your mother and the kingdom."

"Then to what do I owe the honor of your visit?" Corin asked. "In all the time I've spent out here, you are my first visitor."

"I've been looking for your cousin," Geron explained. "I've searched everywhere in the palace and the town, but she is nowhere to be found. I thought she might be out here with you."

"Count Geron, my cousin has been given leave to tour the city with her chaperon. More I cannot tell you."

"Indeed," he said, looking around. He had not yet noticed the swords. "I had heard rumor that she was out here with you."

"I wonder who is spreading such a rumor," Corin said with true curiosity. When Geron did not respond, he asked, "Why do you seek her?"

"As she is a member of the royal family, I wish to make her acquaintance and place my services at her disposal."

"You've come out here for naught. As you can see," Corin said with an expansive gesture, "I am alone with the dragon."

"And you're scrubbing him," Geron continued. Corin saw him glancing into the clearing underneath the trees.

"You sound surprised," Corin said. "What did you expect me to be doing?"

"I had thought that there would be a better way for the heir to the throne to spend his time."

"It's good enough for me," Corin said, inwardly flinching at the lie. "It is the work that has been entrusted to me."

Geron studied him for a moment, and then commented, "You're wet."

"It's a hot day. I went for a dip," Corin said quickly, and thought, *He doesn't miss a thing.*

"I see," was Geron's curt reply.

Corin was impatient for him to move on. "Commander, is there anything else I can do for you?" he asked.

"No," Geron said brusquely. "I need nothing else."

"Then with your leave, I'll continue with my work. As you can see, I have a great deal of dragon to cover."

"Indeed, a great deal of dragon," Geron said with no expression in his voice. He wheeled his horse around and galloped off the way he had come, accompanied by the four other riders. The sudden movement of the departing horses spooked the birds in the tree, and with loud cawing they flew towards the city walls. Corin continued to scrub, but watched the riders until they were well out of sight.

Only then did he lean over the dragon's broad side and call down, "Elinor! They're gone! You can come out!" There was splashing down at the water's edge, and he saw his cousin drag herself onto the shore. He left his scrubber and climbed down to her. She sat in the sun and wrapped her arms around her legs. She rocked back and forth shivering and her lips were blue. The stream was runoff from the mountains and the water was cold, although it never seemed to bother Star.

"The sun will dry you off," Corin said. "You'll warm up quicker if you walk around." Corin pulled her to her feet, and supporting her by the arm, he walked her around the clearing until her shivering stopped.

"He was looking for me," she said at last.

"And he wanted you badly enough that he even came out here."

"Why is that so strange?"

"My mother assured me that there is general agreement that no one bother us. He wanted to find you so badly that he was willing to forget that he is not welcome to come out here."

"That was close," Elinor said. "If I hadn't fallen, he would have seen me."

In their walking around, they had reached the dragon's head. Star was listening to their conversation and looked over to them. "I thought you'd never hit her hard enough," he said. "And I could tell you enjoyed it."

Star's comment puzzled him. "Did you want me to knock her off your back? Did you know they were coming?"

"Not particularly," Star responded. "But I did have a strong feeling that you should get her out of sight."

"You could have just said so, you know."

"You took care of it," he said. "Besides, it was far more entertaining this way."

This reminded Corin of how the whole event had begun. He turned to Elinor. "Why did you hit me? I hadn't done anything to you."

"*He* told me to," she said, pointing to the dragon.

"If Star had said something to you, I would have heard it, and besides, when did you start understanding his speech?"

"He didn't say it in words. He put the idea in my head. All of a sudden I had this strong impulse to hit you with the scrubber. I thought it would be part of our training, somehow."

"It is important to always be ready for the unexpected attack," Star added, and then chuckled, "Or visitor."

"So you *were* in on this!" the prince exploded.

"I will admit that I did have the thought that since there are two of you, it would be useful to practice unexpected attacks. What I find remarkable is that she picked up on it. I am truly impressed."

"What is he saying?" Elinor wanted to know.

"He said that the next time an idea pops into your head, check it out with him first to find out if it really is a good idea."

"Why don't I believe you?" she asked, squinting at him.

"That's what he said," Corin insisted.

"That is not at all what I said," Star remarked, amusement in his eyes.

"He's contradicting you," Elinor said.

"I think we should go back," Corin said.

"You're changing the subject," Elinor countered.

"Hide the swords in the grass," Corin ordered. "And then climb back up."

"It's still early. Why are we going back early?"

"It's my turn to have a feeling," he said.

"I think you're lying to me."

"Why would I do that?"

"Because you're jealous that I had a feeling to do something that Star inspired me to do and it turned out fortunate in the end because Geron didn't find me."

"I can't even follow what you're talking about. Go hide the swords."

"Don't forget your needles," she sniped.

They continued quarreling as Elinor stashed the swords underneath a bush and Corin gathered the scrubbers and buckets. Star pulled himself out of the water and waited for them to climb up onto his neck.

"I agree with both of you," Star finally commented.

"Star even agrees with me," Corin said.

"You've left out the part where I agree with her as well," the dragon snorted.

"I have a feeling you're not telling me everything," Elinor said, starting her climb up to the dragon's neck.

"And tomorrow I expect a more thorough scrubbing," Star added.

"He wants you to try harder scrubbing him tomorrow."

"I don't think I'm going to listen to you anymore," Elinor declared.

"Suit yourself," Corin said, seating himself and crossing his arms.

"That's what I mean about making things up when Star speaks," she said crossly. "How can I know when you're being honest?"

"I didn't make anything up," Corin insisted staring ahead. And then he called out, "Let's go, Star. We're ready."

Star raised himself nimbly to his feet and began the walk home. "You've got a lot to learn about women," he commented. "She's not going to let you get away with that."

"I'll deal with it," Corin responded.

"You'll deal with what?" Elinor asked.

"It wasn't about you," he said.

"You're such a liar," she said.

"Am not."

"Are too. You are so see-through when you lie."

Corin did not say any more, but sat with a frown on his face, staring stoically ahead. They traveled on in silence towards the gate, where every morning they picked Elinor up and every afternoon dropped her off. It was called the Orchard Gate, since it was only used by farmers who tended the apple orchards that grew along the wall. They had chosen this gate because it was kept unlocked and unguarded, had no regular traffic except in the harvest season, and opened up to a quiet alley in the city. It seemed like the ideal place for Elinor to come and go unnoticed.

As they approached the gate, Corin had just told Elinor to wait for him in her room with Nellie when he was startled to see a solitary figure standing beneath the great walls. After their encounter with Geron, his first impulse was to hide his cousin.

"There's someone at the gate," he said to her. "Quick! Climb towards Star's back and see if you can hide among his horns."

Elinor did not budge, but instead craned her neck to better see what had alarmed her cousin. "No worry," she said. "I know him."

This made Corin even more curious. He took a careful look and was startled to realize that he also knew the man standing there. He recognized him from his greying beard. He even had his crow precariously balanced on his shoulder. "You *know* him?"

"Don't sound so astonished," Elinor said. "I've been here long enough to meet people."

"Where do you know him from?"

"On the first day I came to meet you here, the day I thought I was running away, even though you told me how to find the gate, they weren't very good directions, and I got lost."

"What do you mean they weren't good directions?" he said, offended.

"If they had been good, I would not have gotten lost," she said simply.

"Maybe you aren't any good following directions," Corin argued.

"Stop bickering," Star ordered, startling them both. Corin frowned and Elinor guessed what the dragon had just said.

"Anyway, this strange old man showed up out of nowhere and asked me where I was going. When I told him I was looking for the gate that opened to the orchards and the pathway that led to the river, he brought me right to it."

"Why didn't you tell me about this?"

"I didn't think it was important enough to mention."

"Did you ever see him again?"

"Two more times," she replied. "Both times he said that he wanted to make sure I didn't get lost. He is a very nice old man."

Corin did not mention who this old man really was. In truth, he knew very little about him other than having watched him perform in the market. Then the memory struck him that right after Elinor arrived, the old magician had asked him to bring her to see him. Corin sat there stunned until Star stopped at the gate.

"Coming on the early side today," the old man commented.

"You're waiting for us?"

"I wish to see young Elinor safely home. I hear it's been an eventful afternoon."

He looked up to Corin, who stared at him with wide eyes. He nicked his head toward the bird on his shoulder, and Corin remembered the crows in the trees.

Corin did not know what to say. Elinor climbed down and walked with the magician to the gate. He opened it and let her pass through. Before following her, he looked up at Corin, who still stared silently after them with his mouth hanging open. "Go on," the magician said with a wave of his hand as if he were shooing away a dog. Then he disappeared through the gate and closed the door firmly after him.

"Let's go home, Star," Corin said.

"Finally something intriguing is going on around here," the dragon commented with a chuckle.

"At least one of us is pleased. Will you tell me what's going on?"

"Only what is self-evident. I have nothing more to add."

"Why don't I believe you?"

"Wasn't that the same thing your cousin complained of?"

Corin did not answer, and for once Star's chime-like chuckling did not delight him.

Mali came to meet them when they came into the barn. "Home a bit early today," he commented.

"Looked like a storm was coming," Corin said, hoping to avoid having to explain more. Mali stared at him a moment, perplexed, then walked over to the open barn doors and looked up at the clear sky.

"It was clouding up on the horizon," Corin called back over his shoulder, retreating in the other direction. He hurried to his room to quickly change his clothes. They were still damp from his tumble into the river. Then he would go find Elinor and have a talk with Nellie. He was startled when he entered his room and found Elinor sitting on his bed looking worried. He quickly closed the door behind him.

"What are you doing here?" he asked in a loud whisper. "I told you to wait for me in your room."

"I don't think you have to whisper in here," she said.

"Why aren't you with Nellie?" he asked, continuing to whisper.

"That's why I'm here. Every day when I've returned, Nellie has been waiting for me in my room. Today, she wasn't there."

"Where do you think she went?" he asked.

"I don't know. That's why I came to you."

"Maybe she just stepped out for a moment. You know, to use the commode. Or get something to eat."

"The room looks untouched, as if she had not spent any time there today. She always brings sewing and moves the chair next to the window for more light. The chair was still in the corner and there was no sign of her handwork."

"You are such trouble," Corin muttered.

"It's not like I couldn't hear that," she complained. "And it's not my fault if she disappears when I'm gone. I did what I could so that she would stay put."

"Which obviously didn't work. You should never have threatened to do her harm," Corin said angrily. "What if she's run off?" He paced the room several times trying to figure out what to do next. Both of them jumped when there was a loud knock on the door.

"Sire? Are you within?" a voice called from the hallway.

"Quick," Corin whispered, pulling Elinor to her feet. "You've got to hide. Over here." There was another loud knock from the door. "Coming!" Corin called out. He dragged Elinor to a far corner of the room and made her crouch down. Then he took a blanket that was covering a chair and threw it over her. He mussed his hair and went to open the door.

"Roddy," he said, stretching as if he was just rising from a nap. "What is it?"

"Your mother, sire, wishes to speak with you. She's heard that you've come home early and asked me to come find you. She's in her sitting room, sewing with the other ladies."

"Thank you, Roddy. I will go to her in a moment." Roderick nodded his head and looked over the boy's shoulder into the room as if he expected to see something unusual there. Then he turned and left. "He knows," Corin muttered as he went to the corner and pulled the blanket off his cousin.

"Thank goodness," she exclaimed. "I could barely breathe under there."

"Stay here," he hissed at her. "Don't answer the door. Don't go anywhere. You're so much trouble. You have no idea how hard it is to keep secrets around here. Everybody always seems to know everything." He stalked to the door and let himself out.

Muttering to himself, Corin walked the hallways of the palace, heading for the queen's private sewing room. It had south-facing windows, which gave it a warmth and brightness that was well-suited for the careful, detailed work of needlepoint. On quiet afternoons, the queen often retreated here with several of her ladies-in-waiting to sit, sew and gossip, escaping the demands that the crown often weighed upon her. When he came to the door, Corin knocked once and, without waiting for permission, let himself in.

The queen was sitting beside an open window working on a piece of embroidery, deep in conversation with the woman sitting beside her, with needlework in her hand. Several other women sat around the cozy room also engaged in their needlepoint. He had heard cheerful conversation as he opened the door, but all voices fell silent when they saw who had arrived. He took a step towards his mother and made a small bow at the waist. Then he looked around briefly at the other women, acknowledging them as well.

"Mother, you asked to—" but the rest of what he wanted to say died on his lips. Sitting beside a window with her embroidery in her lap, sat Nellie. His mouth fell open.

"Ah, Prince Corin," the queen said pleasantly. "Did you come to sew with us?"

She smiled to see her son's baffled expression. "Of course not." Now her smile faded and she spoke in her court voice. "If you will excuse us, ladies, I'd like to be alone with my son." The women heard the icy tone underneath the queen's words and hastily gathered their needles, colored threads and cloths into their large aprons. One by one they hurried from the room. The queen turned to the woman who was sitting beside her, and only then did the prince recognize her. "Maisy," Aina said, "thank you for your visit. Please come again soon and gossip with me." Maisy gathered her work and, passing by the prince, first kissed him on his forehead and then playfully ruffled his hair. As Nellie left, she gave Corin fearful side-long glances. When the last to leave had closed the door, the queen sat up very straight and peered at her son. All sign of her smile was gone.

"I believe it's time we talked."

Chapter Ten

What the King Discovers

*N*o, Corin, although it may surprise you, I am not angry with Elinor for leaving without her chaperon. I happen to enjoy spending the day stitching with Nellie and hearing about her family's struggles to keep their cow in milk." The queen paused to watch her son's reaction. "And to answer your unspoken question, Nellie has been sewing with me for the past two weeks." She smiled as her son's mouth fell open. "On the other hand," she continued, "I want you to know that when all this began, it took me the better part of a day to calm Nellie down and assure her that Elinor would not harm her in any way. I hope that I have not given my guarantee of her safety in vain. What do you think?" She looked piercingly at her son and waited.

"Honestly, I had nothing to do with that," Corin protested.

His mother peered at him in silence, as if trying to read his thoughts. She arched her eyebrows. "You must forgive me if I am not completely convinced." The young prince was about to say something else, but she held up her hand for him to remain silent. She was not finished. "Nor, Corin, am I upset that Elinor has been joining you in tending to Star. It is something your father and I had hoped might happen at one point, although we had envisioned her spending a certain amount of time learning our general routine and customs in regards to caring for our Luck Dragon by working first in the barn. You will admit that her working directly with Star so soon after her arrival is unusual."

"It was Star's idea," Corin said in his defense.

"You seem much too innocent," Aina said shaking her head. "But I am not finished, and you won't weasel out of this one. As I said, I can forgive Elinor's trespasses. She has suffered much in the loss of her family, and in light of this, I can forgive her actions if they are at times, let us say, erratic and surprising. Besides, she is now a member of our family," and when she saw Corin's surprised expression, she emphasized, "Yes, you heard me correctly, Elinor is a member of our family, even if she does not yet know what is important to me. However, I expect you to know better. Corin, I am angry and disappointed that all of this has happened and you kept it from me. I have waited now for two weeks for you to come to me, and my patience has grown very thin. You know how I feel about keeping secrets. I thought you and I had an understanding."

"Star said it would be better not to say anything," Corin quickly said. Aina stared hard at him and he looked away to avoid her gaze.

"I'm not sure I believe you," she said. "It is much too convenient to blame this on Star."

"It's because of Geron," Corin blurted out.

"Count Geron? What does he have to do with this?"

Corin hastily explained to his mother all the events that led up to that afternoon. "That's the whole story," he concluded. "I haven't kept anything back." Immediately, he felt a pang of guilt, since he had withheld the role the magician had played. To avoid any closer questioning, he put the full focus on Geron. "And it's never happened before, that anyone has ever ridden out when I was with Star by the river."

"I admit that it is irregular," Aina said. "Geron also came to me looking for Elinor. However, let me state clearly, that I am convinced that your suspicions of Geron are unfounded. I do not have the slightest reason to suspect that he is unfaithful to the crown."

"But Elinor swears that she heard—"

The queen would not let him speak further. "Elinor is a young and impressionable girl who is dealing with a great loss. I am not ready to believe something so inflammatory coming from her right now. I have not forgotten that she let herself be walked right out of the city by men who did not have her best interests at heart."

Corin hung his head, knowing that he was not going to convince his mother to suspect her own commander of the city's garrison. He decided to reveal that even Star had warned him about Geron, although he knew he would have no way of proving it. However, his mother did not give him a chance to speak.

"On the other hand," Aina continued in a severe tone, "there is someone in this city about whom I do have serious concerns." Corin looked up. "I have every reason to believe that a powerful magician has gained entry into Gladur. A black magician, who wishes to see Star injured and Gladur ruined. I believe this is the cause of Star's recent poor health."

Corin knew she must be talking about the old man from the market who had helped Elinor. "Is this because of the dagger?" he asked.

"Have you sought him out again?" Aina demanded. "In spite of my forbidding you?"

"No," he said quickly, emphatically shaking his head. He was relieved that he could tell the truth, even if he was splitting hairs. Although he had seen him that very afternoon, he had not sought him out. But this made things even worse since he had repressed in his story the part the magician had played. He wanted to explain to his mother that the knife had not really come from the magician. He could not believe that the old man could be evil.

"Beware him," Aina said darkly, as if she could read in Corin's soul that he was walking a thin line with the truth. "He will deceive you with kind words and deeds that look to benefit you. When he has won your trust, you will be firmly in his power. That is when he will carry out his wicked plans." She had an inner gleam in her eye that made her look ferocious. "Corin, this is a battle for our own survival. It is about everything we believe in and stand for."

"But, Mother, Star would never allow——"

She interrupted him. "Aren't you the one always reminding me that this is not how Star works? It is Star who is suffering from this attack. And when Star suffers, the whole realm feels it."

Corin was speechless. Could it be true that the old man was a dark magician?

Aina broke into his thoughts. "Where is Elinor now?"

"In my room, waiting for me."

"Bring her here. It would be best if we speak of this together."

Corin turned to leave but stopped short. "Mother, I just can't believe—"

Aina interrupted him. "It is what you cannot believe that is the most dangerous. It is the very thing that will destroy you. Now, bring Elinor to me."

Pondering his mother's words, Corin left the sewing room. His mind had become a confusion of thoughts and feelings. He came to the door to his room even more baffled than when he had set out.

"Elinor," he called out, thrusting the door open, "Mother knows—" and got no further, finding that he was addressing an empty room. He looked to all the corners. "Elinor!" he called out, but there came no answer. "Where has she gone, now?" he muttered. "This is so annoying." He circled the room twice, as if he might flush her out of the woodwork. "Where are you?" he called out loud. Then suddenly a thought, or better said, a picture popped into his head. He knew with certainty where she was and rushed out of the room.

It had grown dark enough that the lanterns in the great barn had been lit, and they cast their golden glow upon the resting dragon. Most of the workers had finished their shift. Corin saw Mali at the far end of the barn, but he was not interested in speaking with him and stayed in the shadows. It did not take long for him to find Elinor, sitting on a barrel near Star's head. She was pensively staring at the dragon. Once Corin caught sight of her, he nearly pounced on her.

"Can't you do anything I ask?"

She looked up, surprised to see him there, startled by his sudden appearance.

"It wasn't my idea. I would have stayed—"

"Don't pin this on Star again," Corin sneered. "It's much too easy an excuse." He was doubly annoyed, realizing this was what his mother had just been saying to him. However, he did not have time to think about this. A deep voice suddenly spoke from behind him.

"I asked her to come here." The hair on the back of Corin's head stood on end and he whirled around.

"Father!" he gasped, his heart taking a leap of surprise. "Mother didn't tell me that you're back."

"That's because she doesn't know yet," the king said with a smile. "I have not had a chance to greet her or have myself announced."

The young prince stood there awkwardly, taken off-guard by his father's unexpected appearance. He was not quite sure what to say. He was never sure anymore around his father. He seemed often to do or say something that displeased him. Lately, their conversations usually turned into arguments, and he was relieved by his father's long absences. And when his father was around, Corin kept his mother as an intermediary between them. He searched for something to say to ease the tension that was already building up inside him.

"But the army," Corin said. "We would have heard..."

"I have come without the army, Sprout," his father explained. "I traveled with but a few retainers. I came to speak with you, actually. But when I went to your rooms, I found your cousin. I asked her to join me. I wanted to greet Star."

At mention of his name, Star's great head reared up, and stretching his long neck, he bent down to sniff at the top of the king's head. "I've always enjoyed that smell," the dragon chuckled. "It reminds me of the Lady."

"How did you find us?" the king asked. "We have been here only a few minutes. I took pains to come here unobserved. Not even Mali has ferreted me out yet."

Corin hesitated while he tried to figure out how to explain it. "I had this picture," he finally said, "inside of me, that I would find Elinor here. But I knew nothing about you."

"How odd," Star said with a nod of his head and chuckled.

The boy looked up sharply at the dragon. "You know more about this than you're letting on. Did you send me the picture?"

"He has grown very perceptive," the dragon commented to the king.

"How is his sword work?" Michael asked.

"He is every bit as quick as you were, perhaps even more so," Star replied. *Then why do you complain so much how slow I am?* Corin thought. He was about to speak up, but Star's next comment stopped him. "Elinor, however, shows more promise with a sword. Next to her, the boy looks sloppy." Corin shot his cousin a look to see if she had picked up any of what Star was saying and was relieved that she seemed to be lost in other thoughts.

"My not telling her is not going to make it any less real," Star said, addressing the boy. "And it won't be long before she knows it."

"I'll deal with it," Corin grimaced.

"He has your stubbornness, and that is a handy trait to have," Star chuckled.

Michael turned to his son. "Elinor has mentioned to me your difficulties with Commander Geron."

Corin perked up, grateful that Elinor had broached the subject. "Father, he rode out with his retainers looking for her. He came to the river where I scrub Star. No one has ever dared to do that before. Not even you and Mother have ever come out."

The king pondered this a moment in silence before responding. "It is not expressly forbidden, only silently agreed upon as a courtesy."

"Doesn't it seem odd that no one has ever done it before?" Corin protested.

"Geron is the commander of the city's garrison," the king replied. "He has leave to do what he sees fit for the safety of the city and its citizens."

"I know, Father. But did Elinor tell you what he said to her at the spring ball? It sounded like a threat to me."

"Did you hear him speak it yourself?" the king asked.

"Do you think she's lying?" Corin said, his voice rising in anger.

"Unless she can bring forward another person who heard the threat, it is his word against hers. Right there you've lost your case." The king was firm.

Corin flapped his arms in frustration. "Not even Mother believes us. She stands by Geron. Instead of her own family!" He caught himself getting excited and said no more. It was comments like this that usually got him into an argument with his father.

"Your mother grew up with Geron. He was the son of one of Worrah's generals," the king said pensively. "She has known him her whole life. He was, in fact, at one time one of her suitors. You probably didn't know that."

Corin looked up. There was something in his father's voice that said he did not share the queen's good opinion. "And what about you? Do you trust him?" He must have said this with too much passion. His father shot him a warning glance.

"Watch your tone, Sprout. Even a question has implications if the tone is accusatory. As heir to the throne, the nobles are all too ready to give meaning to even your most casual comments. So watch your tongue." Corin looked away and bit his lip. His father continued. "As to your question, I will answer you honestly. I knew Geron's father. He held a high post under Worrah. When Aina took her rightful place as queen after the Battle at the Straits, he swore fealty to both of us. Personally, I felt at the time that he did this too hastily. To me, he was a man whose faithfulness was determined by backing the leader who had the best chance of keeping him in power. The moment things might go ill with us, I was certain his support would waver. He died several years ago, but I believe his son has similar ambitions."

Corin was astonished by this revelation. "But you let him control the troops that are here to protect the city."

"I truly believe that he holds Gladur dear and would defend its walls to the death."

The cousins gave one another a meaningful look. It was Elinor who spoke what they were both thinking. "But given the right situation, he could turn on you," she pointed out, "if it were to his advantage and did not endanger the city. And based on what I heard him say, he is seriously considering it. Don't you think it would be wise to relieve him of his commission?"

"Talk is one thing, a deed is something else," the king said, shaking his head. "Besides, I believe it is better to have Geron close, where I can keep an eye on him, rather than distant where he can hatch plots against the crown in secret."

"Well, if you ask me," Corin exclaimed hotly, "it is time to keep your eye closely on him, so he doesn't hatch a plot right under your nose and then slip a dagger between your ribs."

The king smiled at these words. "Sprout, I appreciate your spirit. And I warn you again: Watch your tongue. Let's make this agreement: I will enlist the two of you to be my watchful eyes. If Geron is up to no good and suspects that you are watching him, he will be careful to guard what he says as well as what he does. I think you will have little to worry about. As it is, it looks like he's keeping a close eye on you, so you shouldn't have any trouble following his movements."

"Uncle," Elinor said, "don't you think he's dangerous?"

"I do, indeed," the king answered with a laugh. "That is why he is commander of the troops. He is capable, proud and ambitious. He has all the traits of a man who wants to raise himself higher than his present standing. And as you have found out, he is not a man to trifle with. But I am not yet concerned for your safety. I'm counting on Star to keep you out of too much trouble."

"Um, Father," Corin began, "I don't think Star—"

"That's right," the king laughed again, "you don't think that Star works that way. But he always did for *me*. What do you say, Star?"

Star's chime-like laughter filled the barn. "I know better than to offer opinions in these kinds of discussions," he said. "I agree with what you said earlier: Talk is one thing, a deed is something else. And there is one inescapable fact: I *am* a Luck Dragon."

Suddenly Corin jumped up. "Mother!" he exclaimed. "I totally forgot. She's waiting for me to return with Elinor."

The king held up a hand. "I suggest the two of you get a bite to eat and then head off to bed. I will go and speak with Mother."

"It was a ruse?" Aina stared at her husband with disbelief.

"I'm embarrassed to say that we were outsmarted," Michael admitted. "It was my mistake that I never questioned the rangers who reported the attacks. Only later did I discover that they had never seen with their own eyes the destroyed villages or the marauding army. They had encountered men who claimed to be villagers in flight, and they saw rising smoke in the distance. Understandably, as they were few in number, they did not want to run the risk of engaging a large regiment of enemy troops. Unfortunately, I didn't know this until we had already traveled south."

"Why would someone do this?"

"It seems clear to me," the king explained. "I diverted the course of the army to our southern border to bear down on these incursions. I left the frontiers to the north with scattered patrols and meager protection. Worrah is laughing up his sleeve how he has me running around the countryside chasing rumors. And it certainly did not raise the morale of the troops. They went ready for a fight, and found no one to oppose."

"So you left them and returned?"

"Not immediately. I decided if I had been drawn to the south, I should make use of being there. I never spent much time along that frontier, since Worrah has kept me very busy to the north. I bivouacked the troops for some needed rest. I left General Korvas in command and then went traveling."

"Alone?"

"I took Will with me. We dressed ourselves as frontier rangers."

"Where did you go?"

"I wanted to find out the mood of the people who live there. What do they think of this large kingdom to the north that hosts a Luck Dragon? I also wanted to find out if Worrah had been sowing any seeds of discord among them."

"How did you go about it?" Aina asked.

"Will and I spent our time talking to people in markets, taverns and by campfires. I'm now almost sorry that I went."

"What did you discover?"

"The prevailing opinion is that the queen of Gladur Nock is a kindly woman who cares for her people and has brought them an era of prosperity and peace."

Aina stood and curtsied, wearing a beneficent smile. "Thank you for the good report. Wouldn't you call that a welcome opinion?"

"The king, on the other hand," Michael continued with a dour expression, "people scorn as the latest warlord who sucks the countryside dry of young men for his army and then confiscates the harvests to feed them. The prosperity of Gladur is founded upon the oppression of the farmers and suppression of its neighbors. They feel it is only a matter of time before I bring war to their land in an attempt to absorb them into my growing kingdom."

"Certainly you're not surprised," Aina frowned. "You brought this on yourself when you allowed settlers to take those villages."

Her response caught the king off-guard. "Not this again," he replied sharply. "Those villages along our frontiers were abandoned in the time of Scorch."

"*Nearly* abandoned, but not completely," Aina corrected him. "And they were not in our territory. You had no way of knowing if the villagers would return once they heard that Scorch had been defeated."

"I had to do something for the people of the Forest Village. They remained true to the crown, to *you*, all those years. They were the ones to shed their blood and give their lives in the Battle at the Straits. Without them, we would have had no army to oppose Worrah. Their land and property were confiscated when they took refuge in the forest. It would have caused even more ill will had I begun to redistribute property other citizens now claimed they owned. I had to offer them something. Why do we have to rehash this?"

"We could have found another solution," Aina insisted. "There was always the Restoration."

"A name that came into usage only years later," Michael pointed out. "At that time, it was known as the Devastation of Scorch. How could you expect them to go and live in the lands that had been the dragon's lair?"

"It has become our most productive pasture and farm land. You predicted that yourself."

"Predicted, yes. But the proof came only with the passage of time. I needed an immediate solution. There are no easy decisions as king," he said defensively. "You know this. The edges always get ragged and I can't make everyone happy. Why do you insist on bringing this up again?"

"Because if a situation is neither black nor white, and your judgment around it is grey, you are not making things clearer."

"You always know best in hindsight," the king said irritably.

"I was not in favor of it at the time," she pointed out. "The council was split, and even Geron spoke clearly against doing it." At the mention of Geron's name, the king bristled and shot his wife a dark look, at which she grew silent.

"And yet you allowed it to pass," the king countered in a warning tone, "in spite of the council's—and Geron's—disapproval."

"I accept that I am complicit," the queen said quietly, staring down at her folded hands. "I wished to leave you to reign freely, right or wrong."

"Then leave me free of your criticism!" the king exploded. "I made my decisions with good intentions."

"Obviously not for the villagers you dispossessed," Aina said, her eyes now flashing. "After all, I am not the one surprised that the villagers who now live along the new frontier mistrust you."

"I am aggravated that my attempts to secure the frontiers and provide a ring of safety from Worrah's attacks are seen from the outside as barricading ourselves in so we can prepare an attack upon our neighbors. Can't they see that our stability and peace will give them a chance to bring the same to their own land?"

"Quite the contrary," the queen explained with bitterness. "I am not surprised that they view you the same as Worrah, except that you are an even greater threat. I believe that the memory of Scorch terrorizing the land lives vividly among them still. And now we even have the dragon housed inside the city, ready at any moment to bring destruction at your bidding."

The king was silent a moment before admitting, "I heard the whispered rumor that I am a powerful magician. They don't want to understand that Star is not dangerous and that I exercise no magic over him. I shouldn't be surprised. How can I expect them to believe that a wild dragon can be tamed?"

"Whether they view me as a beneficent queen or not," Aina reflected soberly, "I expect that they live in fear that one day we will unleash the dragon to ravage their fields and farms and then follow up with the army to subjugate them thoroughly. I often wonder how we can change this. Geron suggested—"

"Please," the king interrupted, holding up his hand, "save me the ideas of your advisors. I can hear them all at once in a council meeting."

"If you would only deign to attend one," Aina said accusingly. "And they are your advisors as well. Only last week, Geron lamented—"

The king once again held up a hand to stop her from speaking further. To gain control of the anger he felt welling up inside of him, he took a deep breath and continued in a strained voice. "Aina, I am well aware of the problem we face. Too few of our neighbors ever travel here for our festivals to see what benefits a Luck Dragon can bring.

Only twisted facts and rumor of our prosperity reach our neighbors. And the more secure we become, the more King Rodham to the south fears an invasion. He seems convinced that I am nothing more than a land-hungry warlord with my eye on my next conquest. Bellek, at Worrah's prompting, no doubt, has done a good job of convincing everyone that I am dangerous ..."

"Which you are," Aina added with a shrug.

"... and that Worrah is the rightful ruler of Gladur because we unseated him by force."

"Which we did," Aina admitted. "Except that our actions were provoked by the severity, cruelty and greed of his rule. Let no one forget that I am by right of birth the Queen of Gladur."

"And I am seen as the common-born rogue knight you married for the purpose of helping you hold your crown and expand your kingdom. Our neighbors know only Worrah's story, either out of ignorance or because it's convenient. I discovered that all of this has led King Rodham to step up the conscripting of soldiers to strengthen his army. This has been sapping the farms and villages of their young men. Now women are forced to labor in the fields as well as work at home. Young women go unmarried. There are fewer weddings, fewer babies, and little joy. It is not a pretty picture."

"We have problems of our own," Aina said, sitting up a bit straighter.

The king's eyebrows arched. "Tell me."

"The rumor of a powerful magician in Gladur may in fact be true, although it is not you. I believe a black magician has entered the kingdom. Worse still, that he has been brewing mischief in one of our forests."

This took the king by surprise. "Do you know where?"

"Only that from time to time, hunters have seen smoke rising into the sky and sitting heavily among the branches of the trees. But every time they investigate, they find nothing. The report has come from very different forests, which is why I cannot pin it down. Some say that he is holed up in the Enclave."

"I should have cleaned out that nest long ago," the king grumbled.

"You know that Geron thinks differently about that," the queen replied.

"Geron again!" the king finally exploded. "Why do you speak of Geron so often?"

"I don't know what you're talking about," the queen said defensively.

"He has come into this conversation repeatedly. And I hear that he has been seeking out Elinor for unclear purposes."

"How do you know this? It is a twisted truth. Commander Geron is only doing his duty. He felt it his obligation to become acquainted with young Elinor so that he may be of service to her as a member of the royal family. If I am speaking of him often, it is because Geron offers me excellent advice."

"Geron this and Geron that," the king said with a frown. "It sounds to me as if you lean too heavily on his advice these days."

"His is the advice left me to lean upon, with you absenting yourself so frequently."

"See that you don't bend too strongly in his direction," the king said darkly.

"When I have need of a strong arm, I look for the one that is closest," Aina said hotly.

"Insufferable!" the king bellowed. "What are you insinuating?"

"Only that if you were more present I would not need to turn to others when I have needs."

"So now he's satisfying your needs? I'll have his head!" the king roared. "I will not endure this!"

"Don't read into my words what I haven't said," the queen warned.

"Where your words end your actions begin," the king retorted. "I'll not suffer him longer."

"You have no choice. He is commander of the city garrison," the queen said hotly. "You will keep your hands from Geron."

"To save him for yours?" the king asked accusingly. Aina turned pale at his words. "We'll see what choices I have," the king threatened and stormed from the room. "We'll see what choices I have left."

·*,·*·*·*,·*·*·*· ·*,·*·*·*,·*·*·*·

"Go on," Corin said. "Tell me about it." He and Elinor were sitting in the shade of the trees beside the river. Star sun-bathed, listening to their conversation. While they spoke, Corin sewed. He had finally grown comfortable doing this in front of Elinor.

"It was awkward," Elinor said. "I didn't know what to say to him."

"You didn't go alone with him, did you?"

"No, I was spared that. Because Uncle had set it up, he could name the conditions. That's how he talked me into doing it. He said that Geron would not rest until he had been able to welcome me in his own way, so the best thing to do was for him to officially set up a meeting. That way he could send a chaperon."

"Nellie?"

"That's what he wanted to do at first, but I said I would go only with someone who could wield a sword in case things got dicey."

"What did my father say?"

"He laughed at me, but agreed. He ordered Roderick to accompany me."

"Good choice," Corin said, nodding. "He's strong, and completely dedicated to my parents. How did Geron react?"

"He tried to casually tell Roderick that he needn't bother to join us, but when he saw that Roddy was firm upon accompanying me, he gave in. I think he wanted to avoid being too obvious that he wanted me alone."

"What did you do?"

"It was uneventful," Elinor said, making designs in the sand with her finger. "Geron took me on a tour of the city's fortifications, had me admire the thickness and strength of the walls, took me around to the different gates, and in the end gave me a tour of the practice grounds and then the barracks where the city's garrison is quartered. I was surprised how many troops he commands. It's like a small army."

"That is indeed what it is, and every bit as well trained. It is in case the city is ever besieged while the standing army is away," Corin explained. "What happened next?"

"Then he returned me to the palace."

"Did he ever mention your two previous encounters?"

"Not a word. He was polite to a fault and treated me as if he really wished me to believe that he was putting his services at my disposal." Elinor sat and watched her cousin's steady stitching. "What is that good for?" she asked. Corin bristled at first, but then realized there was no mocking in her voice. He reached to his sewing wallet and pulled out a long thread. He handed it to her.

"Break this," he said. She looked at him surprised, but took the flax thread and in a quick movement snapped it in two.

"Was that supposed to be hard?" she asked.

Instead of answering, Corin handed her the two pieces of cloth that he had been sewing together. "Pull them apart," he told her. "Go on, give it a tug." Elinor took the material and pulled on the two halves, with Corin's new seam in the middle. Nothing happened.

"All right, I admit you do good work—" Elinor began.

Corin held up a hand to interrupt her. "A single thread," he explained, "breaks easily. But when it is woven together with many others, it has great strength. And it takes only a single thread to bring two pieces of cloth together to hold as strong as one."

Elinor shrugged her shoulders. "Anyone who sews knows that," she said.

"You asked why I sew," Corin said. "That's why. I'm learning the art of holding things together." Star's chimes chuckled at these words and Corin looked up at him. "And I do it without needing a blade." The dragon laughed even harder. Corin made a face, and ordered, "All right, time to get into the river. Elinor, grab your brush. We'll continue our work on the back half of the dragon."

Corin put his sewing away carefully, and once the dragon had taken his place in the river, they journeyed up his leg to the spines at the base of his long tail.

"We stopped right about here," Corin said, placing his bucket down and began to scrub. Elinor did the same.

"Was Melkhi with him?" Corin asked. "When you toured?"

"Who's that?"

"The stout man you said held you behind the curtain. I recognized him from your description. The two of them have become very close lately. It couldn't be any other."

"No. I haven't seen him since that evening. The only other person with him was his son."

"Burk or Leprun? He has two sons."

"Leprun. He is close in age to us. Do you know him?"

"Of course. I know everyone. Leprun and I were close friends when we were younger. We were in the same work detail and pushed brooms together in the barn. But we have grown apart over the past few years. Why do you think he came?"

"I don't have a clue. Geron kept trying to get us to have a conversation. I did find him good looking."

"Maybe he wants to use Leprun to spy on you. Do you think Geron suspects that you come out here with me?"

"He asked me how I spend my days. Auntie had coached me to say that I pass my time with her ladies-in-waiting making beautiful embroideries. That way he could not check up on me very easily without being obvious about it."

Corin nodded his head, but said nothing. He had been keeping his eye on Elinor, trying not to let her know that he was watching her. He practiced observing her out of the corner of his eye, on guard against any sudden movement. Since that day when Geron had appeared, Elinor had taken up trying to catch her cousin unawares while they were scrubbing. She claimed that Star inspired her to do this, and since the dragon never denied it, there was no way to stop her, other than to stay alert and ready to parry her blow.

Corin hated being sent flying down into the river. He hated being bested by a girl. In addition to disliking having to learn martial arts from Star, he did not like getting battered by his own cousin. She was remarkably fast and well-coordinated. When she practiced with the dragon, he secretly watched her moves, wanting to model his own after hers. She was so agile and made it look easy to escape Star's blows. If he studied how she moved, maybe he could improve as well. But he would never admit this to her.

In the lull of their conversation, Elinor found her moment. Corin had just stuck his brush into his bucket when her stick made a sudden, wide arc through the air towards his shoulder. He had been tracking her movement and his response was immediate. His stick flew up to parry the blow. Since his brush had been inside of it, the bucket was lifted with it and went flying through the air, directly at Elinor's head. All in one movement, she landed her blow, which Corin was able to parry, and bent her head enough to the side to let the bucket pass over her shoulder without hitting her, although she was splashed by the water pouring out of it.

It was all over in a moment. The bucket continued its path behind Elinor and tumbled down the dragon's side to the stream below, landing with a splash.

"I didn't think you saw me coming," Elinor said with a smile. "You're getting better at this. And you got me wet. That was a nice trick with the bucket. Did you intend to do that?"

"I'm going to have to go get that," Corin muttered, looking down into the stream. The bucket had been carried by the current and was caught in some exposed tree roots along the shore. He looked up at Elinor. "How come you're so good at this? You hardly moved to get out of its way. It would have hit me square in the face."

Elinor laughed, and for a brief moment, Corin had the sense that he was happy for her company. "Don't be so hard on yourself," Elinor said. "I've been keeping a secret from you."

Corin planted his brush and leaned on it. "I'm listening. I'm even intrigued."

"I'm not doing this for the first time," she said.

"You mean, you've been trained already? How is that possible? You're a girl."

"You make it sound like I'm defective," Elinor said with a scowl.

"I didn't mean it that way," Corin said quickly. "I just meant how often do you hear of girls being trained in arms?"

"I know three cases," Elinor said. "Two of them were our mothers." She saw a look of disbelief cross her cousin's face. "Remember, they were sisters and grew up together. Apparently, our grandmother thought it was important that her daughters were trained in arms. As royals, I guess, they could do whatever they wished. Anyway, when I was old enough, my mother said that what was good enough for her was good enough for her daughter. I've been working at this for three years now."

"No wonder you do the moves so easily," Corin said with surprise.

"I'm glad you noticed," Elinor said with a smile. She then feinted to the left and swung her brush at him again.

Chapter Eleven

An Unexpected Challenge

*F*or Corin, a summer had never seemed to pass so quickly as this one. Any resistance he had about going with Star to the river evaporated like a rain puddle in the hot sun. He got up every morning looking forward to their outings. He even stopped complaining about how much he disliked sparring with swords. As much as he enjoyed Star's company, he grew to prefer Elinor's companionship, regardless of what they were doing. Even their daily quarrels did not bother him.

Over the past weeks and months, his father had gone on campaign and returned several times. They had little contact, which was a relief for Corin, although tucked away in the back of his mind was the ill feeling that things should be different between them. His father had recently returned home again and had been more often in a foul mood than not. He noted that his parents did not speak to one another in his presence and wondered why only long enough to conclude that he did not have a clue.

On one particular beautiful summer afternoon, following their time at the river, Star dropped Elinor off as usual at the orchard gate and continued on his way to the compound. Star's health remained an enigma. The dragon sidestepped any direct questions from Corin. Some days he was as spry as ever, and on others he dragged himself to the river and had little interest in taking a greater part in their training in arms than giving meager instructions as Corin and Elinor sparred with one another. Corin was very satisfied with his progress. Star had stopped pointing out that Elinor was so much better. When they sparred, Corin more often than not came out on top. Although it was true, he told himself (and knew better than to say it out loud), that he was *only* fighting with a girl, still Elinor had more training than he had. Corin had caught up with her and was feeling good about himself.

After giving Star over to the evening handlers, Corin chatted for a while with Mali before leaving the barn. He wanted to go to the stables before supper. Muck had told him about some horses that had recently been acquired. Corin was in need of a mount and wanted to take a look at the new arrivals.

Corin's path took him past an open courtyard where the stall boys often congregated for a game or some light sparring after their work shift before going in to eat. Since many of them were children of noble families, learning knightly skill at arms was a natural part of their overall education. This afternoon, everyone was crowded in a tight circle, watching someone in their center. Corin was intrigued, because the crowd was raucous, calling out equally encouragement and derision. He walked to the edge of the circle to look what held their attention.

In the middle, two of the barn boys were fighting. Corin was startled to see that one of them was his friend Muck. The other was a boy everyone called Red, due to the color of his hair, who was known to have a quick temper. Each boy had a wooden practice sword and buckler. It was immediately obvious that this was not a case of friendly sparring. Red had an ugly, angry look on his face. Muck was concentrated and wary. Red stood a head taller than his opponent, but Muck was stouter and more muscular. He crouched down in his guard position to make himself an even more compact target. The boys around the ring were hooting their enjoyment of the match, and keeping the perimeter tight. Corin wondered how this got past the attention of the Barn Master who was careful to keep fights as far away from the dragon as possible. That was when he noticed Morik, captain of the queen's guard, standing in the front row of the ring.

He came often to oversee their training in arms, and he did not look alarmed watching Muck and Red squaring off. Apparently, this was going on under his guidance.

Corin watched with fascination as Muck cleverly worked Red until he had his own back to the setting sun that slanted into the courtyard. When he saw that Red was squinting to see better, he chose that moment for his attack. Covering his head with his small shield, he dove underneath Red's guard and tripped him up. Red went down with a loud grunt, throwing a small cloud of dirt into the air. Leading with his shoulder, Muck crashed his whole weight onto Red's chest. Corin celebrated with the rest, chanting Muck's name in victory. Morik separated the two boys, ending the fight. As they stood up, Muck was smiling broadly, and Red was looking dazed that it had ended so suddenly.

Morik took a moment to speak quietly to the two boys, reviewing what had just happened, giving advice and praise. When he was finished, he had them both shake hands and, after taking their weapons, sent them off in different directions into the crowd of boys. Red moved to the rear of the circle and stood there sulking. Muck was immediately surrounded by a knot of boys slapping him on the back and giving him their excited review of the fight. Morik then called out, "Any other takers?" Corin was about to continue on his way to the stables when he heard a voice call out in answer to Morik.

"I'll go next. How about it, Sprout? Are you game?"

Corin froze and looked around to see who had spoken. Geron's older son, Leprun, stepped out of the crowd of boys and stood before the prince. "Come on, Sprout, let's give it a try. You and me."

Corin was taken by surprise. He had been standing at the back of the crowd and wondered how anyone had even noticed he was there. He was not given time to think about it. Many of the boys were already shouting out to him to take the challenge. "You're not afraid, are you?" Leprun asked with a confident smile. Now he had no choice but to accept, or lose face in front of all the others. In the back of his mind he wondered if Geron had put Leprun up to this. He nodded his head in acceptance and stepped through the crowd to the center of the ring where Leprun joined him.

Morik handed both boys their swords and shields. "No gouging," Morik instructed them. "Spare the soft parts. No harm if you draw blood, but no blows with the intention of doing real damage. I don't want any broken bones. You both have work to do tomorrow. You have no helmets, so at the first landed blow to the head, I will stop you. Disarm, outmaneuver, overpower, but do not destroy. This is only friendly sparring. Understood? Now, are you ready?"

When Corin looked at the malice in Leprun's eyes, he was not so sure about this being friendly. He and Leprun stood opposite one another and both nicked their heads, acknowledging Morik's instructions. As they sized one another up, looking for weaknesses in their guard, the crowd of boys erupted in loud shouts of encouragement.

Corin was used to Elinor's stance and fighting habits. He quickly made adjustments to be ready to engage with Leprun. He noticed almost immediately that Leprun kept his shield low, covering more the middle of his body than his shoulders and chest. This could be a fault in his form. Or was he taunting the prince to take a swing at his head and make an immediate end to their combat? Was this a trick to entice Corin to attack him where he looked unguarded? All of these thoughts streaked through his mind in an instant. It took him only a moment longer to decide that Leprun was trying to trick him into attacking where he only appeared weak. Leprun was the son of the commander of the home troops. It was not possible that his father would let his training be haphazard. In an instant, Corin knew his plan of attack.

Corin began jabbing at the lower half of Leprun's shield. If Leprun wanted him to attack high, Corin decided to see what would happen if instead he attacked low. He started swiping at his knees, and from the puzzled look on Leprun's face, he could tell that he had taken him off-guard by this attack. This forced Leprun into being the first to take a strong offensive action. He stepped forward to close the gap between them and took a sharp shoulder-height swing at Corin. Obviously, Leprun expected Corin to raise his shield to take the blow, and he would use this moment to position himself for a more effective attack by keeping Corin on the defensive. With anyone else, most likely this would have been a sound strategy. Corin, however, jiving on his heel out of the way, swiveled with the same momentum. Leprun's blade whistled through empty air, and he felt the stinging blow of Corin's sword as it slapped him on the back. He whirled around to keep Corin in front of him, furious and perplexed by how Corin had evaded his attack and ended up behind him.

Corin felt his mind turn off and his senses take over. He did not have to think about what to do. His body had been so well trained that he became aware of his actions only after he had done them. Leprun went on the offensive, but Corin played with him. He was so fast and agile that Leprun was not able to land any blows, and when he did, they harmlessly glanced off Corin's shield. Corin, on the other hand, repeatedly struck Leprun's unprotected body, slapping him with the sword so as to be painful, but nothing that would injure.

The crowd around the two was alive with excited shouting and gesturing. Whenever one of the contenders came too close to the inner ring of the circle, many hands would push him off towards the center. It was obvious to all that Leprun, in spite of being the more aggressive of the two, was fighting an opponent he could not catch.

"Stand still!" Leprun finally growled through clenched teeth. Corin did not even bother to respond. He continued to play Leprun, watching his opponent's rage grow as he searched fruitlessy for an effective attack. Corin could have ended the battle several times, but chose to keep it going. He was annoyed that Leprun had singled him out to fight with, and he wanted to send an unmistakable message to anyone else who might have a hankering to challenge the heir apparent that he was not one to trifle with. He silently sent thanks to Star for having insisted that he had to be ready for the day someone wanted to fight instead of talk. That day had come sooner than expected.

Corin was finally satisfied that he had taught Leprun the lesson he needed. He stood his ground, keeping a cautious distance, and looked for his opening. While he felt hardly winded, he noticed with satisfaction that Leprun was panting through his open mouth. Until now, the ring of boys had been only a blur of faces that he had not taken the time to focus on. At this moment, however, something in the throng grabbed his attention. He noticed for the first time that the spectators were not only barn boys. He saw a number of adults there as well, obviously attracted by all of the noise. In all likelihood, word had spread that the prince was sparring, and they had been drawn to come and watch the entertainment.

Then one face in particular, just over Leprun's left shoulder, caught his attention. It was Elinor! What was she doing here? He had no time to dwell on the question and would have let it pass, except that Elinor was standing shoulder to shoulder with Muck. And she had hooked his arm with hers. Not only were their arms intertwined, Elinor and Muck were holding hands! Corin could not believe his eyes. He stood there transfixed.

Leprun saw that Corin was distracted, and he was not going to ask him why. He knew a window of advantage when he saw one and used this moment to attack. In spite of his shock at seeing Muck and Elinor holding hands, Corin would have been able to easily parry Leprun's attack if it had not been for what he noticed next. Standing off to the side behind Elinor, stood the nobleman from the market, the one from whom the magician had lifted the dagger that caused his mother so much alarm. Corin had no doubt that this was the same man. In an instant, his eye had taken in the telltale details: his neatly trimmed beard, the ring in his ear and the pheasant feather in his hat. And to Corin's alarm, the nobleman was not watching the fight. He was watching Elinor!

Corin wanted to call out and warn Elinor. He raised his sword arm in a gesture that she should look behind her. This movement, in fact, is what saved him from being struck. Leprun's sword came crashing down on him, and his raised sword coincidentally, if awkwardly, parried the blow. This brought Corin's focus jarringly back to the fight, but it was all too late. The sword strike had been so violent that it threw Corin off-balance. He took a step to regain his footing, but someone stepped out of the crowd behind Corin and stuck his leg at an angle between Corin's.

It was Burk, Geron's younger son, who saw his chance to help give his brother the advantage. Several hands grabbed Burk to shove him back away from Corin, but not before Corin had tripped over Burk's outstretched leg. As he stumbled, Leprun followed him from behind with a wicked stroke to the back of his shoulders. Corin was laid full outstretched on his face into the dirt. There came from the crowd cries of "Foul!" met by others crying "Victory!" Morik stepped in and stopped the fight.

Corin was stunned and lay a moment with his face in the sand. Morik was leaning over him. "Your Highness, are you hurt?" he was asking. He turned the prince over onto his back.

"Not here," muttered Corin. "No *Highness* here." He was feeling very low at the moment.

"Yes, sire," Morik responded. "Are you hurt?"

Corin sighed, "No *sires*, either. Please."

"Yes, Your Highness," Morik replied, carefully feeling Corin's limbs for possible breaks. He asked again, "Are you hurt? I was certain you had the advantage, sire. What went wrong?"

Corin was staring up at the late afternoon sky. His eye was caught by a figure on a balcony overlooking the courtyard. Someone was standing there watching the fight. A thrill shot through Corin when he recognized that it was his father. He blinked, and the figure was gone. It was then that he remembered what had distracted him from the fight.

He sat up abruptly with his cousin's name on his lips. He looked around to find her. The circle had already broken up, and people were either walking off or standing around excitedly recounting the fight. Neither Elinor nor Muck was to be seen. Leprun stood nearby, his arms crossed over his chest, still breathing heavily, his sword hanging limply from one hand, staring at Corin with a frown on his face. Corin looked in all directions, but the nobleman had also vanished.

"Sire, speak to me," Morik was saying. "Where are you hurt?"

Corin now looked at Morik. "My only injury is to my pride, good Morik," he said. "Help me up." Morik grabbed the prince by the arm and carefully raised him to his feet. Corin's shoulder hurt where the wooden sword had struck him. He walked over to Leprun and held out his hand. "Good fight," he said.

Leprun stared at the outstretched hand, but did not take it. "I didn't ask him to do that," he said. "He will suffer for that interference."

Corin kept his hand outstretched. "He was only helping out his brother. If I had one, I might have done the same. I don't hold it against either of you. But it will teach me to better watch my back."

Leprun stared at Corin's hand, still waiting for him. Finally, he reached out and took it, but only for a moment. Leprun immediately pulled away and stalked back towards the barn and the commissary. Corin stood there staring after him, as the supper bell rang.

"Sire," Morik asked, standing at his elbow, "shall I attend you?"

"I'm fine," Corin replied. He turned and walked off toward the palace, rotating his arm in circles to work out the pain in his shoulder where Leprun had landed his blow.

Supper was an uncomfortable affair for the prince, and not due just to the soreness in his back. Corin knew that both Elinor and his father had seen Leprun beat him, but neither of them mentioned it during the meal. Corin wanted desperately to speak with his cousin, but not in the presence of his parents.

"An early report came in today," Aina commented to no one in particular. "About the crops."

"Anything interesting?" the king asked indifferently.

"Reports on the state of our crops are always interesting," the queen said pointedly. "But this time they are also worrisome. The crops are not coming in as we had expected."

"It's been a dry summer," the king said with a shrug.

"We've had dry summers before," Aina stated flatly. "This year is different. The yield is not what it has been."

"Certainly in the Restoration the harvest will make up for where it may be lacking elsewhere," the king said.

"However, that is not the case," Aina said, her eyebrows arched. "How about the cattle? Are you as unconcerned about what is happening among the herds?"

His parents' conversation continued, but Corin stopped listening. He tried to get Elinor to look up, but she was ignoring him. Finally, he kicked her underneath the table. He gave her a look as if to say, *What's going on?* but she merely crinkled her nose at him and went back to picking at the food on her plate. Suddenly her attention was riveted by something her aunt said.

"Plague?" Elinor blurted out. "Did you say plague?"

Aina looked up at her. "I'm glad something has shaken you out of your reverie," she said. "Yes, I did mention the plague. Along with failing crops, diseased cattle, unrest along our borders, and people questioning the wisdom of keeping a dragon that is not bringing us good fortune, peace and prosperity. Recent reports are that the plague is spreading again."

"Aina," the king warned. "Not here. We can talk of this later."

"No, Michael, I disagree," she said. "I much prefer that the children hear about it from us rather than on the street somewhere as rumor."

"What about the plague?" Elinor asked. She was openly agitated.

"Nothing confirmed," Aina responded. "But there is rumor that it has broken out in some frontier villages, but not yet in the lands of Gladur Nock. We are prepared to reinstate our policy of preventing those who try to flee it from entering the kingdom. It will string out our already thin defenses, it will hamper commerce, all of which will lead to more grumbling, I'm afraid."

"But how can this happen with Star living here?" Elinor asked.

"You are not the only one asking this," Aina admitted. "I'm afraid that a sick Luck Dragon gives limited support."

"Nonsense," the king grumbled. "There's nothing wrong with Star."

"Michael, denying it does not make him better," Aina warned. "There is something seriously wrong. Tell me, in all the years you lived in Nogardia, did the crops ever fail? I would welcome that you could tell me this is normal."

Michael did not respond, but sat silently brooding, his gaze averted. No one at the table spoke after this nor did anyone appear to have much of an appetite left. Finally, Corin nudged Elinor again, and she looked up at him, annoyed to be disturbed.

"May we be excused?" he asked.

"Of course," his mother said.

Corin rose from his seat, pulling on Elinor's sleeve. "Come on, let's go," he said to her.

"But I'm not—"

"Yes, you are," Corin said, tugging at her arm. "We have to go."

Elinor let her cousin pull her from the room. "Where are we going?" she asked, once they were in the hall.

"Somewhere we can talk," Corin said. "To my room. Come on."

As soon as his door was closed, Corin confronted his cousin. "All right, what was that all about this afternoon?"

Elinor shrugged her shoulders. "Don't ask me," she said. "You're the one who lost. I don't know how you let him get past your guard. He just about *explained* to you what he was going to do before he did it. His moves were so obvious."

"I'm not talking about that," Corin said waving away the embarrassment. "What were you doing with Muck?"

Elinor looked at him blankly. "I don't know what you're talking about," she said. "I don't know anyone with that name."

"Right there in the front," Corin said heatedly. "I *saw* you. You were holding hands with him!"

"Oh, *him*," Elinor said. "Maybe you have him confused with someone else. His name is Alek. He's really nice. I think you'd like him. He was very handy with a sword right before you showed up. Too bad you missed it. Would you like me to introduce you to him?"

Corin flapped his arms. "No, I don't want you to introduce me to him. Alek. Muck. It's all the same person. And I did get to see him fight. And I already know him. He's one of my best friends."

"You know him?" Elinor asked amazed. "And you never told me about him?"

"I never got around to it," Corin said. "That's not the point."

"It most certainly is the point," Elinor insisted. "Why didn't you introduce me to one of your best friends? How many more do you have out there?"

"I have lots of friends," Corin said. "What were you doing holding hands with him?"

"I think he's cute," Elinor said with a smile.

"What does that have to do with it?" Corin exploded.

"I wouldn't hold hands with him if he weren't," she said innocently. "He's also very nice. *He* wants to introduce me to all of his friends. Did you know how nice he is?"

"Of course I know that he's nice," Corin nearly shouted. "That's why we're good friends. But you were holding his hand!"

"Don't read too much into it," Elinor said, waving away his concerns. "You were in an exciting fight and I wanted someone to hold onto. It was very innocent."

"There is nothing innocent about holding hands," Corin insisted. "And how do you even know him?"

"I don't stay cooped up in the palace all the time, you know. After we get home from practice and scrubbing, there is still a lot of daylight left. I've made lots of friends."

That was when it hit Corin. He had assumed that every day after they came home, Elinor sought out Nellie and joined the ladies-in-waiting at their sewing. Lately, he had been working with different craftsmen, a new routine that his father had insisted on, which kept him busy and prevented him from spending time with his friends in the afternoon. It never occurred to him that Elinor was making friends on her own. "Did you leave with him after the fight?"

"Of course," she said. "I walked with him back to the commissary and sat with him for a bit while he ate. I like talking with him. And did you know, the food there is really good. I had a portion of stew before coming home, which is why I wasn't too hungry at supper tonight."

Corin could only shake his head in disbelief. Elinor had made herself quite at home, and he had known nothing about it.

"You're not upset that I spend time with Alek, are you?"

"No, of course not," Corin stammered.

"Because he is your friend, after all," Elinor continued with a smile.

Corin was troubled, and he did not understand why.

"I can tell you're still upset," Elinor said, peering at him. "Do you think you have to protect me from him?"

"No," Corin said feebly, now thoroughly confused, because that was exactly what he was feeling.

"After all, it's not like he's going to kidnap me," Elinor continued, enjoying Corin's discomfort.

"Of course not," Corin mumbled.

"Although he might want to hold hands with me again," she said, watching Corin bristle at this. "Or even kiss me," she added. She burst into laughter when she saw Corin's jaw drop.

"Now you've gone too far," he protested loudly.

"I didn't say I was going to *let* him," she squealed with delight. She opened the door to leave, "But I might." And she slipped into the hallway, closing the door behind her before Corin could object.

Chapter Twelve

Aina's Secret Trysts

The day was still young. Only the tops of the tallest trees were awash in golden light. The king stepped lightly through the barn. Workers were just arriving in the commissary for their breakfast, and except for Mali and a handful of his closest workers, Michael knew he would have some quiet time with Star. As he approached the great dragon's head, he was surprised to see a hooded figure standing there.

"Aina," he said. "What brings you here?"

The queen was equally startled to see her husband. For a brief moment, she groped for words. "I was—looking for Corin," she said. "It's market day, you know."

"He's gone off to work with the caulkers this morning," Michael said. "Remember, we spoke about this before. He's been with them all week."

"Of course," she said. "How could I have forgotten?" They stood there a moment in awkward silence. Finally Aina said, "If only we could find Aga. You know, to help us understand what is wrong with Star. I feel certain that he could give us the advice we need."

"Aga?" the king said, surprised. "Strange you should think of him. Aga was already old at our coronation. He must be long dead by now. Otherwise, we would have heard from him. He said he would check in from time to time, and his absence all these years seems to tell its own story."

"Still, I wish he were near," she sighed. "I miss his good advice." When her husband did not respond, she asked, "What brought you here so early?"

"I thought I'd take Sprout's place for the day and go down to the river with Star. It's been forever since I gave him a good scrubbing."

"Then I will leave you two," she said, turning to go.

"Aina," Michael said, struggling to put into words what he wanted to say to her. She waited to hear him out. "Come with us," he finally said. "We could—take a picnic. And sit out under the trees."

Aina hesitated before speaking. "It's market day," she said. "I can't disappoint those who come looking for me."

"What about disappointing me?" her husband said.

"That is what being a king is about," she replied in a quiet voice. "Try having a talk with your son instead." And slipping past him, she walked away.

The king sighed. "How could I have done that better?" he wondered out loud.

"Perhaps by suggesting a time when she is not already doing something else?"

The king looked up to the dragon. "If she wanted to be with me, why wouldn't she just drop everything else when I make an offer?"

"How often are you ready to drop everything at her suggestion?"

"You have a point," the king admitted reluctantly. He sat down on a barrel and crossed his arms. "Teach me something, Star," he said. "It's been forever since you taught me something new."

Star did not hesitate. "There was a time when both men and women of the Dragon Keepers could speak with me," he began and then paused to watch the king's reaction. "Is this the sort of thing you wanted to know?"

The king had a startled look. "Star, you've never mentioned anything like this to me before. I thought that only the men had the ability to speak with you."

"My care has always been with the men who could better handle the physical demands," Star continued. "Over time, I had less and less occasion to be with the women. Over the course of many generations, ages really, their inborn ability to speak with me went inward out of disuse, and there, I believe, it was transformed. This did not happen quickly, mind you. The women lost the outer means of understanding my speech, but gained something equally powerful and magical. They could command me through the power of their imagination."

"Why hasn't Aina ever done this?"

"She has. She is just unaware that she possesses this power. Do you remember the first time she brought you to see me in my wild state? How do you think I happened to be there waiting for you when you arrived? Did you think it mere coincidence?"

"We thought that you had sensed us. By smell or some other way."

"I could have been anywhere in the Devastation when you came. But I was waiting at the borders to the untouched lands, precisely where you appeared. Aina had summoned me."

"And what about now? Does she still send you—messages?"

"She could if she wanted. And if she knew that it was possible. But she is content to leave my care in your hands, as the women always have. However, she does visit me regularly."

"She does? Aina?"

"Ah, I fear I've betrayed one of our little secrets. She comes frequently when you are gone from home. And when you are here, she prefers to visit with me when you are not around, such as this morning."

"She wasn't looking for Sprout?"

"Your wife is not prone to forgetfulness. She knew he was not coming here. She also knew this was a time she could be alone with me."

"Why doesn't she want anyone else around?"

The dragon looked around to emphasize that they, too, were alone.

"I understand why I don't like anyone else around," the king said. "I come to speak with you privately. Why doesn't she suggest we come see you together?"

"She comes without you so you won't get in the way," Star said pointedly. "You are so thick-headed sometimes. If the only way she can communicate with me is by *not* talking, why would she want to be around when you start jabbering and translating everything for her?"

"I didn't mean anything…"

"Stop apologizing. Just stay out of our way, and don't tell her I've told you about our trysts. And, believe me, should Aina have the need of me, she could summon me through the power of her imagination alone. How did you think Galifalia managed?"

"I always wondered, but it never occurred to me to ask."

"Young Elinor has the same power," the dragon added. "That is how I found her when she was kidnapped the day after her arrival. Did you think we found her by chance?"

"Why did you never tell me until now?"

"Because it was none of your business."

"What's changed?"

The dragon did not answer his question. "So, are you going to take me out for a scrub? Your son's work leaves much to be desired. His interests lie elsewhere."

"Don't tell me that," the king sighed.

"Someone has to break the news to you."

"It's not like I don't know."

"Not wanting to know is even worse." The dragon peered at the king. "I agree with Aina. You should have a talk with him. He has been mixing with people you should know about."

The king sat up straighter. "Who? What sort of people?"

"Wandering, homeless street performers, jugglers, ballad singers. People from the Enclave, most likely, who sneak into the city. One in particular I know about. He's a magician, from what I hear."

"The magician!" the king gasped. "What do you know about him?"

"Only that the young prince is very interested in him. And that he has from him a certain dagger that I suspect would interest you greatly."

"The dagger. I've seen it. Star, does this magician have anything to do with your growing illness?"

"Aina's advice was sound. Go and speak with your son. Ask him about the magician."

The king jumped to his feet, looking alert and agitated. "I know where to find him," he muttered. He turned to go.

"What about my scrub?" the dragon asked as the king hurried away.

"Later!" Michael called back over his shoulder. "I have to go find Sprout."

"That should move things forward," the dragon murmured, and smiled to himself.

Chapter Thirteen

The Magician's Deception

*B*ut Father, you don't even know him," Corin protested. He knew he should say as little as possible and let it pass, but he was already in a dark mood. He had spent the morning helping to waterproof baskets the women used to transport water. And for the two days previous, he had been learning the art of caulking the hull of a riverboat.

He had complained once too often about going to market, and he wondered if Elinor had let slip his comment about wasting his time scrubbing Star. In the course of the past month, Corin had worked with the barrel makers, the tin workers, and even with the dyers, which had left his hands stained blue for a week. He had helped ret the flax harvest in a pond that stank abysmally and learned how to heckle the soaked stalks afterwards. Aside from the tedium of that work, he was at least satisfied now to have a supply of thread of his own making and of a quality he could depend on. For the most part, however, the new workload had felt like forced labor.

Working with the caulkers had been Corin's least favorite. Not only was the smell disagreeable, but no one had thought to warn him to wear old clothing that he could discard, and the black tar had ruined his favorite work shirt. To make matters worse, a thin film of it was smeared over his hands and would not wash off. They were no longer sticky, but he did not like the lingering smell or the unclean look. He was irritated to notice when he was changing his clothes and glanced into his mirror, that he even had a wide smudge of black across his cheek, smeared there in a careless moment. It made him feel so common. He acknowledged with bitterness that, although he secretly wanted the life of a commoner, this was going too far.

Once he had changed, and before joining his mother for the last hour of the market, Corin stopped to grab a quick bite from the leftover breakfast dishes in their private dining chamber. After eating, he lingered a little longer to work on a sachet he had been making for Elinor. With all the additional apprenticeships, he did not have as much time for the projects Master Ambroise set him. The sachet was already filled with fragrant dried lavender blossoms. He had just finished carefully stitching the edge and was sewing the form of blue flowers to decorate it when his father found him. Seeing his son working with needle and thread, the king exploded.

"But, Father," Corin said defensively, "Master Ambroise specifically told me—"

"Enough of Ambroise," his father said cuttingly. "I never could tolerate the man. Leave stitching to the women. You cannot rule a kingdom with a sewing needle in your hand. You've seen enough of him for the time being. You will learn something useful."

"Father,—" Corin objected. The king cut him off.

"And you've spent far too much time on the street watching free-loading performers. And you will keep your distance from that magician as well. I will have him arrested and thrown into prison. I should have done that a long time ago."

"But, Father," Corin protested, "you don't know him at all."

"I know enough," the king said sternly. "The dagger you brought home is a threat to you, to me, to everything we stand for. I shall have every wandering performer banned from the city. I'll do it! Are you so preoccupied with yourself that you haven't noticed what they have already done to Star?"

Corin was cut deeply by this remark. "I know better than you!" he spit back. "I'm the one with him every day." His father brooded silently at these words, so he continued. "You have no real proof the magician has anything to do with this. Did Star tell you this? Besides, it wasn't the magician's knife—" but he got no further before his father interrupted.

"I don't care!" the king exploded. "Until I know more about him, you are forbidden from seeing him again."

"Forbidden?" This was worse than the armed guard his mother had threatened to surround him with. "Why would you forbid me?"

"And I want you to begin working with a trainer to improve your sword skills. I will appoint a good man."

"Why do I have to work with a trainer?" the boy was appalled. Then he remembered seeing his father on the balcony. "Is this because of the fight I had with Leprun?"

"It's time to step up your training to become a knight," the king said firmly. "There is no excuse for having lost that fight."

"Didn't you see what his brother did?"

"You have to learn to find an advantage even when your opponent is larger or you are outnumbered."

Corin wanted to point out that he was already being trained by someone vastly larger than he was, but instead he exclaimed, "Father! I'm not ready for that."

"That's for me to decide," his father shot back. "You're the perfect age. In fact, you are behind. You've demonstrated that other boys your age are far more skilled. When I think what I could do at your age—"

"I'm not *you*," Corin interrupted. He hated when his father made comparisons with when he was growing up. "Why can't I decide when I'm ready?"

"Of course you're ready. Any boy your age would jump at the chance."

"Then offer it to them!" he shouted, finally losing control.

"That is an impertinent response!" his father shouted back.

"Why can't you just leave me alone with this? I hate swords. What if I don't want to be a knight? Why can't that be my choice?" The moment he had spoken, he knew it was not what he meant and wanted to pull the words back.

"Not become a knight?" his father shouted. "You don't want to become a knight?" His face turned red. "And what about king? Will you take a pass on that as well?" His balled fist slammed down. Dishes jumped, scattering their breakfast across the table. A filled cup sloshed over its sides. Corin winced.

"I never said anything about not wanting to be king." The boy struggled to keep his voice calm.

"And how do you want to hold your crown without a strong sword arm?" his father challenged.

"It doesn't have to be *my* sword arm," Corin answered weakly.

"And how do you expect men to follow you if you don't show that you are a strong leader?" the king pushed his point. "Do you think Leprun would follow you?"

"By being strong in other ways," Corin answered, but his voice had grown even fainter. He did think that Leprun would follow him, if he asked, but he knew that his father was not interested in his opinion. He hated that he let his father intimidate him.

"What sort of weakling have I fathered?" the king bellowed and Corin flinched at the words. Then the king snarled, "You might as well go and deliver yourself up to Bellek. Worrah would find some use for you."

At this taunt, Corin lost all control, and he yelled back, "Maybe I'll do just that! I'm sure he'd be happy to see me."

The king's eyes bulged. He raised his open hand as if to strike, and, although Corin braced himself for the blow, it never fell. "Go then!" the king cried instead, pointing to the doors. "And good riddance to you!" He turned on his heel and stormed from the room.

Corin stepped to the doorway and watched his father's back until it disappeared around a corner. "I'm not a weakling," he announced to the empty corridor in a shaky voice. He gritted his teeth. "How can I make you understand?" he said in a low voice. He took a deep breath and let it out slowly. He waited a few moments longer and then left in the other direction.

He headed for the market, knowing that his mother was expecting him. He descended by a back staircase and let himself out of the palace and into the city by a servant's doorway. He went to the Weavers' Quarter where the market was being held. The crowds grew as he approached the square. However, he was not yet ready to face his mother. He was still shaky from his argument with his father. Corin stopped at the fountain in the middle of the square. He bent over the stone rim and held out his cupped hands to catch a stream of clear water pouring out of the mouth of a stone satyr. *Maybe the water will wash this tar off*, he thought idly. But of course, it did not. He splashed his face, repeating this several times, as if he were trying to wash away the unpleasant quarrel. He ran his wet hands through his hair, taking deep breaths until he felt himself beginning to relax.

"Sprout!" a happy voice cried out nearby. He looked up to see Muck and Balu coming around the corner of the fountain. Corin smiled as best he could and nodded his head in greeting.

"Why aren't you at your stand?" Muck asked.

"I'm on my way now," he answered.

"Why the late start?" Balu questioned, but then saw the answer to his question. "You've been waterproofing, I see. Nasty job, isn't it?"

Corin only nodded his head, but then he said, "Not so bad."

"Where's Elinor?" Muck asked.

Corin shot him a glance. "I should ask you that question. The two of you have become regular chums."

"Did you think you could keep her all to yourself?" he replied, his chin jutting forward. "I like her company. She's also a very pretty girl." And he winked at Corin.

"You think she's pretty?" Corin asked astonished.

"I like her, too," Balu added. "She showed me a really nifty trick for throwing a knife."

"Great," Corin said bitterly. He was not aware that she knew anything at all about throwing knives, and this annoyed him even more. "I'm happy you are all getting along so famously with one another. Maybe I can join you one of these days."

"That would be great," Muck said with a smile, slapping him on the back. "Whenever you get unstuck from your pots, join us. Is she with your mom today?"

"That's where she's supposed to be," Corin said ruefully.

"Great," Muck said. "We'll go with you."

They made their way through the market, pausing at stands to make comments or to throw a few jibes at other roving boys. When they came to the queen's stand, she was sitting alone, aside for the usual attendants who stayed in the background.

"Your Majesty," Balu said as they approached, making a small obeisance.

"Good morning, Auntie," Muck greeted her with a happy grin.

"Good morning, boys," the queen replied, returning a warm smile. "Would you like a sweet bun? They are freshly baked this morning. I put raspberries in them."

"Thank you!" the two boys cried out in unison, reaching for the basket she proffered.

"Mom, they came to see Elinor. Isn't she here with you?"

"She wanted to see the other stands in the market," Aina said. "She said she was looking for some cloth for a dress."

"Did she go alone?" Corin asked.

"No, dear. I sent Nellie with her." The moment she said this, the queen looked suddenly worried and glanced at her son. The look on his face did not make her feel any better. Then she shook her head and said to him, "No, she wouldn't. You told me she promised."

"I think you're hiding her from us," Muck said to Corin, missing the queen's concern. "But like I said, she's too pretty to keep all to yourself. We'll find her."

"She'll be back a little later," the queen assured them.

"Come on, Muck," Balu said. "I smell parched corn coming from over there. I'm hungry for a handful."

"Thank you for the sweet buns," Muck called out as Balu pulled him away by his sleeve.

Corin came behind the stand and sat down beside his mother. There was an uncomfortable silence between them. He reached out and took a bun. "Came out good," he said, nibbling on it. "I like the raspberries. Makes it sweet and moist." Then there was silence again. Fortunately, at that moment two women approached the stand at once. Corin helped one of them.

"You haven't done that in awhile," Aina said when the women had gone their way.

"Done what?"

"Helped a customer," she said. Corin just shrugged his shoulders. "Was it that bad?" Aina then asked.

"What?" He was startled by her question.

"You look shaken up," she said. "Was it the waterproofing or your conversation?"

The implications of what his mother had said suddenly dawned on him. "Was that your idea?" he asked accusingly.

"Guilty on both counts," his mother admitted.

"You put Father up to that?" He glared at his mother.

"Don't be angry," she said. "If it is about the work, since you complained so often that you were bored with market days, I suggested to your father that we expand your experiences and apprentice you out. I think you've visited the caulkers enough for now. As to your conversation, I asked your father to have a chat with you. The two of you hardly talk anymore."

"There's a reason for that," Corin said sourly. "Father holds a discussion with a mace in one hand and a battle axe in the other."

"Your father was never a man of many words," Aina sighed. "Did it get out of hand?"

"Only if you consider disowning me out of hand."

The queen looked up, shocked. "He wouldn't," she said darkly. Corin wanted to respond, but her expression stopped him. She was looking beyond him, over his shoulder, and had gone pale. He turned to see what had disturbed her. Standing nearby hovered Nellie. She stood there, not moving, looking agitated and worried.

"Nellie!" the queen called out sharply. "Come to me!" Nellie lowered her eyes and with small, quick steps hastened to the queen. "What happened?" Aina demanded. "Where is my niece?"

Nellie kept her eyes averted. She opened her mouth to speak, but when no words came, she pressed her lips together again, and then bit her lower lip.

"Speak to me, Nellie," the queen commanded.

"I don't know!" Nellie burst out, throwing up her hands. "One moment she was there, and the next moment she'd disappeared. I can't find her anywhere." With her words, tears began streaming down her face. She pulled up her apron and hid behind it.

"Nellie, that's not useful right now," Aina scolded harshly.

"Don't yell at her. It's not her fault, Mom," Corin said quickly in her defense. "That's just what Elinor does."

"I'm not blaming her," Aina said, but she had a vengeful look in her eyes. Nellie continued to stand there and bawl. The queen turned and with an impatient gesture summoned one of her ladies-in-waiting to come forward. "Take Nellie," she said with clipped words. "Give her something to drink. Calm her down." The woman put her arm around Nellie's shoulders and gently led her behind the stand. "Roderick!" the queen called sharply. The young man hastened forward

Corin put his hand on her shoulder. "Mother, let me go look for her," he said. "I think I know where to find her."

"I'm sending Roderick with you," Aina said firmly.

"Please, let me go alone," Corin pleaded. "I'll find her and bring her home. I promise."

The queen studied him for a long moment. "And what if you get into more than you can handle?" she asked.

"And what if there is nothing to handle?" her son countered, returning his mother's stern gaze.

Aina locked eyes with her son. When she was satisfied with what she saw, she turned to Roderick. "Give me your sword."

"Mother!" Corin exclaimed. "I'm not going to need a sword. Why would I want a sword to go look for Elinor?"

"Then you won't mind carrying something at my request that you won't need." She took the sword and belt that Roderick handed to her and held it out to her son. "That's my condition," she said.

Impatiently, he snatched the belt from her hand and strapped it on.

"I don't want to regret letting you do this," she said.

"You won't," Corin said with a smile. He walked around the stand towards the stream of meandering shoppers.

"Where will you look for her?" Aina called after him.

"At the place where I'll find her," he called back over his shoulder. And before she had a chance to disapprove of his response, the prince slipped into the crowded plaza.

"Shall I follow him?" It was Roderick, still standing beside her.

"Let him go," the queen said. "We have to at some time."

Corin knew he had one chance of finding her. Quickly he oriented himself and, weaving between booths and shoppers, worked his way to the edge of the market. Then, with a quick look behind to make sure he was not being followed, he entered the quieter maze of streets. As he hurried along narrow alleys between houses, he heard a clock striking the hour. He counted as he walked and was alarmed to hear it strike noon. How had it gotten so late? The market would be winding down by the time he arrived. He quickened his steps.

When Corin entered the quarter called River Gate, he hurried to the marketplace. Shoppers had thinned out and many stands were closing down. He looked around for a crowd watching a show, but he could not find any. He wandered around, hoping he could catch sight of Elinor somewhere. He began to resign himself that she had not come here, or that she had already left again. He was passing by a narrow alleyway between two shops when something odd caught his eye. He turned around to look again. He saw three men crammed into the small space, their backs to the plaza. All their attention was on something or *someone* they were blocking from his sight. The fact that they were looking *down* caught his attention. They were dealing with someone shorter than they were and, he guessed, younger as well.

Corin walked towards the men. As he approached, he dragged his feet in the gravel. It had the effect he hoped for. One of the men heard the noise and glanced over his shoulder. He nodded in greeting.

"Good day to you, young master," he said with a wary smile, turning fully to block Corin from seeing behind him. "Can I be of help to you?"

"I was just wondering what's in the alleyway that's so interesting," Corin said.

"Nothing that need concern you, young master," the man replied. "You can just be on your way."

"Oh, but I'd like to see what's going on," Corin said, speaking louder than was necessary. "You wouldn't mind my taking a look, would you?"

The man's smile faded. "Just go on your way, laddie," he said with a shooing gesture. "We don't want no trouble with you."

That was when he heard a muffled "Sprout!" coming from behind the men. Immediately, someone began shoving them aside, and a moment later Elinor's head and arm emerged from between them, trying to force her way past. One of the men, however, grabbed her by the arm and held tightly onto her.

"Let her go," Corin ordered in a steady voice, suppressing the shakiness he felt in his legs. He placed his hand on the hilt of his sword, suddenly grateful for his mother's precaution.

"This is no business of yours," one of the men snarled. "She's with us."

Corin glanced to his left and what he saw gave him hope. He pulled his sword from its scabbard and pointed it towards the men. "Not any longer," he declared in a loud, firm voice. "Let her go."

"Don't be a fool, boy," the man holding Elinor warned. Corin noticed the man's eyes darting from his face to his hands and back to his face. Then he smiled. "Where did you steal the sword, Tar Boy? You're not what heroes are made of."

"I disagree," Corin said confidently, although silently cursing the smeared tar on his face and hands. He held his sword up and pointed it threateningly at the neck of the man who had spoken.

The man frowned darkly. "Kill the meddler," he growled to his companions. "Do it quickly. And throw his body in the alley." The two companions pulled knives out of their belts and took a step out of the alley, while the man who had spoken held on to Elinor. The two men moved threateningly towards the prince, who stood his ground, keeping his sword steadily between them.

"Do we have a problem here?" a deep voiced boomed. The men were startled and looked up to see a market constable walking towards them. He was a middle-aged man with a confident walk. He bore a sword at his side and carried a light halberd, something between a weapon and the symbol of his position. Corin had seen him walking nearby and knew brandishing his sword would attract the constable's attention. The knives disappeared as quickly as they had been pulled and the men stepped back away from Corin. Elinor took this moment when her captor was distracted to bite his hand. He yelped and swung his free arm to hit her, but Elinor had already skipped away. She ran to Corin and held him tightly by the arm.

"Haven't we done this once before?" he said bitingly in a low voice.

"It wasn't my fault," she hissed. "What's that on your face?"

"Never mind," he said, keeping his eyes on the three men and his sword ready.

"We were just having a friendly discussion," one of the men was explaining to the constable. "We don't mean no trouble."

"He was letting us admire his piece," another of them said, gesturing towards Corin's sword. "I think he wanted to sell it to us, but we ain't in need of any. We'll be going on our way now. We have important business to attend to." The three men turned to beat a hasty retreat.

"Just make sure your business would meet with my approval," the constable called after them. He watched them go and commented to no one in particular, "I'll remember them for another time." Then he looked to Corin and Elinor. "Are you two all right?"

"Yes, constable," Corin said, returning his sword to its sheath. "I am grateful for your assistance."

The constable's expression turned grave, and he studied their faces carefully. Corin suspected that his keen eye had seen the crest of the queen's guard on the pommel of Roderick's sword. The crest spoke louder to his sensibilities than the tar stain. "Sire, shall I call the watch to see you home?" he asked in a low voice, so as not to attract attention.

"That won't be necessary," Corin said. "We can find our own way. My thanks to you, constable, for attending to your duty in keeping the market safe." He hooked his cousin's arm and walked her away from there, back in the direction of the palace.

"Why does this keep happening to you?" he scolded as they walked. "Can't you just act normal for a while?"

"I don't *know* what normal is," Elinor shot back. Although her voice belied that she was shaken by her close call, anger was pushing it away. "Go ahead and teach me what normal is. My mother is dead. My father is dead. Both my brother and my sister are dead. Everyone I knew and loved is *dead*. My chaperons, my teachers, my friends. *Everyone*. I've lost my family and they've left me an orphan, and I can't even return home because they're all gone. I don't know anymore what normal is."

They walked in silence after this tirade. Corin held onto her arm as they went, and Elinor reached up repeatedly with her sleeve to wipe her eyes.

"I'm sorry," Corin finally said in a small voice. "I didn't mean it like that. I was just scared for you."

"Did Star send you?" she asked. Her voice was still shaky.

"No. I came looking for you when Nellie returned alone."

"If Star didn't send you, then how did you know where to find me?"

"It wasn't so hard to figure out," Corin laughed. "You came to see the magician."

She looked at her cousin searchingly. "You didn't tell me that you know him, too."

"I've spoken with him only once," Corin admitted. "Before you came to live here, I often sought him out to see his show. Something about him fascinated me. What do you know about him?"

"Not much. He told me that he lives deep in the forest, and that keeps him from coming to the market very often. He told me that I should come visit him." Then she laughed. "But he failed to tell me where to find him, so I doubt that will ever happen."

"Why did you come to see him today?"

"The last time I saw him he invited me to come see him in the market, but he didn't have much to say to me, so I don't really know why he asked me to come. Maybe he just wanted me to admire his act."

Corin was suddenly aware of his argument with his father. In spite of himself, he felt suspicion rising. "What did those three men want with you?"

"They kept saying there was something they wanted to show me. I had the impression they wanted to avoid a scene and get me to go with them willingly. It was only when I resisted that they pushed me into the alley."

"How soon after speaking with the magician did you run into the three men?"

"Almost immediately," Elinor answered. "He pointed out a shortcut for me to take back towards the palace, and hardly had I set out in that direction ... hold on, are you suggesting that he had something to do with them?"

His mother's words came back to him. *He will deceive you with kind words and deeds that look to benefit you.* "I don't want to believe it," Corin said. "But you have to admit that it looks suspicious. He gets you to come here, has nothing in particular to say to you, tells you which way to walk, and then you are nearly kidnapped again. I don't like the way it adds up."

"But he is such a kind old man," Elinor said. "He's been so helpful to me."

"I know," Corin said. "I love coming to see his magic show. I don't like saying it, but maybe my parents are right. They don't trust him. Maybe we should just stay away until we know more about him. It was pure luck that I came along when I did and saw that constable."

"Well, that's what Star is all about, isn't he?" Elinor said.

"What do you mean?"

"Pure luck. Doesn't he make that sort of thing happen? Isn't that what he does here?"

"Elinor, I keep trying to explain to you—" but then he stopped himself from telling her again that that's not how a Luck Dragon works. The fact was that it had all turned out well because of good luck. He would have to take this matter up with Star directly. Corin turned to Elinor to say that he was beginning to think that she may have a point, when he was startled by the sudden look of alarm on her face. He never saw the blow coming.

He was not unconscious for long. When he opened his eyes again, he was staring at the gravelly ground of the alley they had just entered. He blinked his eyes several times trying to recall how he had gotten there. He was too stunned to think clearly until he remembered the look on Elinor's face. He sat bolt upright, which was a mistake, because it caused his head to throb. Yet at the same time, it was a fortunate move, because otherwise he would have missed seeing his cousin being dragged away between two men. He saw her trying to bite the hand of one of the men holding onto her, and the swing of his free arm as he boxed her on the ears. Then they were gone, around a corner. They were moving in the direction of the river gate.

Corin jumped to his feet, but immediately fell to his knees again, his vision swimming. He was feeling sick to his stomach. He put his hand to the side of his head where the pain was most intense. Pulling his hand away, he was startled to see that it was smeared with blood. He vaguely registered that he must have been hit with a club. He tried again to get to his feet, this time rising slowly, resting his hands on his knees. He glanced at his surroundings. The market fountain looked reachable, but it annoyed him that it danced before his eyes and would not hold still.

Staggering like a drunk, he walked with halting steps into the plaza and focused all his will on reaching the fountain. He never made it. Fountain, plaza, houses and sky all swirled around before him as if some master juggler had snatched them up and was tossing them one after the other before his eyes. The movement made him dizzy and the giddiness sickened his stomach even worse. He fell to his knees, retched, and collapsed onto his side. He was grateful that all the misery went away when he closed his eyes.

Part III

The Enclave

Chapter Fourteen

Precious Cargo

Corin was floating through a layer of thick clouds. Vaguely, it occurred to him that he must be riding on Star. Was Elinor sitting next to him? He looked to all sides, but could not see her. Everything was fuzzy and shrouded by a whitish mist. Where was Elinor? Where had she gone? Then it hit him. Elinor!

He sat bolt upright and cried out from the stabbing pain in his head. An elderly man he had never seen before rushed into the room. Corin looked around and recognized nothing. "Where am I?" he puzzled.

"Young master," the man said. "You've had quite a blow to the head."

"Who are you?" he next asked.

"My name is Silas, young master," the man said. He was dressed in homespun tunic and pants. His face was creased, wrinkled and browned by the sun. He had curly greying hair and a kindly smile. He looked concerned. "I saw you collapse in the plaza and brought you home. My wife is good with herbals and she got the bleeding from your head to stop. You've had quite a—"

"Where's Elinor?" Corin interrupted. He did not expect that Silas would have an answer, but that was the only question that mattered to him at the moment.

"I don't know an Elinor, young master," Silas responded. "Is that your sister?"

"Where am I?" Corin asked for the second time.

"As I said," the man answered, "I brought you home. I couldn't leave you just lying there on the street—"

"I have to find Elinor," Corin insisted, swinging his feet to the floor. He jumped up, but sat down again quickly when the room around him began to swim.

"You'll have to take things slowly," Silas said, placing a steadying hand onto the young man's shoulder. "You've had a stern blow to your head."

"Here, here," clucked an elderly woman bustling into the room. "Why is our young patient getting out of bed?" Like her husband, she was dressed in homespun cloth and wore a scarf over her head in the way of older matrons. She was carrying a bowl filled with water and over her arm a towel. She placed the bowl onto the small table beside the bed where Corin sat with his hands to his head.

"I have to go find Elinor," he moaned, but he did not try getting up again.

"Soon enough, soon enough," the woman cooed, soaking a washcloth in her bowl. "But first we must clean you up a bit. Sit still while I wipe the dried blood away. You'll feel so much better for it." Without waiting for her patient to agree, she took the cloth, held his chin in her hands, and washed his face.

"Smells good," he mumbled from behind the cloth, inhaling deeply. "Mmm. Chamomile and lemon balm. One's not so pleasant, though. That must be figwort."

She pulled the cloth away a moment and peered into Corin's face. "Right you are, young man. Both good and healing it should smell." Then she went back to washing his face. "Seems you know a thing or two about herbs. Now hold still."

"You don't understand—" Corin began, but was cut off by the woman.

"What I understand is that you've suffered a blow to the head and my man carried you senseless into my house. And there's one thing I've learned from having three sons and a husband, and that's that men think their heads are much harder than they actually are. And you are no exception. Now sit quiet and wait until I am finished."

"Yes, ma'am," Corin sighed, but he was grateful for the care and attention. The pain in his head had dulled and the room stopped swimming.

He heard her cluck in disapproval. "There are some stains I do not have the herbs to remove, I'm afraid." Corin knew she must be referring to the tar. Then she rambled on as she gently washed his face. "To think, in broad daylight! Such a thing has not happened for years around here. And poor thieves they were, not even taking your fine sword."

"My sword!" Corin exclaimed, jerking away from her. "I still have it?"

"There in the corner," Silas said, gesturing with a nod of his head. "And what might a young man your age be doing walking around with a sword? You are quite a paradox, if I do say so myself."

"I borrowed it," Corin admitted, but decided not to explain more. "Look, I've got to go look for Elinor." He started to get up, determined to grab Roddy's sword and go.

"So you've said already," Silas agreed. "But what direction do you plan looking in?"

This stopped Corin. He eased himself back onto the bed and Silas' wife, tutting her disapproval, continued daubing away at his scalp with her washcloth. "You young folk were just born impatient. Rest here until you're feeling better," she said. "I'm warming some soup for you. When you have your strength back, Silas can go with you to look for your lost sister."

Corin's eyes were drawn to the window. He squinted at the glare of light shining off water. "That's the river," he said amazed.

Silas noticed where Corin was looking. "Indeed, our house is one of those built into the city wall. We enjoy a lovely view to the river. I grew up in this very house. My father grew up here as well, and my parents, freshly married and expecting their first child, which was yours truly, mind you ..."

Corin stopped listening to Silas. His eyes were riveted on a river boat that was moored within sight of the window. Its prow was turned upriver, and there were men walking up the gangplank carrying supplies on their shoulders. The boat was being loaded in preparation for setting sail against the current. This, in itself, was no unusual event. There was heavy traffic in trade going both up and down river. Wind blew boats against the current, and where the wind was not enough, men at oars provided the extra power. Regardless of political tensions between Gladur and its neighbors, barring open hostilities, there remained brisk trading of goods.

However, what held Corin's full attention were the three men who stood on the shore next to the boat. Even at the distance, he recognized all three of them. One was the nobleman from whom the old magician had lifted the dagger that had so upset his mother and who had been eyeing Elinor while he dueled with Leprun. The second, he was certain, was one of the three men who had tried to kidnap Elinor in the marketplace. And the third was none other than Geron, commander of the city's garrison.

Corin felt his muscles tense. His first impulse was to jump up and dash out to confront them. This, however, he knew would be a rash action that would achieve nothing. He had to come up with a plan. He was certain that Elinor was inside the boat, held against her will. He knew they would deny having her, and Geron was the voice of authority to prevent him from forcing his way on board. Seeing him together with the other two men, Corin was more convinced now than ever that Geron was part of a conspiracy. Desperately searching for a plan, he tried to imagine what his father would do. That, however, was no help.

His father, he was sure, would attack all three men with his sword flashing wildly and force his way on board. So he quieted himself and thought of what Star would advise him to do. That was more helpful. Star's calm voice urged him to wait. As long as the boat was moored, he could reach it at any time. He would have to act quickly only at the moment the boat prepared to set sail. His best counsel was to wait and watch for an opportunity.

"... our own children, of course, have long since grown," Silas had continued his narrative. "We are blest with three grandchildren, two girls, Mari and Sali, and a boy—"

"Do you think I could stay here a bit longer?" Corin interrupted him.

Silas looked at him with surprise. "Well, isn't that just what we've been trying to talk you into all this time? Of course, you can stay. As long as you need to. Addie, let's give this boy some quiet."

"First some soup, to strengthen him. Then he can have all the quiet he needs," his wife said bustling out of the room carrying the washbowl and the towel.

Corin was delighted with how his fortunes had turned. He now felt how famished he was, and Addie's hearty soup, with a generous wedge of her hearth-baked bread, refreshed and strengthened him. He was grateful to be able to rest. His window allowed him the perfect vantage point to keep a close eye on the suspect boat. He watched as Geron and the two men spoke some more and laughed over some joke. Geron looked very satisfied with himself, and this fueled Corin's suspicions even hotter. Then the captain of the guard went his way and the two men, the nobleman and the kidnapper, walked up the gangplank onto the ship and disappeared into the single cabin belowdecks. The crew finished loading the boat, and then all went quiet. It did not look as if they were preparing to set off upriver before the next day.

It was tedious keeping watch on the boat. Corin sat on the broad ledge of the window box, making himself as comfortable as possible.

The throbbing in his head came and went. At one point late in the day, although he was sitting up and leaning against the window to keep a close watch, Corin succumbed to dreamless sleep.

He woke up with a start. Night had fallen, and, sitting in the dark, Corin was momentarily disoriented. He reached up and felt the curtain and the cold glass of the window. Outside, a single torch burned within his sight, and he panicked when he could not tell in the dark shadows if the boat was still there. His first impulse was to jump up and run out to the wharf. But once again he stopped himself from being impulsive, and instead sat a moment and listened. Although he sat in the dark, a faint, dancing light was coming through the door from the next room. He heard two voices conversing in low tones, and knew them to belong to his two kindly hosts.

Stop and think, he told himself. What would be the best plan? He knew the right thing to do was return home and let his parents take over the search. But he felt the panic rising inside of him that he had to act fast. He was certain that he knew where Elinor was being kept prisoner. He could not run off to get help and leave her in peril. Besides, he was feeling lucky and certain that everything would turn out right. It all had so far, hadn't it?

Corin realized that leaving by the front door would only cause delays. He would have to talk his hosts into letting him leave in the night. He was certain they would want him to stay until morning. And once he left their home, he would have to talk his way past the guard posted at the gate to the river.

He hated leaving without thanking Silas and Addie, but he knew he had no choice. As quietly as he could, he got up and felt his way to the corner of the room where Silas had left the sword. Confidence surged through him once he felt its firmness in his grip. It reminded him of the day he had knocked Elinor off Star's back. Resolve strengthened his limbs. Is this the feeling that made his father so enjoy fighting? He tucked this thought away for a later time. Now he had to go find his cousin.

Corin went back to the window and felt along its frame until he found the latch. Making as little noise aa possible, he unfastened the window and swung the double pane inward. It would be a tight fit. The window was made too small to allow a full grown man, but Corin was certain that he could squeeze through. He stuck his head out the window and looked down to see how far it was to the ground. He laughed at his folly, because in the darkness he could not tell. He pulled his head back in and took his sword. He emerged from the window a second time, leading with the sword in his hands.

He looked left and right. The quay looked deserted. Torches burned in sconces along the wall, although they were widely spaced and shed only limited light. He unsheathed the sword and let the belt and scabbard fall. The muffled sound came so quickly, he knew with satisfaction that the ground level of the quay was only a foot or two below the floor level of the house. He let the sword follow and hoped the sound would not attract any patrolling guards. There was no time to lose. He pulled his shoulders and head back into the room. With a glance back towards the warm light from the neighboring room, he spoke a silent thanks to the old couple and, hoisting himself up, thrust his feet through the open window, letting his body follow. Holding onto the window sill, he gently let himself down.

Once on the ground, Corin retrieved his sword and strapped the belt around his waist. He stopped and listened carefully. There was the creaking sound of wood against wood as boats rocked gently in their moorings. He could hear the sloshing of water against their hulls. He was certain that he had not come too late. He felt like he was riding a wave of good fortune. He looked into the darkness towards the river. He could discern a small flickering of light coming from the deck of a boat. It came from a brazier the deckhands used for cooking their meals. He now had a light to aim towards. He was so focused on getting to the edge of the wharf that he did not see the shadowy figure in the dark until he bumped into him. He was startled by the presence of another person on the otherwise deserted waterfront.

Corin was doubly jolted when he looked up at the face of the man he had collided with. There was enough light from the torches to make out his features.

"You!" Geron cried in astonishment, recognizing the young prince. Then he yelled, "Stop! Come back!" as Corin raced away into the darkness in the opposite direction. "Guard!" Geron bellowed from behind him.

Corin heard the pounding of feet pursuing him. It was risky to run blindly in the dark, and he realized his only chance of escape was to hide. It was only a matter of time before the guard fetched torches to look for him in every nook and cranny. There was only one place he could be safe. He turned to the river.

The water was cold, but he was so keyed up from the chase that he barely registered it. He slipped into the river at the prow of a boat and followed its contours, hanging onto loose ropes dangling over the side until he was on the river side of the boat, hidden from the shore. He could hear the muffled cries of the guard and wondered what he should do next.

He noticed there was a sudden commotion on the boat moored behind the one where he dangled in the water. He released his hold on the ropes and let the gentle current carry him towards the prow of the next boat. He grabbed a line and discovered that it was a rope ladder. He pulled himself up out of the water until he was even with the deck. He hung there, watching the activity.

"Cast off the lines!" someone ordered. "Man the oars!"

"What's the haste?" another voice in the dark grumbled. "We're not due to leave until morning."

"You cast off when you're told to cast off," the first voice shot back. "Now cast off and put your backs into the oars."

Corin heard a number of grumbling voices and, with the torches on shore as a backlight, could see the shadowy figures of the deckhands at work unfastening ropes and taking their places at the double row of oars. Corin had to make a quick decision whether to stay with this boat or continue his search on others. He had no idea if he had found the boat he had suspicions about earlier. He listened carefully to whatever snatches of conversation he could catch.

"How will we find our way in the dark?" one of the sailors called out, miffed at the suddenness of their departure.

"All you need to find is the oar in front of your face," a gruff voice threatened. "Leave the steering to the pilot."

The boat rocked back and forth, slowly moving away from the wharf. From his vantage place, Corin could see members of the guard on shore running this way and that with torches in a full search. It did not seem safe anywhere, but he did not want to get carried up the river with the wrong boat. He peered at the next boat moored along the wharf, but all was quiet and dark there. He hung by one arm, ready to launch himself into the water and swim if need be. Suddenly, a door opened from belowdecks and a man appeared. He pulled aside the man with the gruff voice. They were standing right next to where Corin was hanging over the side! He pressed himself against the hull and waited until they would move on.

"What's going on?" one asked in a low voice. "Why are we casting off?"

"There's a commotion on shore," the gruff voice responded. "The whole guard has been turned out. Something's been lost and they're looking for it. The last thing we want is for them to board us in their search."

"But how will we find our way in the dark?"

"The river is wide and clear here and there's enough of a moon to show us the way," the gruff voice answered. "We'll row an hour or so upriver and then find a safe mooring until morning. All that matters is that we get out of here now."

"I hope you know what you're doing," the first man said.

"Do you know what would happen to us if they found her on board?" the gruff voice asked. Corin felt a thrill go through him at those words. He watched the shadowy figure of the other man reach up to his throat. "That's right, they'll have us dangling from the end of a rope. We'll take the risk of rowing a bit in the dark."

If they found *her* on board. That could mean only one thing. Corin was hanging from the very boat where Elinor was kept captive. Now all he had to do was figure out a way to free her. He knew that time was on his side, as long as he could stay hidden. The darkness worked to his advantage. Climbing the rope ladder had lifted him from the waist above the surface of the water, and although he was chilled and the forward motion of the boat dragged on his legs, it was a warm evening and he set his mind on accepting being uncomfortable. He hung onto the gunwale and watched and waited.

The sailors had settled into the work of rowing and their backs were to him, so he did not have to worry about being discovered by them. Corin could not see any other figures on deck, other than the silhouette of the pilot in the stern steering their course. One deckhand sat in the prow with a sputtering torch, to warn the pilot of any impending collisions. It was the only light on deck. There was no conversation, only the repetitive call of one of the men marking the cadence to row by and the sound of the oars dipping in the water. Corin looked back and saw the torches on the wharf were just a suggestion of light in the fading distance. To the rhythmic sound of the oars gently splashing in the water, the boat slid silently through the dark night. He leaned forward to rest his head on the deck. It had begun to throb again, and he took advantage of the chance to rest. He did not intend to, nor did he think it possible while hanging onto the ladder, but he drifted into sleep.

Corin was abruptly jolted awake. He was momentarily disoriented, first sensing that he was wet and uncomfortable. He realized then that he had fallen asleep. He tensed and involuntarily ducked his head down as there was a great deal of movement on the deck.

"Can't see a blasted thing!" someone cursed.

"Just ship the oars," a voice ordered.

"Throw out the anchors!" the command was barked into the darkness. A moment later there were splashes to Corin's right, coming from the prow of the boat.

"Any lines to secure?" someone nearby asked.

"We'll hang well enough from the anchors," a voice growled. Then he spoke loud enough for all to hear, "Get some sleep, mates. We move on at first light. We've precious cargo to deliver."

Corin felt a new thrill at the mention of *precious cargo*. They had made things easy for him. They must have docked near the shore. He had only to wait for the crew to go to sleep and then he could rescue Elinor. He pulled himself a little higher out of the water and grew still, watching and listening. The movement on deck soon quieted down, as sailors found flat spaces to lie down. Then he heard the sound of angry voices, but not on deck. Someone in the cabin was yelling. A door opened and a man, still cursing, emerged onto the deck to the subdued chuckling of the crew members. Then it grew quiet again. It was not long before the frogs along the shore resumed their evening song, and the sound of men snoring joined the general chorus. The commotion had already told him where to find the cabin door. He had only to beware stepping on someone and waking him up.

Inch by inch Corin slowly pulled himself out of the water until he was sitting on the edge of the boat's deck. He sat there awhile, waiting for his clothing to stop dripping. He did not want to be splashing any sleepers in the face as he passed by them. Although he was chilled from sitting in the water, he was so keyed up he barely noticed. As he waited, he realized that, oddly, the night had grown brighter. He was able to make out dark shapes and open spaces on deck. He glanced up and saw a three-quarter moon had risen above the line of trees on the shore. What a stroke of good fortune! Then he tensed. The light of the moon would help him find his way, but it would also make him visible to others. His only hope was that anyone seeing him would think that he was just a restless member of the crew.

Corin watched the moon hovering in the sky and waited until the sound of the snoring and the singing of the frogs had found a solid rhythm with one another. He slowly lifted himself to his feet and waited to steady his footing and work out any stiffness in his body from the time spent hanging over the edge in the cold water. Then, holding his sword close to his body to keep it from knocking against anything, he let the moonlight guide him through the empty spaces on deck and around all the sleeping lumps.

He arrived at the cabin door without incident, his heart racing. As he took hold of the door handle, he had a sudden misgiving. How was he going to find Elinor in the darkness of the cabin? With a shrug of his shoulders, he knew he had no choice but to try. He quietly drew his sword, to have it ready in case he had to fight. He entered the room and was struck by its stuffiness. He stood in the doorway, hoping that his eyes would adjust quickly.

He was startled by the whispered voice, "Sprout?"

"Elinor?" he whispered back into the darkness.

"I'm over here," she said urgently from somewhere to his left.

Çorin took a step into the small space and realized that the light of the moon shone from behind him, casting an eerie glow into the cabin. He looked around. Sitting in a chair, not two steps away, was a man. The moon shone full on his unshaven face. Corin froze, his sword ready to strike.

"He's drunk asleep," Elinor whispered, and in spite of her lowered voice, he could hear the cutting scorn. "Cut me loose. My legs are tied, too."

"Anyone else?" Corin asked quietly, trying to scan the room.

"No. Just this drunken slob. Cut me loose."

Corin walked towards the dark corner from where he had heard her voice come. There was a muffled, hollow bump. "Ow!" Corin clapped a hand to his forehead. He heard his cousin giggle.

"Low ceiling," she said in a quiet voice. "Duck."

"You could have warned me," he scolded quietly. The last thing he needed was another blow to his head. He hunched over and felt with his hands until he found her. He let his fingers guide him to where to cut her free.

"You're soaked, you know," she said. "What did you do, swim?"

"Quiet, would you?"

"He's so drunk, he's not waking up again until tomorrow. Late tomorrow. He was bored keeping an eye on me, and he drank up all the ale, his portion as well as everyone else's."

"So that's what the yelling was about," Corin reflected, pulling away the ropes from her body. "Come quietly. The men on deck have not been drinking."

"Where are we going?" Elinor asked.

"I'm not sure yet. Just off this boat," he said. "They've anchored near the shore."

"I'm not stupid, you know," she scolded. "I've got ears. I could hear when they moored the boat." Corin sighed. Hardly were they together again and they were quarreling. Didn't she realize what he had gone through to get her out of there? He had her by the hand and paused at the cabin door, crouching down, looking to see if there was any movement on deck. "Do you realize this is the third time you've been kidnapped since coming to Gladur?" he whispered over his shoulder. This was not the time to bring this up, but her comment had stung. "What is up with you?"

"It's not *my* fault," she protested. "Move already," and, embarrassed by Corin's words, she gave him a shove from behind. Although she did not intend it, her push threw Corin off-balance. In order to keep himself from falling, he involuntarily lurched forward. His sheathed sword, which he had been holding close to his body to prevent it from knocking something unintentionally, now clattered noisily against the deck.

Corin put out his hand to steady himself, but instead of finding something solid, landed with the full force of his weight onto something smooshy. It was a sleeping sailor's neck. The shock of Corin's hand grabbing his throat rudely awoke the sleeper, who screamed with full force from the fright, "Help! Murder!"

The sailor's yell abruptly awoke Elinor's sleeping guard, who became immediately conscious of his duty, and upon hearing the call of distress, leapt from his seat and staggered to where Elinor had been kept tied up. It took but a moment for him to find the empty chair and the cut ropes. He was fortunately too disoriented to see his prisoner crouching in the moonlight just a few steps beyond the door. Instead, he lifted his face towards the open cabin door, and although his words were slurred from the prodigious amount of ale he had drunk, he yelled loudly, "All han's! Prish'ner eshcap't! All han's, alert!"

The sailor Corin had landed on, still yelling for help, instinctively threw the prince off, causing him to fall backwards, landing on his seat. Startled by the yell from behind and fearful of recapture, Elinor sprang forward, grabbed her cousin by the arm and yanked him to his feet. "We have to get out of here," she said urgently.

"Who are you telling?" he replied, now grabbing her by the arm and dragging her towards the opposite side of the boat from where he had boarded. The yelling continued, joined by a chorus of other confused voices. Bumping into some shadows and tripping over others, Corin suddenly had a brilliant idea.

"Attack!" he yelled fiercely. "Have at them! Attack!" Then pulling at his cousin with even more determination, he succeeded in dragging her to the far edge of the boat. He glanced back at the shadowy figures that were now converging from all over the deck. He saw with glee that his ploy was having the desired effect. In their sleepy stupor, thinking that they had been boarded and were under attack, sailors were punching and swinging at one another. "Jump," he hissed at Elinor.

"Do what?" she asked breathlessly, thinking he must certainly mean something else.

"Follow me," he said. He did not wait for her to comply. Still holding tightly onto her arm, he launched both of them from the boat's gunwale and into the darkness below. As they fell, Elinor shrieked, and Corin prayed they were falling into water and not onto rocks.

Elinor's screech and Corin's misgivings both ended with a splash. Elinor came up spluttering and Corin grabbed her again and made for the line of trees marking the shore, visible in the dim, milky moonlight. He knew it would not take long for the sailors to realize his trick and in a body set after them. After only a few moments of splashing towards the dark shore, the cousins felt the gravelly bank beneath their feet. Grabbing roots, they hauled themselves out of the water and dove into the waiting cover of the foliage.

They did not pause, but heedlessly plunged into the bushes. It was not a moment too soon. Behind them on the boat, order had been restored. Someone was shouting commands and several torches had been lit. A moment later, sailors bearing flaming brands followed the path of the escaping cousins, first into the water and then through the dense foliage on shore.

At first, Corin thought that it would be easy to escape, because the night was dark underneath the trees and the undergrowth thick. But the lack of light was the very thing that stalled them. As soon as the cousins reached the protection of the trees, they set out at a cautious jog to put some distance between themselves and their pursuers. However, now that they were under the canopy of the trees, the light from the moon was no help in finding solid ground to place their feet. As a result, Elinor suddenly collapsed on the ground with a shriek of pain. Corin found her quickly and knelt down to help her up again.

"My ankle," she gasped in a strangled voice. "I think I broke it. Oh, it hurts so much."

"Lean on me," he said, hauling her to her feet. She collapsed again onto the ground with another shriek of agony.

"Quiet," he whispered urgently. "Get up."

"I can't," she said between sobs. "It hurts too much."

"You have to," Corin said urgently. "They're coming."

Whoever was commanding the sailors must have had some experience pursuing escaped prisoners. He ordered his men to fan out in an arc, and they moved through the forest like a great net ready to close on its prey. When Corin looked back, it appeared as if they were being surrounded, which was indeed the case, and this caused him to panic. With Elinor unable to move forward, their only choice now was to hide in the bushes, hoping the sailors would not find them as they passed by.

Suddenly a dark form hovered over them and a thrill of fear coursed through Corin's limbs. They had already been found out! He grasped the pommel of his sword and drew it, ready to fight.

"Put that away," the shadow said gruffly, keeping his voice low. "Follow me. It's your only escape."

"Who are you?" Corin blurted out, unable to decide whether to stab him or trust him.

"A friend," the voice responded. "Come quickly. We have no time to lose."

"She can't," Corin said, feeling helpless. "It's her leg. She can't walk."

"Now this," the voice sighed. "I'd expect something a bit more fortunate coming from you. But then, who knows what good will come of it?" Corin puzzled over the man's words and stood out of the way as the figure bent over and carefully lifted Elinor. Once he had her cradled in his arms, he looked over his shoulder at the pursuing torches. They were dangerously close. Corin could hear the sailors speaking to one another.

"We could use some diversion, here," the stranger muttered. A moment later, a sudden blast of wind blew through the branches of the trees around them, blowing leaves and twigs into Corin's face. The noise of it drowned out everything else.

The stranger leaned close enough to Corin's ear to be heard. "This way," he said. "Keep up. We have a bit of a walk ahead of us. If you lag behind, they'll snatch you."

"How did you do that?" Corin asked, astounded at the sudden wind. But the stranger had already moved on, and Corin had to hurry not to lose him in the darkness of the night. As he walked, Corin reflected that there was something vaguely familiar in this stranger's voice, but he dismissed it out of hand. Who could he possibly know out here?

The shadowy figure before him moved effortlessly through the dark underbrush. Corin staggered behind, tripping over any unevenness in the ground beneath his feet, annoyed by the tree debris that was still blowing into his face. He glanced back from time to time and felt relief that they had left behind the lights and the shouting. A heavy weariness now crept into his limbs, and he longed for nothing more than to crawl under a bush and fall asleep until morning. The moon had either disappeared behind clouds or was completely hidden by the thick foliage of the forest they were winding their way through. They trudged onward, and Corin was worried that they were traveling much too fast in that darkness. However, it became clear that the stranger knew his way perfectly and led Corin without mishap. The roaring wind ended as suddenly as it had begun, and Corin shrugged it off as a fortunate coincidence.

Finally, they emerged into a small clearing. Corin could make out the heavier shadow of a building, likely a small cottage. The man bearing Elinor did not stop, but walked right up to the dark wall of the building and disappeared. Groping with his hands, Corin found the doorway and followed as best he could. From the feel and the smells, he sensed that they stood in the room of the cottage that served as sitting room, kitchen and bedroom. He spied glowing embers and knew that must be the hearth.

"Welcome to my humble abode," the shadowy figure finally spoke.

"Elinor?" Corin said softly into the room.

"I believe she has fallen asleep," the stranger said. "I laid her down beside the hearth." Corin heard some rustling and then the stranger spoke again. "She's wet. It is an odd time to have gone for a swim, but I'm certain you had your reasons. I will stir up the fire to dry her off." Corin heard him blowing, and saw the embers in the hearth flare up. In their light, he could make out the bulky figure of the stranger hunched over them. He watched him reach to a pile of kindling that lay beside the fireplace and place wood shavings onto the embers. He blew gently a second time, and flames burst forth. Onto this fire, the stranger lay first small pieces of wood and progressively larger pieces, all of which crackled in the hot flames. It was a welcome sound, and Corin sensed the sudden heat. Only now did he feel the chill from his wet clothing. The warm flickering light of the fire filled the room as the stranger added a last few larger pieces of wood.

"I think we can spare ourselves a rushlight until that burns lower," the stranger muttered out loud. In the dancing light that now chased the shadows into the corners of the room, Corin looked down at Elinor, deeply asleep with her mouth slightly open. He glanced at her legs and wondered how badly injured she might be. By now the stranger had stood up and turned around. Corin looked up, curious to see the face of their rescuer. He was immediately struck by the long beard, his beak of a nose, and those piercing eyes.

"It's you!" he gasped. Corin staggered back a step and let himself down in a chair.

"I did invite you to come visit me, did I not?"

"What are you doing here?" Corin stammered.

"Seeing that this is my home, the more interesting question is, what are you doing here?" the old magician said with a warm smile.

Chapter Fifteen

The Writhing Dragon

1 don't know, Your Majesty," Nellie howled. She was using her apron to dry the tears dripping down her cheeks. Anxious, she twisted it between her hands as if she were wringing out a dishrag. "I already told you everything." She buried her face in her apron and sobbed.

"She doesn't know anything," the queen said severely. "The poor thing's a wreck. Leave her in peace."

The king paced restlessly up and down in front of Nellie. He paused at the queen's words and looked up. "If she doesn't know, then who will?" he demanded.

"We'll not learn more by yelling at her," Aina scolded. "Nellie, you are excused." At these words, Nellie's reddened eyes peeked out from behind her apron. "That means, you may leave now," the queen added with a shooing gesture. "Go now." Nellie did not wait to be told again and, glancing at the king, scurried from the room.

The king glared at her as she left. "Who will give us answers now?" he boomed.

"You're not being helpful by scaring everyone," Aina rebuked him. Even the guards in the room were looking uncomfortable. "I think we have to conclude that she has been kidnapped. Again. Since it happened once before, it is the best lead we have."

"Where is Commander Geron?" the king shouted at the guards. "Who will tell me where Geron is?"

A guardsman stepped forward. "Your Majesty," he said with a short bow of his head.

"Save me the etiquette and tell me where the commander of my city troops is hiding," the king said sourly.

"Sire, Commander Geron has been summoned to the palace, but the only message that has returned is that he cannot be found."

"Insufferable!" shouted the king. "How can the guard not know where their commander has gone?"

"Sire," the guardsman continued, "there is a rumor that he was last seen with a small patrol leaving the city in a boat."

"Leaving?" the king yelled. "Where was he going?"

The guardsman flinched. He was obviously collecting himself before answering. "He was rumored just after nightfall to be seen headed upriver, sire," the guardsman said in a shaky voice.

"Splendid!" the king roared. "Kindly ask Commander Geron to report to me when he returns from his moonlight picnic." The guard turned to leave the room. "So that I may relieve his shoulders of the burden of his head," the king continued. The guard faltered on his way out and then hastened his steps.

"Michael!" the queen gasped. "Have you lost your senses?"

"I have lost my patience," the king responded with a growl. "There is mischief afoot and I want answers. If Geron is missing at a moment like this, then he is a part of the problem. Has anyone heard from Sprout? Where is he?"

"It's my fault," Aina said with a worried expression. "I should never have let him go."

"Go where? Where has he gone?"

"He begged me to let him go and find Elinor. He was certain that he knew where to look. I have not heard from him since."

"You let him go alone?"

"He insisted upon it. I made him take Roderick's sword, so at least he is armed."

"Much good it will do him," the king growled. "He is handier with a sewing needle. He is more likely to trip over a sword than use it."

"He's not that bad," the queen defended him.

"Nor is he that good," the king shot back. Silence filled the room as he paced. Finally he stopped and faced Aina. He looked like he was struggling with something. "I suspect that he never went looking for his cousin."

"Whatever do you mean?" the queen looked alarmed.

The king chose his words carefully before speaking. His tone was softer. "When he came to the market, did he mention that we had spoken?"

"He said that you speak with a hard and heavy hand," the queen said frowning.

"I did not strike him!" the king barked with an upraised fist. He got control of himself before he continued. "However, we did have harsh words for one another. I fear that the foolish boy may have done something rash."

"You mean, even more rash than daring to disagree with his father?"

The king cast his eyes down. "I lost my temper," he admitted in a low voice.

"Tell me something I don't know," the queen said bitterly. "How can you expect him to take you seriously if all you ever do is yell at him and find fault?"

"I don't always yell at him," the king said defensively, his voice raised again. Immediately he realized what he had just done, and he turned his back to the queen in embarrassment.

A guard entered the room and stood waiting to be acknowledged. He took this pause in the conversation to speak. "Your Majesty."

The king whirled on him. "Not now!" he bellowed.

"Your Majesty," the guard said again, his voice shaking. "Mali sent me to—"

"Tell Mali whatever it is can wait until tomorrow," the king said with a raised voice. "Go now."

The guard took a step to go, but then stopped himself. He summoned his courage and quickly said in one breath, "Your Majesty, Mali requires the presence of the Dragon Master." This got the king's attention, and he now turned fully to the guard who delivered the rest of his message. It was brief. "Your Majesty, it's Star."

The king glanced at Aina, who had turned pale and sought out a chair to sit down. She returned the king's gaze. "You must go to him," she said, her voice weak. "Now." Without another word, the king swept from the room, close behind the guard who had summoned him.

Michael was alarmed to find the dragon lying on his side. Mali and all the senior staff of the Compound were gathered near Star's head. When he saw the king approach, he hurried over to meet him. "Sire, I'm so glad you have come. I have never seen anything like this before."

"How long has he been like this?" the king asked.

"We only just found him, sire," Mali replied. "I sent for you immediately. It was as if he keeled over."

The king walked over to the dragon's head. "Star," he called out, "Can you hear me?"

"Is that you, boy?" the dragon asked wearily, moving his head with difficulty so he could see the speaker.

"Star, what's going on?" the king asked. "How can we help you?"

"I am feeling quite weak," the dragon replied. "It is difficult for me to sit upright."

"Star, has someone done this to you? Has this happened to you before?"

The dragon remained silent, as if summoning his strength. Finally, he said, "Get the harness, the one I use to draw the wagon during the festival processions."

"Why the harness, Star?" the king asked. "What do you want us to do with it?"

"Strap it onto my body and hang the traces over the beams below the roof. Then you can pull me into a sitting position. Help me sit up."

The king immediately began shouting orders. The harness was hauled out of storage, and several of the men worked to buckle it to the dragon's body. Others were already throwing the long straps up to men who had climbed onto the overhead beams where they guided the straps down the other side. When everything was secured and in place, teams of men pulled firmly on the straps and helped the great dragon to sit upright.

"That's better," Star sighed. "I can breathe easier now. Make sure the buckles are well fastened and the straps secure."

The king gave the order. Then he asked, "What else can we do to help you?"

"For tonight, nothing," the dragon sighed. "Perhaps tomorrow my strength will return."

The king gave orders for the workers to take shifts through the night to monitor the dragon. For the time being, however, he told them to get some rest, and that he would remain with Star for the first shift.

"Sire, we will do everything we can," Mali said, "although, I am troubled. I have never seen or heard of anything like this before. I am profoundly puzzled. I only wish old Keg were here to advise us. He was with Star even longer than I."

"Thank you for your concern, Mali," the king said. "Go and get some rest. I will stay here now and see if Star can shed some light on how we can help him."

The king watched the workers recede from the barn, leaving him alone with the dragon. He pulled up a stool, sat down and cradled his head in his hands. "After everything else, now this," he moaned.

"Tell me," said Star. "What troubles beset the Dragon Master?"

Sunk in his own misery, the king did not detect the lightness that had returned to the dragon's voice. "I've ruined everything," he groaned. "I spoke unguarded, angry words to Sprout, and I suspect I have chased my own son into the hands of my enemy. I only wanted the best for him. I wanted him to see he had choices that I never had offered to me."

"How odd," the dragon responded. "I think *choices* are the very thing that Corin would say that he lacks." The king looked up and blinked his eyes at these words. The dragon continued, "Why are you so worried about how he will turn out? Look at how few options you had, yet you still found your way to the life you dreamed of having."

"Yes, but I had you on my side," the king replied without thinking.

"True," the dragon agreed. "And poor little Sprout has to go it alone."

The king's eyes grew large at Star's words and he turned red. "I didn't mean it that way," Michael stammered.

"Actually, I think you did say what you meant." The dragon remained silent and gave the king time to think about his words. Then he asked, "What else have you ruined, O Dragon Master?"

Michael caught the tone in his voice this time, and looked up to see if the dragon was mocking him. He could not tell and, shrugging his shoulders, he continued. "My niece is missing. We think she's been kidnapped. She is a guest in our household, and we could not even keep her safe. That speaks volumes about the state of the realm." The king fell into a brooding silence.

"Although her adventure had an uncertain beginning, she is now well cared for and protected, that much I know," Star said confidently. "For the time being, you need not worry about her."

"How can you know this with such certainty?" the king asked, sitting up straight.

"Her powers are strong," the dragon replied. "She is able to place images into my soul that I cannot resist. In this way, without intending to, she remains in contact with me. It was the same with Galifalia. I obeyed her out of the same love as when you ask me to do something."

"Why is it so powerful with Elinor?" Michael wondered.

"I suspect it has something to do with your common destiny."

"You mean, that we are all descended from the Dragon Keepers?"

"There is something even more compelling that you share." The king looked puzzled. The dragon asked, "What do you, Galifalia, Aina, and the young Elinor all have in common?"

The king thought for a moment, and then recognition lit up his face. "We are all orphans."

"Exactly. There must be something in the shock of losing your parents that forges a stronger connection with me."

Michael grew silent, lost in a faraway memory. Then he looked up and addressed the dragon. "If that is true, then it finally makes sense what the emissaries explained to us following the Battle at the Straits."

"What did they tell you?"

"That they repeatedly found it necessary to send away a member of the royal house to connect with you. Just bringing you together, they said, never seemed to work the same way. The connection had to develop in its own time and on its own terms. Although we had parents, they saw it as a painful necessity to separate us and set us out as orphans. They did that to Galifalia and later with me. It has haunted me ever since, that somewhere I have parents that I can never meet."

"It makes sense to me. Through the shock in the child's soul of losing its connection with its parents, it seeks a new one that gives stability and orientation. And if I am near, whether in my wild or gentled form it does not seem to matter, it is irresistible for a member of your race."

The king was silent. It was as if he had not even heard Star speak. He was still struggling with the memory of what the emissaries had said. "Just bringing you together never seemed to work," he mumbled. He looked troubled. Finally, he asked, "So what does that say about Sprout? I never thought of it until now, but he is the only one of us who is not an orphan."

"Ah, your disobedient son," the dragon murmured. "The young prince and I have a different understanding with one another."

"What kind of understanding?"

"It's something none of you will ever be able to comprehend. The prince, you see, has a choice."

"Is that good or bad?"

"Both. With choices, it is always both. That is why, I suspect, you are so reluctant to give him very many." The dragon was silent a moment, locking his gaze with the king's. A shiver shook Michael, and the air was filled with the tinkling of Star's bell-like laughter. "You love me, do you not?"

"As much as I love life," the king said sincerely.

"And so it is with your wife and your young niece. Although Elinor does not realize it yet, it won't be long until it dawns on her. But your son has a choice to love me or not. And he will claim that choice as his inheritance, as he rightfully should. None of you can decide for him. What he chooses will make all the difference."

At these words, the king stared at Star with his mouth open, uncertain how to react. He looked away and his face grew grim, his mouth a thin line. What he was brooding, the dragon did not get to hear. At that moment, a guard came rushing into the barn, seeking the king.

"Your Majesty," the guard said breathlessly, coming to a halt.

"What news?" the king demanded, springing to his feet.

"Commander Geron has been located," the guard said. "You had given orders to report this to you as soon as he returned."

"Geron!" the king exclaimed. Unconsciously, he balled his fists. "Tell him he is strictly confined to quarters until I come and speak with him. He is relieved of duty until further notice. Report to his second in command, Count Lexi, and tell him that he will assume Geron's responsibilities."

The guard involuntarily took a step backwards at the king's words. He had a look of astonishment on his face. "Sire?" he questioned.

"You've heard my orders," the king barked. "Go now."

The guard glanced up at the dragon, then back to the king. He hesitated, but then collected himself to speak.

"But Your Majesty, Commander Geron—"

"I am relieving Geron of his command!" the king bellowed angrily. "You will carry out my orders!"

The guard nodded his head in obeisance, turned on his heel and left the way he had come. As he walked, he shook his head in disbelief.

The moment he disappeared, the king, who had spoken so forcefully to the guard, sank back down onto the stool, deflated. He held his head in his hands once again and moaned softly.

"Complete for me the inventory of your miseries," the dragon coaxed.

The king looked up again. He peered at Star but decided that he was imagining that the dragon was not taking him seriously. He took a deep breath. "You know as well as I do that from the time I became king, we have known constant frontier skirmishes. The villages along our borders have either grown deserted or they are inhabited by a suspicious, cautious folk, unhappy with their lot. I am uncertain of their faithfulness to the crown. I am viewed with mistrust by our neighbors. They see me as a robber king, waiting for a chance to pounce and devour them."

"You wished to bring peace, and instead you have brought fear and mistrust," Star said quietly.

"I was certain that with you here, it would be different. Like when I was a boy growing up."

"You are no longer a boy," the dragon said. "Not even your son is a boy anymore."

"But why do they see me like a hungry dragon waiting to spring?" the king asked in anguish.

"A fitting image," Star said with a chuckle. "You have grown from stall boy to warrior king."

Michael looked up. "Not by choice," he insisted.

"Are you so sure of that?" The dragon smiled. He waited, but when the king did not respond, he said, "Continue telling me your misfortunes."

Michael sighed. "It only gets worse. Since returning to Gladur, I have received a report that our fields will not be yielding the harvest we expected. There will not be famine, but neither will we have surplus. The coming year will be much leaner than expected."

"I've heard rumors that there are more misfortunes."

"A mysterious fever among the cattle is raging uncontrolled. We have lost a quarter of our herds with no end in sight."

"That is bad news, indeed. However, as terrible as this sounds, I sense you have not told me the worst," prompted Star.

The king groaned. "You want a full confession?" When the dragon waited without responding, Michael sighed, "It's my wife." He sounded defeated.

"Is she ill at ease?"

"Ill at ease with me," Michael admitted. He swallowed hard and continued. "We have grown increasingly distant from one another. When we do speak, we argue and disagree over the silliest, unimportant issues. The real reason that I go so often on campaign is to avoid strife with Aina." The king had a surprised look on his face.

"You didn't know that until you said it, did you?" Star said softly. The king's look turned to shock, and he silently shook his head in agreement. The dragon asked, "What do you think is the root of the problem between you?"

"We have different views on how to manage the affairs of the realm," the king admitted. "Since it is her land by right of birth, I have chosen the obvious solution: I absent myself. I go to fight her wars. I thought if I yielded decisions of the state to her, it would improve our relationship."

"So, you left to find wars to fight. Did your strategy improve things between you?"

"We still quarrel," Michael admitted. "If anything, the mood worsens. And I fear that she has turned her attentions to another, someone I thought I could trust."

"Thus the harsh treatment of Commander Geron," Star commented. "Am I correct?"

"What do you know of it, Star?"

"Only what you have just told me," the dragon responded. "What was your latest quarrel?"

"She blames me for Sprout's disappearance. And the truth is, I too blame myself. Star, I don't know anymore the right thing to do."

"I doubt that Aina wants you to yield anything to her," Star said. The king looked puzzled at this remark. The dragon continued, "Remember, she, too, is a warrior. As you met her with swords when you first came to Gladur, she wants you now to meet her with conviction."

The king frowned. "I'm more comfortable wielding a sword than words." He sat brooding again, his arms crossed over his chest. "And as if things could not get any worse, you are not well, and you cannot even tell me the cause. Star, everything I have worked for is falling apart. I have found only one explanation."

The dragon perked up. "Those are hopeful words. Tell me, what is the source of all these miseries?"

"I'm convinced that this is the work of the black magician."

"What black magician?" the dragon asked, surprised.

"The one you warned me about. Sprout has been in contact with a wandering magician in the market. I am certain he has been sneaking away from his chaperon to go visit with him. The boy has already shown signs that this magician has managed to corrupt his mind."

"Why do you suspect that he practices the black arts?" the dragon asked.

The king reached into the folds of his tunic and drew forth the dagger that Corin had brought home. He held it up for Star to see. "Because of this," he said.

Star was silent as he studied the form of the writhing dragon etched into the metal of the blade. "It looks painful," he said solemnly.

"The magician gave this to Sprout. I think the magician is the one causing your illness," the king said. "And your illness is leading to the failing crops and dying cattle."

"And what about the disharmony between you and your son? And that between you and Aina? Is the magician behind that as well?"

The king did not heed the dragon's words. "Years ago, the wizard Aga told me this could happen. He warned us that if the day ever came when your good fortune appeared compromised, we should be on the watch for just such a dagger."

"Did he say more?" the dragon asked darkly.

"He said it would be a sign that the bearer of the dagger heralds an end to the old rule, and that nothing could be the same again." The king stared at the knife in his hands before continuing. "He cautioned me that to pursue the bearer of the dagger would be fruitless. He would always manage to elude me. He said my only choice was whether or not I would be willing to lay aside my old ways."

At these words, the dragon's eyes rolled upwards, and in great pain he turned and twisted in the harness that held him aloft. Michael looked up with astonishment at the suddenness of this attack. His eyes darted from the dagger in his hands to the writhing of the dragon before him.

"Star!" he called out. "How can I help you?"

It took several moments for the fit to pass. Star hung his head, exhausted by the exertion. Helplessly watching, the king began to tremble. He pulled his cloak about his shoulders, as if he were experiencing a sudden chill. Michael hung his head and sat lost in thought. Finally, he spoke, and his voice was hoarse, yet full of resolve. "I have to find him. I have to bring him back. If I am to renew my bond with Aina, I must find Sprout and bring him home. I *will* find him," he vowed, balling his fist. "I'm certain that is what I'm being called to do."

"You cannot fix that which you have broken by breaking it again," Star rebuked quietly.

"What a fool I've been!" The king sprang up and spoke with determination. "Star, I must make a change. I have been blinded all this time. I have chased away my son and my wife with my angry and stubborn ways. It is time to do what Aga told me. He said to lay aside my old ways. That must mean my armor."

"Can a dragon remove his scales?" Star asked.

"Nay, but you do slough your skin. It's time I shed mine." He unbuckled his belt, removing his sword. He stood there staring at its bright blade with the form of a charging dragon etched into the steel near the handle. "I have to do this," he murmured. Michael walked to the corner beyond the dragon and leaned the sword against the wall. His voice was brimming with determination. "Look after this for me, Star. I leave it in your good keeping. It has only been the cause of damage and misery. I must set it aside. I know what has to be done. I will find Sprout, and he will return with me. Then Aina will return her attentions to me, the crops will recover and you will grow well once again. I must go tell Aina of my plans."

"Is that wise?" the dragon asked. "She will object to your going and stand in your way."

The king pondered Star's words. "I fear you are right," he concluded. "Right now, we argue about any plan I have. It is better that I leave quietly. But leave I must. Only in this way will you grow well again, and order will be restored. I will defeat the evil plans of this magician. I will undo the division he has thrown between me and my son." He turned to face the dragon. His eyes were gleaming. "Star, your good fortune has never failed me before. I know I will succeed. How can I fail? I have never felt more certain. You will see, upon my return, all will be well." Without waiting for the dragon to respond, he strode away with confident, firm steps. By the time he reached the back of the barn, he was barking orders.

"You can shed your skin, but you cannot shed your scales," Star spoke quietly. "Good fortune will follow you, O Dragon Master. But you will totter on the abyss before you see the good in it. Your only hope is that you grasp this before you fall."

·✱·✱·✱·✱·✱·✱·✱·   ·✱·✱·✱·✱·✱·✱·✱·

The queen sat alone in her audience room, gazing emptily into the dark corners. Although the sun had set, the lamps had not yet been lit, and at the moment she preferred the growing darkness. It matched her mood. Deep in thought, she tapped her fingers impatiently on the arm of her chair. Suddenly a side door opened and one of her attendants hurried in. He stopped short, retreated, and returned a moment later with a lit lantern. He walked over to the queen and placed it on the table beside her.

"Shall I have the servants come in and ..." he said, gesturing to the lamps along the wall.

"No," the queen said abruptly, interrupting his offer. He stood before her at a loss for words. "Well, Gilbin," she demanded, sharply looking at him. "What have you found out?"

"Nothing new, Your Majesty," Gilbin stammered. "There is no question that His Majesty has gone. There has been no sign of him in either the royal quarters or the common quarters. No one has laid eyes on him for the past five days. The last place he was seen was in the barn, the night Star took seriously ill. When he left the barn, he gave orders that Star be attended. And later in the night he ordered his groom to ready his horse."

"This is all old news," the queen said impatiently. "Five days, Gilpin, and not a sign. You can do better than this. Have you checked with the porters watching the doors, as I asked you?"

"Yes, Your Majesty," her attendant continued, nervously fingering the edges of his tunic. "But no one has seen the king come or go since he left the Dragon Compound."

"What about his horse?"

"Still missing, Your Majesty. That would indicate—"

"I'm not a fool, Gilbin," the queen snapped. "What about Roderick? Why has no one found him yet?"

"Your Majesty," Gilbin said, looking even more nervous, "we cannot find him, either. No one seems to know where he has gone." The queen slapped the arm of her chair with the open palm of her hand, causing her attendant to involuntarily jump.

"Any word on the prince? Any sightings? Any rumors? Has anyone seen him anywhere?"

"N-no, Your Majesty," the servant said, looking down.

"And Commander Geron?" she next asked.

"Still confined to quarters, Your Majesty. He refuses to stir until the king release him."

"Damn!" she exploded. "Where are the men when you need them?" She glanced up at the servant cowering before her. "Don't look so whipped," she commanded, an edge to her voice. "You are only the messenger. You didn't cause it."

"Y-yes, Your Majesty," he stuttered, standing there with wide eyes. Aina looked like a tiger about to spring, and he did not want to be in the way when she did. Another door opened suddenly, and in hurried a servant. He glanced at Gilbin, who was more than glad to step back and allow this newcomer the queen's full attention. He stepped before the queen and gave a cursory bow.

"Your Majesty," he said in a low voice, as if not certain Gilbin should be privy to this information, "an answer has come to your latest communication."

Aina held out her hand. "Let me see it," she demanded. The servant placed a sealed letter into her waiting hand. The queen inspected the imprint on the wax seal briefly before breaking it and unfolding the letter. She held it up to the lantern to be better able to read. The two servants stood in silence waiting for the queen to finish. They saw her eyes narrow. She glanced up with a look of determination on her face.

"Now this. It could not have come at a worse time," she said. "Why would he suddenly be so willing after months of stalling and evading my requests?" She looked up, but the two servants before her knew better than to attempt to answer her question. It was not posed for their benefit. The queen was having a dialogue with herself. "But invitations do not come every day," she continued. "What a time for both the king and my son to be missing. And Geron confined to his quarters. Just when I need them all the most. I see no way out. I will have to take this upon myself. I will go and confer with Star. Is the messenger who brought this still able to ride?"

"Yes, Your Majesty," the servant answered. "He anticipated that you might wish to reply and is getting a fresh mount prepared."

"Attend me, and I shall give you something for him to take." She turned her attention to her attendant who tried hard not to shrink at her penetrating eye. "Gilbin, send me the captain of my guard. And I warn you, him you will find, or else I will think you are withholding from me. Understand?"

"Yes, Your Majesty," Gilbin said with a quick bow, and hastened from the room.

Chapter Sixteen

Naft Abyad

Corin woke with a start. Sunlight was streaming in through a window onto his face, and he did not know for a moment where he was. He sat bolt upright, and then relaxed as the memories of the night before flooded into his awareness. Before him was the hearth, and beside it lay Elinor, covered with a blanket and sound asleep. There was another blanket covering him where he lay on the floor next to the wall. So as not to awaken Elinor, he quietly pulled away his blanket and stood up. He glanced down at his cousin and saw the lines of exhaustion creasing her face. Seeing no sign of their host, he stepped quietly to the front door and let himself out.

It was a splendid day. The morning sun was filtering through the branches of the trees that grew closely around the cottage. The air was brisk but had the promise of a warm day tucked behind it. Corin looked around to get a sense of where they were. The trees grew so closely together, he could not even find the path that had brought them there the night before. There was a fluttering of wings above his head and he glanced up. What he saw brought a broad smile to his face. Perched on a branch sat a large black bird that turned its head this way and that, watching Corin carefully. It chirred softly.

"Oh, you're his pet crow," Corin exclaimed with delight.

"I'm sorry to say that you are wrong on both counts," a voice from behind him spoke.

Corin whirled around. There stood the magician, chuckling into his beard. "Oh, you gave me a start," Corin said.

"My apologies," the old man said. "I saw that you were up and merely wished to inquire whether you slept well."

"Thank you," Corin said, nodding his head. "Quite well. Elinor is still asleep."

"Considering what she has been through," the old man said, "I don't imagine she will be up very soon. I see that you have made the acquaintance of my winged friend, here."

The old man came to stand beside him. He reached his hand up and offered the bird something to eat. The bird snatched it up greedily and then let the old man run his fingers over the feathers on its back, the way one might pet a dog. The bird responded with throaty clicks.

"You said I was wrong about something," Corin said. "What did you mean?"

"First of all, Radabinth here is not a crow." The old man held up his forearm, and the bird hopped onto it. "Look at the size and the strength of the bill. You will never find a crow this large. Crows are suspicious of people and keep to themselves. They're noisy creatures, and, although they are sociable, they stay within their storytelling."

"Well then, what kind of bird is he?" Corin asked.

"My friend Radabinth is a raven. Radabinth is also a *she*, and although I've given her a man's name, she has not seemed to hold it against me. It helps me to remain mindful of an old friend. Now ravens do have behaviors similar to crows', but there are other characteristics that set them apart. One of the more significant peculiarities of these birds is that they are interested in the affairs of human beings and have at times made themselves extremely useful. They are also excellent judges of character, something I have come to trust when I can't make my mind up about someone. Take it as no small compliment that Radabinth likes you."

By this time the raven had sidestepped up the old man's arm to perch on his shoulder, gently picking at his grizzled beard. The raven peered at Corin, lowered its head and cawed loudly.

Corin smiled broadly at the bird's attentions. "How did you tame her?"

"Radabinth is not my pet. She comes and goes as she pleases, and it seems that lately it has pleased her to spend time with me. I am honored by her company. As I am honored by yours." He made a short bow to the young prince. Then he looked searchingly at Corin's face and glanced down at his hands. The boy knew what he was looking at and reddened. "It looks as if you helped to caulk that boat you arrived on."

The prince stared sourly at the black smears of tar still covering his fingers. "I was helping to make baskets watertight yesterday, before all of this started. It's something my father insists I do. So that I can appreciate the work of other people, he says."

"That is a wise decision by your father. I hope you do not resent the extra work it involves. It will make you a more compassionate ruler one day, if you know firsthand the sweat of another man's labor."

Corin had never thought of it that way. He had preferred to believe that his father just wanted to make his life harder for him, to toughen him up. At last he nodded, willing to understand for the first time his father's intentions. "I guess you have a point," he said. "Just the same, I don't like the tar on my hands."

"With that I can help you," the magician said. "Come with me." He led Corin around the side of the cottage to a storage cabinet built into the wall. From inside he pulled out a flask and a rag. He uncorked the flask and poured some clear liquid into the rag and handed it to the boy. "Try taking it off with this."

The liquid had a strange, intoxicating smell. It was familiar, but Corin could not place it. He rubbed his hands with the rag and the liquid had an oily feel to it. He was astonished to watch the tar smear come off easily. "Why, that's like magic," the boy stammered.

"Well, you do consider me a magician, after all," the old man laughed.

Corin put his hands to his nose. "I know this smell," he said. "What is it?"

"*Naft abyad*," the magician said quietly. "White naphtha."

It took a moment for Corin to make the connection. "You mean lamp oil?" he asked with astonishment.

"The very thing," the magician responded with a smile. Then he took the rag from Corin. "Here, let me help you. You have a smudge on your face which I am certain you will look better without. I will be your mirror." And so speaking, he rubbed at the spot on Corin's cheek.

"But white naphtha is precious," the prince said with wonder as the magician cleaned his face. He smelled his hands again. "I didn't know it could clean off tar. How do you come by it?"

"Precious, indeed it is," the old man agreed, stepping back and admiring his cleanup work. He seemed satisfied and returned both the rag and the flask to the cabinet. Then he turned to the prince. "And the question more to the point is, how do you come by it?"

"What do you mean?"

"Tell me, young master, from where do you know the use of white naphtha?"

"Star's barn is lit from lanterns that burn lamp oil," Corin replied.

"Anywhere else?"

"Well, yes, of course. Many of the rooms and all of the halls in the palace are lit from lamps that use white naphtha."

"And how does the rest of the population of Gladur Nock light their homes?"

Corin considered this a moment before replying. "With the light from their hearths and with candles."

"And those who cannot afford to purchase candles, what do they do?"

"They cut rushes from the river bank and soak the pith in their cooking fat to make rushlights. Like the one you almost lit last night."

"Well explained," the old man beamed. "And where does your lamp oil come from?"

Corin thought carefully before he answered. "From merchants?" He knew as soon as he said it that this was not the answer the magician was looking for.

"And where do the merchants get it?" he asked next. "Do you think it springs naturally out of the ground and they know where to go and collect it?"

Corin laughed. "I never thought about it," he admitted, shaking his head. "I suppose someone has to produce it. And it must be difficult to make, because I know it to be very expensive. I have overheard my mother grumble at the cost."

"Expensive it is," the old man said, nodding his head. "Due mostly to the fact that it is not easy to make. And a lot of work produces only a very little at a time. That is what makes it both precious and expensive to begin with. And then, by the time it has traveled from him who makes it to the lanterns that light your precious dragon's barn, it has passed through numerous hands, all of which want money left in them."

"Where do you get the money to pay for it?" Corin wondered.

"I don't pay for it," the old man said with a revealing smile. "I make it."

Corin looked at his host with wide eyes. "Surely you jest with me."

"Quite the contrary, young master," the old man said with a twinkle in his eyes. "The very lamp oil that you use to light your dear dragon's barn, as well as the rooms in your parents' palace, comes from me. I don't sell it to them directly, so they have no idea of my part in things. As I mentioned, it passes through many hands before it reaches the royal chambers."

"Show me," Corin demanded. He was astonished to hear the old man was at the source of something that he had until now taken for granted. "If you make it here, then show me where it's done."

The old man smiled and briefly nicked his head. "Very well, then," he said. "Follow me." He turned on his heel and took a path into the forest. Corin followed closely behind. They walked through dense underbrush and towering trees. The air around them was thick with the sound of clicking, whirring and buzzing insects, as the warm sunshine filtered down to where they walked. Corin could catch glimpses of high, craggy cliffs rising behind the branches of pine and fir trees.

They came into a clearing where a long, barn-like building with stone walls stood. Beside the wall of the building was an enormous pile of dark stones, and beside that was an equally large pile of cut wood. An odd, second pile of stones looked like they were steaming. Corin puzzled at the pile. It looked to be a rather flaky stone, not at all the sort used for building. He noticed smoke filtering out through the thatch of the roof of the barn, and the air in that glade was so still that the smoke hung in the lower branches of the surrounding trees. There was a vaguely familiar heady smell mixed with the smoke.

"Here is where I do my magic," the old man said with a smile. He walked up to a door in the wall, large enough to let a wagon through, and pulled it open. Smoke billowed out of the opening. "Radabinth," he said to the bird that was still on his shoulder, "this is no place for you." He swept the raven off his arm, and it flew up into a nearby branch, cawing loudly in protest. Then the magician turned to Corin. "After you," he said with an inviting gesture.

Corin stepped into the dark space of the barn. It took a moment for his eyes to adjust to the diminished light, and they smarted from the smoke in the air. He sensed quickly that the space inside the building was far from empty. From the light of the open door, he saw many faces turn his way and this stopped him in his tracks.

"Morning, Thos," several voices murmured from the dimly lit interior.

Corin turned to the old man. "Thos? Is that your name?"

"Actually, a shortened version of my full name."

"Who's the boy, Thos?" a man's voice asked loudly from within.

"A friend who is visiting me," the old man responded. "He requested to have a tour of the Works, so I brought him around. How is production this morning?"

"Steady," the voice in the darkness called back. Thos stepped past Corin and walked up to a vat with a fire burning underneath. There was a man tending the fire, and two other men standing beside it, intent on what was cooking inside. There was an odd, upside-down funnel-like structure sitting on top of the vat. In addition to the strong smell of smoke in the room, Corin detected the underlying heady smell again. The boy glanced around and saw several vats along the two long walls of the barn, each with the upside-down funnel apparatus.

"What are you cooking?" Corin asked, bewildered by the strange sight before him.

"Stones, mostly," Thos said.

"Stones? Are you kidding me?"

"Did you not see the pile outside?" Thos asked. When Corin nodded, he continued, "That is a very special stone. There is a lot of it around here, which made this an ideal place to set up my works. When these stones are heated, they release a very exceptional vapor, that, when run through this strange apparatus, ends up as a precious clear liquid."

"White naphtha?" Corin guessed. His nose had now identified the familiar smell.

"Exactly," Thos said, taking him by the sleeve to stand at the end of the glass tube coming from the large upside-down funnel. The tube emptied into a glazed ceramic jar sitting on a table, and Corin could see drops of clear liquid falling one by one into the opening.

"What is this?" Corin asked, gesturing to the contraption suspended above the vat.

"It's called an alembic," Thos said. "It is the same method used to distill spirits from fermenting fruit, such as grapes. The spirits we get from grapes we can drink. The spirits we get from stones we use to light up the night. One might say that the liquid we distill from fruit lights us up on the inside. The two spirits are more similar than one might think."

Corin peered into the ceramic jar. "It does not seem like you get very much at a time."

"It is a slow harvest," Thos admitted. "That is why I have set up several such works at places throughout Gladur where these stones are abundant. In this way, the yield is sufficient enough. I have more surplus than you might imagine."

"You said that you are cooking mostly stones," Corin said. "What else are you cooking in the vats?"

Thos led him to the opposite wall of the building to smaller containers. "These two vats don't need to be as large as the others since they are not accommodating stones," Thos said. He picked up a bucket that sat next to one and held it up for Corin to look into. It contained a black liquid.

"What is it?" Corin asked.

"Rock oil," Thos said. "It's like a liquid form of bitumen, very similar to the pitch you were using yesterday to waterproof baskets. This is more precious than the stones, because quantity for quantity it yields much more white naphtha than the stones can. But we do not have any deposits here and have to import it. That, of course, immediately makes it more expensive to produce. The kingdom of Warrensfold that borders Gladur to the north is rich in rock oil deposits."

Corin just nodded his head, amazed at what commerce went on about which he was ignorant. Suddenly, he began to cough. Until now he had been able to hold back the irritated tickle in his throat that the thick smoke caused, but he could not resist it any longer.

"Come on," Thos said, taking Corin by the arm. He led him to the open door. "You're not used to this much smoke. Let's get you into the fresh air again."

Once outside, Corin got his coughing under control and took several deep breaths. When he was certain he could speak without breaking into another fit, he had a question. "Who are those people in there? Where do they live?"

"How silly of me," Thos reflected. "I had forgotten that you do not know where you are. Come with me and I will show you." He glanced up into the branches of a nearby tree and saw the raven. "Radabinth, come," he said, raising his arm for the bird to land on. The raven spread its wings and with a flap landed on Thos' arm. The old man took something out of his pocket and gave it to the raven to eat.

"What are you feeding her?" Corin asked.

"I've heard it referred to by many names. *Akutak* is the one that I use. I ran across it on one of my journeys and have grown fond of making my own. It's a mixture of dried meat, fat and berries mashed into a pulp and then dried," Thos said. He took another piece out of his pocket and showed the boy. "It's actually quite tasty," he said, popping it into his mouth. "Want to try a piece?"

"Gladly," Corin said, and Thos gave him some. Indeed, Corin found it delicious. It had the savory, smoked taste and texture of meat with the sweet-sour tang of berries. The contrast of flavors made his mouth water. "I like this," he declared, smiling at the old man. It helped to fill the complaint in his belly, nagging that he had not eaten since Aggie's soup the day before.

"This way," Thos said. He turned and chose another path through the forest, a different one than how they had come. As Corin walked, slowly savoring the akutak, he was struck with amazement that such works, as Thos called them, could exist without his knowing anything about them. It was amazing that the lamp oil used in the palace and the compound would come from such a place secreted away deep in the forests. He was filled with curiosity where the old man was taking him now.

Thos led Corin via a well-worn path through the trees. Steep, craggy cliffs peeked through between the branches. The morning sun reflected red off the bare rock faces. "Is this a canyon?" Corin asked.

"Indeed, it is," the old man replied. "It is fairly difficult to gain access to this place except by the river. It's a wonder that you found it at all."

"It was a coincidence, you know," Corin pointed out. "It was where the boat happened to dock for the night."

"Coincidences seem to be attracted to you," the old man chuckled. As they walked, Corin recognized distinct sounds: voices, laughter, the crying of children, the repetitive striking of an axe. Then his nose picked up the scent.

"Who else lives here? I smell a cookfire."

"You smell many cookfires, I would venture to say," Thos responded. They rounded the high, thick-growing bushes and a clearing opened up before them. Corin was stopped in his tracks.

"Welcome to the Enclave for the Disenfranchised," Thos said smiling broadly at the prince.

"What does that mean?" Corin asked.

"The hideaway for those who have no rights," Thos explained. Then he chuckled and added, "Known by most simply as the Enclave."

Before them in the open canyon, bathed by the morning sun, bustled a small community. Smoke from many cookfires hung in the air. Corin's mouth fell open in surprise.

The clearing was filled with a peaceful community going about their morning business. There was an odd array of makeshift lean-tos and huts distributed in a haphazard fashion. In front of these modest dwellings women tended cookfires. Groups of men and women mingled and visited. Weaving in and out of this maze of humanity, the children ran about at their games of tag and keep-away. There was a sense of harmony that pervaded the scene, and Corin was drawn to go and join them. It was like the markets at home, except here all the activity would not end at noon when the market was closed.

"Where are all these people from?" he asked.

"The smell of breakfast reminds me that Elinor must be awake by now and wondering where we are. Let's head back to my cottage, and I will tell you what I can along the way." Thos turned and headed back the way they had come. Corin took one last, long look at all of the bustling life tucked between the red canyon walls and reluctantly hastened after the old man.

"Many of them are former residents of your capital," Thos explained when Corin had caught up with him.

"But why don't they live there any longer?"

"The king favors a well-ordered realm. When he came to power, he set himself a high standard for improving the lives of the citizens of his capital. He declared that he would no longer tolerate homelessness."

"I am well aware of this edict," the young prince stated. "It is a way of saying that homelessness had no place where a Luck Dragon is kept and cared for."

"This edict made it a law that every citizen of Gladur had to find some productive occupation. And that every citizen had to find a roof under which to sleep."

"What is wrong with that?"

"What is wrong is that some people pursue activities that are not considered productive occupations, such as the jugglers and acrobats you may have seen practicing in the village, and not all such activities bring in the amount of income that supports putting a roof over their heads."

"I'm not following you," the boy admitted.

"Many of the people who live here, if they had remained in Gladur, would have been living marginally or completely on the streets. Gladur boasts a moderate climate, and these people are comfortable living that way and don't desire more."

"How can they possibly be happy living on the streets?"

"Unless I'm mistaken, it is a lifestyle that you have been strongly attracted to," Thos said pointedly. Corin's face reddened. It was uncanny how this old man could read his soul. He was unaware that he had ever mentioned it to anyone.

"They can be happy on the streets," Thos continued, "when they are allowed the freedom to make that choice. Not if they live hungry and destitute, of course, but to have their own community among themselves. Some are wandering merchants of a sort. Others are performers, poets, singers and artisans. I'm sure you have enjoyed many of them performing on market days. The coins they receive in payment for their shows buy them the food they need. More they do not ask for. They are happy with a simple existence, and they come here to be left to live in peace. These are a passionately independent people who don't like being told what to do or how to live their lives."

At these words, Corin felt his heart resonate with what Thos was telling him. How often had he wished to be left alone to live life his own way! Who could attest better than he to his father's harsh and stubborn views? These people looked at life as he did. He had an odd sense of having come home.

"Many are grateful for the edict," Thos continued, "since it drove them out of the city. They prefer living here in the open, although they might not readily admit this. It gets a little dicey in the winter, but they manage." Corin was reminded of his conversations with Roddy who had grown up under similar circumstances. He remembered how often he had envied Roderick for his childhood.

"Has the king ever threatened to drive you away from here?"

"Yes," the old man replied. "But for the time being, he leaves us in peace. Besides, the people of the Enclave are not particularly worried about the king's army. This canyon is easily defended, and there are many men among us who enjoy the practice of skill in arms. They are neither lazy nor cowardly, and we have a well-organized and a surprisingly well-supplied militia. In addition, they have developed a unique and terrifying tool of defense. The king would be a fool to attack us. It would be a tragic loss of lives and resources on both sides.

The king would be better off to consider how to align himself with the people of the Enclave, but I suspect he holds them in too great disdain for that."

"Do you have your own rulers?"

"There are those who regulate the militia and others who pass judgment in the unavoidable squabbles and disagreements. No one person holds all the power."

"What do you live from?"

"We wander between all the major markets of the neighboring realms, trading what the people of one realm produce and the people of the next one desire. Each kingdom receives us in accordance with its own laws. As regards Gladur, we may freely come and go, as long as we are gone by nightfall, or at least have a roof over our heads. The market constables are not there only to keep the peace. They make sure we move on after the market has closed."

"How odd," Corin mused. "My father lived on the streets as a child."

"Indeed, I have heard that story myself," Thos said. "I suppose that in his misguided way, he wishes to save others from the fate he suffered."

"But if he had not been living on the streets, he might never have gone to live in the Dragon Compound and gotten to know Star."

"Sometimes, our biggest challenges are our greatest opportunities." Thos smiled at him. Then he said, "Once, you asked to go with me, to leave the safety of the city walls. Do you remember?" Corin nodded his head silently, remembering it well. Thos asked, "Are you disappointed with what you have found?"

Corin was afraid of speaking out loud the thoughts that were crowding in on him. Instead, he asked, "Why have I never heard of this place before?"

"I suppose because your parents are protective."

"What were they protecting me from? Are there dangerous people here?"

"There are dangerous people here as there are anywhere. Among our number are malcontents from the time when Worrah was driven out. We have our share of thieves, pickpockets and knives-for-hire. But nothing worse than what you might any day find on the streets of Gladur. No, I suspect that you have not heard about this place because your parents want to protect themselves."

"Protect themselves from what?"

"From the possibility that you would want to run away and live in the Enclave."

Corin was stunned by this comment because it resonated so strongly with the thoughts and feelings he was having. However, he did not have time to dwell on them. They had arrived back at the cottage, and he could hear Elinor calling from inside.

"*Hello!* Is there anyone there? Hello? Can someone come and help me?"

"It seems she is awake," Thos commented with a smile.

They entered the cottage and found Elinor sitting beside the hearth with her back against the wall. "Where have you been?" she exploded upon seeing her cousin.

"Sorry, Elinor," Corin said, going to her. "Thos was showing me around a bit."

"Who's Thos?" she asked, still irritated.

"At your service," the old man said, removing his hat and bowing to her.

Elinor's mouth fell open. "It's you," she stammered.

"Welcome to the Enclave," Thos said.

"The what?" Elinor asked, openly stunned at seeing the magician.

"It's a long story," Corin said. "I'll fill you in later. This is where he lives. He helped us escape last night. Do you remember?"

Elinor nodded her head. "I remember falling," she said. "I hurt myself, and then someone picked me up. Was that you?" she asked, looking up to Thos.

"Indeed it was," Thos said. "I had gone for a stroll in the night and was attracted by the torches and yelling. By chance I stumbled across you, apparently, just in the nick of time. How is your leg?"

"I can't get up," Elinor complained. "I tried, but it hurts too much. And I'm hungry."

Thos laughed and said, "I think we can help. How about if we start with your leg?" He looked down at Elinor, and without saying anything, she nodded her head. "Good," Thos continued. "Let's see what we can find out." He crouched down beside her. "I would like to remove your boot." He unfastened the buckle, and with Corin's help, the two of them gently pulled it off her foot. Elinor let out a tremendous yelp.

"I'm sorry," Thos said kindly. "I think that will be the worst of what I will do to you." He examined her foot and ankle. When he placed one hand underneath to lift it up, Elinor winced in such pain that he stopped. "Well, it is clearly injured," he chuckled. "Corin, notice the swelling and the discoloration. I am heartened that the angle appears normal. Can you wiggle your toes?" They watched while Elinor, making faces of pain, gingerly moved several toes back and forth. "That's good, too," Thos said. "Now, tell me, Elinor, how you think you injured it?"

Elinor recounted their flight from the shore through the underbrush of the forest. "Then I think I caught it in a root, and it twisted when I fell."

"Do you think you broke it? Did you feel something snap?"

"I don't know," she said. "We were running so fast and I was frightened. They were chasing us." As she spoke, Thos had gone to a sideboard where he pulled open a drawer.

"Cabbage leaves," Corin said suddenly.

Thos turned to him. "I beg your pardon?"

"Do you have a cabbage?" he asked. "If we soak the outer leaves of the cabbage and then place them on the ankle, it will help with the swelling."

"I believe you are right," Thos said, arching his bushy eyebrows. "Tell me, what else would you use?"

"We could fill a cloth with chopped onions and wrap that around it," Corin said after considering this a moment. "Of course, there are better remedies, but the others need to be prepared."

"Such as?" Thos asked, obviously enjoying Corin's answers.

"We could rub garlic oil into it, if we could get some. I could make my own, but it takes at least ten days for the garlic to properly cure into the oil."

"Well, well," Thos considered. "Cabbages, onions, garlic. Sounds like the most common of vegetables, and the very ones your mother sells at the market."

"They're very smelly," Corin said, shrugging his shoulders. "But they have good medicinal qualities."

"How do you know all that?" Elinor said, astonished. "I knew only about the cabbage leaves."

Corin reddened. "I hear things," he stammered.

"Then you have sharp hearing," Thos said, eyeing him carefully. He pulled a small, shallow earthenware jar out of the drawer of the sideboard. "How sharp is your smelling, I wonder." He handed Corin the jar. Inside was a yellowish ointment. Corin put it to his nose. Then he took some and rubbed it between his forefinger and thumb, smelling it again.

"It is in a base of beeswax," he murmured. "The consistency of wax and the aroma of honey are unmistakable." He could not disguise the light of excitement in his eye. "However, there is something else. I'm not sure I've smelled it before. I can tell that it has powerful healing properties. What is it?"

"How can you be so sure that it will heal?"

"There is something in the aroma. It is penetrating and strong, and I am attracted to it. I can't say why."

"You have an excellent nose and I'd say an innate sense for healing herbs," Thos said. "The herb you smell is called arnica."

"I've heard of it," Corin said. "Did you get it from around here?"

"What in the world is arnica?" Elinor asked from where she sat.

"An herb with bright yellow flowers, often found in mountain glades," Thos explained. "It is prized for its ability to bring down swelling."

"How did you come by it?" Corin asked, still smelling it on his fingers.

"There are times I range far and wide in my journeys and gather interesting things while I travel. Such as how to make *akutak*."

Corin suddenly had an excited look in his eye. "Tell me, Thos, with all the trees here, do you also distill the sap from the pines? It is pretty much the same process as what you showed me at the Works."

"Do you mean to make turpentine?" Thos asked. When Corin nodded, Thos laughed.

"I've heard that turpentine oil mixed with egg yolk can also be used," Corin said, "although I've never tried it."

"I know it mostly as a tincture for open wounds," Thos said. "I will get you some and we can see if it helps."

"Sprout, how do you know all of this?" Elinor asked.

"Actually, I'm wondering more why no one else is aware of what you know," Thos commented, peering at the young prince.

"I was apprenticed," Corin stammered in explanation.

"Elinor, I believe your cousin is more than what he appears," Thos said mysteriously. "And you will discover him only when he is ready to let you in." As Corin blushed and turned away, Thos bent down to Elinor with the jar in his hand.

"This will help," he said. "Elinor, since your ankle is so tender, I want you to rub this ointment gently into the area that hurts. Will you do that?"

Elinor nodded her head solemnly. She scooped some ointment out of the jar on the tips of her fingers. Then she reached down and rubbed it around her ankle. She had a pained look on her face and afterwards sighed heavily.

"How is it?" Corin asked.

"It didn't hurt as much as I thought it would," she answered. "Does it take the pain away a little bit?" she asked, looking at Thos.

"It is soothing," Thos replied. "But I am mostly hoping that it will begin a gentle healing and reduce the swelling. We can repeat this later, and at least three times a day until you are feeling better."

"How long will it take?" she asked.

"That depends on how badly it is injured. I suspect it will be a while before you are feeling fit again. But you aren't in a hurry to go anywhere, are you?"

Elinor smiled. "I'm still hungry," she said.

"I was known as a decent cook in my younger days," Thos said. "I will make us something to eat. How about some porridge?"

Elinor nodded her head in agreement, then looked up at her cousin. "Help me up," she demanded. "I'm in need of the bushes."

Chapter Seventeen

A Blade in the Moonlight

$\mathcal{T}$his should do it," Corin said, walking out into the open space before Thos' cottage. He was holding in his hand a letter that he had just finished writing. Thos was sitting in the sunlight on the bench that ran along the side of his cottage. Radabinth perched above them on a branch and peered at Corin with interest. Thos was reinforcing the legs of a chair with strips of leather. Corin sat down next to the old man and finished folding the letter.

"I told her we are safe and that we would return home as soon as Elinor's ankle has healed," he said. "I told her not to worry and that we are with friends."

"Did you tell her where you are?" Thos asked.

"No, I followed your advice and left that vague. I agree that it would not go well if she sent her guard here looking for us. Are you sure you can have it delivered?"

"Yes, I will see that it gets into the right hands." He took the folded letter from Corin and stuck it into his belt. Then he returned to his mending.

"Drat this chair," he complained, pulling on the leather cords. "I can't get it to hold."

"Let me try," Corin offered. "I'm good at fixing things."

"Gladly," Thos said, handing him the repair work. He watched as Corin deftly secured the legs with the cord.

"You *are* good at that," Thos commented.

"I don't know why, but I can often see solutions others cannot," Corin said as he continued to work.

"That can come in handy," Thos observed.

"Maybe here, but back home, not so much."

They sat in silence for a while, and then suddenly Corin said, "I like it here."

"I'm not surprised," the old man chuckled. "I suspect it is, after all, what you have long wanted. No one to tell you what to do next, no lessons, no trades to learn, no dragon to care for." He glanced at Corin to watch his reaction. "Do you miss your dragon?"

Corin looked embarrassed. "Not really. I suppose sooner or later I will. But right now, I'm enjoying the change." He looked worried. "I'm supposed to miss him, aren't I?"

Thos studied him and laughed. "It all depends what sort of change you want," he replied. "Do you want to look after the dragon for the rest of your life?"

"No," Corin said quickly, surprised that his response came so easily. He added, "There are just other things I want to do."

"And the dragon gets in the way of that?"

"There are lots of things that get in the way," Corin replied. "But I suppose in the end it all revolves around Star." He saw that Thos was peering at him. "Don't get me wrong," he added quickly. "Star is great, but ..." his voice trailed off.

"But your life would be a lot easier without him?" Thos suggested.

"You could put it that way," Corin agreed in a low voice. Then he said, "There, I'm done." He set the chair upright, sat in it and wiggled to show that the legs were stable again.

"You're good with your hands," Thos commented.

"I like doing things like that," Corin replied. He returned to the bench beside the magician.

"More than scrubbing a dragon?"

"Anyone can scrub," Corin muttered, staring at the ground.

Thos studied him before speaking. "Would it help for you to know that the people of the Enclave also feel that their lives would be easier if there were no dragon?" Corin looked uncomfortable but made no comment. Thos continued. "So what is it you would like to do, now that your life is freed up? This is a unique opportunity."

Corin sat awhile thinking about this. Then he looked up and smiled at the old man. "Can you teach me some magic?" he asked.

"Magic?" the old man was surprised. "Is that the best you can come up with?"

"It will do for the moment," Corin replied with a smile. "Will you?"

"Probably not the kind of magic you are looking for," the old man said, amused. "I cannot make things appear out of nothing, for instance. But I can show you some sleight of hand. I can show you how to give the *appearance* that you are making something appear or disappear."

"That's good enough for me," Corin said.

"Let's begin with something small and simple, and then we can move on to larger items." Thos took out a copper coin and made it disappear, showing Corin how to use his hands to block the viewer's eye from seeing what he was doing. He repeated the movement several times very slowly, so Corin could follow the steps of the trick. Then he handed the coin to Corin and invited him with a gesture to give it a try. Corin's first attempts were clumsy, yet he was fascinated with the challenge to do it successfully.

"If you practice, your hands will learn the movements so well you won't have to think about it, and when you do it quickly enough, the eye misses that you are fooling it." Thos reached up and seemed to snatch a piece of *akutak* out of the air, which he handed to the prince.

"That looks like real magic to me," Corin said in admiration.

"Indeed, I am a magician, a master of cheap tricks and sleight of hand. That is all you will ever see me do."

"You don't sound happy to be a magician," Corin commented, catching the dissatisfaction in Thos' voice. "Is there something else you would prefer to do?"

"The truth is, I have always aspired to be a wizard," Thos admitted with a chuckle.

"Isn't that just another word for the same thing?"

"In fact, the two are quite different, although in common parlance they are often equated with one another. A true wizard is a world apart from a magician. You see, a wizard does no magic of any sort, real or illusory. Unless you consider being in the right place at the right time magic."

"You certainly did that the other night. I don't know how you found us in the dark. Doesn't that qualify you?"

"In truth, I got lucky. Yet I cannot help recalling all the times I did not succeed in being in the right place at the right time. It requires a great deal of vigilance to be a wizard, and I am sorely aware of how often I have failed."

"What do you have to be vigilant about? What are you waiting for?"

"For the invitation."

"Invitation for what?"

"The invitation to go where I am needed. I am not always prepared to act when it comes."

"Why is that?"

"To be honest, I sometimes question if the invitation is real. At other times, I fear that I may not be strong enough for the task that is set me. It was simple enough to rescue the two of you, but there are times I am put to the test, and I question if I have what it takes to see things through. I have the sense, call it a premonition if you wish, that I am about to be faced with a challenge far greater and more painful than any I've yet had to deal with. At such moments my age weighs upon me."

"How old are you?" Corin asked. "You act much younger than your greying hair would suggest."

The magician gazed at Corin, as if choosing his next words carefully. "I am old enough to have had the acquaintance of your great grandmother."

"My great grandmother?" Corin exclaimed. He stopped a moment to think about this. He had been well schooled in his family's genealogy. "Do you mean Galifalia?" Thos nodded. "You knew her? How is that possible?"

"And I knew her husband, Marrow. I had the opportunity to get to know him even better."

"So you mean, you met them when you were a boy?"

"Actually, for a time, I was Marrow's tutor."

"Not possible," Corin said shaking his head. "That would make you ancient."

"I have seen a bit of this world," the old man said with a laugh. "I've had plenty of time to make my share of mistakes. And time enough to consider how to avoid making more." The old man laughed again. "And even more time to discover that making mistakes is inevitable and part of the journey of being alive." He saw the look of disbelief on Corin's face, so he added, "And I don't blame you in the least for not believing me. I'd have trouble myself if I hadn't lived it all."

They sat in silence together. Corin practiced the magic trick, getting his hands used to the movements. He thought about all that had happened so quickly in the past few days. He was grateful the whirlwind of events had quieted down.

"I'm glad we'll have to stay here for a while," Corin reflected. "I am looking forward to getting to know the Enclave better." Suddenly, a question occurred to him, and it gave him pause. "They won't know who I am, will they?"

Thos shook his head in answer. "It will be enough that I say you are my guests. They will accept that I brought you here. Although there are many people who live here, visitors are not uncommon. However, the longer you stay, the more questions people will ask."

"What if they find out who I am?"

Thos watched Corin's reaction as he spoke. "Some would loudly call for your immediate execution as an enemy and a threat to the safety of the Enclave." Corin winced, and Thos continued, "They would accuse you of coming to spy on us, in preparation for a full scale attack. Others might not jump to such extreme conclusions but still want to hold you for ransom, not for money necessarily, but to force the king to be more lenient in his laws against us." He watched Corin's eyes grow wide. "Your family is not held in the highest esteem here," he continued. "Many would be happy to see the heir to the crown silently disappear and the rule of the Dragon Keepers come to an end."

Corin paused, thinking, and then asked, "Are you going to tell them about me?"

"I have my own meandering plans, and I have no great desire to see you disappear into a sinkhole. I see no gain in it. Besides, I am open to the unexpected." Thos paused to make sure he had Corin's full attention. "These are an independent and unpredictable people who live here. You never know how they might react to the right impulse given at the right moment. A little bit of luck and good timing go a long way."

At that moment, Elinor hobbled out the front door and stood holding onto the wall for support, her hurt leg lifted. Her hair was messy and her face puffy.

"Did you have a good nap?" Thos asked.

Elinor nodded but said nothing. She hopped along the wall until she reached the bench where her cousin sat and plopped down next to him. She yawned and looked around. She squinted up at the raven sitting on the branch above their heads. Then she looked at Corin and asked, "What're you doing?"

"Thos has been teaching me his magic," Corin explained, excitement in his voice. "Well, it's really all sleight of hand, but it can look like magic if you don't know what to be watching for. I'll show you. Watch this coin." He sat up straight and held the coin up for Elinor to see. With a clever turn of his hands, the coin vanished.

Elinor's mouth fell open. "How did you do that?" she demanded.

Corin beamed. "It's magic," he said.

Thos had been watching. He nodded his head and smiled. "Quick learner," he murmured. "Smart hands." Up in the branches of the tree, Radabinth fluttered her wings and emitted a loud clicking. Thos looked up at her thoughtfully. "We have a visitor," he commented.

A moment later they heard a voice calling out from the path leading to the village. "Thos! Are you home?"

"Come ahead," Thos called back. A man emerged from the trees and stood in the sun of the little clearing before the house. He was a burly man with a black beard and wild hair, dark eyes and a big smile. He looked oddly familiar to Corin, as if he had met this man before. The visitor took in the scene before him without surprise and nodded at the two newcomers.

"How are your guests doing?" he asked.

"This is Makarios," Thos introduced him to the cousins. "I thought you'd come by sooner than later. Here, have a seat. My young friend just finished fixing it." Thos offered him the chair that Corin had repaired. Makarios nodded his thanks and took the chair.

"Word has spread already that you took the boy to the Works the other day, and now there is curiosity about who you've got here with you," he said. "Unless you want a stream of visitors, I suggest that you bring them around so folks can sniff at them, if you know what I mean."

"And you came to do a little sniffing of your own," Thos observed.

"'Tis only natural," Makarios said with a shrug. "I can help allay people's suspicions." He turned to the cousins. "You heard my name. Tell me yours."

"This is Elsbeth," Thos said, not giving them a chance to speak. "And this is her brother, Cochran. They lost their father recently in a tragic accident, and I've taken them on for a few weeks while their poor mother can tend to her sorrows and an ailing baby."

"I'm sorry for your loss," Makarios said, eyeing them sharply and not looking at all sorry. "There now, I can tell anyone who asks there is nothing to worry about. They look harmless enough. Still, it would be good to show them around."

"I thank you for your concern," Thos said with a nod. "I've been thinking the same thing myself, about showing them around. Unfortunately, Elsbeth, here has turned her ankle and won't be doing much walking around until it heals."

"I have an idea," Makarios said with a gleam in his eye.

"You usually do," Thos said with a laugh.

"You young folk have come at a fortunate time," he said addressing Corin and Elinor. "Three nights from now is our full moon celebration."

"What happens then?" Corin asked.

"The whole village turns out," Makarios explained. "There'll be music and dancing and a very special ceremony. You won't be sorry you came. And once you've been to the ceremony, folks will pretty much accept you as if you've always been here. I'll take you as my guests and look after you."

"How will El—um, Elsbeth get there?" Corin asked.

"You look to have a strong back," Makarios said with a broad smile. "You can carry her there. It's not that far from here to the green where we'll be celebrating. I'll have a seat waiting for you. Agreed?"

Before speaking, Corin glanced at Thos, who nodded subtly. "Fine. We will come. When should we be there?"

"Just after sunset," Makarios said, and Corin saw him wink at Thos. He stood up. "I'll be heading on my way, now," he said. "I just came for a short visit. I'll be looking for you at the ceremony." He turned and headed down the same path that had brought him. Before disappearing, he paused and turned back to them. "I suggest you use the next few days well," he said. "Spend some time in the common area. Let folks get to know you." Then he turned and walked away.

As soon as he was long enough gone to be out of earshot, the cousins turned on Thos. "Elsbeth?" Elinor said, aghast.

"Cochran?" Corin asked, equally flustered.

Thos laughed heartily. "It was the best I could come up with in the spur of the moment," he said. "It won't do to be using your own names, you know. Be happy you don't have to wear them longer than the time you're with us here."

"But *Elsbeth*?" Elinor protested. Thos held his sides as he laughed at her horror.

·*·*·*·*·*·*·*·*· ·*·*·*·*·*·*·*·

The next morning Corin carried Elinor on his back down the path that led to the center of the village. With Thos' guidance, they had made up a plausible story about the family they had left behind. No one appeared surprised to see them. In fact, one young woman invited them to come refresh themselves at her campfire. She made a spot for Elinor to sit comfortably, and it was not long before a succession of visitors passed by to meet them. Everyone was open and friendly to them and sympathetic towards Elinor's injured leg. Many offered advice how to treat the injury and several showed up with remedies. Folks did not pry overly, and before long the cousins were chatting happily with new-found friends. Their hostess kept them well supplied with hot tea and an occasional snack. She was busy tending to her two young children, and it was soon obvious that she had simply provided them a place where they could receive the many curious villagers.

Corin learned a lot that day about how his family was viewed by outsiders. He flinched inwardly a few times when villagers referred to the young prince as aloof and somewhat lazy. To his surprise he heard that his dislike of sword fighting was well known. But it did not surprise him that villagers feared his father might one day attack the Enclave and try to wipe it out. There was a general respect spoken in regards to his mother, as well as about her efforts to reach out to the common folk, but they faulted her for not doing more to soften the king towards them. Many had encountered the queen in the market, even buying goods from her stand, if only for the opportunity to find out what sort of person she was. Corin was relieved that none of them connected him with the prince who also sat at the stand occasionally. But it was in connection with his behavior at his mother's stand at the market that he learned why they considered him standoffish, and he felt shame at being so self-absorbed. He promised himself to be friendlier in the future.

In regards to the dragon, there was a unanimous view. "He's not brought us much good fortune," one man argued. "So why bother with him? Our lives will be much simpler when he's moved on. He's the reason the queen allows the king to be so repressive."

Corin was surprised to find himself agreeing with the people of the Enclave more often than wanting to argue with them. Their opinions might at times be extreme, but they remained reasonable at the same time, at least from their own perspective.

One visitor, a middle-aged woman who wore dangling earrings and a colorful skirt, sat down next to Corin and after a few minutes asked, "Shall I tell your fortune?" Corin was startled by her words, and then he knew why she looked familiar. She had once spoken to him at the market in Gladur, offering to tell his fortune. He had brushed her off then by saying that he had no fortune to tell. He returned her gaze now, wondering if she remembered him, but if she did recognize him, she was keeping it to herself.

"Gladly," Corin replied. "Tell me my fortune."

"Give me your hand," she said. "Palm up." She took his hand in her own and gazed at it. Corin knew that fortune tellers read the lines in the palm, but he had never believed in it enough to seek someone out to do it for him. He waited patiently as she studied the lines. When she was satisfied with what she had seen, she looked up to gaze at his face.

When she did not begin speaking, Corin finally asked, "Well, do I have a fortune?"

"A most remarkable one," she replied in a soft voice. She held his hand in both of hers and smiled warmly at him. "But you have a difficult choice ahead of you. There is a decision you must make, like a fork in the road. You will have to give up something precious in order to gain something that is uncertain."

"And what will I choose?" Corin asked.

"That I cannot tell," she said with a smile. "I can tell you only that your decision will affect more than just yourself. It seems that your fate is tied with that of many. Whatever you decide will have great meaning for the destiny of many other people as well."

She had caught his full attention with these ominous comments. "How will I know the right thing to do?" Corin asked, sitting up very straight.

"Only by the results," she answered. "You cannot know ahead of time."

"How will I know if I have chosen wrongly?"

"It will be obvious," she said and lowered her eyes.

At the end of the day, Makarios came by to visit as well. "Thank you for coming," he said. "I have spoken with many today who consider you their new friends."

"I'm grateful you invited us to visit," Corin said. At that moment, their hostess walked over to them and placed her youngest into Makarios' arms. Then she returned to her chores.

Makarios smiled broadly. "My son," he said proudly. Then Corin understood why they had been so welcomed at this camp. Makarios continued. "I hope you have seen that we are not a bad people. We have our families, love our children and follow our professions, even if they are considered uncommon ones."

"I like it here," Corin said sincerely.

"Stay for a while," Makarios said, eying Corin sharply. "You will find that we cherish our freedom. And we will defend it." He studied Corin's face. "Do you like to be free?" he asked.

"Being here, I feel I'm free for the first time in my life," Corin replied, words that came so easily, that he surprised himself.

"I am heartened to hear that," Makarios said with a smile. "Deeply heartened. Come visit us often. You will find we are better than our reputation. Remember my invitation to come two nights from now. You won't want to miss the ceremony."

· ✳ ˑ ✳ ＊ ＊ ˌ ＊ ＊ ✳ˑ ˑ✳ ˌ ＊ ＊ ＊ ˌ ✳ ＊✳ˑ

The moon had not yet risen above the edge of the high cliffs, and the only light in the dark night was a bonfire in the fields beyond the village. Corin was carrying Elinor piggyback, steering his way through the darkness by the light of the distant fire. He regularly lost sight of it as trees obscured it, but his feet always found their way again along the beaten path until it came into view again.

"Am I heavy?" she asked.

"You're fine," Corin mumbled. She had felt light when they first set out, but the longer he walked with her hoisted on his back, the heavier she seemed to grow. It did not matter. He would not admit that she was too heavy for him to carry. She was in his care, and he was determined to get her safely to the celebration and back again.

Elinor could hear him breathing harder. "I can try and hop part of the way," she suggested. "I'm getting really good at it."

"It's fine," he grunted. "I'll rest when we get there."

"You're grand to do this," she said at last. "Thank you."

"No problem," Corin grunted. He was warmed by her gratitude, and it gave strength to his aching muscles.

They could already hear the sound of drums echoing off of the canyon walls.

"I like it out here," she said. "Everyone's been so friendly." When Corin did not respond, she asked, "Do you like it, too?"

"Mm-huh," Corin murmured. His feelings were too mixed to say more.

As they drew closer, more drums joined into the night's chorus. By this time, they were no longer walking alone, but other shadowy figures were also hastening along beside them.

At last, they cleared a stand of trees, and the green opened up before them. A bonfire burned brightly in the middle, throwing plumes of sparks up into the air. Children pranced around the edges of the fire, and seated further back in irregular concentric circles were the drummers. More were joining them at every moment, and the reverberations of the sound increased in volume as they beat a rhythm in unison. Corin looked for a place to put Elinor down where she could be comfortable. Out of the darkness, Makarios suddenly appeared and grabbed hold of Corin's sleeve.

"Cochran, welcome! Come with me," he said in his ear. "I have a place for you." He led Corin over to a log which was already lined with drummers. "You can both sit here," he said when they came to an empty place.

Corin looked to all sides. The firelight shone on the faces of the villagers seated there, and he saw that everyone had a drum. "Shouldn't we leave these places for drummers?" he asked over the booming around him.

"Yes," Makarios replied, "it's for drummers." And then he commanded, "Sit. I'll be right back." Corin eased Elinor onto her seat and had just sat down himself when Makarios reappeared carrying a drum. He thrust it at Elinor and disappeared into the darkness once again. Elinor looked over to Corin and shrugged her shoulders. She pulled the drum closer and tucked it between her knees. Makarios returned dragging two drums. He put one in front of Corin and, leaning close enough so he could be heard above the music, said, "You're going to like this." Then he sat down next to Corin with the second drum. Corin looked at him questioningly, and Makarios smiled back, but said nothing.

Corin stared at the drum now nestled between his knees, the shifting firelight dancing off it as the rhythm danced in his ears. He ran his hand over the wooden frame, enjoying its smoothly sanded surface and the taut rawhide straps that held the stretched skin in place. He laid his open hand onto the drum skin and felt the vibrations of the drums around him. He wanted to explain to Makarios that he had never played a drum before, but the rhythm speaking to his hand and sounding in his ears stopped him.

Makarios had already settled himself and was beating his drum, rhythmically alternating his hands in sync with the others around them. It was not a complicated rhythm, and Corin's eyes and ears began to translate it to movement through his arms. He glanced at Elinor and saw the look of concentration on her face as she too was picking up the simple rhythm. The sounds in the air and the vibrations coming through the drum instructed his hands. He gave himself over to the rhythm, and before his mind could tell him that he did not know what he was doing, his hands joined in with the strong, intoxicating cadence that by now scores of drums were following in unison.

Corin felt exhilaration at being part of this grand sound. Although he was sitting still, his whole body was moved by the rhythm as it coursed through him. Young women dressed in flowing white gowns had taken the place of the prancing children around the fire, and danced with provocative, undulating movements in time with the beat of the drums. The rhythm carried on, and the longer he drummed, the more confident he felt, and the more forcefully he drummed. After a while, he marveled that, although his arms and hands were in constant movement, he felt no fatigue. The rhythm gave him strength.

As they drummed, the cadence altered occasionally, and he had no trouble adjusting to the subtle changes. In a quiet part of his mind, he wondered if someone were leading all the drums, or if the changes were from a unified musical consensus. No one called out the changes; they happened naturally and seamlessly. He looked around at the faces in the circle, looking for Thos, but he could not see his distinctive bearded face anywhere. He had left the cottage long before sunset, saying only that he would see them later. Corin wondered where he might be.

As they continued to drum, the women around the fire danced, and as the women danced, Corin watched the fire slowly die down. No one came forward to add more logs, and the night began to crowd out the firelight. Corin was so focused on the drumming that it was some time before he became aware of a second sound coming out of the forest surrounding them.

At first he wondered if there were some other instruments being played by people sitting behind the circle of drums, beyond where the light of the fire penetrated. He looked around, but in the dimming light of the dying flames he could see only that those who were not drumming sat quietly or stood in place and danced. What was the shrill sound he heard behind the resonance of the drums? And where was it coming from? It was some time before he recognized it for what it was: the shrill rhythms of the frogs in the nearby stream. He had never heard them so loud before. It was as if they were singing in accompaniment to the drum circle. An ecstatic shiver ran through him as he acknowledged the magic of this moment.

The rhythmical beat of the drums slid through the night, like a ship elbowing its way down a river in the dark, a large presence that the night reluctantly made space for. Across from Corin, behind the circle of drums, he could make out a number of people who had risen to their feet, all of them looking off to his left, waiting for something to appear. He glanced in that direction and immediately saw what held their attention. It was the milky glow of the full moon cresting over the canyon walls. As soon as its white rim became visible, those watching raised their arms over their heads in greeting and let out a whooping sound. At that moment, the rhythm of the drumming changed once again, growing in cadence, intensity and volume, marking the arrival of the long-awaited guest.

Then Corin's attention was drawn to the right, opposite the rising moon. There was movement and commotion coming from over there, but so far, in the reduced light, he could make out only shadowy figures. Then he did a double-take, wondering if his eyes were playing a trick on him. He was certain that he had just seen a spray of flames, separate from the low-burning bonfire. He watched closely now, and a few moments later it came again, an unmistakable tongue of flames surging for a moment into the darkness, at the head of what looked like a line of dancers.

Corin peered into the darkness at the edge of the circle. The line of dancers approached, standing two by two. At their head, stood a single figure wearing an ornamental mask, the details of which Corin could not yet make out in the darkness. Suddenly, out of the mouth of the mask, another spray of flames shot forth. The milky light of the risen moon illuminated them as they came more clearly into view. The dancers were rising and falling in a manner that gave their line a rippling effect. The mask at their head, Corin could now tell, was unmistakably that of—a dragon! And the flames spewed forth from the dragon's mouth! He marveled at the magnificence of the display.

As the dragon dancers slowly approached from one end, a second group of dancers drew near from the other side of the fire pit. They wore no particular costumes and danced their way into the open space, acting oblivious to the approaching threat. The dragon entered the circle around the dying bonfire and once again spewed forth flames. It emitted an unearthly roar that set Corin's hair on end. The two dancers directly behind the mask bearer appeared to be twirling something at their sides. Again the flames shot forth.

At the noise, the dancers from the other side noticed the approach of the dragon. Through their gestures, they showed first surprise and then fear. As the dragon slowly came closer, they panicked and looked for an escape, many raising their hands to the sky as if calling for help. All the while, the drums continued a spellbinding rhythm.

Then one figure emerged from the center of the terrified dancers. He had the appearance of a young man. Corin immediately noticed that he wore what looked like a crown on his head, the firelight gleaming off its metal surface. He strode confidently forward, a long knife drawn, which he held high for all to see. The moon shone off its silver blade, and Corin felt a strange elation.

The crowned figure now joined into a dance with the dragon. They kept the fire pit between them, but it was clear that they were dancing in unison with one another. At one moment it seemed as if the dragon were stalking the youth. Then the tables were turned, and brandishing his long dagger, the young man appeared to be trailing the dragon. Back and forth this game went, as the music of the drums filled the night, and the shrieking of the frogs filled the darkness behind the night. Everything around them grew brighter and brighter, as the rising moon poured its chalky whiteness upon them.

The longer the dragon and the youth played this cat and mouse game, the more excited Corin grew. He knew what must come next, and he grew irrationally joyful watching this enactment. He glanced briefly over at Elinor and was surprised to see that she had stopped drumming and, with her mouth hanging slightly open, sat entranced by the scene unfolding before them.

The dragon continued to spew flames, and its unworldly roar rose above the sound of the drums. The youth danced progressively closer until he finally lunged at the dragon. Gracefully he dodged the dragon's attempts to catch him. At one point the flames engulfed him briefly, but he reappeared unscathed. Finally, slipping past the fuming head, he jumped up onto the dragon's back, although in reality he was borne aloft on the shoulders of one of the dancers. He raised his dagger up above his head, letting the light of the moon shine fully upon it for everyone to see.

The rhythm of the drums quieted, and the voices of everyone watching the drama began chanting, "Slay him! Slay him! Slay him!" over and over again. The youth held the handle of the dagger in both hands, raised high up over his head.

"In the name of freedom," the youth called out, "I slay the dragon!"

Then with a decisive gesture, he plunged the dagger down. There followed an immense outflow of flames from the dragon's mouth and the roaring became louder and more intense. The dragon writhed as if in great pain. Then, all at once, the dancers collapsed to the ground, leaving the youth standing over them. In one hand he held aloft the dagger. In the other hand he held a large dark mass for all to see. With a final explosive flourish, all the drums at once were silent.

The only sound in the night was a piercing scream of agony that startled Corin to the core.

"No-o-o! *No-o-o!* NO-O-O-O!!"

He looked beside him and saw with alarm that it was coming from Elinor.

Chapter Eighteen

A Sudden Departure

I'm all right," Elinor insisted. "Of course, I'm all right."

"Are you sure?" Corin asked with a look of concern.

"Yes, I'm sure. Stop asking me already." She used her sleeve to wipe away the last of her tears. "I was just startled, is all."

By now the moon shone brightly down on the clearing in the forest. Makarios had taken their drums away and not returned. Villagers of the Enclave were milling about, visiting among themselves in subdued conversations. Many stared at Elinor and Corin and then huddled together in animated discussion. A squarely-built older man with greying hair broke away from a group and walked briskly over to them. His features were set and he did not introduce himself before speaking to them.

"That's right!" he declared, gesturing forcefully towards the open space where the enactment had taken place. "That's what we do around here. One day, the pretender king will get his reckoning and we will have the satisfaction to see this done for real. That will free us all." Elinor and Corin stared dumbly up at him. He continued in an unfriendly tone, "Who are you anyway? I've never seen you before. You're strangers here. How did you get here and what are you doing in the Enclave?"

Elinor just stared at him. Corin opened his mouth to speak, but he was too startled to respond.

"They are my guests," spoke a voice from behind them. They turned to see Thos. "And they are under my protection," he continued.

The man looked sharply up at him. "Then teach them our ways and our priorities," he growled. "The king will be the ruin of us all. Barring law-abiding citizens from their own city, spending money that's not his to spend. He's not even royal born. The only advantage to living here is not to have to pay his blood taxes."

Corin stiffened at the man's attacks on his father and the crown. He stood up to caution him to speak more discreetly. But before he could open his mouth, he felt Thos' hand on his shoulder, squeezing it firmly. This caused him to hesitate long enough for Thos to speak first.

"Fear not," Thos said calmly. "I vouch for them and will instruct them in our ways. As to the king, we will leave him to defend his own good name."

The man frowned. "Not that there's much he could do to save his reputation now." He looked from Thos to the newcomers and back to Thos. "And if they are with you, that is good enough for me." He gazed at Corin searchingly, opened his mouth to speak, but then apparently thought better of it. He nicked his head to Thos and, with a final hard stare at the cousins, stalked away.

Corin turned to Thos. "What did we do to—" but broke off mid-sentence when he saw what Thos was carrying in his hand. "It was you," he said with amazement, staring at the ornamental dragon mask Thos was holding.

"It was I," Thos nodded in reply, a tired smile on his face.

"How did you do it?" Corin asked in wonder. "The fire. It looked so magical."

"It was supposed to look magical," Thos laughed. "I am a magician, after all, and that is what people expect of me. But like all of my magic, it was but a trick. And once you know the trick, the magic in it is gone. Do you still wish me to reveal it to you?"

"Yes," Corin replied enthusiastically.

Wordlessly, Thos held out to Corin a flask that hung from a long strap around his neck. Corin took it and felt from its weight that there was liquid inside. He put his nose to it and sniffed, pulling his face away quickly with a frown.

Thos laughed at the young prince's expression. "Do you recognize it?"

"Naphtha," he said. "Unmistakable."

"Precisely," Thos agreed. "Did you never catch my fire-breathing act at the market? No? Well, I don't do it often. Not only is it rather wasteful of a precious substance, but I'm not terribly fond of the taste it leaves behind and it ends up leaving my whiskers somewhat singed. But once a month for the full moon, I make the sacrifice. White naphtha not only lights up the king's palace, it is useful in spectacles such as this."

"What about the roaring?" Corin asked.

"Did you never play with a bullroarer when you were younger?" Thos replied.

Corin broke into a wide grin. "Of course! A bullroarer! That's brilliant."

"Two, in fact," Thos added. "It makes an even larger sound."

"You do this every month?" Corin asked. Thos nodded.

"But that's terrible," Elinor uttered in horror.

Corin turned to her. "Why? What's terrible about it?"

"Weren't you watching?" she asked aghast.

"Of course I was," Corin said defensively. "I thought it was magnificent."

"Magnificent?" Elinor shrieked. "Didn't you see what they just did? They kill the dragon! They plunge a knife into its heart and kill him! And that doesn't bother you?!"

"I don't think so," Corin said, uncertain what there was to be upset about. "It was a great spectacle."

"A spectacle?" Elinor cried in despair. "It was murder!"

Corin finally shrugged. "I don't see what you didn't like."

"Sprout, don't you get it?"

"What am I missing?" he asked, perplexed.

"Sprout, think! What dragon is this all about? What is the only dragon that everyone knows?"

"Star?" Corin said in wonderment, all of this dawning on him only now. "This was about Star?"

"That took far too long for you to realize," Elinor moaned. She hugged her sides as if to hold herself together and whispered in a choked voice, "What am I going to do?"

"But if that was supposed to be Star," Corin asked skeptically, "who was the youth who killed him? He was wearing some sort of garland. Did you see that?"

"It was a crown," Elinor insisted.

"All right, a crown, then," Corin said. "If that was Star, then who is the youth wearing a crown who kills … ?" and his voice died as the realization struck him. He looked up to Thos who had been silently following their conversation. "Thos, it's *me*? Was that supposed to be *me*?"

"Let's get Elinor back to my cottage," Thos said. "I will answer all of your questions there. Do you think you can carry her?"

Too stunned by the implications of what had just happened to respond with words, Corin just nodded his head. He backed up to Elinor and crouched down. She hopped on, wrapping her arms around his neck. Corin slipped his hands underneath her knees to support her weight. Thos walked ahead and, carrying Elinor, Corin followed in the bright moonlight. Once they entered the pathway between the trees, the branches cast dark shadows along the way, but the illumination of the moon made the walk much easier than when they had come. Elinor laid her head against Corin's back, and judging from her ragged breathing, she was quietly sobbing. Corin hoped it was merely from exhaustion, but he had a feeling of dread that this went much deeper.

They spoke no more words the whole way back to the cottage. Once inside, Thos stoked up the fire to drive away the night chill. Corin set Elinor beside the hearth. Even in the dancing firelight, he could see that her eyes were puffy from crying.

"I'll make us some tea," Thos said, lifting the kettle to hang from its hook above the fire. He stood and went to the sideboard, where he took a handful of dried leaves from a drawer. He stepped back to the hearth and dropped them into the kettle.

"Mint," he commented. "We could use something refreshing."

"Thos, tell me what that was about," Corin asked. "Is Elinor right? Was that supposed to represent me?"

"Before I answer that," Thos said, "tell me something first. You've been here long enough to speak with people and hear how they feel about things. For the people in the Enclave, what is their opinion of the dragon?"

Corin did not respond immediately. He thought about his conversations at Makarios' camp and the comments of the man who accosted them after the celebration. He reflected on what the people were chanting after the crowned youth jumped onto the back of the dragon in the enactment.

"He's not a Luck Dragon for them," he said.

"What do you think he does represent for them?" Thos asked.

"He represents all of their unhappiness," Corin answered.

Thos' deep laughter filled the small room. "Perhaps not *all* of their unhappiness," he said. "But it is fair to say that they see him as the root cause for their living in exile from Gladur. And after that, in the same way you see him responsible for all of your good fortune, it is easy for the people of the Enclave to blame him for many of their miseries."

"But what does that have to do with me?" Corin asked. "Why have *me* killing him?"

"It is well known that you do not take after your father's ways," Thos replied.

"They know that?" Corin asked astonished.

"Perhaps you think that you live in a small, protected world, but your life is far more public than you imagine. People watch carefully what you do, what you say, what you like and dislike."

"What people?" Corin asked.

"Everyone from the bean seller in the market to King Bellek's spies in Gladur. As to the dwellers in the Enclave, there are high hopes that you will one day reverse the harsh decrees of your father—"

"Harsh?" Corin interrupted.

"—and restore a period of tolerance and generosity, as your mother represents. Many people here are convinced that for that to happen, the dragon has to be eliminated."

Elinor, who had only listened until now, let out a cry of despair. Thos continued, "They feel that is the only way to unify the realm again and bring an enduring peace with the neighboring kingdoms. Their hopes are set on you."

"Do you mean that they're waiting for me to kill the dragon?"

"As a radical act, perhaps. They want you to break with the past. Ah," Thos said, attracted by the steam coming out of the kettle, "I think our tea is ready."

As Thos busied himself with pouring out three cups of tea for them, Corin's eye was caught by the firelight shining off of something at his waist. It was the handle of a knife.

"Thos, is that the dagger that was used in the enactment?" Corin asked.

The magician glanced down at his waist. "Indeed it is," he answered.

"May I see it, please?"

Thos pulled it from his belt and handed it to him. Corin held it so that the firelight could shine upon it. He was startled by what he saw. It had an intricate design on the blade. He recognized it immediately.

"But isn't this the same dagger as the one … ?" his voice died off in wonderment.

"That I took from the rather self-important nobleman in the market?" Thos completed Corin's question for him. "It is a duplicate, not the same one. I'm sure your mother has the one I gave you, safely locked away in the palace."

"What are you doing with it? She told me that it was from a secret society dedicated to destroying the dragon," Corin stammered.

"I have heard the same," Thos answered cryptically. "Tea?" he said, offering him a steaming cup.

There was no sign of Thos the next morning when Corin woke up. He and Elinor made themselves some breakfast and they treated her ankle with the salve Thos had given them. The swelling had gone down and she was able to hobble about and even place some weight onto her foot. Corin had found a suitable fallen branch among the trees near the house and was fashioning a crutch for her. They had not spoken again about the events of the night before. The conversation with Thos had left Corin feeling elated, although he could not explain why. And with Elinor in a melancholic mood, he was not comfortable sharing it with her. But he was happy and content, humming to himeself as he worked on the crutch. They were sitting outside on the bench along the wall of the house, enjoying the morning sunshine.

They heard footsteps approaching along the path, and both looked up to see who was coming. The old magician was wearing a hooded traveling cloak and a wide-brimmed hat with raven feathers bristling from its band. He had a staff in his hand and a bag slung over one shoulder.

"Thos!" Corin exclaimed. "Are you going somewhere?"

"I've come to say goodbye," he said briskly, walking up to them.

"Goodbye?" the cousins exclaimed. "But where are you going?"

"That remains to be seen," Thos answered. "But away I must."

"Have you received a summons?" Corin asked.

"It is more like an invitation," Thos explained with a smile. "And the choice is mine whether to accept. In this case, I have decided I must go."

"Do you know for what purpose?"

"That's not always easy to figure out. I've been led to some out-of-the-way places and sat around for the longest time until I could figure things out. It can be both tedious and trying. Still, my guides have never misled me."

"Who are these guides?"

"I don't think you're quite ready to hear about them," Thos replied. "However, I will tell you this much. Do you remember the sudden wind on the night you escaped from the boat?" When Corin nodded with the memory, Thos continued, "Ask me when we meet again and perhaps I will be able to tell you more."

"But, Thos," Corin objected, "what are we to do if you leave?"

"The two of you will remain here," Thos replied. "You must give Elinor's ankle time to heal properly. You will be safe here. But heed my warning: Do not wander beyond the confines of the Enclave. I cannot guarantee your safety if you do."

"When will we see you next?" Elinor asked.

"I will summon you," Thos answered. "I have a strong sense that I will need your help if you are willing to give it."

"Of course," Corin said. "We'll do whatever we can to help."

"Consider well," Thos replied. "Once you have agreed, there will be no turning back."

"You make it sound so solemn," Elinor said.

"It is both solemn and grave," Thos said. "It will change everything from here on out. Are you ready for that?"

"I think that is what I've been waiting for," Corin responded quietly. "I am beginning to believe that is why I've come here."

"I am glad to hear that," Thos said. "I hope your resolve is still as strong when the summons comes."

"How will we know that it is coming from you?" Elinor asked.

"My careful girl," Thos said smiling. "When it comes, you will have no doubt. If you do, it is not from me." He then pulled from his deep pocket a letter that had been folded and sealed with wax. "I will leave this inside on the mantel. Promise me that you will not open it until you receive word from me."

The cousins glanced at one another silently, then solemnly nodded their agreement. Thos continued, "Inside this envelope you will find instructions what to do and where to go. And what to bring."

"What to bring?" Corin asked. "That sounds mysterious."

"And it is a deep mystery, indeed," Thos said seriously. "To get through this in one piece will be far greater magic than in all of my cleverest sleight of hand. Elinor, take good care of your ankle so that you will be ready to travel when I call for you. Young prince, consider your options and where your allegiance lies so that you may choose well when the time comes. How you decide will affect the destiny of many. That is your fate and cannot be changed, so be ready. And believe me, the time is coming soon."

Thos stepped into the cottage, and the cousins turned to one another with wide eyes. This was happening all too suddenly. When Thos came out again, he said, "Farewell, my friends," and turned to go.

"Wait!" Corin exclaimed. "This sounds so final."

"It is never final," Thos replied with a brief smile. "It is, however, the next step to take."

"Is there some way we can prepare ourselves?" Corin asked.

"Can we ever be prepared?" the old magician asked. Then he smiled. "Do you remember the first magic trick I showed you?"

"Do you mean the one where I can make something disappear from my hand? Of course, I remember it."

"Then I suggest you prepare yourself by perfecting it."

"But what then?" Corin asked.

"Practice your stitching. After that, the rest will fall into place."

"Thos, tell me before you go, who else knows who we are?"

"As far as I can tell, other than myself, only Makarios."

"I suspected as much," Corin said. "At his camp he spoke to me in ways that had deeper meaning than for a chance visitor."

"I did not tell him, but he made some very clever guesses, and I was not inclined to lie to him when he asked me directly. But fear not, your secret is safe with him."

"After last night, I can't help wondering what would happen if the people found out that I am the prince of Gladur?"

Thos peered at him with a stern gaze. "See that you give no cause for them to question who you are until you are prepared to meet their doubts about you."

He turned to go, but then stopped himself and turned back. He stepped over to Corin, drawing the dagger from his belt and handing it to him. "It occurs to me that if you had this in your possession, you might, just might be able to use it to your advantage. Take it. You are likely to have more chance to use it than I will." With these final words, he turned on his heel and followed the path through the woods. Corin stared down at the dagger in his hands and could not resist being fascinated by the intricate designs of the writhing dragon etched on the blade.

Chapter Nineteen

The Summons

"How long has it been since you sent your letter?" Elinor asked. They were sitting on the bench outside Thos' cottage. Corin had just returned from the village with some vegetables he had been given in return for repairing tools that others had been unable to fix.

"Makarios invited us to come for supper this evening," he said.

"Great," Elinor said. "How long has it been?"

Corin shrugged his shoulders. "I don't know. How long has Thos been gone? Not yet ten days, I think."

"Why haven't we heard from your mother?" Elinor asked. "We should have heard something by now."

"Maybe she doesn't know how to get word to us," Corin said. It was probably true, he thought. He had not told her where they were, but he did not mention this to Elinor. "What does it matter?"

"Sprout, we have to get back to Gladur," Elinor said.

"We are still in Gladur," Corin pointed out.

"You know what I mean," Elinor said. "We have to get back to your parents."

"Thos said we should wait here until we hear from him. He's counting on us to help him."

"That's not enough," Elinor insisted. "We have to go back to your parents."

"You're still limping on that ankle. You'll never make it."

"That's not true. I limp only when my ankle gets tired. I've figured it out. Many people own donkeys here. I'm sure somebody has one they can spare. We can borrow their donkey and I can ride on it. We will pay them back once we are safely home."

"I'm not ready to go back," Corin said firmly, not looking his cousin in the eye. "I want to wait until we hear from Thos. I like it here. Besides, it's not safe beyond the confines of the Enclave. Both Thos and Makarios have warned us about wandering away from here."

"We can travel with some of the locals when they go to Gladur for the market."

"I'm not ready to go back yet," Corin repeated stubbornly.

"Sprout, I'm sure your mother is worried, after having both of us disappear so suddenly. What if she never got the letter? We can't leave her hanging like this."

"I'm sure she'll be all right," Corin said.

"Sprout, we also have to go back for Star. He needs you."

"How do you know that?"

"I can feel it," Elinor said, trying to sound convincing. "I can't explain how. I just know that he needs you."

Corin stood up and paced back and forth in the clearing. He felt torn in two directions. Finally, he simply blurted it out. "I don't need him."

"You what?" Elinor was aghast.

"If it weren't for Star, I could live my life how I want," Corin said sullenly. "It wouldn't matter to anyone if I stayed here or went back. I could be free. Ever since the full moon ceremony, I can't stop thinking about it."

"Sprout, that was only play-acting!" Elinor said, raising her voice. "What's gotten into you? Your dragon is still there and needs your attention."

"*My* dragon," Corin repeated the words as if they tasted bitter. "He's not *my* dragon. Sometimes I wish I had never seen him. Star and my parents are just fine without me. In fact, the last time I saw my father, he even told me I didn't belong in Gladur."

"Sprout, how can you talk like that?" Elinor said, her eyes wide. "Do you have any idea how lucky you are to have your family? Take it from me. Sure, I had moments when my parents annoyed me, when they wanted me to do things I didn't want to do. My older brother teased me relentlessly and I hated it. I resented that my younger sister took Mother's attention away from me. But right now, now that they are all gone and I'll never see them again, I would do anything to have them back. You stop talking this nonsense and go ask someone to lend us their donkey. We're going home!"

Corin opened his mouth to object, but Elinor would not let him speak. "Auntie has been too kind to me to leave her worrying any longer. I want to go home," she said forcefully. "I'd go alone if I could. But I need your help, and you will take me. Get a donkey. Now!"

Corin saw the determination in his cousin's face, but it only triggered his own defiance. "Don't tell me what to do!" he shouted back at her. "Why would I want to go back there? Everyone always wants to tell me what to do, and now you start up. Leave me alone." He turned and was about to storm from the clearing.

Behind him, Elinor demanded, "Sprout! Stay here!"

Suddenly, Corin found himself sprawled flat on his face. Elinor had sprung up, taken her crutch that was leaning against the hut and hooked him between the legs. "You stay here!" she shouted at him.

Corin was furious. He was on his feet in an instant and grabbed for the first thing that came into his hands. It was a stout walking stick that was next to the front door. With this he attacked Elinor. It was fortunate for her that she still held the crutch and could parry his blow. Corin did not stop, but swung at her again. They had sparred many times before, but this time all playfulness was gone.

Elinor was completely on the defensive, taken aback by Corin's attack. He came at her so fast and furiously that she did not even have time to cry out. Her reactions took over, and it was good that she had been such an attentive student, or Corin would have injured her before he got control of his anger.

Corin had the clear advantage and Elinor could see the menace in his eyes. Suddenly, out of nowhere, a blur of black and a confusion of wings flew into Corin's face. It threw him off-balance and he had to step back to avoid the talons that were trying to rake his face. Instead of swinging at Elinor, now he was swatting at the bird to get it away from him as he steadily backed up.

The bird flew onto a nearby branch, its feathers all puffed up. It lowered its head and cawed at Corin. It was agitated.

"What's wrong with you?" Corin shouted at the bird. In response it cawed loudly back at him.

"What's wrong with *you*?" Elinor asked, still clutching the crutch in case he turned on her again. "You tried to hurt me."

Corin looked at his cousin as if coming out of a trance. Then he stared at the stick in his hand and threw it away into the bushes. "I'm not going back," he mumbled defiantly. "You can go. But I'm staying here." He plopped down on the bench. He looked confused. "Sorry," he said in a low voice, cradling his head in his hands. "When you tripped me, I just saw red. I don't know what got into me. I hope I didn't hurt you."

"I'll be fine," Elinor said, cautiously sitting down next to her cousin. "I'm just glad that Radabinth showed up."

"Radabinth?" Corin said, looking up. He studied the bird that still sat on the branch, now preening its ruffled feathers. "Do you think that's Thos' raven?"

"Who else can it be?"

"Radabinth, is that you?" Corin called out.

In answer, the raven puffed up its feathers, then dipped its head and cawed raucously. It sounded like a victory cry. Both Corin and Elinor laughed, and it eased the tension that had built up between them. The raven then lifted its wings and flew to the open window of the house, landing on the sill. It peered into the house and then disappeared inside.

"Hey!" Corin called. "Where are you going?"

"If that's Radabinth, does that mean Thos has returned?"

"I don't know," Corin said, looking into the window, trying to see what the raven was doing in there. "I haven't seen her since Thos left. I assumed they had gone together."

A moment later the raven was back on the window sill. It had in its mouth a sealed letter. It was the letter that Thos had left behind.

"Hey!" Corin cried out. "You can't take that."

The raven spread its wings and leapt from the window, flying directly over their heads. But as it flew off, it dropped the letter—directly into Elinor's lap. The two of them looked at one another, their mouths hanging open.

"Do you think she did that on purpose?" Elinor asked, staring at the letter. The raven was back on a nearby tree branch. It flapped its wings and cawed loudly at them.

"I think this is the summons Thos was talking about," Corin said slowly. "Do you have any doubt that it's from him?" Elinor said nothing, but shook her head, no.

By late that afternoon, the cousins had still not managed to come to terms with Thos' letter. Corin sat staring at it. Elinor was reading it for the fifth time. "This is desperate," she said, a worried look in her eyes. "What are we going to do?"

"I'm not sure," Corin said, taking the letter from her and reading it once again, hoping that he had missed some clue how to make the impossible happen.

"He wrote this before he left," Elinor said. "How could he know any of this before he left? Maybe he got it wrong."

"He obviously had sources we don't know about," Corin said. "We are being put to the test. Do you trust Thos?"

Elinor thought about this and finally nodded her head. "Yes. Everything he has done tells me that I can trust him. In Gladur, he always showed up to help me when I needed it. He saved us from the men on the boat who kidnapped me. He gave us a safe place to live here and has kept our identity from the people of the Enclave. He has had so many opportunities to injure us, but he has always been a friend."

"I'm not totally convinced," Corin said. "I think Thos has a lot of mysteries surrounding him."

"But look at his actions," Elinor insisted.

"There is still the day you got kidnapped. He wanted you to visit him, and then told you how to walk home, and then they found you."

"It could have been a coincidence," she said. "Maybe he was showing me a way to escape them, but it didn't work."

"Maybe," Corin agreed. "But to do what he wants... It's not like we can just go and take it. I don't even know who to ask for help."

"The other option is to return to Gladur like I've been asking," Elinor said. "We can get help from there."

"You're forgetting Geron," Corin said quickly. "He controls the army. Thos clearly states that Father is missing and that Mother is in grave trouble. I don't know about you, but I still suspect that Geron is behind this mischief. Remember I told you that he was there at the wharf talking with the men who had just kidnapped you. I am not going to go and put myself at his mercy. Once we fall into his hands, we may never escape again."

"There's still Star," Elinor said.

"True," Corin agreed. "He could give us advice, but by going there, we run the risk of being captured by Geron."

"Then we have no choice but to do what Thos instructs. That said, I don't know how he expects us to bring a whole load of it with us without telling us how to do it," she said looking at the letter again, "and I don't even know what a dragon wagon is. Do you?"

"Not a clue," Corin said quietly. He got up and paced. "I have an idea," he said at last. "Makarios is already expecting us for supper. I will speak with him about this. If anyone could make this work, he could."

"Do you think we can trust him?"

"That has to go both ways," Corin replied. "We'll know more after we talk. Let's head into the village." The cousins took the path that led to the center of the Enclave. They walked slowly for Elinor's sake.

"How is your ankle?" Corin asked.

"It feels as good as new," Elinor said. "See?" She stood in place and hopped up and down several times.

"Is all the pain gone?"

"Nearly," she replied. "It still has a tight feeling, and if I spend a long time on my feet, it begins to bother me. But the most part, it has healed well, thanks to your herbs and Thos' ointment."

"That's fortunate," Corin said. "Because once we leave here, we have a long journey ahead of us. That idea of yours about a donkey was not such a bad one."

When they came to the edge of the village, they were greeted by a band of children out playing. With shouts and laughter, the children escorted them to Makarios' modest camp.

"Elsbeth! Cochran!" Makarios called out when they arrived. "You are just in time. My wife had just announced that the stew is ready."

Dinner was a casual affair. Makarios' wife ladled out for each of them a steamy bowl of stew and they sat around his campfire and enjoyed the end of day warmth as the sun slipped away behind the cliffs. The baby was asleep, but the toddler crawled from one to the next looking for handouts. They laughed at her antics and the faces she made when she tried out new tastes in her mouth. Both Makarios and his wife shared the latest gossip from their neighbors, most notably that a group of boys had found a beehive in the knot of a tree in the forest and had attempted to get the honey without any adult help. The result was numerous boys of the Enclave with swollen hands and faces, but very little reward for their efforts.

"They'll survive," Makarios laughed. "Now maybe they will listen to us that there are better ways. I tried to teach them about smoking the bees out, but they thought they knew better. Sometimes it takes some pain for youth to be ready to take advice from their elders." He paused and looked meaningfully at Corin. "Have you ever had that problem, Cochran?"

More often than I'd like to admit, Corin thought. He glanced around to make sure that no one was passing by. While they ate, there had been a number of visitors, but at this moment they were alone. He leaned forward and said to Makarios in a low voice, "We have to talk."

"Speak, then," Makarios invited. "What about?"

Corin lowered his voice even more. "We've had a letter from Thos."

"That's interesting," Makarios said with raised eyebrows. "How was it delivered?"

"It came by raven," Corin relayed.

Makarios nodded his head in thought. "He has peculiar messengers, that one. What does he report?"

"That he is in serious trouble and in need of our help," Corin replied.

"That's odd," Makarios considered. "Why your help? You are both young still, his guests, and have few resources at your disposal. What help can he hope from you?"

Corin looked again to make sure that there were no other listeners. Makarios' wife was busy with the children and out of earshot. "My name is not Cochran," he confided.

"And I'm his cousin, not his sister," Elinor added.

Makarios studied the two before speaking. He glanced around. "Come," he said, standing up. "Join me for a walk." He led them along the trail leading out of the village and soon took one of the many side paths.

It did not take long before they were alone among the trees. Makarios stopped in a clearing. "We can talk here," he said, glancing around to make sure they were alone.

"Thos said that you figured out who I am," Corin said, watching him closely.

"I had no need to figure it out. I knew you from the beginning." Makarios enjoyed Corin's look of surprise. "You don't remember me, do you?"

"We've met before?" Corin asked. "The first time I saw you I thought you looked vaguely familiar, but I see lots of people at the market and through the court."

"Think back on the spring festival. I'm sure you will remember."

"There were masses of people there," Corin said with a shrug. "The crowds come from all over."

"But there was only one King of Misrule," Makarios said with a smile.

"That was you?" Corin said with astonishment. Makarios nodded his head. Corin remembered how the King of Misrule had followed him through the room with his eyes. He had not liked it at the time and had been happy to leave.

"Why haven't you raised the alarm, then?" Corin asked. "If it was out of respect for Thos, he's gone now."

"I haven't told anyone else because I haven't made up my mind about you. If you had been like your father, not even Thos could have gotten me to remain silent. But you're not. Many of the more hopeful rumors about you seem to be true."

"What do they say about me?" Corin asked.

"I have to discount most of what I hear," Makarios said. "Although it appears that you are not as unfriendly as reported, albeit you are a private person. I don't hold that against you. You are able to keep a secret, and I find that a good quality for a man who will one day have to lead. And it seems clear that you think for yourself. I have tried not to be hasty in forming an opinion about you."

"What are you waiting to find out about me?"

"The way I see it, you have a choice, and you haven't yet made your decision."

"Tell me," Corin said. "What are my choices, as you see them?"

"The obvious choice you have is to follow in the footsteps of those who came before you. To become like your father. However, you haven't done that. So that tells me that you are considering other options."

"And what do you believe them to be?"

"To make a new beginning. Your father represents the old way. You're wondering if there is a new way. Your way."

"How do you know I'm considering this?"

"Because you have been here long enough to have sent word back to the king and queen to have yourselves rescued. I don't see you wanting to be rescued."

Corin leaned forward. "I'd like to make a deal with you," he said.

"This becomes interesting. Tell me truly. Do you speak out of fear for your life?"

"I speak out of self-interest. And if it spares my life and my cousin's, so much the better."

"Do you really think you are in a position to bargain?"

"Wait until you hear what I offer you and decide for yourself."

"Fair enough. I'm listening."

As Corin explained his plan, based upon the instructions that Thos had left behind, he carefully watched Makarios' expression. The raised eyebrows alone were enough to tell him that he had his interest.

"If your plan fails, you realize that you will be throwing your life away."

"It's my risk," Corin said, trying to sound confident.

"There are many in the governing council here who would welcome to see the heir to the throne sacrifice his life," Makarios said, staring hard at the prince. Corin flinched at these words. Makarios continued, "Do you have any idea of the immensity of what you are asking?"

"I don't have any other choice," Corin replied. "You're the only one who can help us."

"And why should we throw our lot in with the young prince on a suicide mission?" Makarios asked. "You've been here long enough to know how we feel about the royal house and all their nobles."

"Because it will be worth your while."

"You can't buy our loyalty," Makarios said with a dismissive laugh.

"I do not intend to try. But I hope to win it. And your trust. Go this far with me: Withhold both until I prove I am worthy of them."

"That's a big risk to take and a far way to go on faith that you will prove yourself worthy and not get yourself killed in the bargain."

"Everything we do that is worthwhile we do on faith and involves risks." He resisted adding that this was a lesson Star repeated frequently.

Makarios laughed. "You already argue like a king. You might just pull this off."

"Come along and find out," Corin offered. "Then you can have a part in it. If it comes off well, it can only be to your profit."

"And if it comes off ill, what if it leads to our ruin?" Makarios asked.

"I can offer no guarantees," Corin replied. "I am confident I will succeed, but I need your help. Let me meet with your council." Then he added, with a sidelong glance at Elinor, "Alone. The deal will be with me alone, the heir to the throne."

Makarios nodded with a smile. "I will take this up with them. But let me warn you," he continued. His features became serious, even threatening. "Make no mistake. If you come short of being convincing, even if we do agree to join you, we will depart without raising a hand to help, even if there is a knife to your throat. We have nothing to gain from your private ventures and will not tolerate being used as your puppets."

Corin's hand reached unconsciously for the dagger at his belt. His fingers felt the etched lines of the design on the blade. "Believe me," he said. "What I do will be convincing. You will not doubt on what side I stand or my faithfulness to your own ends."

"That remains to be seen," Makarios said with a shrug. "But I'm willing to let you prove it to me. We'll see if the others are as open-minded."

Part IV

Desperate Measures

Chapter Twenty

The King of Warrensfold

*T*he Queen's Guard, with Aina nestled protectively in their midst, traveled along the merchant road. In spite of ongoing border skirmishes, there was still a lively trade between kingdoms. Merchants were always willing to take the risk of stumbling into armed clashes for the sake of plying their trade. Of course, there was the ever-present danger of marauding bands of soldiers and highwaymen looting a merchant's goods. In order to minimize the risks and provide safety, years earlier the queen had modestly fortified caravanserai placed strategically along this road to provide secure places to overnight. Aina hoped that peace with Warrensfold would improve the safety along the route and encourage more trade. She knew that the prosperity of her country depended upon increased commerce with their neighbors. It could only benefit them all.

It was in one such caravanserai that Aina stayed overnight with her guard. As long as they traveled in Gladur, they were met in the evening with well-stocked quarters for both men and their horses, and an innkeeper who was delighted with the honor of serving the queen his best stew and good cheer. Speaking with other travelers in these outposts, Aina learned a great deal. She heard of their hopes and dreams. She listened patiently to their complaints. She made numerous resolutions for future improvements.

At the border to Warrensfold, they found an escort from King Bellek awaiting them. The queen was relieved that her message had been received and so quickly acted upon.

The spokesman for the Warrensfold military escort was a nobleman. "My name is Rigen," he introduced himself. He was richly dressed in the manner of courtiers, with a ring in one earlobe and a pheasant feather jauntily stuck into his hat. He had curly brown hair and kept his beard closely trimmed. "I have been sent by the king to personally escort Her Majesty and do whatever is necessary for her comfort and safety."

"My thanks to you and to your king," Aina replied. "My safety is assured with the addition of your escort to my own. As to my comfort, the inns along the way have thus far been more than accommodating. I am grateful to your king for his gesture and for your company."

Morik, the captain of her guard, was less than grateful. He took the first opportunity to sidle his horse alongside the queen's and, as soon as there was no one who could overhear their conversation, complained bitterly. "I don't like it one bit," he said. "They outnumber us. We should have brought more of the guard."

"Then be vigilant, good Morik," the queen said lightly. "And remember to smile when you speak with me privately, lest our escort grow suspicious that you are suspicious." And so saying, she smiled warmly at the captain of her guard. He smiled in return, even if it was forced. "Besides, Morik," the queen continued, "I am glad to have them where I can watch them, rather than hidden behind the trees in the forest. As it is, I do not suspect any foul play before we have even commenced our talks. Getting into Warrensfold is the easy part. If we come to disagreements, getting out again may prove to be more challenging."

"But you know better than I that Worrah cannot be trusted."

"So let us be grateful that Worrah is not the king of Warrensfold," Aina pointed out. "He took refuge here and appears to have convinced King Bellek to allow him command over enough of a military force to harass our borders, but nothing more. I will not have to deal with Worrah. As it is, this gesture from Bellek may very well be a welcome sign that Worrah has fallen out of favor. That is why I am willing to risk this visit."

"But is it really necessary that you personally undertake this journey?" Morik asked, remembering to smile again, seeing that Rigen was glancing over his shoulder to watch them from where he rode. "Why not send an emissary to work out the details first? You could travel later to seal the treaty."

"In his letter King Bellek declared his sincere desire to make an immediate peace. He outlined numerous points of common interest, all of which I was in agreement with. So I believe I am coming to seal a treaty."

"But why travel to him, Your Majesty?" Morik persisted. "Why not meet in neutral territory where we are both at equal disadvantage?"

"I agree that would have been more to my liking as well," Aina said. "Believe me, Morik, I dislike this as much as you. The timing could not be worse."

"Then why undertake it?" he asked.

"King Bellek wrote that he fell from his horse recently and was injured. He is not well enough to travel, yet he does not want to let that stand in the way of our finding a solution with one another. Perhaps his injury is serious and he wishes to have the protection of a treaty in place before he becomes even more vulnerable. It is what I would do. As it is, I have tried for months to get him to reply positively to my offers of peace, and the tone of his last letter was even apologetic for his delay."

"Words come easy in a letter," Morik grumbled.

"King Bellek is an honorable man," Aina said, her expression somber. "He has given his surety of safe passage. I don't believe he is foolish enough to break his oath to me. These are sacred things between royals. We do not take them lightly."

"Still, Your Majesty," Morik argued, "you are taking a great risk."

"Without great risks, nothing great is gained," she answered with a cautious smile.

"I still fear some treachery from Worrah."

"Worrah is most likely along the frontier burning some innocent village. It is my hope that we can at last put a stop to his menacing the countryside."

Morik sighed and shook his head. "I don't like it, Your Majesty."

"Would you rest easier if I tell you that Star sanctioned our coming?"

"Star!" exclaimed her captain. "But the rumor is that the king is gone from Gladur, as well as Prince Corin."

"They are missing, indeed," she replied gravely.

"Then how did you speak with the dragon," Morik asked in wonderment.

"Star understands our speech, good Morik. It is we who cannot understand his replies. I simply placed before him this opportunity and asked if he sensed it was a good idea to come. I have done this before with him, and I have always trusted his answers, though they are given without words. There was no doubt that he encouraged me to come." She looked at her captain and smiled. "Are you satisfied?"

He paused before he said, "Begging your pardon, no, Your Majesty."

"You have my pardon," the queen replied. "Truth to tell, I am as uneasy as you. If not for Star's clear approval, I would have hesitated coming. I have never met nor heard of this Rigen. I thought I knew all the powerful nobles who stood beside King Bellek. Alert the men to stay on their guard."

At this Morik smiled. "I am relieved to know that my queen has not totally lost her senses."

"Speak with them," she added. "Yet do it cautiously."

Morik glanced over his shoulder at the soldiers riding behind. "I think there is no need of my warning, Your Majesty, but I will pass the word anyway."

Before he could ride away, the queen delayed him long enough to add, "We did not come looking for a fight, Captain. See that you do not begin one. As you pointed out, we are outnumbered." Morik nicked his head before he wheeled his horse to quietly give instructions to the guard.

The caravanserai they came to their first night in King Bellek's territory was poorly kept and ill stocked. Over the next several evenings, they housed repeatedly in the ruins of what had once been well-kept establishments that had fallen into abandoned disrepair. Rigen apologized for the state of their accommodations. He commented to the queen that he hoped her coming to the capital to meet with the king would help bring about a period of renewed prosperity.

In the evenings, Aina attempted to speak with the few merchants she met, as she had done while in Gladur, but they were cautious with their words and openly uncomfortable around so many soldiers.

During the last stretch of their journey, they passed through a forest so large that they had to camp in the shade of its trees. At the campfire, the queen's guard grouped in a mass around her, with Morik by her side.

Aina looked at the huddled soldiers surrounding her. She turned to Morik. "It's not that cold," she commented dryly.

"Your Majesty," Morik said in a low voice, "my men are more comfortable knowing that they are between you and anyone who might want to take advantage of our being so exposed out here."

"Anything I can do to allay your worries?" she asked.

"Just don't snap at the men if they're crowding you. They feel better this way."

Aina smiled. "I appreciate your concern."

"I'd appreciate not having any," Morik replied.

The next day Aina and her guard had to accept riding along the narrow forest road sandwiched between the Warrensfold escort. More than once Morik grumbled to his queen about "no escape." They emerged from the forest late in the afternoon. The queen's guard was relieved to be out in the open again. Across the meadows, the walls of Warrensfold's chief city rose high. The fields around them were eerily empty of all activity. As they walked their horses towards the towering main gates, they noticed an unfamiliar smell in the air. It had a dull, penetrating odor that was unpleasant but not overpowering. Aina wondered where it was coming from, but looking around saw no recognizable source.

Morik brought his horse up beside hers. "Your Majesty," he said. "May I have permission to speak freely?"

"Of, course, good Morik."

"Your Majesty, for the last time, I have to say, I don't like that you've come here, as if delivering yourself into his hands."

"Morik, we have passed safely thus far, and the escort, if not overly cordial, has been professional. Perhaps it is this unpleasant smell that unsettles you. I know it certainly does me. However, I hold firmly to my belief that King Bellek has invited me here in good faith for peace negotiations."

They arrived at the main entrance to the town. The captain of the gate came out to speak with them, accompanied by several heavily armed soldiers. He eyed the queen's guard warily as he looked through the papers that Morik presented to him.

"You are welcome here, Your Majesty," he said lowering his head to her. "But you cannot bring your guard in." He handed the papers back to Morik. "At most, five of you can accompany her, and you come unarmed."

"Impossible!" Morik objected hotly. "What sort of queen's guard are we without our arms? Do you pull a dog's teeth before you send him out to watch the sheep?"

"No wolves in here," the captain laughed gruffly. "No need for sharp teeth. Those are my orders. Take them or leave them."

"I'll take them," Morik said, stepping threateningly forward to stand in his face. The captain took a step back and the gate guards quickly drew their swords. "I'll take them and shove them back—"

"Morik!" the queen spoke sharply, restraining him with her voice. "Certainly we can come to some compromise. We've come here on a mission of peace. Rigen, can you not intercede in this?" she asked, turning to her escort's commander.

"I am certain we can work something out, Your Majesty. Please forgive the captain of the gate. He is merely following his orders. As I am certain your own captain does." He turned to the captain of the gate. "I will take responsibility from here. The extra caution is unnecessary. I am under orders from the king. We arranged accommodations for all of the queen's guard before I left. Have those plans changed?" The captain looked dissatisfied, but shaking his head in answer, he and his guard stepped aside.

"I will continue to lead you," Rigen said.

"Thank you," Aina said. "Our journey has been long, and I am certain my men and their horses are tired. As must your escort be. Can you see that my men are given food and a place to rest?"

"It will be my pleasure, Your Majesty," Rigen said with a smile. "Please follow me." He turned and ordered the gates opened.

Still squeezed between the soldiers of their escort, the queen and her guard passed through the gate into a large open marketplace. They were surprised to find the streets as deserted as the fields had been. Aina looked around at the windows of the adjoining buildings. She caught sight of numerous faces, cautiously watching the arrival of the neighboring queen, but many windows were shuttered closed. It was obvious that the streets had been cleared of all traffic.

"You can dismount here," Rigen said. "Our grooms will see to your horses." As the queen and the guard dismounted, numerous attendants appeared.

Morik came to stand at the queen's elbow. "Where is everyone?" he wondered. "It's not right."

"Patience," the queen advised. "Not all cities are run as ours."

Rigen led them beside an inn. "Your guard will be cared for here," he said, gesturing to the building. At the open door stood the innkeeper, nervously wringing the white apron that hung around his waist. "They will find refreshment awaiting them inside," Rigen continued, "and they will be quartered upstairs. If you please," and he gestured with open arms that they should enter.

Aina turned to Morik and waited. "Five of us will stay with the queen," her captain said flatly. "The others can go rest." The queen nodded her approval.

Rigen shrugged his shoulders but made no comment. When the guard had entered the inn and the door closed behind them, Rigen said pleasantly, "This way, if you please." He led them to a palatial building edging the marketplace. Several guards came to attention at their approach.

Rigen turned to address the queen. "Your Majesty, I must ask your guard to surrender their swords before we enter."

"Not happening," Morik stated flatly.

"Your Majesty, please understand—" Aina held up her hand and turned to Morik.

"Captain, how many visitors to my court have you allowed to enter into my presence wearing their swords?"

Morik hung his head and furrowed his brow. "None, Your Majesty."

"Would you agree then, that it is common practice to enter unarmed before the king or queen?"

"Yes, Your Majesty," Morik answered reluctantly.

"Then you and your men will surrender your swords," she commanded. Then she turned to Rigen. "Of course, they may keep their knives, can't they? So they don't have to feel too naked. I'm sure you understand."

Rigen was taken off-guard by her request and muttered, "Yes, of course. No harm in that." Morik looked up in time to see the queen smiling at him.

They were admitted to the palace and Rigen led them through a series of large halls and entryways. In contrast to the empty streets and marketplace, the palace was alive with activity. Armed soldiers seemed to be everywhere, coming and going, many just standing along the walls, as if awaiting orders.

"Mostly officers," Morik commented quietly to the queen.

"Where there are officers," Aina replied, "somewhere there is an army waiting to be led. I wonder where. And against whom."

They were taken to a small antechamber. A table within was laid with food and drink. To the side, along the wall, were a washbowl and towels.

"Your Majesty," Rigen said, "refresh yourself here while I announce your arrival to the king."

"Most fitting," Aina replied. "Thank you. The refreshments are welcome." They were left alone, although several guards were posted outside the door. Aina's men were drawn to the food and drink. The queen went to wash her hands and face.

"At least I can freshen up a bit before meeting with King Bellek," she commented. She glanced around the walls of the room and sighed, "A mirror is all I'm missing." She looked over to the men at the table. "Morik, pour me a drink, please. I'm parched."

"Yes, Your Majesty," he said and brought her a filled cup.

Their rest was all too brief. Before long, Rigen reappeared at the door to the room. "The king will receive you now," he announced.

"Excellent," Aina said, glancing at her guards. "Shall we go?"

Flanked by members of the Warrensfold guard, they were escorted to large double doors guarded by two sentries. When they saw Rigen, they opened the doors and allowed them entry, carefully eyeing the queen and her guards.

They entered a spacious receiving room. A modest fire burned on the great hearth to the side and the room was backed by large windows letting in the daylight. This was obviously an audience chamber. Near to the back wall sat the king. He was surrounded by his advisors, deep in discussion, so that Aina could not yet see him. It was only when they came to stand before the throne that the courtiers and officials parted. Aina was unable to suppress her gasp.

"You!" she spit out. "What are you doing here?"

"Not a very friendly greeting," said the man from the throne, sounding disappointed. "After all these years, I expected something more cordial. I am, after all, your stepfather."

"You're a snake, Worrah," Aina said bitterly.

"You are hardly arrived, and already you have harsh words for me, my dear," Worrah replied, unruffled by her greeting. "Come, bring a chair for the Queen of Gladur Nock, so that we may converse civilly. She is, after all, a queen, even if she gained her crown through force."

"Others gain their rank through trickery and deceit," she sneered.

"We all have our methods, we royals, do we not?" he answered.

"There is nothing royal about you except the title you stole," Aina scoffed.

"Oh, dear," Worrah said, looking innocently at his advisors who gaped in amazement at this conversation. "We have certainly started off on the wrong foot. I suggest we begin again. Please, Aina, be seated," he said, indicating the chair that had been brought for her.

Aina remained standing. "I have no business with you, Worrah. I came upon the invitation of your sovereign, King Bellek. I certainly did not come to banter words with you."

"Bellek is indisposed and cannot meet with you," Worrah said lightly.

"Where is the king?" she demanded.

"You are before him," Worrah said with a smile.

"I came to speak with King Bellek. What are you doing sitting on his throne? I was invited by the king and came to negotiate with him. He wrote to me that he was willing to discuss peace."

"As I explained, Bellek is indisposed. It was I who invited you to come here."

"Where is King Bellek?" Aina asked again.

"You are persistent," Worrah sighed. "Bellek has suffered a most unfortunate accident. Fortunately for the realm, he placed me into this trusted and high position beforehand, making the transition to my leadership seamless. He signed decrees that if anything should happen to him, I should sit as king in his place until such time that he could regain his health."

"Yet another kingdom usurped? You had him murdered," Aina accused.

Worrah looked shocked. "Do you take me for a regicide? I am hurt that you have such a low opinion of me. I assure you that Bellek is alive." He turned to look among his advisors. "He is alive, is he not, Rigen?"

"Yes, Your Majesty, he lives," Rigen said with a nod.

"You see?" Worrah said to Aina. "But still, you cannot meet with him. You will have to do all of your negotiating with me."

"I came to speak with the King of Warrensfold," Aina insisted.

"Do you see me on the throne? That makes me the King of Warrensfold."

Aina took a deep breath. "You have lured me here under false pretenses. We shall leave." So speaking she turned to the door, but at a sign from Worrah, guards stepped in her way.

"I am sorry, Your Majesty," Worrah said. "I have need of you here."

Aina turned back to him. "Very well," she said, taking a deep breath and getting her passions under control. "Then tell me what plans you have for our discussions?"

"I was so pleased when your dispatch came," Worrah said with a satisfied smile. "I have long wanted to meet with you again, ever since you so unfairly drove me from my throne in Gladur."

"Another throne you did not deserve."

"A throne that was mine by right of marriage," Worrah pointed out. "Just as your husband sat on his throne by the same rights."

"Sat?"

"He is elsewhere than on his throne at the moment," Worrah said with a dismissive wave of his hand. "I suspect he will not see it again soon."

"What do you know about my husband's whereabouts?" Aina asked, her eyes growing wide.

"Seemingly more than you do," Worrah answered with a sly smile. "However, I have no intentions of discussing him further. I want to come to some accord how to make the most of your visit."

"How about crossing swords?" Aina spat out. "I never could tolerate you."

Worrah laughed. "Ten years ago I would have welcomed that offer and enjoyed the opportunity to measure the length of our swords, one against the other. I would have relished watching your blood flow into the grass. But age has refined my tastes. I have greater plans for you than a commonplace sword fight. That's something we can enjoy any day. What I have in store for you is unique."

A thrill of fear ran through the queen at these words. She stole a glance at Morik, but he was not looking at her. He was not going to wait for the queen's permission to act. In one fluid movement, he drew his knife and leapt at the throne.

Worrah's guards were prepared for this. Morik hardly had his knife unsheathed before they pounced on him and the four others. There was a brief scuffle, and then it was over. Two of the queen's guard were violently thrown to the ground and pinned there. Two others found themselves with swords at their throats. Morik had managed to wound one of the guards who jumped him, but he was no match for all of them. They disarmed him and had both his arms pinned behind his back.

Worrah stood and looked carefully into Morik's face. "I like men of spirit and initiative." He studied his features. "You look familiar," he said, but it was not with friendliness. "Judging by your age and rank,

I am willing to wager that you used to provide me and my court with precious entertainment. You've risen far from the pen I kept you in." He waited for Morik to respond, but the captain of the queen's guard only glared back at him. "I'll tell you what I'll do," Worrah continued. "I will present you with yet another chance. I am a man who believes in second chances. Serve me, and I will raise you higher than you ever imagined possible."

Morik's answer was to spit in Worrah's face. The king made an ugly sound in his throat and swung his arm, delivering a vicious back-handed slap. His ring left an angry welt across Morik's cheek. "Thank you for the clarity of your response," Worrah said wiping his face. "Still, I will raise you. You, and all of your brethren in the guard shall be raised together. I will raise your heads high for the faithful service you have done the queen. Faithful service deserves its reward, does it not? How about raised on a spike at the gates to the city? Of course, we will have to remove your heads from your shoulders to get them that high, but we all make sacrifices to be highly honored." With a dismissive gesture he had them dragged away from the throne. He turned his attention back to the queen.

"As for you, Aina, I have a special entertainment in store. I would not want you to have come all this way in vain. We have in Warrensfold an exclusive fate for those who are considered a danger to the wellbeing of the common folk."

"When did you ever care about the common people?" Aina shot back.

"Oh, dear Aina, I have always cared for them. It is upon their backs that my table is set. Where would I be without them? I may occasionally have to cull them, but I will protect them. Your arrival presents me with a unique opportunity. Here I have before me a woman who cavorts with dragons. I have heard, you keep one lavishly cared for in your own palace. You know what that makes you, do you not?"

"You would not dare."

"I do not need to dare, only act. You are a witch, Aina of Gladur, and I shall act against you, in the name of the people."

"I came here under safe conduct," Aina cried out as guards stepped forward to restrain her.

"Did you? Does a witch deserve safe conduct? However, I am just. Rest assured, I will see you safely conducted. Have no fear of that. You shall be very safely conducted. Guards, take them all away." He then turned to an attendant who had just entered the room. "Has her guard been provided for?"

"We fell upon them as they ate," he reported. "They are all securely in chains."

"Excellent. See that the queen is kept separate from her guard," Worrah cautioned. "Who knows what mischief they could brew up if we let them get together?"

"It shall be so, Your Majesty," he said and followed the guards who had seized the queen.

Worrah turned to Rigen. "How neatly it unfolds," he said with a smile. "You'd think we had a Luck Dragon on our side." And they both laughed.

As they were being forced out of the chamber, Morik found himself for a final moment beside the queen. "The king will hear of this, will he not?" he asked, desperation in his voice.

"Where the king is and what he hears are not in my power to predict," Aina gasped. "Let us hope that he has better fortune than our own." These were the last words she could speak with him before they were forcibly separated.

Chapter Twenty-One

In the King's Dungeon

*T*he King of Gladur Nock lay on the cold stone floor and stared into the darkness. *What did I do wrong?* he pondered. *How did they find me? And so quickly? Who betrayed me?*

He had been walking across the marketplace just as the evening bell rang, when guards appeared out of nowhere and arrested him without explanation. He had tried to escape them, but they were armed, he was not, and all he got for his efforts was a cuff to the side of his head with the butt of someone's sword. They dragged him off and tossed him into this dark hole. As a last insult, they had shackled his wrists to a long chain that ran through an iron ring above his head.

How am I going to get out of here? Thoughts swirled in his head and he wished sleep would wipe them away, but it was as elusive as the answers to his many questions. He could hear the heavy breathing of another prisoner in his cell. He had noticed him when they dragged him in and shackled him, but when the guards left, they took the light with them. It was dark, and he had been in no mood for talking.

He lay there listening to the guards' conversation which reached him with the slice of dim light through the crack under the door. They were playing cards, and he followed the randomness of their talk. Listening to them was by far preferable to heeding the unanswered questions that ran through his mind over and over again. The guards covered every topic—from what the king ate for dinner to the poor quality of their own ale and the latest gossip they heard from their wives. Time passed slowly and their idle chatter never ceased.

All at once, he heard a commotion. Someone had unexpectedly arrived. "Woman, what are you doing here?" one of the guards ask.

"I've brought his food," he heard the woman respond.

"Leave it over there," the guard said gruffly.

"I'll do nothing of the sort," the woman objected. "I know what you've got in mind. Once I leave you'll eat it. I wasn't sent to line your idle stomachs. I was sent to feed the prisoner. Orders from Bellek. He wants him well treated, you understand, as befits a captive king."

"First I've heard of that," the guard grumbled. "So what do you want from us?"

"Open his door, you cabbage heads. Has the ale dimmed your brains? Open his door so I can deliver my goods. I want to satisfy myself that he receives what I bring. Now open up. And be quick about it."

The king heard the guard fumbling for his keys. His feet scraped on the stones as he shuffled across the floor. "I don't remember being told about opening for any of the likes of you," the guard grumbled.

"And that's because your head is too full of ale to remember," he heard the woman scold. "And you'll be soon on the other side of one of these doors if you don't open up quicker. Hurry up, this basket isn't getting lighter."

"I'm going, I'm going." There was more jangling of keys. "Don't be such a scold. Worse 'n my old Meg," the guard complained.

"And if you don't hurry, next time I'll bring your old Meg with me to get you to move faster," the woman threatened.

The guard chuckled to himself, "You're a feisty one, you are. Just don't be too long. This one's dangerous."

"Can't be too bad," the woman said, "seeing that they put you in charge of him."

"Don't be fooled," the guard said, his speech slightly slurred. "I'm mighty fearsome with a sword."

"Then may I never cross you," the woman said. "Now leave me to my ministerings."

The prisoner heard the bolt drawn and then the door to his cell opened up. He squinted at the light from the lamp she held in her hand as she took a step into the cell.

"Give a call when you want out," the guard said crossly, closing the door behind her. There was the sound of the bolt being slapped back into place.

The prisoner sat up and gaped. Before him stood a middle-aged matron who moments before he would have sworn was a kingdom away. He could not believe his eyes.

"You are a marvel," he said. "How did you do this? How did you find me?"

She walked up to the king with a big smile, placing the lantern on the floor beside him. "Hush," she scolded, placing a finger to her lips to get him to keep his voice low. "I've brought you something to eat," she said loudly, intended for the guard in case he was listening at the door. She placed the basket on the floor beside the lantern and pulled the cloth away from the top. The king's face showed surprise when he saw what was within. Barely hidden, lay a dagger among the bread, cooked meat and fruit.

"That simple? You just walk in and bring this to me?"

She reached in the basket and pulled out a bottle, handing it to him with an invitation that he drink.

"It may look simple, but I labored in getting it to you," she explained. "You have to strengthen yourself. Even if you're a king, hunger can humble you."

"Humbled I am, believe me. I'm in a tough situation."

"I've heard you've been in worse," she said lightly. The king looked up. "Rumor is that as a young untried knight you were captured in the forest, hogtied, and about to have your throat cut, so the story goes. By brigands, no less. Two men and two women, I heard. And still you got away. You ran them off and ended up eating the very meal they had prepared for themselves. Is that only a rumor, or is it true?"

The flicker of a smile cross his face. "True it is, Maisy," he said. "Very true, indeed. As only you could know." But then concern darkened his features, and he asked in a low voice, "Maisy, do you know of my son and young Elinor? And how do things stand with the queen?"

Her response alarmed him. "Not well, my King, not well at all." Then she leaned over, close to his ear, "Yet all is not lost. Not yet." With these words her voice abruptly changed. It had an unmistakable chime-like quality, as if Star had spoken.

Michael's eyes shot open. A grey, morning light filled the cell. He sat up with a clanging of his chains and reached beside him. There was no basket next to him on the stone floor. No lantern. No sign of Maisy. He took a deep breath. It had all been a dream, yet so real, he could still hear her last words ringing in his ears. *All is not lost.*

His eyes were drawn to the man who sat along the opposite wall of this small room. He remembered listening to his breathing in the night. The man sat there gazing at him. He was not shackled.

"Must have been an interesting dream," the man commented. "Did you lose something you wish you still had?"

Michael was embarrassed. "It was very real," he laughed bitterly. Then he looked closely at his cellmate. He sat wrapped in a faded green traveling cloak. He was an older man whose greying beard and hair were streaked with black. He had a beak of a nose, and his eyes shone with a strength that was palpable, even in the dim light of their cell. Suddenly, the stranger's features were absurdly familiar. Astonished, the king's mouth hung open as he stared at him. "Am I still dreaming?" he muttered.

Seeing Michael's shock, the older man laughed. "It's been awhile, hasn't it?"

"You," Michael spoke in a choked voice. "But that's not possible."

"Because I must be long dead?" he asked.

Michael mutely nodded his head. When he could speak again, he said, "You look even younger than when I saw you last. Your hair used to be snow white."

The old man shrugged his shoulders. "One of the peculiarities of being in my line of work," he said.

"What are you doing here?" Michael marveled.

"Just yesterday, I was asking myself that very question. I thought I had the answer, but it felt oddly incomplete. But I've learned that if I'm patient, what is missing usually presents itself. Today, you are the answer to the riddle of what I am still doing here. It's now obvious to me that I've been awaiting your arrival. Now, I'm curious to find out what you are doing here?"

"Yesterday," Michael recounted, " I came looking for my son. I was captured in the marketplace."

"What a strange place to go looking for your son," the old man said. "Why is he not in your own good land?"

Michael hung his head in embarrassment. "He ran off," he said in a low voice. "It was my own fault. I chased him off."

"And how is your Luck Dragon?" the old man asked next. "Do you not care for a most precious guest in your kingdom?"

Without looking up, Michael said in a murmur, "The dragon is ill."

"How did you fall to such a sorry state, O King?" the old man asked, with great sadness in his voice.

"Worrah—" the king mumbled.

The old man would not let him speak further. "Worrah?" he exploded. "You have not laid eyes on Worrah since he escaped after you defeated him at the Battle at the Straits. He has not even come down here to gloat over you yet, although once he gets my message he will be tempted. Worrah? No, O King, look no further than yourself to find the cause of your downfall."

"How dare you say such a thing to me?" Michael growled threateningly, his eyes blazing.

"How dare you remain blind to how your life has unraveled?" the old man countered. "It is time to wake up and see how you have managed to take every piece of good fortune that was entrusted to you and turned it against yourself."

"This is preposterous!" the king objected.

"Is it indeed?" his cellmate continued. "We sanctified and celebrated your wedding to Aina for seven days. It was a magnificent event. There was feasting and dancing on the green. It was as if the world had been renewed. And what have you done to the woman you thought you could never have, yet in whose name you fought a wild dragon—and won? You suspect you've chased her into the arms of your rival."

The king grabbed the chains that restrained his arms, shook them violently and snarled, "What do you know about them?"

"That due to your continued, self-imposed absence, the queen relies on him for what she should rely on you. Yet the list of your failings does not stop there." The king glared at the old man, but said nothing. "You became king of a people you released from an oppressive and cruel rule."

"And they are grateful," the king said sullenly. "The kingdom thrives."

"Yet not as a result of much effort on your part. You avoid your duties as king. You escape whenever possible. When was the last time you sat in judgment at court? It is a kingdom run by the queen."

"They are her people. They have an inherent trust in her," the king said defensively.

"And they have developed an inherent mistrust in you because you have not given them the chance to get to know you. You are close to the army, to your commanders, but to your people you are an absent king. You even disdain their forms of celebration."

The king was stung by these words. Finally, he said, "Their ways of rejoicing are strange to me."

"Then make an effort to become familiar with their ways. You may be surprised by what you'll find."

"I suppose," the king said with a defeated shrug.

The old man pressed mercilessly on. "And should we speak next of your son?" The king's eyes shot up and he pulled his chains taut.

"You've driven him away, right into the hands of your greatest enemy. Or, at least, that is what you came here to find out."

"What do you know of this?" the king bellowed. "Is he here?"

"And then there is Star," his cellmate continued. "I left in your care the greatest gift any ruler or kingdom could wish for: a Luck Dragon. Through his presence and your meticulous and conscientious care, you could expect fortune, prosperity and peace. Yet what do you have instead? The plague is knocking at your door, the crops are failing, your cattle diseased. You have been in constant frontier skirmishes since taking the crown. Your family is in shambles and your dragon is ill."

Hearing the truth spoken was too much for him. Tears streamed down his cheeks and into his beard. "But what has gone wrong?" Michael cried out. "How has the dragon failed me?"

"Ask instead how you have failed the dragon," the old man said accusingly. "It is a pity that King Pell died. You could have spent some time in his tutelage on how to properly care for a Luck Dragon."

"King Pell? Of Nogardia? King Pell *never* cared for Star," Michael said vehemently. "*I* lived in the compound for ten years. *I* cared for the dragon every single day. On his rare visits, King Pell's contribution to Star's care was to walk through and nod his head in approval of the hard work we were doing. It was Garth who ran the compound, not Pell. Garth and Mali and Keg. They understood how to care for a dragon. And they put him into *my* care."

"Only because King Pell knew who to place in positions of trust. He knew where he was needed. He used his time to care for the kingdom, passing judgment where judgment was needed and looking after his family. You were friends with his son, were you not? Did he reject his father and his ways?"

"No," the king said slowly, remembering the friend he had known as Frog. "He idolized his father. He said he always wanted to become just like him, both kind and wise, yet able to make difficult decisions and stand by them, or ..." He trailed off.

"Or what?" he demanded.

"Or have the courage to admit when he's made a mistake and then do what he can to rectify it." The king nearly choked on these words.

The old man was not finished with him. "And what did you think about your friend Frog, heir to the throne of Nogardia, although he was destined to lose the blessings of the dragon?"

"I used to think he was the luckiest boy in the world." His eyes grew wide. He looked up at the old man, pleading, "Help me find Corin. I must speak with Aina. Can you help me?"

"I fear you will see them far sooner than you wish and in circumstances that will bring dread to your heart. I wish I could help you, but you have labored long, though unwittingly, to bring this end upon your own head. Nothing will ever be the same again."

Then the old man rose to his feet and walked to the cell door. He banged on it and yelled, "Jail Keep! Open up! Take me to the king. Tell him I'm ready to give him what he wants."

Chapter Twenty-Two

The Black Lake

"Are you sure we're doing the right thing?" Elinor asked. She sounded nervous. They were surrounded on all sides by guards and shuttled through halls and corridors. They could see little of the rooms or even the walls of the hallways because the guards hemmed them in so closely.

"It's a little late to reconsider," Corin said. "We don't have much choice at this point but to see things through."

"Do you think he'll be here to meet us?" she asked.

"I certainly hope so," Corin replied.

"But maybe Thos had something else in mind," Elinor said.

"Then we've made a big mistake because I don't think there is any going back."

"Do you know what you're going to say?" she asked.

"I'm rehearsing it in my head as we walk," Corin admitted. "After all, Bellek is a king, and I'm the prince of the neighboring kingdom. We can be cordial."

"How well do you know him?"

"We've never met," Corin confessed with a weak smile.

They had just entered a large hall, and the guard opened up enough for them to look around. It was warm in the room, and a bright fire was burning in the large hearth. Corin's attention was fixed on the knot of men they had been brought before.

One man among them was seated, and Corin decided this must be King Bellek. His hair and beard were greying, but he had a sharp, penetrating eye and was powerfully built. He looked up at their arrival, but appeared only curious why such a large escort had arrived with these visitors. Attending the king, some with papers in their hands, stood a number of richly dressed men. Corin's attention was drawn to one in particular. He had a round face, a ring in one ear, and a pheasant feather in his hat. He was the nobleman who had overseen Elinor's kidnapping!

The man's mouth fell open when he looked up at them. "Unbelievable!" he exclaimed. "Delivered into your hands. You now have them all, Your Majesty."

The king looked at the speaker and his eyes grew wide. "What are you telling me, Rigen?"

"That this is the very girl you sent me to kidnap. And unless I'm mistaken, beside her is the heir apparent."

"King Bellek," Corin stammered, stepping forward. "Let me introduce myself!"

The king leapt from his throne and pounced upon Corin. He grabbed hold of his tunic and lifted him from the floor, revealing how strong he was. "This is, indeed, my lucky day," he said into Corin's face, his eyes large with delight. Then he let Corin down, raised his right arm and brought it crashing down against the side of Corin's head. Elinor shrieked and the prince crumpled on the spot. He had no more need for his well-rehearsed lines.

A short time later, Elinor stood, bound, in a small waiting room furnished with a single wooden chair against the wall. She had been sent there with an escort of two guards and told to wait. Her guards stood stoically on either side of her, silent at her attempts to get them to answer her questions. The door opened, and in stepped the king and the man she had heard him call Rigen. They both looked very pleased with themselves.

"So, this is the elusive young lady," the king said.

"Third time's the charm," Rigen said. "You won't escape me this time."

"Nor did you capture me," Elinor said sharply. "We came willingly."

Worrah smiled. "She's spunky. I like that. Much like her aunt when she was her age. Always standing up to me and talking back."

Elinor eyed him suspiciously. "You're not the king, are you?" she said, the truth dawning on her. "You are the queen's stepfather. I've heard of you."

"Let me assure you," he said, bringing his face close to hers, "I *am* the king."

"Why did you have me kidnapped?" Elinor demanded.

"To lure the others here," Worrah admitted. "But it looks like I did not have to go to all that trouble. You have obligingly delivered yourselves to me."

"We came here as envoys for peace," Elinor spoke quickly. "We were summoned."

Worrah held up his hand to stop her from saying more. "I know all about your mission. You have come to offer me help in making peace." He spoke it as if it had been a lesson learned in school. "So there might be harmony between my kingdom and yours." Then he continued with a laugh. "I must say, the old man has delivered in spades. Indeed, we finally do have a chance for an enduring peace."

He turned to Rigen and said in a serious voice, "Now that we have finished with the trial, we can move forward unhindered with the sentences."

"Trial?" Elinor exclaimed. "What trial?

"That's right, young lady," Worrah said with a smile, turning back to her. "I suspect that you are unaware that your aunt is here as well."

"The Queen is here?" Elinor cried out.

"Her visit has been quite eventful," Worrah continued. "She has been found guilty of witchcraft."

"But you can't do that!"

"Actually, I believe I can. And your uncle will be dealt with as a pretender to the throne," Worrah continued.

"The king?" Elinor's head was swimming.

"The heir apparent will quietly disappear. Peace will be assured by eliminating the royal family of Gladur Nock. I am sorry to have to include you in these unfortunate proceedings, but as you do stand in line to the throne, we must be attentive to tie off all loose ends. Farewell, young lady." He turned to go. "Come, Rigen."

Elinor's mind raced. How could she save herself? In spite of her bound hands, she tried to leap at Worrah, but the guards anticipated her movement and held her back. "He'll come to save me," she shouted at Worrah's back. This caused him to turn around, an amused smile on his face.

"Who, my dear?" he asked. "You certainly can't mean any of the royal family. Do you have a young lover in the king's guard? By the time he receives word of what happens here today, you shall be long cold."

"Star," she spit at him. "He has saved me before. I can summon him without words. He will come and bring destruction to you all." She was grabbing at straws, but she got the effect she desired. At her words, Worrah's eyebrows raised in interest.

"Indeed, is this what you believe?" he asked.

"Star will come. He will seek me out and protect me. And Corin. Don't do something you will regret."

"I hate doing things I will regret," Worrah said, nodding his head. "Star? We're talking about the dragon, are we not?"

"Yes," Elinor exclaimed. "The dragon. He is immense and breathes fire and will destroy you all." She knew none of this was true, but her hands were bound and she needed a big stick.

"Are you sure he will come?" Worrah asked. Elinor missed the interest in his voice. She wanted to believe that he was worried.

"Without a doubt," she replied. "Release us, or I guarantee he is already on his way."

"Guaranteed?" Worrah asked.

"Guaranteed," Elinor stated confidently.

"Then we must hurry," Worrah said. Elinor felt victorious. She held up her bound hands, expecting him to cut her loose. Instead, he turned back towards the door and ordered curtly, "Bring her." The guards had her by her arms and forced her to follow behind Worrah and Rigen.

"What a glorious day," she heard Worrah say to his companion. "The dragon, too."

The guards followed closely behind the king, keeping a firm hold on their prisoner. They passed through the same receiving hall where they had first been brought before Worrah. They retraced their steps to the main entrance to the palace.

With confident steps, Worrah led them out through the main streets of the town. They passed by an open marketplace where an empty cart surrounded by piles of dried brush had been placed in its center. The guards dragged Elinor forward whenever she lagged. They soon came to one of the gates to the city. They paused a moment there as Worrah gave orders to a guard who then rushed off back into the city. They continued on their way out into the open fields surrounding the town.

It was a bright, clear day. To the left of the gates, a gradual slope led down into a shallow ravine. Elinor saw the line of trees of the forest. If she could make a dash for those trees, it could mean safety. But the guards showed no sign of loosening their hold on her, and she doubted that with her hands tied she could outrun them.

Worrah led them down into the ravine. Elinor saw that at its lowest point there was a small lake. She saw several figures standing on its shore, but they were still too far away for her to recognize anyone. The water of the lake was oddly dark, black even, as from stagnant water. As they marched closer, she noticed an odd and revolting smell in the air, a mixture of rotting vegetation and something that she could not identify.

The closer they came, the thicker the odor hung in the air, and Elinor guessed it was coming from the stagnant water of the lake. Then she recognized her cousin among those standing at its shore.

"Sprout!" she cried out, and he looked up to see her coming. He did not look well. His hands were bound and there was a cut above his left eye where Worrah had struck him. A trickle of dried blood ran down the side of his face. Seeing their approach, however, he perked up.

"King Bellek, you're making a mistake," Corin called out. "I've come to help you."

"Indeed you have," the king replied, taking the last steps to close the space between them.

"He's not Bellek," Elinor said bitterly. "It's Worrah."

"Worrah?" Corin's eyes were wide with shock. "You're Worrah?"

"*King* Worrah," he said. "Why does your family have such a hard time accepting that?" When Corin just stared at him blankly, he continued. "Anyway, there's been a change of plans. I'm not going to sink you in the lake after all. You are going to help me catch a dragon."

Worrah turned to Rigen. "Take them out yourself and see that they are comfortable." The guards took hold of their prisoners and started leading them to a rowboat pulled up in the shallows of the lake.

"Worrah," Corin called over his shoulder. "Listen to me."

Worrah ignored him and was giving orders to a guard, who rushed off at a run toward the city gate. Then he turned back to Corin with a nasty smile. "Two's company, three's a crowd. I like crowds. I wonder what that makes four? A sticky mess? Let's find out."

The smell from the lake was strong. The black slime along the shore was thick and sticky to step into. "What *is* this?" Elinor asked out loud, but no one answered her question.

"I'll take the girl first," Rigen said. Her guards forced her into the boat and Rigen seated himself at the oars. The other guards pushed the boat into deeper water, cursing at the slime on the shore that stuck to their boots.

Elinor looked down at her own boots and the black scum sticking to them. "What is this?" she asked again.

"Welcome to the Black Lake," Rigen announced. "What is stuck to your boots and what gives the water its distinctive color and unpleasant odor is tar. Black Lake is a giant tar pit, with just enough water covering it at this time of year to skim a boat along the surface. It is not a thick layer, which is why I am transporting you one at a time. I don't wish to get stuck."

"But where are we going?" Elinor asked.

"We are nearly there," Rigen said, pointing over his shoulder with his chin as he rowed. Elinor looked beyond Rigen and saw a platform out in the lake, nearer to the farther shore. "That is where I will deliver you."

"But for what purpose?" Elinor asked.

"You will learn that soon enough," Rigen replied.

A few moments later, the boat came alongside the float. "Careful stepping out. I wouldn't want you to fall in. Just yet at least." Although it was awkward with her hands tied, Elinor managed to get onto the float safely. She turned around to see that Rigen was already rowing back the way they had come. She looked around at the black water that surrounded her. *Oh, Star,* she thought, *I am in serious trouble again.* She heard a voice within her respond, *I am nearly there.* Even if she were only imagining it, she was comforted by the words.

She sat and watched Rigen's boat pick up Corin and then turn back toward the float. When it was alongside, she helped Corin onto the float beside her.

"Step further back," Rigen ordered them. "Away from this edge." When the cousins complied, Rigen pulled a dagger from his belt and drove it into the wood of the float. "So you can cut your bonds," he said. "It will be more entertaining to watch you flail when you do eventually fall in." He paused a moment and admired the blade. It was the one that Thos had given to Corin, taken from him when they were made prisoners. "Nice knife you have," Rigen commented. "It's a shame to see it go into the goo. But those are the king's orders."

"It's your own," Corin remarked, wondering at Rigen's words.

"That's not my knife," he said flatly. "Never seen it before."

Corin was puzzled. "That's the dagger the magician took from you in the market. Or at least one very much like it."

Rigen looked up at him with surprise on his face. "You were there? How our lives have intertwined. Indeed that shameless thief did lift a knife from me that day, but this was not it. Mine was inlaid with silver. That knife I would like to get back." Without another word, he pushed off from the float and rowed across the lake, leaving the cousins stranded.

"We could swim for shore," Elinor said, gazing at the nearer land.

"I doubt we would make it," Corin said, crouching down to retrieve the dagger, and with its sharp edge he cut the ropes that bound his hands. "Trying to swim, we would sink lower than the boat, and once stuck in the tar, we would be pulled down." As soon as his hands were free, he pulled the knife from the wood and turned to cut Elinor's ropes. "Odd," he commented, gazing at the design on the blade. "I believe him that he'd never seen this dagger before. But why would Thos go to all the trouble to make me think it came from Rigen instead … ?" Then he knew what Thos had wanted him to think.

"The dagger really came from Thos," he said aghast. "It all makes sense now. The full moon ceremony …"

Chapter Twenty-Three

The Blade Strikes Home

*L*ook!" Elinor called out. Rigen was once again rowing the boat across the lake towards the float. In the boat sat another man with his hands bound.

"Father!" Corin exclaimed. The King of Gladur Nock sat in the boat, an impassive expression on his face. "What is *he* doing here?"

"The prince steps back and shows me the knife I left," Rigen ordered when he came near the float. "The girl will help the king from the boat." Corin did as he was told and Elinor rushed to help her uncle step onto the float. Rigen did not linger, but began rowing back immediately.

"Uncle," Elinor exclaimed. "What are you doing here?" Corin stepped over to cut his father's hands free.

"I came looking for Corin," he explained calmly. "However, I despair to see you both here. We are in a desperate situation." He turned to his son. "Do you think we could swim?"

"I've been thinking that Elinor might have a chance," Corin replied. "She is light and if she just skims the surface, she might make it. But if the water level grows thinner near the shoreline, I fear she would be sucked under."

"I'm not going to just wait here," the king declared, pacing the float, looking for some escape.

"You don't have to," Elinor exclaimed.

"What do you mean?" her uncle asked.

"Star's coming," she said.

"Star?" the king exclaimed. "Why do you say that?"

"I can feel him," she said. "He knows I'm in trouble, and I can feel that he is coming. It's the same way I felt when he and Sprout saved me right after I had arrived in Gladur."

"Star told me about your connection," the king said. "Did you summon him?"

"I guess so," Elinor said, shrugging her shoulders. "I don't know how I do it, but I am certain he is on his way."

At these words, Corin and his father looked around at the Black Lake and then at one another. They were thinking the same thing. Corin turned to his cousin. "You have to tell him to go back. Tell him to stay away."

"Whatever for?" Elinor asked. "He'll come right to where I am."

"That's exactly what they're hoping for," Corin said. "They want you to lure him to come to you."

"Tell him to turn back," the king said. "Tell him it's too dangerous. Because once he sees all three of us—" He was interrupted by a loud cry on the shore. They looked up to see a clump of soldiers pointing into the sky. Michael looked up and dread filled his heart. The immense winged shadow against the sky could be nothing other than—Star.

The dragon circled three times around the open fields, sinking lower with each pass. The king was gesturing wildly and calling out as loudly as he could for Star to turn aside and go elsewhere.

"What's that wrapped around his body?" Corin asked. "What are those lines hanging from him?"

The king was stumped a moment, and then remembered. "Before I left, we placed the harness onto him, the one he uses to carry the wagon during the processions."

"Whatever for?"

"He had grown weak and was having difficulty sitting up," his father recounted. "He asked that we truss him up and use the lines tied to the rafters in the barn to help him sit up."

"It looks like he brought part of the barn with him," Elinor reflected. The ends of several of the lines hung down and Star flew low enough that they could see that some were still tied to pieces of wood. "He must have torn down half the rafters to get out of there."

"What a clever fellow," Corin said. "It's as if he knew."

"Knew what?" his father asked, but Corin did not respond. They watched as Star circled for the last time and flew down, skimming the surface of the lake's brackish water, and came to a stop only feet away from the float, his chimes ringing wildly.

"Quickly," Star implored them. "Jump onto my wing."

The impact of the landing had disturbed the surface of the water, and the float began pitching wildly. They leapt from the float to land safely onto his outstretched wing.

"Star!" the king shouted. "You cannot stay here. This lake is a tar pit. It's a trap. Get out."

"Too late," the dragon said. "My legs are already caught. Go to shore across my wing." He stretched it out even more until it touched the nearest shore.

"Quick," Corin shouted. "Gather the lines. The harness lines."

His father saw immediately what Corin was thinking. "But we need something to attach them to, so he won't sink any deeper. There are no trees on the shore."

"Use these," Star said. "I thought you might have need of them." The dragon opened his immense mouth and they saw he had been carrying a collection of swords. Twisting his long neck, he deposited them on his wing next to them.

"Never did much care for the taste of swords," he muttered. Corin was already busy collecting the lines. Tied to pieces of wood, they were floating on the surface of the lake.

Picking up the swords, the king found his own among them. "My sword," he marveled.

"You left it in my care, O Dragon Master. It is time I returned it to you. I thought you might have use for it. And from what I see, I am not mistaken."

Taking the lines from the harness and using Star's wing as a bridge, they walked the shoreline, at intervals driving the swords into the ground and fastening the lines to them.

The soldiers standing guard near to the lake watched these strange proceedings and saw that their prisoners had escaped and were now armed. They marched down to the shore with the intention of recapturing them, but they had not reckoned with the king. As soon as they were within range, out flashed his sword. One fell, he disarmed two of them and wounded a fourth before they realized that they were not up against a man, but a human whirlwind, armed and furious. Abandoning the weapons they had lost, and supporting their wounded comrade, they beat a hasty retreat.

The king took the helmet from the fallen soldier and fitted it onto his own head. He picked up the short shield, more of a buckler. Taking the swords the others had abandoned, carrying two and tucking one into his belt, the king returned to help secure the lines to keep the dragon from sinking lower into the tar of the Black Lake.

"Star, where did you get these?" the king called out, referring to the swords the dragon had brought. They were not much good for battle, dented, the edges dull, and rusting in parts.

"It was the best I could find," Star responded. "They were stored in a closet near to my bed."

"I've got you something to fight with," Michael called to the cousins, holding up the soldiers' swords.

"Uncle, look," Elinor called out. A line of soldiers had appeared. Along the ridge of the higher land around them, Worrah, on his horse, stood among them. He had seen the dragon's arrival and how he had sacrificed himself so the three prisoners would not fall into the tarry waters. Although Worrah had succeeded in catching the dragon, the

King of Gladur Nock, whom he considered in some ways even more dangerous, was not only free, but now armed as well.

Michael looked up at the troops gathering against them. He walked over to Star's head. "I can't pretend otherwise," he said. "The situation is desperate."

"And yet, things have been much worse and still you have prevailed," the dragon replied with a tired laugh. "Have I not taught you that?"

"You have taught me much, but I am truly baffled what to do next."

"You could escape to the forest," the dragon suggested. "There is a chance you could elude them."

"Star, I will not abandon you," Michael replied. "We can't flee, nor can we fight them all. I don't know how we will see ourselves through this one."

"As you have always done," Star chuckled. "With luck, O Dragon Master, with luck!"

Michael looked to the cousins standing beside him, their gazes intent on the line of soldiers, their swords ready. "If either of you has a better plan, speak it freely," he said.

The dragon noticed Corin looking back and forth from Worrah's gathering forces to him. "Tell me something, boy," he said.

"What is it, Star?" he asked.

"Do you love me?"

Corin's face showed surprise. "Star, of course I love you," he professed. "How can you doubt that? I don't have any choice but to love you."

"Love is always a choice," Star said.

Corin considered this before responding. "Not around you, it isn't. If I breathe, I love you."

The dragon gazed into his eyes a moment before saying, "Then will you do what you have to out of love?"

Corin had a look on his face as if he had been caught at something. He grew very serious and looked resolute. He nicked his head. "Yes, Star. I promise."

"This is an odd time for expressions of love," Elinor grumbled, nervously watching the soldiers on the rise above them. "What did you promise?"

Corin did not answer her, but turned his gaze to the line of trees.

"You and your secrets," Elinor complained. "Thinking of running for it?"

"No," Corin said. "We're here until this is over. I was just hoping to see something else."

Michael looked up at the soldiers holding their line. He looked around at the empty fields and over to the line of trees. "This makes no sense," he said. "Why aren't they attacking? Or at least trying to flank us?"

"Maybe they're afraid of the dragon?" Elinor suggested.

"They've been watching us since Star arrived," the king said. "They can see that he is stuck in the tar lake. That was their plan. They've had every opportunity to charge and finish us off."

Corin continued peering at the line of the forest. Now he turned to his father. "Maybe they have something else in mind," he said.

"Then I wish they would get on with it," his father said. "I don't like the waiting."

As if in answer to the king's impatience, there was stirring among the soldiers on the rise. They parted their ranks, making a space in their midst.

"What are they up to now?" the king wondered out loud.

They watched as a small cart, pulled by two lines of soldiers, was hauled onto the hill above them into the open space left by the troops. In the middle of the cart, a wooden pole had been secured. It was the cart Elinor had seen in the middle of the marketplace. Bound to this pole, with her hands tied behind her, stood the queen.

"It's Mother!" Corin cried out appalled. "What is she doing here?"

"Aina!" the king called out in anguish and raised his hand as if he could snatch her from the cart. Then he looked to Star, as if he hoped that the dragon would free himself from the tarry water and fly to save the queen. Star, however, was floundering in the black water, listing onto his side.

At the king's cry, Aina looked in their direction. She gazed at the children, her husband, and then at the dragon, becoming ever more entrapped in the tar lake. She gazed, but she did not cry out. A line of soldiers walked behind the cart, all of them laden with brush and wood. After them came three soldiers with lit torches. It was obvious what they had come to do. As soon as the cart came to a stop, they started piling the wood against its base. More soldiers appeared behind them, all of them heavily armed, until the hillside was covered with Worrah's army.

Worrah rode his horse to stand right beside the cart holding the queen. He directed the soldiers to pile brush underneath and inside the cart at Aina's feet. The remaining brush and wood he ordered them to stack around the wheels of the cart. He was going to burn everything. When they were finished, he had the torchbearers surround the cart. Then he stood up in his stirrups, and when he began speaking, all grew silent.

"We have waited many years for this moment. Truth and a firm, guiding hand will prevail." The soldiers cheered. "We finally have in our power those who wished to destroy us." More cheering. "It is as I promised you. Behold, the dreaded dragon thrashes away his last moments of life in the pool of death. Behold the witch who plotted our destruction; she will soon be burnt to ashes. And finally, the rogue knight masquerading as a king, who has so long troubled our frontier villages, will soon be cut down." The cheering grew even louder. When it subsided, Worrah continued. "I have been true to my promise. Let all be my witness. Unchallenged victory, at long last, is delivered into—"

He broke off suddenly. He sat down in the saddle, his gaze riveted on something beyond the army. All eyes turned to see what had caused

Worrah to stop. They looked, but all they saw behind them was an empty field. Beyond that, however, the line of trees at the edge of the forest was alive with activity. Silently, out from beneath the cover of the trees poured a mass of armed men, taking their places in the open field and standing at the ready. The sun glistened off their shields, raised spears, swords and battle axes. They stood there, waiting for some sign.

"Finally," Corin said. "I thought they'd never show."

"Who are they?" Michael asked in wonderment.

"They are the army of the Enclave," Corin said. "They followed us here."

"Are they friend or foe?" his father next asked.

"They may not know yet themselves," Corin replied.

The king saw his first glimmer of hope. "Is there a way to influence it?"

"You've certainly waited too long to ask that question," the young prince turned on him angrily. "There is much you could have done to have won their support."

The king stood there considering. "I've wronged them, haven't I?"

"Not with intention to wrong, that much I will give you," Corin said. "But how can you expect to make friends if you are too busy chasing enemies?"

"I am chastised," the king said, his head still lowered. "And by my own son. I am about to lose everything." Then he looked his son in the eye. "Is there anything that can save us?"

"Only desperate measures," Corin replied. Then he chose his words carefully. "Only if you give up that which you love the most can we expect to have even a chance of surviving this."

"I will not sacrifice your mother," his father said fiercely. "I will die trying to save her."

"With luck, you won't have to do either," Corin said. "I meant something else."

"What else do I love more ... ?" and then it dawned on him what his son meant. "Sprout, you can't! He's already trapped."

Corin did not respond. Instead he turned back to the tar lake. As he walked, he looked to the line of trees, to the army that stood there, poised, still waiting for some sign. He drew the dagger from his belt and held it high over his head for all to see. Looking grim, he walked with firm steps towards the sinking dragon.

Suddenly it dawned on Elinor what Corin planned to do. She cried out with alarm and lunged after him, grabbing hold of his sleeve and pulling him back. "You can't!" she protested. "I know what you're thinking. The full moon. But you can't. You just professed your love to him! I heard you!"

"It's different now," Corin said in a strangled voice. "There's no other way to get them to fight. It's the only way I have to break with my past. Now I have a chance to do something that is my own."

"Is this the deal you made with them?"

"Yes. Let me go."

"Even if it brings to ruin everything that you hold dear?"

"It draws me onward. I must follow where it leads me. Let me go."

"I can't!" she screamed, pulling at his arm with all her might. "I can't let you do this!"

"We saw them enact this. They've been waiting for me. Now it is time to do it myself."

"No!" Elinor cried out, trying to drag him back.

"Let go!" he ordered, violently shaking her off. She lost her balance and collapsed in a heap on the field. Corin looked down at her, his face impassive. "I don't expect you to understand. It's our only chance. Star knows I have to do this."

Corin walked resolutely to the tar lake. The tip of Star's wing still lay on the dry shore. He slid the dagger back into his belt and drove the point of his sword into the ground. Balancing himself on the precarious bridge, he crossed over to the dragon's body.

Corin's unexpected movement held the full attention of both armies. They stood transfixed and watched to see what he would do next. Elinor and the king watched dumbly with the others as Corin climbed up onto Star's immense flank. Star had not been able to right himself and had slipped onto his side. The dragon's breath was labored and his sides heaved. His own weight had caused him to list further to the side until he lay there twisted. The sounds coming from the dragon were nothing like his familiar, cheerful ringing chimes. It was a mournful sound, much like the shriek or the wail that one hears the wind make in the trees during a storm. The prince climbed until he was standing on Star's exposed breast. They could see Corin was talking, whether to himself or to the dragon no one was close enough to tell. Star, in his turn, between the mournful shrieks, seemed to speak in short, labored phrases.

Corin stood upright and pulled the dagger out of his belt. Elinor gasped as he held it up high over his head for all to see. He turned to make sure that the army of the Enclave had a clear view.

"It's … it's the dagger from their ceremony," Elinor stammered. "The magician gave it to him." Then she glanced over to the king and saw that he had gone pale. "Why is he doing this?"

The king stood up and walked toward the lake of death where the dragon lay trapped in the tar. "Sprout!" he called out in a loud voice. "It doesn't have to be this way."

Hearing his father, the prince looked up. "It *does* have to be this way," he called back. "I cannot be you. I must do things my way." And he turned his attention back to the dragon.

"He can't hurt him," the king said turning to Elinor, but it sounded more like a hope than a statement. "He hasn't been taught. It's not possible. Star would have told me if he'd taught him."

They all watched as Corin knelt down and with his free hand began feeling around for something among the dragon's scales.

"He doesn't know what he's looking for," the king murmured. "He can't."

They could hear the dragon speaking to Corin. To the king, it sounded like he was pleading, but he was too far away to make out the words. Corin searched with intense concentration. They all waited, barely breathing, to see what would happen next.

Worrah had not let the moment pass him by. This close to his great victory, he was not going to leave anything to chance. He had summoned archers to stand by him. He wanted to shoot the prince off the dragon, but he was as curious as the rest what Corin was doing. *Arrows travel fast,* he thought to himself. If the boy were to save the dragon somehow, his archers would have him riddled immediately. For the moment, however, he waited.

"What is he looking for?" Elinor whispered.

"There's a spot … on his breast," the king's words came in gasps, "… where he could … the heart … Star's heart."

Then they could all see that Corin had found something. He nodded his head as if satisfied. With his free hand, astonishingly, he appeared to pull back one of the scales and then once again he held the dagger high above his head.

"No!" cried out Michael, his voice choked with anguish. He stumbled towards the lake. "Stop!" he called out in panic.

"In the name of freedom!" Corin called loudly. His voice carried across the fields. Wild cheering arose from the gathered troops of the Enclave. Here was their full moon ceremony, this time with the true prince and the real dragon. Its effect on them was intoxicating. They began chanting and banging their weapons on their shields with a steady rhythm. The chanting was clear for all to hear, and for Elinor, a nightmarish echo of the full moon ceremony: "Slay him! Slay him! *Slay him!*"

Corin knelt there a moment, poised as they chanted. Then, with a decisive, powerful stroke, he thrust downwards. Dagger, hand and arm disappeared into the dragon's breast. Elinor shrieked with terror, and no less a sound of despair came from the king who crumpled to the ground. Corin had thrust the dagger into the dragon's heart!

They could see Corin speaking again, and then the dragon emitted a tremendous, ear-splitting roar. Elinor was horrified as she watched his death throes. And then the dragon lay still.

A wild look came into the king's eyes as if he were possessed. He struggled to his feet, took his sword into both hands and lifted it over his head, turning towards the troops on the hill surrounding the cart holding the queen.

"For Queen Aina!" he bellowed. "For Gladur Nock!" And without waiting further, all alone, his sword raised above his head, he charged the line of soldiers. It was clear to all who watched that the king, in his despair at the death of the dragon and the imminent death of his wife, wished nothing more than to die on the swords of his enemies. Although he ran alone, he was like a frenzied bull, and none of the soldiers was anxious to meet his rage in battle. His reputation as a fierce and unrelenting warrior was legendary. Certainly, their numbers could bring him down, but many knew they would fall before that happened. The line wavered and soldiers scattered to get out of the way.

Hardly had the king taken off at a run, than Elinor's wits returned to her. She took her sword and also raised it high above her head. She had watched the dragon die and saw the king run to his own death. She had little reason left to live. "For the Queen!" she cried out fiercely. "For the King! For Gladur!" and she charged forward in her uncle's footsteps.

By this time, Corin had climbed down from the now still dragon and retrieved his sword. He ran full tilt towards the wavering line of soldiers, directing his steps towards the cart where his mother was bound. He, too, had his sword raised high and was calling as loudly as he could, "For the Enclave! For the Queen!"

The forces from the Enclave had grown silent and watched in astonishment as all of this unfolded before them. In spite of having played it out repeatedly at the full moons, many had gasped in horror when they saw Corin actually plunge his knife into the dragon's breast. Many of the warriors stood there unabashed as tears rolled down their cheeks and into their beards. They had hated the dragon. He had stood as the symbol of their exile. Yet, he had been *their* dragon, and something in their hearts now recognized that the dragon had given them a focus for their resistance and helped them define themselves.

And now he was dead. It was a death blow to their own hearts as well. They watched with amazement as the royal family charged the waiting line of the enemy, rushing to their certain deaths. In the hearts of many awoke the sentiment that there was something wrong with how this was unfolding. This was utterly not the way they wished to see this happen. The king had sent them in exile, but he was still *their* king. They lived in his territory, he had let them come and go in Gladur to ply their trades, and in spite of many threats, he had left them in peace.

Their attention was suddenly drawn to a solitary figure who now rode up before them mounted on a prancing horse. With joy, they recognized it was their own Thos whom they knew so well. But he was no longer dressed as the old magician. He sat on his horse wearing a breastplate, his greying hair flowing out from underneath an iron skullcap. He, too, had a sword in his hand and, knowing that he had the attention of the troops, raised it above his head.

"Damn!" Worrah cursed, recognizing the old man who had so recently been his prisoner. "How did he escape me?"

"For the Enclave!" Thos cried out. "For Gladur! For the king! Charge!" Without waiting further, he spurred his horse and galloped towards Worrah's troops. His appearance was all the army from the Enclave needed. With one voice they raised the cry: "For the Enclave! For Gladur!" Some voices were heard calling out loudly, "For the dragon!" which was immediately picked up by the rest of the army. "For the dragon! For the dragon!" and they charged as one body behind Thos' horse, their war ululation filling the air.

Worrah's troops stood watching all of this as if frozen in time. From one direction approached the royal family of Gladur Nock, screaming as if possessed by demons. From the other direction charged an old man on a horse, followed by the rowdy warriors from the Enclave, screeching as if they, too, were maddened by some mysterious force.

Worrah had observed all of this as well. Up until this moment, everything had unfolded perfectly. The young prince had turned on his father, and unexpectedly, the dragon was finally dead. Yet instead of the desired effect, he was now under attack. He watched as his line of soldiers hesitated and threatened to break before a single blow was struck. It was not supposed to happen like this. He had to marshal his forces before they panicked. It was not possible that his troops could fail him now. They vastly outnumbered the unruly forces from the Enclave.

Worrah turned to his officers and began shouting orders. The front line had already broken and soldiers were running in disarray. He had to stop this before it absurdly turned into a full rout. In his mind, he saw a way to turn this to his own advantage and use the break in his lines to flank and then surround the attacking forces.

This, however, was an unnecessary plan. His well-trained officers did not need to wait for his orders. Freely using their whips, they rode among the panicking troops and quickly turned them to face the oncoming attack. A moment later, Worrah's forces engaged the troops from the Enclave. Now that his soldiers had been brought back to order, their courage returned, and they met the attack with a firm wall of shields. There was a thunderous noise as they clashed, shield against shield, war cries mixing with the anguished screams of injured men.

Worrah had not forgotten his original intention of burning Aina as a witch. When he saw that his officers had the troops under control and were directing the battle, he turned his attention back to the cart where the queen was bound. He spurred his horse, forcing his way through his own soldiers until he stood beside the cart. He snatched up a flaming torch from one of the soldiers standing there.

"Go make yourself useful," he snarled at him. The soldier scurried away. "I have waited long for this moment," Worrah gloated, speaking directly to Aina. The queen was silent but met his eyes and held them. "With you finally out of the way," he declared, "Gladur will be mine at last." Without waiting for any reply from her, he threw the torch into the waiting brush at the foot of the cart. Then he wheeled his horse to return to the battle, certain that victory was at hand. The torch had fallen into the dry brush, and it was only a moment before it smoked and then burst into flames.

The flank which Michael and the cousins had assailed, in spite of their greater number, was faltering under the viciousness of the attack. Michael drove directly toward the cart that held his wife. Flanking him were Corin and Elinor. Michael's blade flashed in the sunlight, moving quickly and mowing down whoever dared come into his path. His reputation combined with his superb skills confounded and intimidated the soldiers who stood in his way. Corin's and Elinor's blades were hardly less active than the king's. All three of them, dragon-trained, fought as one. They were an irresistible force and no one dared for long to stand and challenge them. Barely winded, the king reached the cart. He glanced at the cousins and then at the mass of troops surrounding them, keeping their distance, yet ready to menace them.

"Come up with me," he urged them, and vaulted over the side to stand beside Aina. The smoke was heavy, and the flames had already reached the sides of the cart and were spreading fast. Quickly, Michael cut the ropes that held the queen. Then he pulled from his belt the extra sword he had taken and handed it to her. At first she did not want to take it.

"What's the use?" she said weakly. "All is lost already."

"We've faced worse odds," the king said, his eyes alive with passion.

"How can we prevail?" she asked.

"With luck," Michael said, and laughed.

"But we've lost Star. We've lost everything."

"Have we?" the king countered. "Everything? Listen."

Over the clamor of battle the cry of the warriors of the Enclave could be heard: "For the dragon!"

Michael smiled grimly, "Then for Star's sake, let us avenge him." Aina studied her husband's face and saw something in his eyes that she had not seen there for a long time. She took the sword from his hands.

"For Star," she said. Michael turned to jump back into the fray and then paused. Where were the children? They had not followed him into the cart, and for a moment he was overcome with dread, fearing that Worrah's soldiers had surrounded them while he was freeing Aina. He had to save them!

However, his fears were unfounded. In a moment he located the cousins, driving Worrah's trained soldiers back away from the burning cart. No one wanted to stand up against them. He paused long enough to marvel at their skills.

"Where did Elinor learn to wield a sword?" the king asked, turning to his wife. "Did you teach her?"

"Not I," Aina said.

"And when did Sprout learn how to swing a sword?" he asked.

"When you weren't looking," Aina replied, climbing over the edge of the cart. The flames were growing dangerously close and it was time to get out before the fire engulfed them. Side by side, the king and queen leapt from the cart, already swinging their swords before their feet hit the ground. Joining Corin and Elinor, the four of them formed an arc, with their backs to the burning cart, and defended themselves from any who came near.

While he fought, the king wondered what their next move should be. They could not remain where they were. It was only a matter of time before the fire in the cart would burn down to the point that soldiers could get behind them. Should they retreat to the Black Lake and use that to protect their backs? They were only four against so many, and he did not see any chance of escape. If they remained there, they would be overwhelmed. Michael was not going to wait for that to happen. Their strength was still fresh, and if there was anything Star had taught him, it was to be bold and do the unexpected. Michael and Aina were on the outside of the arc with the children between them. He turned to his son who stood his ground beside him. "Sprout!" he spoke sharply, to get his attention.

The prince glanced briefly at him, but did not stop the rhythmical swinging of his sword. Then he said, landing a powerful blow against the opposing soldier with each word, "My—name—is—*Corin*!" The blow delivered with the last word was so powerful that it knocked the enemy soldier onto the seat of his pants, in spite of his being a head taller than the prince. The soldier scrambled to his feet and ran away, knowing he was no match against the fury of his young assailant. Having a moment's respite, Corin turned to his father. "Have I made myself clear?" he asked forcefully, breathing heavily.

Michael was speechless at his son's vehemence. He had never seen him like this before. Then he nicked his head briefly. "Totally," he said. "Absolutely clear."

"We have to drive against Worrah," Corin now directed. "It's our only chance. We have to do it now while he is distracted by the army of the Enclave. They won't hold for long."

"But we're in luck," the king responded. "You have no idea who's leading them."

"That's Thos," Corin shouted, engaging another soldier. "The magician from the market place. The one you forbade me to see."

The king was astonished. "That's your magician?" he stammered.

"The very one," Corin affirmed. "And unless he has some more sleight of hand up his sleeve, we don't have long. It's our only chance. We must reach Worrah."

"Agreed!" the king called over the noise of the melee. What Corin had not said out loud was that he had no expectation that they would be successful. Michael turned to Aina and called loudly to get her attention. He motioned that they should drive towards Worrah. Aina understood his intention and with a nod of her head, began forcing back the soldiers that opposed her. Elinor saw the queen's movement and kept pace with her. She fought with utter determination, her sword never resting.

In spite of the superiority of their sword skills, the four of them made only slow progress against the packed troops that stood before them. Also slowly, the gap behind them began to fill up with soldiers who cautiously approached them from their blind side. If they were going to force their way to Worrah, something else would have to happen to open up the way.

It came unexpectedly.

Chapter Twenty-Four

The Deceit of Prince Corin

*T*hos was still on his horse, engaging any who dared approach him, but holding back from the general storm of the fighting. He called out encouragement and issued orders, but not having a line of officers to carry them out, much of what he shouted was lost in the noise of clashing arms and shouting warriors. When the fighters of the Enclave attacked Worrah's line, it faltered and bulged inward, but due to the sheer numbers, it did not break. Through the efforts of Worrah's officers, the line reformed and slowly pushed back to regain the ground they had lost. Now that the soldiers had found their footing again, they were making gains. The line of the Enclave was thin by comparison, and it was showing its weakness at several points along the battlefront.

Thos' attention had been drawn to the rear of the Enclave army. He was watching it with great interest. And Worrah had been watching Thos. He was convinced that the old man was looking for a chance to pull his army back and regroup. Worrah saw this as his chance to drive them into a full retreat. He gave orders to several officers and had the word passed along to the captains in the front lines of the battle to be ready for a big push forward. The moment Thos drew his forces back, Worrah was determined to pursue him and offer no quarter. He wanted a quick end to this battle. He had noticed that his attempt to burn the queen had been cut short by the king's foolhardy actions. He wanted to finish what he had begun with the royal family of Gladur Nock, and he viewed the army of the Enclave but a temporary distraction. He barely minded. He would destroy this vagabond, ragtag army and then deal with the royal family at his leisure. He had already noticed that they were trying to force their way in his direction. He laughed to himself that Michael was too stupid to even try to escape.

The moment came that Worrah had been waiting for. He saw Thos raise a trumpet to his lips and blow a general retreat. The soldiers from the Enclave broke off their fighting and, turning their backs to the front line, began running back towards the forest. Worrah did not delay an instant. He gave the order for his own trumpeters to blow the signal to charge. With a shout of victory, Worrah's troops gave chase.

This had not gone unnoticed by the four members of the royal family who had been toiling against the throng of soldiers that still stood between them and their goal. When Thos called a general retreat, Michael could not restrain himself.

"No!" he shouted. "Stand fast!" Yet there was no one but his own family to hear him. It was Corin, fighting beside him, who heard his muttered despair, "Now all is lost."

"Courage, Father!" Corin called out. "Now all begins. Forward! We must reach Worrah!" And with these words, he threw himself with increased vigor against the soldiers who stood before him.

Yelling wildly, the army of the Enclave ran headlong across the meadow, back the way they had come. Worrah's army followed, hot on their heels, yelling threats and taunts.

"Now we have them." Worrah felt the thrill of victory, already imagining the road leading to the capital of Gladur Nock lined with stakes, holding the decapitated heads of these hapless Sunday soldiers. "What fools," he gloated, "pitching themselves against a trained army!" He spurred his horse to ride behind his forces, eager to take part in this wholesale rout. Relishing the moment, he was not ready for what happened next.

As the last of the soldiers from the Enclave surrendered the field, they left behind three wagons that had been pulled into position at the rear of the battle line. The army was in such haste, they had abandoned the wagons where they stood. Or so it seemed.

The wagons presented a strange sight. They carried what looked to be large wooden water tanks. In each wagon, next to the tank, stood two men, one at either end of a long handle fixed to the side of the tank. They looked poised for action, and did not appear in any haste to escape with the soldiers streaming past them. At the front of each wagon, and facing Worrah's oncoming army, was a long, wide spout. Oddly, the end of the spout was in the shape of a dragon's head, its mouth gaping wide open.

As the last of the soldiers from the Enclave passed them by, the men standing in each wagon began furiously working the lever between them. As one end went up, the other end went down. Within moments, it became obvious that they were working a pump. And then it became clear why the end of the spout was in the shape of a dragon's open maw. Flames shot out of the dragon spouts, spewing fire onto the enemy soldiers rushing towards them.

The panic among Worrah's troops was immediate. Contrary to logic, the flames that were poured onto them from the wagons behaved like liquid. Whatever the flames touched, they not only scorched, but adhered to that surface and spread. Panicked soldiers ran in disarray, their clothing aflame, crying out to their companions to help them.

More flames poured forth from the jaws of the dragons. Abandoned weapons littered the field. The air was filled with the stench of burnt flesh and the anguished cries of soldiers calling for water to douse their burning clothes. Those soldiers not caught by the flames were busy helping to rip the burning clothing off of the backs of their comrades.

Soldiers from the Enclave now rushed forward to cut down their defenseless and distracted foes. At a cry of warning from the wagons, they ran away to escape the next attack of flames.

Worrah had been galloping his horse through the ranks of his soldiers when the flames first struck. He was caught as unprepared as his army by the rain of liquid fire. A lick of flames caught his shoulder and he was aghast to find his cloak on fire. He struggled to unfasten the clasp at his neck and ripped the flaming cloth from his back, letting it fall to the ground. He pulled harshly at the reins to control his panicked horse, and after a moment he saw the reason for its terror. The flames that had ignited his cloak had also caught the horse's tail on fire. His mount reared up repeatedly as Worrah pulled at the reins for control. But the pacicked horse wanted to bolt from there and the third time it reared up, it succeeded in unseating Worrah. A moment later, the horse was streaking across the field away from the scorching dragon wagons.

Worrah cursed and surveyed the field of battle. His army had retreated out of range of the wagons. This was an unexpected hindrance. But it was a battle, and the unexpected was always waiting to happen. This was admittedly a setback, but he would soon find a way around those wagons. His force was still far superior to the meager army of the Enclave. An officer rode up and gave his horse to Worrah. He had barely seated himself in the saddle when he knew what to do. They may have shooting flames, but he had something else that shot, and just as deadly. He turned and rode back to his army.

As soon as he reached his waiting troops, he was issuing orders. He surveyed his soldiers and was not happy with what he saw. A shocking number of them wandered around, weaponless, dazed and scorched. Others sat or lay in the field, half naked after shedding their burning clothes. Many were in pain and sat huddled and moaning. He ordered that the wounded be moved to the rear. His troops were frightened and demoralized by this new weapon. Soldiers from the Enclave were now pushing the wagons into range of Worrah's cowering army. It was up to Worrah to find a plan to neutralize the dragon wagons. But that was not all. He wanted to turn their demonic weapon against them.

This would assure him the victory that he was still convinced must be his. He called up his archers.

Quickly he lined up the bowmen three deep and gave the order for them to shoot. Their aim was deadly. A rain of arrows fell on the dragon wagons, striking several of its tenders and dozens of soldiers who were pushing the wagons forward. A cry of despair rose from the army of the Enclave as they retreated to a safer distance. Next Worrah ordered his archers to shoot again, this time to where the soldiers of the Enclave had taken refuge, but even more importantly, into the space between them and the dragon wagons. This had the desired effect. Although most could take shelter behind their shields to ward off the deadly rain of arrows, they were prevented from sending men to replace the pump operators who had fallen. Worrah ordered his archers to keep shooting to hold back any reinforcements, and at the same time he sent his own men, under cover of the archers, to take command of the dragon wagons. But they did not get very far before they in turn were forced back by a barrage of arrows shot from the army of the Enclave.

In the midst of this standoff, an officer hastened up to Worrah. "We have prisoners, sire," he reported breathlessly.

"Dispatch them," Worrah ordered coldly, hardly glancing at the reporting officer, pondering how to get his men past the arrows and to the dragon wagons.

"But, sire ..." the officer tried to explain.

"I said, dispatch them," Worrah barked, this time looking the officer full in the face. "Run them through! Cut their throats! We're not taking any prisoners. We will litter the field with their bodies. We are taking no prisoners."

"But sire," the officer stood his ground. "You don't understand."

"What I understand is that I am about to continue this battle with one less officer because—" and then he broke off when the prisoners in question came into sight. His tone changed. "If you survive, see me after the battle," Worrah said to the officer, "and I will reward you." He turned his attention fully away from the standoff over the wagons and walked over to meet the little group that came, heavily guarded, towards him.

"Excellent!" he gloated. "Your timing is exceptional."

Before him stood the royal family of Gladur Nock. They had been disarmed and were ringed by soldiers who stood cautious and wary. Elinor had blood trickling down the side of her neck from a scalp wound. Her hair was wild, and she was sobbing, with her face hidden behind her hands. Aina, also wounded, had enfolded her niece with her uninjured arm and she stared defiantly back at Worrah, tears staining her face as well. Michael stood stoically beside her. He had been wounded in the leg, and he pressed against it with his hand, trying to staunch the flow of blood which stained his leggings. Corin stood beside his father, examining their captor with curiosity. He, too, showed signs of their recent fighting, although of the four, he seemed to have received the least amount of injuries.

"Come with me and watch," Worrah said, leading them, under guard, to have a clear view of the field of battle. "I should have known," he continued, "that you would have some trick up your sleeve. How ingenious to use such a colorful army against me. However did you get them to fight for you?" He waited for Michael to respond, but the king remained silent. Worrah continued, "Well, it matters little. We will soon overwhelm them and seize this new weapon of yours. It will come in quite useful. In the right hands, *my own*, there is not an army that will be able to withstand it. I must get that old man to show me how to use it. Then I shall have him burned at the stake with the rest of you for practicing witchcraft." At these words, Aina could restrain herself no longer and sobbed openly with Elinor. She had escaped being burned at the stake, only to face returning to it. She would have preferred to die with a sword in her hands.

"There's still hope," Michael said quietly, turning to her.

Hearing this comment, Worrah laughed mockingly. "Hope? Of what? Haven't you noticed how things stand? How I totally dominate the field of battle and have you completely in my power? Look in the meadow below. Your invincible Luck Dragon lies dead. *Dead!* Drained of all good fortune." At these words Elinor sobbed even louder. "Your ragtag army will soon be destroyed. Your regular army is ignorant that there is a battle here. I've seen to that. They are camped along the southern borders of your country, many days' march away. Do you think I don't know this? I planned this! Do you think I don't know who is with the army? It's Korvas. His father served under me. Did you never wonder why you always arrived too late to find me? Korvas always knew my position, because I let him know it. And his job was to keep you from knowing. And now his job is to keep the army far away."

The king was not able to hide his surprise at being deceived by one of his own generals. Worrah saw this and smiled. "There is no one left to come and help you. No one even knows where you are. Have you forgotten that you came here alone?"

"I did not come as alone as you think," the king said stubbornly.

"Of course," Worrah celebrated. "How could I overlook the reinforcements you brought with you? A woman and two children. And your hapless dragon. And we have your son to thank for dealing with him so decisively." He looked at Corin, who returned his gaze steadily. "You did as you promised."

"I told you I came to help you," Corin replied.

Astonished at these words, Michael looked at his son. The truth dawned on him. "Is this why you wanted to drive against him?" his father asked.

The prince turned to him. "When last we spoke, so long ago, you questioned whether I would be fit to wear the crown of Gladur," Corin reminded him. "Since that day I have sought out Worrah. You even sent me to him, remember? I knew this was my only chance." He turned to address Worrah. "You saw what I did to the dragon," he said. "I wanted us to be captured. I planned all this."

"How could you?" Elinor sobbed out loud.

"Star was the one thing that stood between me and freedom," Corin said turning to his cousin. "Now I can live my life the way I want to and not how everyone expects me to."

"I hate you!" Elinor sobbed, burying her face in her aunt's enfolding arms.

"You are worth more to me than my whole army," Worrah said gleefully. "You have dispatched their precious dragon and delivered back into my hands the whole of the royal family. I might even let you live."

"At my father's urging, I came to stand beside you," Corin said to Worrah. "With your help I wish to wear my father's crown." At these words, both his mother and Elinor ceased weeping. They looked up to stare at him in shock. Michael's expression was grave, but he said nothing.

"I assure you," Corin said to Worrah, "that you and I are of one heart and mind." He glanced briefly at his father to see the effect of his words and was satisfied with what he saw.

"Come, stand nearer to me." Worrah gave a sign and the guards released their hold on Corin and he went to stand closer. "I see we have an understanding. There are two kingdoms between us. I will make you my viceroy to rule Gladur in my name. And with this new weapon that we saw today, there will be more lands to follow. Of that I am certain. I appreciated Scorch for the destruction he brought, but he was impossible to manage. You have brought me dragon's breath without the annoyance of the dragon." A malicious glint came into his eyes.

Worrah turned to Michael. "Years ago, you were the source of my fall from power. But I have returned. And now you will be the source of my greatest victories. Do you not despair?" He wanted to see Michael squirm, even beg for mercy.

"Still," Michael replied, his head held high, "there is hope. As long as I breathe, there is hope."

"Always your insufferable confidence!" Worrah shouted, losing his patience. "Yes, there is hope. You could beg me for mercy and hope I show some. You could beg that I kill you first so you do not have to watch your wife and niece suffer. You could beg that I kill you before you have to watch your own son's betrayal unfold as my victory."

Michael stood there unmoved, which only incited Worrah to greater fury. "What is wrong with you?" Worrah screamed at him. "Why are you not tortured that you have brought the destruction of all you love on your own head? That your own son has turned against you?"

"Because you cannot destroy what I love," Michael said quietly.

"Why? Because your son already has?" Worrah mocked. "You think I can't destroy what you love? I can't? Watch what I *can't* do." He grabbed Elinor and violently ripped her away from Aina. Elinor screamed in terror, striking out with her arms to defend herself, but to no avail. Guards restrained Aina, preventing her from protecting her niece. Worrah seized a handful of Elinor's hair and forced her to sit in the grass. "I can't destroy what you love?" Worrah shouted. "Watch me begin with this sniveling girl. Watch me!" he commanded. Worrah drew his sword and pulled viciously on Elinor's hair until she was forced to her hands and knees, her neck exposed, screaming and sobbing at the same time. Worrah kept his eyes on Michael as he raised his sword. He wanted to see the king suffer, watch him cringe, cry for mercy. None of that came. Michael stood there, unmoved, whipping Worrah to even greater madness.

Suddenly, as if it were an extension of Worrah's rage and frenzy, there was a tremendous cry and whoop from the field of battle. With her knees and hands on the ground, Elinor could feel the earth vibrating, and she held back her screams to listen. A moment later, everyone around her could hear the thunderous pounding of galloping horses. Seemingly out of nowhere, horsemen appeared on the field, flanking the troops of the Enclave. They were taken completely by surprise.

Worrah's attention was drawn to the horsemen riding down on his opponents. "Cavalry?" he said, his head turned away from Elinor. Reinforcements had arrived. The standoff would now end and the battle was his. He laughed wildly. "Cut them down!" he shouted, as if his voice could carry that far. "Cut them down! All of them!" He raised the sword in his hand above his head in a victory salute. It was only then that he puzzled over the banners the lead horsemen were flying.

Aina was the first to recognize who led the arriving cavalry. "It's Geron," she said loud enough that Corin heard.

"Geron?" Corin said in shock. "No!" His eyes darted over to where the king stood, whose gaze was riveted on his son. "Father! Now!" Corin shouted "*Now!*"

Chapter Twenty-Five

The Second Ride of Sound-the-Alarm

*E*veryone's attention had been drawn to the arriving cavalry, even the guards around the royal family. Michael took advantage of the distraction. With a vicious blow, he elbowed the guard beside him in the face and then ripped the sword out of his hand. He did not turn and attack the guards, but immediately tossed the sword into the air.

"Corin!" he cried out. That was the only word he could speak, because a second guard, reacting to Michael's sudden and threatening move, now swung his sword at the king's head, striking him full on his helmet. Michael fell hard at the blow and lay still and crumpled on the ground.

The sword the king had tossed made a graceful arc through the air over Corin's head. He did not leap up to try and catch it, but instead took two steps in the direction it was going. It was perfectly thrown, and he raised his hand to receive the pommel of the sword as it descended the arc. Corin allowed his own forward motion to become one with the sword and created another arc with a new trajectory, gracefully jiving at the same time on the ball of his foot. Before anyone had time to react, before Worrah even knew that something had happened, Corin forcefully struck Worrah's head off his shoulders. Still helmeted, it fell with a dull thud and rolled in the grass. The headless body toppled to the ground like a tree falling over.

Corin snatched up Worrah's fallen sword and tossed it to his mother. The two of them directed a ferocious attack on the soldiers guarding them. Surprised by the arrival of the horsemen, and shocked by Corin's sudden and fatal assault on their king, they fell back, several of them already wounded. Corin leapt to stand over his father's fallen body.

"To the King!" he cried. In a moment, Aina stood beside him. Elinor picked herself up off the ground, grabbed a fallen sword, and joined them. They now encircled the body of the king, threatening anyone who came near. Events on the field of battle with the arriving cavalry drew away any opposition and soon left them standing there alone.

They had barely caught their breath when the horsemen swooped down and isolated the royal family, riding a circle around them, screening them from the battlefield. They could hear the astonished cries from the horsemen.

"It's the Queen!"

"And Prince Corin!"

"Isn't that Her Majesty's niece?"

"The King lies stricken!"

"Mother," Corin said through clenched teeth, holding his sword before him, ready to strike at any who came near. "Mother, we tried to warn you about Geron, but you wouldn't listen to us. But they will not take me. I will die defending Father."

Aina glanced at him and asked, "Are you resolute in this?"

He did not answer her question. Instead, he said, "I could have saved us, but for this. I don't know how he found us. He's probably been working with Worrah all along, just as Korvas has. Both their fathers served under Worrah. The conspiracy is so clear now. Throw yourself at his mercy. He will spare you and Elinor." Then he added fiercely, "I do not care for his mercy. They will have to kill me before they can harm Father."

"I am satisfied," his mother said, and lowered her sword, stepping away from her fallen husband. She turned to her niece. "Come, Elinor. We are finished with fighting." Elinor stared at her with wide eyes. She looked at the ring of horsemen and glanced to her cousin. She fumbled for words.

"Go," Corin said to her. "You've done all you can. It's over now. Save yourself."

Elinor looked him in the eye, and he saw there, past her exhaustion, deep sorrow. She dropped her sword and stumbled over to the queen. Aina enfolded her niece with her good arm. Elinor buried her face in the queen's gown and wept.

Corin raised his sword menacingly towards the ring of horsemen who held their positions. *The king may be a rogue knight who married fortunately*, he thought, *but he is still the rightful king. And I am his son.* He felt the resolve to die defending this. He lifted his sword and shook it towards the horsemen, bellowing loudly, "For King Michael!" He would die with his father's name on his lips.

To a man, the horsemen drew their swords. *Now the attack,* Corin thought. *It will be over soon.*

The horsemen urged their mounts forward, drawing the ring even tighter. However, instead of dismounting or riding on Corin and the fallen king, the horsemen raised their swords and called out strongly in one voice, "For King Michael!" followed by, "For Prince Corin! *Huzzah! Huzzah!*"

Corin was stunned by this response. Was this their final salute before cutting him down? *Why don't they attack?*

The circle of horses opened abruptly, and into the space galloped two riders. Even before their horses came to a halt, both of them sprang from the saddle and hastened towards the queen and Elinor. So this is what delayed their action against him. Corin was not surprised to see that one was Geron but was shocked when he recognized the other.

"Roderick!" he spit out the name. "This is bitter. I believed you, of anyone, would have remained true." He held up his sword with both hands ready to strike, stung by the gall of betrayal. He would not go down before he had bathed his sword in their blood. At this moment he knew how much he was his father's son.

Neither Geron nor Roderick, however, had his sword drawn. Roderick glanced at the prince but did not respond. The two men approached the queen with haste and, when they reached her, went down on their knees. Corin was taken aback by their show of deference.

"Your Majesty," Geron began, "please forgive our delay. We came with all speed. Yet it seems we have come too late." Without waiting for her to respond, he sprang to his feet again and turned back toward the circle of horses. "Bring the king's surgeon!" he ordered. "Make haste!"

By this time, Aina had returned to Corin and bent over the body of her husband. She was carefully removing his helm. She glanced up at her son who still stood straddling his father's body. "Do get out of the way," she gently chided. Corin still had his sword raised to strike but suddenly felt foolish. He took a step to the side, giving his mother room to attend to the king. No one was offering him resistance. He lowered his sword and glanced at Elinor. She looked as dazed as he felt. He then turned his attention back to the king and knelt beside his mother.

"Is he still alive?" he asked in a low voice.

"There are times when being hard-headed pays off," Aina said, smiling weakly. "This is one of them. The blade did not penetrate his helm. But he has been stunned."

The king's surgeon came running up and joined them. He examined the king's scalp and felt his limbs. He found the wound in the king's leg and, taking a bandage from his satchel, turned to Elinor and said, "Hold this in place and press firmly. That will help stop the bleeding until I can stitch it up." They were all silent while he continued to examine the king's body. Finally he looked up to the queen and said, "If he has no wounds worse than what we see, he should survive this with yet a new design of scars. Come, help me turn him. I want to make him more comfortable."

As they moved the king's body, he groaned. Suddenly, his eyes shot open, and staring wildly, he struggled to spring to his feet. Aina and the surgeon grabbed hold of him and restrained him from further movement. "Michael," Aina said urgently. "Listen to me. All is well. The battle is over. You must lie quietly."

With wild eyes, the king looked from his wife to the surgeon, then back to his wife. His limbs went slack and he grunted in pain as they lowered him back to the ground. He looked again to the surgeon.

"You?" he said accusingly. "Who invited you, Ambroise? Are you the one who gave me this headache?"

"I'll give you an even worse one if you don't do what I say and lie still," the surgeon threatened, busy unfolding a large leather wallet.

"I'm the king," Michael said with a frown. "I'm the one who gives orders."

"Then order yourself to be quiet and let others finish up," Ambroise scolded.

The king chuckled, and this made him grimace. "Don't make me laugh, Surgeon. It makes my head throb. I suppose you're going to want to sew me up like a fancy piece of embroidery."

"I'll make a very pretty row of rosettes for His Majesty," Master Ambroise said with a smile. While they spoke he had taken a needle and thread out of his wallet and was already examining the king's leg wound.

"It's not right for a man to take up sewing," the king grumbled.

"What if it keeps another man from bleeding to death or developing an infection, Your Majesty?" Ambroise asked. He looked up at the soldiers standing around watching. "Hold him," he ordered tersely.

"I won't flinch," the king said, steeling himself.

"I'm not worried about that," Ambroise said. "It is to keep you from smacking me while I patch you back together."

There was laughter from the men around, and several crouched beside the king muttering, "With your leave, Your Majesty," and steadied him with their hands.

To distract himself, the king looked up at the faces around him. He singled out the commander of Gladur's home garrison. "Geron," he said severely, "I thought I had you confined to quarters until I could have your head removed."

"And hearing you were here," Geron responded calmly, "I came to see how I had displeased my liege lord."

"That you did not come sooner," the king sighed. "Just like you to miss out on a memorable battle." Then he lowered his voice and looked Geron in the eye. "I owe you my life and that of my family and that I still have a crown to wear on my aching head."

"The safety of Gladur Nock and the royal family are the duties with which you charged me, Your Majesty. Only death will prevent me from fulfilling those obligations."

"And I am once again confirmed that I chose wisely," the king said. "Thank you, Commander.

"At your service, Your Majesty," Geron said with a bow.

"And how do affairs stand at home?" the king asked.

"As soon as word spread that both you and the queen had left the city, those nobles not loyal to the crown thought they saw their opportunity. They had nearly seized control of the armory before I took matters in hand. You were right about Melkhi, I'm sorry to say. At your advice I befriended him and kept him close. I discovered that he was more than critical words. He led the uprising."

"What have you done with him?"

"I have had him arrested for high treason, along with those who chose to follow him. They await your return and your judgment. The council has already met on the matter and implores you to be just yet firm."

"I am grateful that you have handled this so effectively," the king said gravely. "I have recently learned of more treachery. This time from General Korvas. It seems you were right about him."

"We will have him relieved before he gets wind of events here. I only await your word. We will handle this discreetly, Your Majesty."

"If not for you, Geron, I might have found myself in a similar situation to King Bellek. It would have caused great mischief."

"I am fortunate to have been of service, my King," Geron said with a bow.

"And Geron," the king added in a somber voice, "here before the others, let me express my apologies. I wrongly spoke rashly and acted hastily towards you. I admit that I did not return your faithfulness with my full trust. I don't know what got into me."

"Say no more, Your Majesty, and it will be forgotten," Geron said with a wave of his hand, as if he had just brushed it away. "A king must forever be wary. And let me say, I would follow no other. I hope I have given you proof of my loyalty."

"Indeed, you have," the king smiled. Then he flinched, barking at Ambroise, "Aren't you finished yet?"

"If you startle your surgeon, it only results in my work looking sloppy," Ambroise commented dryly. "As if you cared." He was already tying the knot. He glanced up and saw Corin. "Could you follow my looping?" he asked. "Utterly important to keep equal tension and to loop under when you come back around. You don't want it slipping. You do have your wallet with you, I hope."

Corin barely noticed what Master Ambroise was saying. He could not take his eyes off Geron. The commander stood there, his chin stuck out, looking calm, noble and completely in charge of the situation. Until now, Corin had been certain that Geron had come to help Worrah depose his father.

The king, unaware of his son's misgivings, continued to search the faces around him. "Sounder!" he exclaimed. "How relieved I am to see you." *Sounder?* Corin thought, shaken from his reverie. He looked around. *Who could he be talking to? Sounder is a character from a ballad.* Corin was startled to see his chaperon, Roderick, step forward and bow.

"Your Majesty," he said. "I am relieved to see we came in time."

"But, Father," Corin interrupted. "Why do you call him Sounder? His name is Roderick."

"Although you have done much today that is right, in some things you are still mistaken," the king smiled. "Roderick is young Sounder, who years ago, when I was but a wandering knight, rode like the wind on my dear Storm to fetch help from Nogardia. And now he has ridden like the wind a second time, to bring help from Gladur. Corin, have you never heard the ballad honoring his wild ride in our first battle with Worrah?"

"Of course I've heard it. A thousand times, it seems. The minstrels sing little else in the marketplace," Corin replied.

"Did you think it was merely a song?" his father asked. "Certainly his deeds were given some dramatic emphasis, but I assure you that what Sounder did then was as real as what he did now. Without him, we would have no story to tell, and the minstrels would be singing about Worrah's conquests instead."

"But, Father, this is Roderick," Corin insisted.

"Well, many of us carry nicknames when we are young, don't we?" his father replied. "Until today, I called you Sprout, although I doubt I will use that name again, my dear Corin. Out of respect, when Sounder came of age, we used his given name. But for me he will ever be Master Sound-the-Alarm. And he was once again true to his name."

Corin was stunned. "You're Sounder?" he stammered, looking to his chaperon. "You're the famous Sounder they sing about?"

"His ballad is about to get much longer, unless I'm mistaken," the queen laughed.

"How's this possible?" Corin asked, still sorting out all this new information.

"When I told Worrah that I had not come alone," the king said, "I was speaking the truth, and since I doubted he would believe me, I had no cause to lie. I hoped it would give your mother some hope. I came here with Sounder. When I entered the city, I left him on the outskirts of the town and instructed him, that if I did not return by morning of the second day, to assume I was either dead or a prisoner, and to hasten home and make some quick decisions about the next step. He did just that."

"When I returned and found that the Queen and her guard had also left for Warrensfold, I turned to Commander Geron for help," Sounder explained. "He took over from there."

"Your position in the royal household would be irreplaceable," the king said, "if only you could keep the young prince from slipping through your fingers."

"I think after today," Roderick said with a broad smile, "the prince will no longer be in such need of my companionship."

"You have a point," the king said with a nod, glancing at his son, "a very convincing point," and then began to chuckle.

As the king continued to visit with their rescuers, Corin turned to Elinor. She sat in the grass with her knees drawn up under her chin, and she hugged her legs.

"Imagine that!" Corin said, sitting down beside her. "My own chaperon, all this time, he's famous and never breathed a word of it to me. Now I understand why he always liked so much to listen to that ballad. He's Sounder." But Elinor was not listening to him. Her expression was serious and she gazed emptily before her. "Say, Elinor, are you all right?" Corin asked, and he reached out to put his hand on her shoulder. "Do you want Ambroise to look—"

Elinor wrenched her arm away, as if his hand had been a hot iron. "Don't touch me!" she screamed at him.

"Elinor, what's the matter?"

"Stay away from me!" she shouted. The group around the king grew silent as everyone looked up to see what had caused this disturbance.

"Go away!" she yelled at Corin. "Leave me alone! I don't ever want to see you again. I *hate* you!"

"Elinor," Corin said, astonished at the vehemence of her words. "What's wrong? The battle's over. We won. We were wrong about Geron. He is not a traitor."

"But *you* are!" Elinor screamed at him. She stared at her cousin with wide eyes, struggling to get the words out. "You—killed—him!"

"Worrah?" Corin asked, puzzled. "Of course, I killed him. He was about to cut your head off. He was going to burn Mother at the stake. When I told him I wanted him to help me wear the crown of Gladur, he just mistook my meaning."

"I don't mean Worrah!" Elinor screamed in frustration. "You killed *Star!*" And with these words she buried her face in her arms as sobs wracked her body.

"Star!" Corin exclaimed. "I completely forgot." He turned to address the guard who still held their positions in a protective circle. "Quick! Bring horses, many horses." And without any further explanation, he sprang to his feet and, pushing his way past soldiers and their mounts, ran as fast as he could back to the Black Lake.

Chapter Twenty-Six

Elinor's Secret

As Corin ran full out toward the Black Lake, he saw that Thos was already there. He had removed his breastplate and helmet and was standing beside the dragon's head. By this time Star's body had settled even deeper into the tar of the lake.

"Star!" Corin called out breathlessly, running toward the dragon's outstretched head. "I'm here!"

"Well, you certainly took your sweet time about it," the dragon commented dryly. Then he followed up with a chime-filled chuckle. "But I suppose you've been a bit busy. Have you gotten everything done?"

"Everything but this," Corin answered. "But I'm back now. We'll get you out." He looked up to see if the horses were coming. He hurried along the lines of the harness to check that they were still holding. The deeper the dragon had sunk, the more taut the lines had become. Two had broken loose and Corin reset the swords and retied the lines.

"He's still sinking, and the longer we wait, the faster he'll go," Thos commented quietly, coming over to Corin. "We don't have much time."

"They're bringing horses," Corin assured him. "Send someone for the wagon."

"I already have," Thos said. "We should see it coming over the rise soon."

Corin was adjusting the harness lines when he heard someone call his name. He looked up to see Elinor running down to the lake, her face still streaked with tears, her hair flying wildly.

"Uncle said he's alive!" she shrieked, her eyes wide.

"Not much longer if those horses don't come soon," Corin said, taking in the slack on another line.

"But I saw you drive the knife into his heart," Elinor said, her voice shaky at the mere memory of the deed.

"Ah, fooled you didn't I?" Corin said with satisfaction. "That was some sleight of hand that Thos taught me. It had to look real. I had to fool everybody. Here, watch me do it again."

Corin took the dagger from his waistband. He lifted it high above his head pointing upwards, and then turned the blade down towards the ground, changing his grip on it. He held his arms so that the blade was hidden behind them. Then he thrust his arms downward into the ground, but there was no longer a knife in his hands.

"Where did it go?" Elinor asked, amazed.

"Up my sleeve," Corin said, taking it out and showing her.

"Why didn't you tell me?" Elinor wailed. "I thought you'd really killed him."

"I didn't have time," Corin explained with a shrug. "We got pretty busy after that, you know." Relieved, Elinor crumpled in the field and gave herself over to her weeping. Corin looked at her mystified. "What's wrong now?" he asked, but she could not respond.

Corin looked up at the sound of horses. Several riders had brought their mounts, with Roderick in the lead. As soon as they arrived, Corin and Thos gave orders to tie the lines from the harness to their saddles.

Thos walked from one rider to the next, checking that the lines were secure. When he came to Roderick, he paused and stood there watching him work. Roderick noticed the old man and glanced up at him.

"The lines are good and should hold," he explained, but got no further. He stood there staring at Thos with a confused look on his face. His mouth hung open, as if he wanted to say more but no words came out. His eyes were riveted on Thos' face. "It's you," he finally spoke in a quiet voice. "I'd know you anywhere. You're the old man."

Thos chuckled at the young man's astonishment. "You've grown since last we met. I rejoice to see you again, Sounder," he said. "That is your name, is it not?"

"Aye, sire, Sounder they used to call me," Roderick said.

Corin had noticed their interchange and walked over. "Roddy, do you know him?" Corin asked. "Roddy! You look like you've seen a ghost."

Thos answered for him. "What's the matter, boy? Don't you ever listen to the old ballads of great deeds of the past?"

"Of course I listen ... but where do you know him from?"

Thos only laughed in answer. He looked up and said, "Wagon's coming," and with no further comment walked away from them towards the wagon that had appeared on the rise of the meadow.

Corin turned to Roderick. "What was that all about?" he asked.

"Bless me," Roderick replied, scratching his head in wonder, staring after the old magician.

At this moment the queen appeared, surrounded by a protective guard. A fresh bandage covered the wound on her arm. She walked straight to the dragon.

"I want to know how he's doing," she demanded. There was a great cascading of bells. Corin laughed. He saw Elinor out of the corner of his eye sitting where she had collapsed with wide eyes, her mouth gaping open. He wondered what had happened now, but shrugged it off.

"He says that he is very happy to see that you have survived this ordeal," Corin told her. "And he apologizes for his frightful appearance. He is embarrassed to be seen in this state by so many. He says that I have a lot of work ahead of me to clean him up. Turns out he's far more vain than any of us imagined."

"I did not say that," the dragon quipped.

Aina relaxed, hearing her son able tease the dragon. "I was very confused," Aina admitted to him. "I saw what you did, yet I did not have a feeling that Star was in danger. I could not believe that you could do such a thing. And then there was your father's odd behavior.

He acted elated and more hopeful than ever. He only now explained to me that he recognized Star's final roar, not as his death cry, but rather as a call of jubilation."

"I had no time to explain," Corin said. "Star has always taught me that if I'm going to do something, make it look real, even if I'm unsure. I guess it worked. Where's Father?"

"I've left him in the good care of Commander Geron and Ambroise," she answered.

Corin grew very serious. "Are you sure that's safe?" he asked.

"Ambroise assured me that he would hurt the king only if he tried to get up before he gave him permission," his mother answered lightly.

"I didn't mean the surgeon," Corin said.

Aina peered at her son before speaking. "You still don't trust Geron, do you?"

"I don't know anymore," Corin said honestly. "I saw him talking to the men who kidnapped Elinor in front of the boat where they had her. And later in the night, he chased me when I was trying to get to the boat to rescue her."

"He was talking to the men because that's his job, to look for suspicious activity. Obviously, they were able to fool him. And later, he chased you because you are the prince and had no business being out there. I had reported you missing and asked that you be returned safely. He was trying to catch you *on my orders*."

"Oh," Corin said, looking embarrassed.

"Corin, I know that you believe you have reasons to suspect him," Aina said. "But Geron is committed to me. He would not do anything that would endanger the crown. Yes, he is an ambitious man, but he would defend to the death the walls of Gladur and my right to the crown."

"But, Father—" Corin began.

"Yes, I am well aware that Geron would much rather see himself king than your father. I've had a lifetime knowing him to know how much he wants that. But he is also a man of honor. And I trust men of honor like Geron. As it is, your father has just revealed to me that he has been working secretly with Geron to ferret out sedition among our nobles. It seems that Geron has prevented in Gladur what befell King Bellek here. So it's no surprise you would suspect Geron of being a traitor, since he was leading them on all the time." Corin's eyes grew large at this revelation. Aina continued, "Now look me in the eye and tell me that you will give him the benefit of your doubt."

Corin lifted his face and looked into his mother's steady gaze. Then he nodded his head. "Promise."

By this time the wagon had arrived at the lake. The queen regarded it with curiosity, but then her eyes were drawn to the old man who guided the driver. She took one look at him and cried out, "It's true!" The queen started running towards him. Her guard was not ready for this sudden move and scrambled after her as best they could, unclear of the reason for her actions. Several unsheathed their swords as they ran, ready for any yet undetected danger.

Aina reached the old man, who smiled broadly when he saw her coming towards him. He opened his arms, and she flew into his embrace. Both Corin and Elinor were astonished by this show of affection and hastened after her.

"Oh, Aga," they heard Aina say as they came nearer. "How I have missed you! Why have you stayed away so long?"

"I have been closer than you know," the old man said with a wink to Corin. "There are others who have needed my looking after them more than you."

"Mother," Corin said, marveling at this reunion, "do you know him?"

"Corin, this is Aga. Certainly I've spoken of him before. He has known your father since he was a babe. And in my most desperate time of need, he came to Gladur to give me guidance and support. In the stories the minstrels sing, he is the one who gave your father back his armor and his horse after it had all been lost. It was Aga who led the forces of Nogardia to our rescue."

"Do you mean those stories are all *true*?" Corin asked aghast.

"What did you think?" his mother said surprised. "Did you think the minstrels were making it all up? That they were just stories to fill a long winter's night?"

Corin opened his mouth and then shut it before he said something else foolish. He took a deep breath and realized he had a few knots to untangle. "Mother," he said at last, "this is the magician I told you about. The one from the marketplace." Aina looked at him surprised.

Then Corin turned to the old magician. "You told me your name is Thos. Why didn't you tell me your real name?"

"Thos *is* my real name," he replied, "as well as Aga. In fact, if you put the two together, you will have my full name. I usually use only half at a time, so as not to wear it out."

"Aga, if it was you all this time, why did you give the dagger to Corin?" Aina asked, her expression severe.

"I sent it as a message to beware," Aga answered. "I knew you would remember my warning. Considering all that has happened, I think it was delivered at the perfect moment. But let's leave questions for later. I see that the horses are hitched up to the lead lines on Star's harness. I want to see him out of this tar pit."

Under Corin's direction, the horses began to drag the great dragon out of the tarry trap of the Black Lake. At first it was exceedingly difficult to make any progress. The horses strained at the lines, yet the dragon did not budge. Following some directions that Star himself gave, they changed direction and managed to rotate Star's body so that he was no longer lying on his side. This helped him to sit up and regain his balance, and he found the sunken bank with his forelegs. As the horses pulled, he pushed his body forward. Painstakingly, he scooted himself forward until finally his rear legs also felt the bank and he could give himself the final thrust to stand firmly on the ground.

It was slow and difficult work. They changed horses several times, to make sure they always had fresh energy to pull Star forward. The process was exhausting for the horses and their handlers, but also very taxing on the dragon. At last Star emerged from the lake, his legs and half his body smeared in the black, sticky tar.

"His beautiful coat," Aina fretted to Corin. "How will we ever get him clean again? Tar only wears off with time."

"Remember I told you that Thos is a magician?" Corin asked. "He has some magic that will come in handy here. What he has in the barrel in the back of that wagon is exactly what we need. There's a river nearby, and I'm taking Star there. We'll be back by nightfall. He won't be clean yet, but I assure you he'll look better."

Corin walked up to the dragon. "Come on, Star. Time to get into the river. Don't be offended, but I'm not going to ride on you this time. In fact, I will drive the wagon and you can follow." Corin walked over to the waiting wagon that was still hitched. He climbed up to the driver's bench and picked up the reins. Before he could give the horses the go-ahead, someone else was climbing up after him.

"Elinor!" he said in surprise. "What are you doing?"

"I'm going with you," she said, settling herself on the bench beside him. "You can't do the whole dragon alone, you know." Her eyes were still wide and brimming with tears. Corin figured she was simply relieved to find Star alive.

"Last I heard, you didn't want to spend the rest of your life scrubbing a dragon," he teased.

"Nor did you," Elinor declared with a smile. "But that doesn't have anything to do with today. Let's go."

"It's a sticky mess," Corin warned her.

"Well, it won't be the first sticky mess I've gotten into since coming here," she replied with a laugh. And then she giggled with abandon.

"What are you so happy about?" Corin asked.

"Can't tell you," she beamed. "I have secrets, too."

Corin shook his head. "You are so odd." And this made them both laugh. "You could use a wash yourself, you know," he said with a smile. "You wouldn't want Muck to see you now."

"Look who's talking," she countered, making a face at him. Self-consciously, she ran her fingers through her tangled hair. "Just be careful I don't knock you into the river again."

"Go ahead and try," Corin said. "Just don't go blaming it on Star."

"This is all my own idea," Elinor said.

"You are all talk."

"We'll see who ends up in the river first."

"It's a good thing it's still warm because you are so going down with a splash."

They both laughed and Corin offered Elinor the reins. She looked at him, surprised at this gesture, and then took them.

"Sprout, how could you be so sure everything would work out?" Elinor asked as the wagon rumbled along. "You took a great risk."

"How could it go otherwise? We have a Luck Dragon on our side."

"I thought you were always the one arguing that that is not how a Luck Dragon works."

"I've learned a lot in the last few weeks. And one of the things I've learned is that sometimes a Luck Dragon is just a Luck Dragon. This was one of those times."

When the wagon rolled off with Star, Aina returned with her guards to the king. She arrived just as he was struggling to his feet. His head was bandaged, as was the wound to his leg. The king turned to his wife. "I must attend to Star," he explained.

"It's about time you did," she scolded.

"I've come to realize that I have been serving two masters," he said in a subdued voice. "I think that blow might have knocked some sense into my head. I have tried to be both king and Dragon Master, and I have been miserable at both. I thought I could be a husband and a father on the side, but I've muddled that as well."

"Do you see a solution?" she asked.

"Honestly, I don't know. I think first I must go back to being the Dragon Master, and take things from there. All good that has come into my life has come from Star, so if I focus on him, then I hope I will be led how to serve the crown and my family."

Aina nodded. "I support you in this. Ask for Star's guidance. Go to him now. He is in need of many caring hands."

The king called for a horse, but his attendants were not willing to bring him one. "What is this treason!" he shouted. "Bring me a horse!" There was scurrying and confusion among his guards.

"We may not, Your Majesty," one of them explained. "We are under orders."

"Orders?" frowned the king. "Whose orders supersede my own?"

"Master Ambroise warned us—"

"Ambroise?" the king cut him off. "Do you owe him more fealty than to me?"

"Don't yell at your attendants," Aina said, coming quickly over to him. "They are conflicted and have your best interests in mind, even if you do not."

"Then let them bring me a horse," the king said petulantly.

At that moment a rider came galloping toward them. "At last," the king said. But he was disappointed to see who was in the saddle. Master Ambroise dismounted and stood before the king.

"I hear my patient is causing trouble," he said, his expression severe. "Your Majesty, I have many wounded to care for here. Why do you draw me away from them?"

"I'll take your horse," the king said.

"Your Majesty, you may take my head, but you may not have my horse. I am sorely needed by others who have also sacrificed themselves today."

"I must go to Star," the king said, his tone softer.

"You have had a severe blow to the head and a nasty cut on your leg," Ambroise explained, as if to a child. "Not to mention various other cuts that could use a stitch or two if you would only hold still and let me. If you ride a horse, the way *you* ride, you will aggravate your head injury and likely open the stitches I so painstakingly sewed you up with, forcing me to repeat my work, and if you thought it hurt the first time, you will not like my second attempt."

"Ambroise, release my misguided attendants from their vow of protecting me from myself and let them bring me a horse. I promise to ride gently. I must attend to Star."

Ambroise glanced at the queen who subtly nodded her head. She was satisfied with the king's promise. "Bring His Majesty a steed," Ambroise said to the attendants. "A gentle one," he added. Then he sprang back into the saddle and was about to ride off when the queen delayed him.

"Good Ambroise," she asked, "have you any news of my guard? They were taken prisoner before the battle."

"Your Majesty, I have seen to them myself," Ambroise replied. "All escaped injury with the exception of your captain."

"Morik?" the queen was alarmed. "Does he live?"

"According to report, he instigated an escape when their guards were distracted as the battle raged. He was severely beaten for his efforts and as a warning to the others."

"How badly?" Aina asked.

"He will survive," Ambroise said gravely, "and I have made him as comfortable as I could. He awakened briefly, but was in such pain that I gave him a draught to put him to sleep. He will need much mending. Several of your guard have stayed with him. More I cannot add." Ambroise did not wait longer but, giving his horse free rein, rode across the field back toward the makeshift camp the soldiers of the Enclave had set up.

"I will go to Morik," the queen announced. She turned to her attendants. "Bring me a horse as well," she ordered.

The horses were brought, and the queen leapt easily into the saddle of one and swept away at a gallop. The king mounted his horse more slowly. When his head began to swim, he was ready to believe that perhaps his surgeon had not exaggerated his warnings. Surrounded by a clump of mounted guards, he walked his horse across the field toward the river.

As he went, the king perused the devastation of the battle. Soldiers who could still walk were gathering their fallen comrades into growing mounds. Salvaged armor and weapons lay to one side. A large number of Worrah's troops sat in the grass, surrounded by guards. The dragon wagons now stood abandoned in the fields, the earth around them scorched. The king wondered at this new weapon and what it would mean to warfare. He looked at the nearby walls of the city and at the surrounding fields. He had, albeit unintentionally, invaded a bordering kingdom and defeated its army. He cringed at the thought of how this would be received by his other neighbors. He was in need of advice. He had to find Aga and speak with him. But first, he had to attend to Star.

The king rode until he came within sight of the river. He saw Star on the bank, lying on his side. It was an uncommon position for the dragon, and the king's first reaction was alarm. Without thinking, he prodded his horse to a trot, but the jostling made his head ache and his vision swim, so reluctantly he slowed down again. Near to the dragon stood a wagon with a large wooden vat on its bed. He saw with surprise that Aga himself was there, scrubbing at the dragon's exposed underbelly. Near to him other men scrubbed. Among them stood Sounder, also scrubbing. Elinor was working around Star's chin. However, he was puzzled not to see Corin anywhere.

The king halted his horse at the wagon and dismounted carefully. His attendants joined him and stood around nervously, waiting to see what their king would do next. Michael walked over to Elinor. He noticed that as she scrubbed at the stubborn tar streaks along the contours of Star's chin, tears were streaming down her face.

"Elinor," he asked gently. "Are you hurt?"

Elinor did not speak, but silently shook her head, not pausing from her work.

"She's all right," Star spoke. Michael was relieved to hear how normal he sounded. "She is deeply caring and is very dear to me."

When Star spoke, Elinor's tears streamed in earnest, and she scrubbed even more vigorously, pausing only long enough to use her sleeve to wipe her face.

"Elinor?" the king spoke again, still concerned.

"Let her be," Star said gently. "She is not in distress. Go chat with Aga. Come back to visit with me later."

Michael shook his head in wonder and realized that he had to trust Star. He walked back to the wagon and picked up a brush leaning against it. He stepped over to where Aga was working, periodically dipping his brush into the bucket beside him. The liquid from the bucket was removing the tar from the dragon's scales.

"That's not water, is it?" Michael asked as he walked up to the wizard.

"Your Majesty," Aga said with a smile, pausing long enough to bow briefly to the king. "I am delighted to see that you are still among the living." He returned to his scrubbing. "No, water would not clean him up, I'm afraid. This is a very special mixture. *Naft abyad*. It is very effective at removing the tar."

"Lamp oil?" the king was surprised. "Where do you have such large amounts from?"

"I have my sources, Your Majesty," he said enigmatically.

"You are full of mysteries," the king sighed with a laugh. "I shouldn't be surprised." He turned to his attendants and directed them to fill buckets from the vat and pick up scrubbers from the pile in the wagon. "I thought I'd come give you a hand," Michael said. He set his personal guard to work on the dragon's tarred underside. Taking a bucket himself, he scrubbed beside the old man.

"I have a problem," the king said somberly as he worked.

"You are a king," Aga laughed. "Problems are attracted to you like wasps to pastry."

"I shouldn't be here," the king continued. "This battle was never intended. But all of the neighboring kingdoms will view me as an aggressor, invading Warrensfold for my own gain."

"Did I mention you have a Luck Dragon?" Aga asked lightly.

The king put down his brush and looked at the wizard. "What am I missing?"

"While I was waiting for you to arrive in the prison, I discovered that Worrah had already imprisoned another king, the rightful king of Warrensfold."

"Bellek? He's alive?"

"In his own prison. And, I imagine," Aga continued, "conveniently waiting for you to free him and place him back on his throne. Unless you wish to exchange him for some puppet king who will be more inclined towards you. The choice is yours."

"This is a spectacular stroke of good fortune," the king murmured. He dropped his brush and called for several of his guards, giving them explicit orders to free King Bellek from his dungeon.

"He may not appreciate you the way you want," Aga suggested.

"All the more reason to beat a hasty retreat back to Gladur," the king said. "As soon as Star is ready to go, I'm prepared to leave. Bellek will have to deal with the nobles who shifted their loyalty to Worrah. He will stand or fall on his ability to reassert himself. From the reports I've heard, I have my own housecleaning waiting for me back in Gladur. I want no part of his process. However, I will provide him with whatever support he asks for to secure his crown."

"Good choice," Aga smiled, and continued with his brushing. The two of them, king and wizard, worked for a while silently, side by side.

"This works wonders," Michael commented, seeing how relatively easy the naphtha removed the tar. "Is this the same liquid that was used in the dragon wagons?" he asked.

"It provides the base, Your Majesty," Aga said, "but the formula, I have heard, is far more complicated."

"Is there more of it?" the king asked warily in a low voice.

"It was mostly depleted in the battle," Aga replied.

"Could you make more?" the king asked, keeping his voice low.

Aga paused before answering. "Your Majesty, the one man who possesses the knowledge how to mix such a volatile and destructive substance will have disappeared from the Enclave before another week has passed, taking the secret with him." When the king did not respond, Aga continued. "I strongly counsel you to let this knowledge quietly disappear. You do not want to carry such a burden."

Michael accepted Aga's caution without response. He scrubbed a little while longer, struggling to find words for the question that burned inside of him since coming in sight of the river. Finally, he asked, "Where's my son? He should be here."

Aga put his brush down and faced the king. "Has he not done enough today?" The king looked at him with surprise. The old man continued. "Not only has he secured the safety of your crown and defeated the man who conspired since before he was born to sit in your place, he managed to unite the forces of the Enclave under your banner. I'd say that is an enviable list for one day's work. What else do you want from him? Are you aware of what your son did as you lay stunned? Has anyone bothered to tell you that he was ready to lay down his life defending you?"

The king eyes grew wide. "I did not know," he said quietly.

"Then it is time you did," Aga said. "You keep wanting him to be like you, but he is of far greater worth being true to himself."

"I was only thinking," the king said, hanging his head, "that ..." his voice died away.

"What?" barked Aga. "Get it said."

"That he has a deeper commitment," Michael said, sounding unsure. "I entrusted Star's care to him. Star needs him now."

"The young prince is needed more urgently elsewhere," Aga stated flatly, going back to brushing the dragon's scales.

The king was surprised at this comment. "Where could he be needed more than right here caring for Star? What is more important?"

Aga put his brush down again. "I won't say more important, but equally important are the soldiers who put their lives on the line today so that you still have a throne to sit on."

"How in the world can he serve them?" the king asked, frustrated that he was missing the connection.

"It's about time you woke up to the truth about your son," Aga said, his sharp eyes holding the king's. "I've heard that you were worried about Corin's lack of interest in swordsmanship. You were concerned that Star's training was less than adequate. Do you still hold that concern?"

The king shook his head. "He showed himself to be very able today," he admitted. "I regret that I ever doubted his skills."

"As heir to the throne, no one questions how important it is that he know how to wield a sword," Aga continued. "But sword fighting will not be his greatest asset."

"What do you mean?" the king asked.

"It's a good thing that you are stubborn and thick-headed. It has gotten you to where you are now. But it is not the only way." Aga waited.

"Go on," Michael prompted him. "You have my attention."

"It's about time."

The king sighed. "Don't gloat. Just explain."

"Most kings of the ancient race, from which you and your son are descended, were men of peace." He saw the king's eyes widen. "Would you like me to repeat that?"

"But even men of peace have occasion to defend themselves," the king objected.

"Which is why it is essential to know how to handle a sword. And equally important to have men faithfully at your disposal who can handle one. Unless I'm mistaken, your son has tried to get you to see this."

The king did not answer, but after a moment, mutely nodded his head. Aga continued, "Was it Star who failed to explain to you that the leaders of the Dragon Keepers were men of peace? Or have you conveniently forgotten that?"

The king pressed his lips together before speaking. "I preferred to hear stories about Soran the Great and others known for their warlike nature."

"Naturally enough," Aga said. "You wanted to hear about leaders like yourself."

"I am ashamed," the king said, his eyes downcast.

"Don't stay that way too long," Aga laughed. "It does not become you. You have to be true to who you are. That said, you have to get out of his way and let Corin be true to who he is. Do you think you can live with that?"

"But where has he gone?"

"To serve as he's been trained," Aga answered. "Your son is a healer, and a very talented one. His skills are sorely needed by those who were wounded in battle. Anyone can wield a brush and scrub a dragon. Every man in the battle today could swing a sword to some extent or another. But few have the knowledge how to guide a needle to close a wound and what herbs will fight off the infection that follows. Those are your son's skills and that is where he is needed."

The king's mouth fell open, yet he was speechless. Aga asked, "Why so astonished? Did you not know he was apprenticed to Master Ambroise?"

"Yes, of course," Michael stammered. "But I thought it was merely to learn the basic arts of healing that everyone should know."

"And so it was originally intended, until Ambroise saw in Corin a sleeping talent for the healing arts that needed little prodding to awaken. Did you not wonder at your son's growing interest in sewing?"

"I mistook it for idleness," the king admitted.

"Master Ambroise found in Corin an ideal apprentice. He set him the task of cultivating his own set of surgical needles, polishing them to a thinness and point that embroidery needles never need. He set him sewing tasks until he saw the young prince had developed his own interest in steadying his hand and honing his skills. It is far more subtle than swinging a sword, yet no less useful in the world."

"Where is he now?"

"Seeing that many of the wounded do not suffer an agonizing and avoidable death as a result of their wounds. Ambroise cannot do it alone."

The king was silent, trying to make sense of this. Aga saw it was time to tell him the rest. "I'm taking him with me," he said. He was not asking a question, but rather informing the king.

"Where?" Michael asked, surprised.

"My work here is finished for now," Aga explained. "I will take to the road and travel. There are affairs elsewhere that call for my attention. Corin once asked if I would take him with me when I left here. He has a hunger for the road, but you have always protected him from it."

"I wanted only the best for him," the king feebly argued.

"But wouldn't you agree that life on the road taught you skills you could never have learned remaining in one place?"

Silently, the king nodded in agreement.

"I can bring Corin into contact with other healers whose skills go even beyond the admirable ones that Ambroise has cultivated. See it as an extended apprenticeship."

"But Star needs him," the king stumbled over the words.

"I believe Star has found someone who will give him her full devotion," Aga said, gesturing toward Elinor. She stood at Star's chin, carefully removing tar with a hand brush. She was laughing now and talking animatedly.

"But Star needs someone who can understand him," the king objected. "I promised him that when he came into my care. I cannot be with him every day. I am sure that Elinor will be very attentive, but Star deserves to have at least one constant caretaker with whom he can talk."

"I think you are in for another surprise, Your Majesty," Aga said gently. "Come with me." He lay down his brush and walked toward the dragon's head where Elinor stood. Puzzled, the king followed.

"... without a shock, I feel certain," they overhead Elinor saying as they approached. "I think that just believing in it could be all Auntie needs. She loves you so dearly. Don't you agree?"

"Who are you talking with, Elinor?" Aga asked. Elinor had been so involved in her conversation that she had not noticed their approach. She looked up at her uncle and the wizard. Her face shone with joy. The king looked around, but there was no one else near her.

"He can talk," she said, and with these words the tears again overflowed her eyes and ran down her cheeks. "It's true," she insisted. "Until now I could only feel what he meant." She reached up and wiped her eyes on her sleeve. "Oh, Uncle, his voice is so beautiful."

"You understand him?" the king asked, astonished.

"Every word," she said. "Every sweet word."

Michael turned to the dragon. "Star, is this true?"

"Indeed, O Dragon Master," Star replied. "What the girl says is true. We have been having the most fascinating conversation. Don't take offense, but neither you nor your son ever asked me such penetrating questions as young Elinor does."

"How is it possible that she can understand you?"

"I have a suspicion," Star said. "But there is no way for me to know for certain. I believe that when she thought that Corin had driven the knife into my heart, the shock was so great for her that it uncovered her latent ability to understand me, which has lived in all the women descended from the Ancient Ones. It has been so long since I have been able to converse with a female of your line that I had forgotten how delightful it can be. It has made holding still for all of this tedious cleaning quite bearable."

Aga turned to the king. "I hope that settles the matter," he said. "May I have your blessings now to take Corin with me?"

Chapter Twenty-Seven

The Starry Sky

"Don't wake her," the dragon said.

Corin looked down at the dark form curled up under the blanket. Although it had grown dark, he could make it out in the luminosity of Star's coat. "Is that Elinor?" he asked.

"Poor thing is exhausted," Star said. "She labored all afternoon on cleaning me."

Elinor stirred and pulled the blanket up under her chin. "Tell me, Star," Corin said. "Is it true what they're saying? There's a rumor that Elinor can understand you."

The dark form on the ground stirred again. "Every word," she mumbled sleepily. "No more secrets from me. You are in such trouble." She giggled. Then she added, "But now I sleep. More scrubbing tomorrow." She rolled over and pulled the blanket over her head.

The prince smiled broadly at her comment and looked up. He admired the luminous stars that lit up the dragon's coat. "They got a lot done," he commented.

"Thanks to the soldiers from the Enclave," Star said.

"They were here?" Corin was surprised.

"They wandered over in twos and threes, at first just to gape at me. But then, when they saw what was needed, they did not hesitate to pick up brushes and scrub away."

"How did they react to finding that you were still alive?"

"Judging from their conversation," Star chuckled, "they feel a certain ownership of me now. Several commented that they had always wanted a closer look. Others even dared to say that they always believed in me. Many said how relieved they were that *their* dragon was still alive. I think their full moon ceremony will take on a new focus."

"You know about that?" Corin asked cautiously.

"There are a great many things I hear about," Star chuckled.

"Amazing," Corin said.

"It's time to speak with your father on their behalf," Star suggested. "They are not a bad people."

"I learned that while we stayed there," Corin replied. "And I'm just coming from speaking with him. I insisted that the people of the Enclave be given the right to live as they please and the assurance that the crown will never persecute them, either in the city of Gladur or out."

"How did the king receive that?"

"I was surprised," Corin admitted. "He agreed without argument. After I told him who led their forces, he invited Makarios to speak with him on behalf of the people of the Enclave and to hear their grievances. I left them just now deep in conversation. I suspect that their control of the lamp oil production will be a large bargaining chip."

"It is a good beginning," Star mused. "It will not be easy, but it is a fine start. There will have to be compromises on both sides."

"Have you heard the news about King Bellek?" Corin asked.

"Did they find him?"

"In his own dungeons," Corin replied. "Worrah had kept him alive in case he might need him. Seems like Thos found him there when he himself was taken prisoner. I heard the king was somewhat lean from short rations, but none the worse for wear."

"There will need be some housecleaning on his part," Star commented.

"Apparently he has wasted no time. He knows who of his cabinet members were instrumental in the overthrow and who went along just to save themselves. There have already been a number of arrests. Inadvertently, I played a small role in that myself."

"How so?"

"It happened when I was tending to some of the more severely burned."

"What were you giving them?"

"Honey is the best remedy, and we used up what stores were in the city on those with the worst burns. We turned to egg whites as well. That works very well, but has to be reapplied several times to be effective. In too short a time, we ran out of both. For many, vinegar compresses are going to have to do."

"And what did you discover while tending to them?"

"I recognized among the wounded Worrah's second in command."

"Had he been burned?"

"Not in the least," Corin continued. "He was hiding among them, hoping to be overlooked, waiting for his moment to slip away. If I had not had so many close brushes with him, he would have succeeded. His name is Rigen. I heard that King Bellek was very happy to have him in custody. Turns out he's a younger cousin to the king and was a main instigator in the overthrow."

"How does King Bellek feel about two foreign armies having invaded his land? Not to mention the presence of a dragon."

"Father has him convinced that getting him back on his throne was your doing. I think he truly believes it himself, that you were behind all of this." Corin paused to hear the dragon's response, but all Star did was chuckle. "I expect that King Bellek will visit you tomorrow," Corin continued, "together with his court. I've heard talk of peace pacts and trade agreements being negotiated. The ministers of commerce from both our kingdoms have already announced their delight at the prospect of working together."

"I am delighted that matters have moved along so well," the dragon said contentedly. "I cannot tell you how your news lightens my heart. This whole adventure has done wonders for me."

"Star, does this mean that you are well again? I never did understand what was troubling you."

"It is actually quite simple," the dragon explained. "You know that I am very sensitive to the energy around me. If there is anger and aggression, I reflect that back. It can easily send me into my wild state."

"But that does not explain your illness."

"In a similar manner, while in my tamed state, if my keepers are discontent, quarreling and misunderstanding one another, then instead of growing wild, I become ill. I am very vulnerable to the moods of those closest to me, and when they are out of balance, I am unable to function at my full potential."

"And has that changed now?"

"You would know best," the dragon laughed. "Until now you have been unhappy with your life and looking for an escape from the constraints placed upon you as the heir to the throne. Do you still have these complaints?"

Corin shook his head. "After today, I feel content with what is waiting for me. I am looking forward to how my apprenticeship will now unfold."

"Your contentment is reflected in my improved health," Star revealed.

"Is it that simple?"

"Do you want it to be more complicated?"

Corin laughed. "Please, no."

"Whether your parents will be able to resolve their difficulties will be a further test to my health, but I have faith in their ability to work things out. Particularly once they realize what is at stake. Besides, I now have Elinor. She is a spirited girl with deep reserves of cheerfulness and love. She will remain close to me, and that in itself is healing. I so love the devotion an orphan can bring."

Corin glanced down at the dark form of his cousin underneath her blanket. "I am happy for her," he said quietly.

"I am happy for *me*," the dragon chuckled. "I will need her companionship once you've gone."

Corin looked up surprised. "So you've heard already."

"Aga told me."

"Aga," he repeated. "I'm going to have to get used to calling him that. Yes, he has invited me to go traveling with him."

"And you, of course, have accepted," Star said.

"I have. He said he wants to take over my apprenticeship from Master Ambroise."

"Very fitting," Star said. "And I overheard him promise the king not to let you neglect your swordsmanship."

"I didn't think I would get away without it," Corin laughed.

"Don't let your guard down," the dragon warned. "Aga may look old, and he's no dragon, but don't underestimate how quick he can be. Add to that, he's sly like a fox."

"I'll be on my guard," Corin smiled.

"Of course, you won't be the first of your family to be trained by him," Star pointed out. "Your great-grandfather Marrow spent a considerable amount of time with him. It was through Aga that he met Galifalia."

"He told me similar stories, but I was not ready to believe him. How can Aga be so old?" Corin wondered.

"That is a secret I will leave for him to reveal. Even if I did have a part to play in it."

"You've known him a long time, haven't you?"

"Aga and I go back very far indeed. Our destinies have crossed more than once."

Corin was silent, gazing upon the dragon's marvelous starry coat, as if the skies had descended to earth. "I'll miss this," he sighed. "Your coat. I never thought I would, but now that I am about to leave you, I realize how precious a thing it is to me."

"Even if it is not the same as being near me," the dragon said, "I have a suggestion that could help. Whenever you miss me, look up at the stars on a dark night. I will not be as close as now, yet I will be there."

"But I won't be able to speak with you," Corin said sadly. "To get your advice."

"Then hear my advice now," Star said. "When you have a question, pose it and then get quiet. Wait and the answer will come. Have you not learned that yet?"

Corin remembered all the times he was at his wits' end and in his desperation asked himself what Star would advise him to do. It was true that every time he found an answer waiting for his question. He grew silent and pondered this.

Star broke into his reverie. "Now that you've had a whole day of it, of real battle and tending to seriously wounded men, tell me. Did it turn your stomach, or do you hold firm with your resolve to heal others? Sewing up a wounded soldier is not the same as sewing a sachet filled with sweet smelling herbs."

Corin chuckled at the comparison. "Star, it was painful to care for so many men who were needlessly wounded or maimed. That is why I so hate swords. What can a sword do? It is made to kill and mutilate. And it bothers me that, try as I might, I could not find a way to prevent the battle today."

"Prepare yourself that it may not be the last time, either," Star said gently.

"Caring for those men," Corin continued, "sewing up their wounds and tending to their injuries felt right to me. Admittedly, it was not pleasant. And sadly there were numerous wounds beyond our skills. But so many others were helped and grateful for my work. I never grew tired, and the work never bothered me. Together with the other apprentices Ambroise had brought with him, we did much to comfort the soldiers. Tomorrow we'll continue our work to ease their suffering. I feel useful for the first time in my life. This is what I was meant to do."

"Far more useful than wasting your time scrubbing a dragon?" Star asked.

Corin blushed, and he was grateful it was too dark for the dragon to see. "Star, I'm sorry I ever said that. It's not really what I meant."

"I know. Your soul was saying that you feel called to something greater, something that is uniquely your own. Have I ever told you that there is a long line of healers among the people we call the Dragon Keepers?"

"You never have," Corin said. "Why did you keep it from me?"

"I suppose I never felt the time was right to tell you about them. You had to decide to take that path on your own. Otherwise, most likely you would have rejected it, complaining that you are following in someone else's footsteps." The dragon chuckled.

"Ouch," Corin said softly. "Guilty as charged."

They both grew silent and after a few moments the air was filled with the gentle chiming of bells, which Corin recognized as Star's way of purring.

"So you don't mind?" Corin finally asked. "That I'm going?"

"You will return better able to lead your people in peace," Star said. "You will be challenged by those who disagree with you, yet have valid arguments that you cannot dismiss out of hand. But that is your path, your destiny, to allow that dialogue to unfold in a constructive manner."

They grew silent again underneath the starry skies, and Star joined his voice to the chorus of frogs singing their evening song among the reeds. Corin breathed this in and felt the pain that his time with Star was soon to end. He had a sense of panic, wondering what questions he had failed to ask.

"Star," he said, breaking into the night concert. "I have something troubling me."

"Let me guess," Star replied. "Are you feeling a conflict with being a healer and at the same time having been the one who ended Worrah's life?"

Corin laughed bitterly. "That was my *second* question."

"Then tell me your first one."

"It also involves Worrah. You once told me that you bring good fortune even to those who are devising evil. Do you still hold to that?"

"Indeed I do."

"Then what good fortune did you bring to Worrah? He now lies dead."

"If you think about it, you will find my influence throughout his misadventure. Through a number of unlikely coincidences, Worrah suddenly found himself with your father, the king of Gladur, in his prison, and the queen at his doorstep suing for a peaceful settlement to their border disputes. To top this off, he successfully lured me into his tar pit so I was unable to take part in the ensuing battle!"

"Which was fortunate, because you can't be around fighting without going wild yourself," Corin pointed out. Then he had a realization. "Did you get yourself stuck on purpose, to prevent any mishaps?"

"I'll say only that although it was a radical and risky act, it was a surprisingly fortunate course of action at that moment, as the unfolding of events proved. And had that battle continued longer, or had you not taken matters into your own hands, I would have been in one sticky situation, out of which I still ponder how I might have escaped."

"I'll never understand Luck Dragons," the prince sighed.

"Perhaps you are not supposed to," Star provoked.

Corin waved off his teasing. "Get back to Worrah. Is there more to tell?"

"Indeed. Not only did he manage to lure the king, the queen and their dragon to fall completely under his authority, but you and Elinor arrived to stand before his throne. All of his perceived enemies were in his hands at once. Would you not call that unbelievable good fortune?"

"Until you said it," Corin admitted, "I did not realize what position he was in."

"Worrah could have dictated any conditions he wished," Star continued. "How could your parents refuse? But instead of negotiating, what did he desire?"

"He wanted us all dead. Why would he do that?"

"I believe it has to do with the most basic drive that guides all life on this planet."

Corin looked up interested. "What new mystery is that?"

"No mystery at all," Star chuckled. "I'm speaking about hunger."

"Hunger?"

"A desire to eat is an immense motivation."

"Whatever does this have to do with food? Warrensfold is not stricken by famine."

"We hunger for more than food," Star explained. "But you will understand what I mean if we speak for a moment only about food. No matter how much you eat at one meal, you will, sooner or later, grow hungry again. You can satisfy your hunger in the moment, but it will always return. It is in the nature of life to never be satisfied for long. Would you not agree?"

"I cannot deny it," Corin said. "But I suspect you are speaking now about other hungers."

"Indeed I am," Star said. "Hunger influences more than the search for your next meal. It colors all of your decisions. Whenever you are dissatisfied, it reflects a hunger for something. This has its good sides, as well as its obvious downsides. After all, if you were content for too long a time, you might never get much accomplished. Your discontent with being a dragon's caretaker led you to develop a hunger to understand healing herbs and become an enthusiastic polisher of surgical needles."

Corin laughed. "Are you telling me all this so I won't feel bad about being so difficult to get along with?"

Star chuckled. "I'm telling you this so you can forgive all those who tried to push you in directions that satisfied *their* hungers."

Corin thought about this before asking, "Tell me how this relates to Worrah."

"He let his greed overrule his good fortune. He was a man with a large appetite, and he was hungry for power. Deposing King Bellek was not enough for him. He wanted to consume Gladur Nock as well. Worrah had not learned how to curb his appetite. Much like a hungry dragon."

"The form you took when Worrah ruled Gladur!" Corin exclaimed.

"An accurate reflection, wouldn't you agree? Is there any wonder why I was drawn there?"

"Just the same, I'm still not at peace that I was the one who killed him in the end," Corin said. "I want to devote my life to healing others, not to the way of the sword. That is my father's way."

"Beware that you do not completely reject the benefits a blade can bring."

"I'm not aware of any," Corin said bitterly.

"That is because you are still young. The day is not far off when, in addition to your needles, you will sharpen your own surgical blades. There are times you have to cut in order to heal. And even when you sew up the injured, there is the moment when you must use the sharp edge of a blade to cut the thread."

Corin nodded, considering all of this for a while in silence. Then he asked, "So in the end, was all of this your doing?"

"Let's put it this way," the dragon explained. "I provide the opportunity. It is up to you to take advantage of it. I would say you did so admirably. Worrah, on the other hand, squandered the good fortune that had been placed so carefully into his hands. This made his fall inevitable."

"I have much to learn," Corin sighed. "I don't understand half of what you're telling me. I have far to go before I am ready to assume the crown."

The night was filled with the delightful chimes of Star's laughter. "Kingship?" he asked. "Aren't you the one who rebelled against repeating the past by being the next Dragon Boy? Have you changed your mind about becoming the next king?"

"It's different now," Corin replied, speaking slowly. "I was faced with making a decision and I made a clear break with my past."

"Now that you've brought that up, tell me something," the dragon probed. "When I was stuck in the Black Lake and I led you to the opening between my scales, were you aware of your options?"

Corin sat silent struggling to find the words. "Star," he finally said, his voice lowered, "I could have killed you."

"Indeed, I believe you considered it."

"When I climbed up onto you, I had every intention of driving that dagger into your heart. A part of me knew that I would not be able to penetrate your scales, so in the back of my mind, I knew that I really could not harm you, and I was staging it all for the sake of the forces from the Enclave. But then," Corin struggled with the memory, "you showed me where to find the opening between your scales. I never knew it existed."

Star's chimes rang gently in the night. "How can I ask you to offer me your heart if I do not offer mine in return?"

"But you placed in my hands the means to destroy you."

"Isn't it always that way when we make ourselves vulnerable?"

"Then did you know what I would choose to do?"

"No. There was the moment when all hung in the balance. Not even a Luck Dragon could know what would happen next."

"But you took such a chance. I felt desperate to be free. I could have chosen differently."

"Choice is always that way, isn't it? To give one's heart is a sacrifice. And it has to be done willingly. I decided it was worth accepting the risks."

"I am ashamed of myself," Corin said, hanging his head.

"Don't be ashamed. I put you in that position. You were tested and you chose love."

"I could have chosen to fulfill the ceremony of the full moon," Corin said, his voice catching, knowing how close he had come.

"It is only when we have free choice that our decisions have meaning and can change the course of events. Instead of driving the blade into my heart, you placed your open hand there. You will never be the same after this. Do you remember what I had you say to me?"

"*We be of one heart*," Corin said slowly. "*Thou and I, we be of one heart.*"

"*And we be of one mind, thou and I,*" Star replied. "*One heart and one mind.*"

And then they spoke at the same time, "*We be one together. We are one.*"

"The future is yours," Star said. "You have broken with your past. You have used the blade to sever yourself from it. So you see, a blade can have a positive purpose. Yet, because of how you chose, you are still whole. You will become the thread that weaves lives together."

"How will I do this without your advice and guidance?"

"Don't underestimate Aga," Star chuckled. "And I will never be far away."

"But you will be in Gladur," Corin said.

"There is not a stitch you can make that I will be unaware of. Not a blow with the sword or an incision with the blade that I will not feel. Whatever you do in my name, I will be with you, watching you, guiding you. Clear your mind of all else, of all the meaningless distractions that clutter it up, and you will find me there waiting for you. During the day, you cannot see the stars, but they are there, waiting for the night to reveal them. If you are quiet and patient, you will know my presence. Like the stars, I am always there, waiting for you, watching you, loving you."

They grew silent and gazed up at the inky dome of heaven that spanned the horizons. As they watched, a bright star streaked between the points of light, and the dragon's chime-like laughter filled up the space between.

Thus ends
The Dragon, the Blade and the Thread

Book Three of
-- The Star Trilogy --

About the Author

*R*aised in Los Angeles, Donald Samson spent the first twelve years of his adult life respectively in a Greek fishing village, a small German border town and finally in the mountains of Switzerland, healing from a mega-urban childhood.

Upon returning to the States, he took up the art of teaching young children. He was a Waldorf class teacher for nineteen years, and his teaching experience spans grades 1–10. He lives along the Front Range of the Rocky Mountains with his spirited wife, Claudia, two sons and sporadically obedient dog.

Mr. Samson has written plays for grades 3–7 and two plays for adults, one of which was a finalist in the Moondance Film Festival. In addition to *The Star Trilogy*, his published works include two translations of Jakob Streit's biblical stories, *Journey to the Promised Land* and *We Will Build a Temple,* and he was a contributing author to *Gazing into the Eyes of the Future, the Enactment of Saint Nicholas in the Waldorf School.* All three are also available from AWSNA Publications.

The Star Trilogy
by Donald Samson

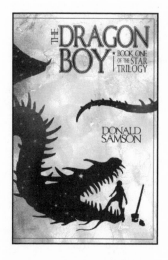

The Dragon Boy

Gold Medal:
Moonbeam Children's Book
Awards: Best First Book

Mom's Choice Award for
Fantasy, Myth and Legend

Finalist: Young Adult Fiction
Eric Hoffer Book Award

The Dragon of Two Hearts

Silver Medal:
Moonbeam Children's Book
Awards for Young Adult Fantasy

Mom's Choice Award for
Fantasy, Myth and Legend

The Dragon, the Blade and the Thread

Bronze Medal:
Moonbeam Children's Book
Awards for Young Adult Fantasy